WITHDRAWN

WATCHING YOU
WITHOUT ME

WATCHING YOU WITHOUT ME

Lynn Coady

ALFRED A. KNOPF   New York

2020

THIS IS A BORZOI BOOK
PUBLISHED BY ALFRED A. KNOPF

Copyright © 2019 by Lynn Coady

All rights reserved. Published in the United States by Alfred A. Knopf,
a division of Penguin Random House LLC, New York.
Originally published in Canada in slightly different form
by House of Anansi Press Inc., Toronto.

www.aaknopf.com

Knopf, Borzoi Books, and the colophon are registered
trademarks of Penguin Random House LLC.

Library of Congress Cataloging-in-Publication Data
Names: Coady, Lynn, 1970– author.
Title: Watching you without me : a novel / Lynn Coady.
Description: First edition. | New York : Alfred A. Knopf, 2020. | Identifiers:
LCCN 2019032440 | ISBN 9780525658436 (hardcover) | ISBN 9780525658443 (ebook)
Subjects: LCSH: Psychological fiction. | GSAFD: Suspense fiction.
Classification: LCC PR9199.3.C546 W38 2020 | DDC 813/.54—dc23
LC record available at https://lccn.loc.gov/2019032440

Jacket design by Jenny Carrow

Manufactured in the United States of America
First United States Edition

for the caregivers

(What if people really did that—sent their love through the mail to get rid of it? What would it be that they sent? A box of chocolates with centers like the yolks of turkeys' eggs. A mud doll with hollow eye sockets. A heap of roses slightly more fragrant than rotten. A package wrapped in bloody newspaper that nobody would want to open.)

—ALICE MUNRO

I Brought This Mess to Town

1

I was in my mother's room when the screen door opened and a man started to yell. It was so unexpected and disorienting that for a second I didn't even know where I was. Then I glanced at the digital clock on the nightstand, with its red, oversized display for aging eyes, and remembered I'd been in here, kneeling at her empty bedside, for over an hour. I was supposed to be boxing things up, but mostly I'd spent the time laying various items across the bed and randomly smelling them.

Hullo there! How's my girlfriend?

That was what he'd shouted, and now I could hear Kelli from her perch in the living room, babbling something pleased in reply. There was no reason to be alarmed. It was someone Kelli knew, therefore some appointment I must have overlooked in the schedule. The schedule was kept inside a chewed-up-looking file folder called *Kelli's World!* (with a heart above the *i*), which my mother had maintained over the past few decades, and which I was only now beginning to successfully decode. In the numb and frantic days after my arrival, *Kelli's World!* had been both blessing and curse. There'd been so much to do and so much to cancel—including appointments I canceled and then realized I needed, so had to call back and apologetically reschedule. Kelli had, for example, back-to-back dentist and dermatologist appointments that inconveniently fell on what it was clear would be my mother's final days—those appointments I canceled, obviously. But I ended up rescheduling Kelli's "friendship circle" at the community center, as much of a pain as it was to drive her there and then back across the bridge to the hospital. It was just that I'd realized that the friendship circle would allow me the opportunity to actually be alone with my mother for the first time in I didn't know how many years. An opportunity I figured I'd better seize.

After she passed, the schedule just kept right on rolling. There'd been the five-on-the-dot arrival of the cheerful silver-haired couple from Meals on Wheels—not just every week, as I assumed when I saw the notation in *Kelli's World!*, but every *night*. In the days leading up to the funeral, the "Wheelies" (as the couple very much enjoyed referring to themselves) had saved my life with their standing order of two blandly fragrant trays—one for Kelli and one for Irene—the second of which, because it was put in front of me, it occurred to me that I should eat. But after the wake, Irene's refrigerator had been bursting with casseroles and the leftovers of casseroles. We were good for food, and the relentless cheer of the Wheelies, as much as Kelli thrilled to their arrival every evening, was becoming something I had to gird myself against. So pretty soon I canceled the Wheelies too. I figured I could handle the evening meals well enough until I figured out what I was going to do with Kelli.

Big Bean! Howdoya do, whaddya say, whaddya know?

The man sounded louder now, more inside than out. I stood up, feeling annoyed with myself because the voice had startled me so badly. You'd think I would be used to the constant intrusions by now—the flurry of hot and cold running caregivers my mother had put in place once she received her ultimate diagnosis. Kelli's bathers, for example. My mother used to bathe Kelli herself, but it must've become too much for her at some point, because now she had bathers turning up every other day, at all hours, sometimes rapping on the door first thing in the morning, calling to my sister through the screen, was she ready for a nice shampoo? To be fair, the first morning this occurred also happened to be the first day the sun had risen without our mother in the world, so there hadn't been much sleep the night before. I should have been ready for it, the *tap-tap-tap* at the door, but *Kelli's World!* had been reading like hieroglyphics to me around then and the banging noise had brought me lurching from the bathroom wild-eyed, as if about to face a firing squad, toothbrush poking from the corner of my mouth like a final cigarette.

But once I understood that these invasions had my mother's stamp—had been scheduled and approved by Irene herself—it was hard to feel aggrieved.

It was also hard to feel aggrieved at the sight of Kelli, always overjoyed at the arrival of her bathers, rocking and smiling, repeating their names so happily and incessantly you can bet I learned them pretty quick myself. So far there'd been Ruby. Gisele. Brenna.

But now it was—

TrebieTrebieTrebie. That's Trebie. Kelli knows Trebie. Followed by a stream of giggles—her distinctive *heh-heh-heh* that properly belonged to a villain from a Scooby-Doo cartoon.

'Course you do! To know me is to love me!

Kelli kept chattering away as I came down the hall, repeating the new name in the rapid-fire way she had when something got her excited. *HiTrebieHiTrebieHiTrebie.*

My sister only has a few things she likes to say—her "catchphrases," my father used to call them—so when they change, when you hear Kelli uttering something entirely new, it feels odd, like a cool hand landing on your shoulder out of nowhere. Like when you know a stranger's in the house because the air has shifted with an influx of new pheromones, the dust eddies suddenly swirling around in entirely different formations.

Of course, there *was* a stranger in the house. Besides me, I mean.

He was my sister's walker. Every Tuesday and Friday at ten in the morning, Trevor and Kelli took a poky, meandering turn around the neighborhood together. He'd been on vacation, he explained, which was why we hadn't seen him before now. And which was why Gisele had been the one walking Kelli the previous week.

Nothing in *Kelli's World!* had told me to expect a man. The bathers were all women, and the silver-haired Wheelies had operated according to a quaint boy/girl protocol: he stayed with the car while she knocked lightly, announced herself with a musical call of *Din-*

din!, and set a tray before my vibrating-with-happiness sister. Later, as I was looking over *Kelli's World!,* the only notation I could find on Trevor's Tuesday and Friday mornings were the letters *BL*—Irene's abbreviation for Bestlife, the home care agency she used.

He didn't wear scrubs—none of the Bestlife people did—but if he hadn't told me he was a worker, I probably would have assumed it. There was something about his stance, in particular: *I am professional,* it assured me; *sanctioned.* He'd also figured out a way of dressing that spoke of an office issuing orders somewhere. I think it was in the colors he chose: light khaki pants, a creamy yellow T-shirt, sunny and bright to distract from his dual vocational gloom clouds of illness and infirmity, pulled over muscles that had been sculpted just enough to let you know they were there. Gingerish hair buzzed down to bristles. Of course, the clipboard was the accessory that put the whole outfit over the top.

He still had a grin on his face when I arrived at the top of the stairs, the playful grin he wore to banter with Kelli. But his mouth went slack and round at the sight of me, and for a moment he looked irritated by his own confusion. I gave him an apologetic smile. It was clear that no one had told him of our mother's death.

I'd already put on tea, so I took it off the stove, fished some cookies from a tin, and invited him to sit with us upstairs. Kelli seemed delighted by this. It wasn't just that cookies in the a.m. weren't the norm, but that the home care workers, who in her mind I suppose comprised her circle of intimates, were not usually encouraged to socialize beyond what duty required. Kelli grinned and whispered into her lap as Trevor lowered himself into a chair across from her. There was no getting around the fact that my sister had been in tremendous spirits ever since our mother's death. Irene's absence hadn't yet taken hold in Kelli, as far as I could tell—all she understood for the moment was that she was surrounded by novelty. Her sister being home, for example. A swirl of relatives she hadn't seen in years, bringing her plates of food, the afternoon of the wake. And now a tea party with her good friend Trebie.

"I'm just sorry as all shit," Trevor repeated one or two times, after I'd told him. He sat in a low chair with his toned, freckled arms dangling between his legs.

"Yes," I said. "It was a—well, it wasn't actually a shock, I guess."

I was lying. It *was* a shock, but it wouldn't have made sense for me to say so. My mother had been preparing me for this eventuality, mentally at least, since her diagnosis and subsequent mastectomy some ten years ago. But it was still a shock.

"She was such a nice lady," said Trevor. I'd heard these six words so many times in almost as many days. It sounded like easy lip service, just a thing you say when an old woman dies, but I knew it wasn't, because whenever it was spoken to me, it was spoken in tones of astonishment, even awe—that's how Trevor was saying it now. My mother had achieved an ideal of decent, patient, competent, yet soft-spoken nice-ladyhood I think very few people encounter anymore. Everyone always experienced my mother as a rare exotic, an antique, somewhere between a concertina and a California condor.

When I didn't reply, Trevor nodded, as if agreeing with himself. "One nice fuckin' lady."

"Nice fuckin' lady," concurred Kelli, in parrot mode. She only did that with people she liked.

It made me smile to imagine my mother and Trevor in conversation, because my mother was decorous above all else. When necessary, she'd be decorous on other people's behalf—she'd certainly been on my behalf enough. So I could imagine her overlooking Trevor's unselfconscious profanity just as she'd overlooked the indelicacies of countless others in her decorous lifetime. Yet my mother was nice in the tradition of many a Nova Scotian lady of her generation and upbringing—it could be a stiff, dogmatic niceness of the schoolmarm stripe, a niceness of propriety and parochialism outlined with a filigree border of intolerance. I may as well come out and say that my mother could be irredeemably racist in that same nice-lady way, but even so, manners came first, and she set great store in "keeping one's opinions to oneself." Once when I was visiting, the Sri Lankan family that had moved in down the street invited her to a party for a newborn baby. ("I suppose you wouldn't call it a christening," she mused to me.) And my mother, by god, she defrosted a shepherd's pie, blotted her lipstick, and floated down the sidewalk on a cloud of benign tolerance. "They were so welcoming!" she enthused to me afterward, dumping all the delicious-looking food they had sent her home with into the garbage.

These memories got me sniffling.

"Ah, shit," said Trevor, observing this.

"Karie don't cry no more, don't cry no more, Karie." Which was what Kelli always said to me when I cried, because she was the older sister.

"Oh, it's Karie, is it?" said Trevor.

"Sorry," I said. We'd been speaking for a half hour and I still hadn't identified myself beyond "Kelli's sister." His identity had taken precedence. "It's Karen."

Trevor placed his hands on his knees in a finishing-the-conversation gesture. "Well, me and the Kelli-bean here should get our walk in and let you"—I could see him mentally reach for something somber and respectful—"do your thing." He pushed on his knees and stood with a weird physical precision, as if it were some kind of training exercise he usually did in sets of fifteen at the gym.

I was nodding and Kelli was already on her feet, at the closet and putting her windbreaker on upside down. I got up to help her, but Trevor beat me to it, peeling the yellow nylon sleeves from Kelli's arms, over her protests.

"Jacket on!" said Kelli.

"We gotta get it on right, Beaner."

"Geddit on right," conceded Kelli, standing still for him.

I watched the stranger dress my sister, feeling incongruously at peace. It was a suspicious feeling—it had no place in this house, in this hingelike moment of my and my sister's existence. Thinking about it now, I realize I had spent the days after my mother's funeral flailing around for some kind of cosmic reassurance when it came to the arrangements I was beginning to make for Kelli's future—looking for signs from the universe that the total upheaval she was facing would go smoothly and she'd be more or less okay. And somehow the sight of Kelli keeping still for Trevor, smiling and humming as he zipped her jacket up to her chin, had given me that reassurance, however briefly. *See? Someone else taking care of Kelli. That's all it is. It won't be as hard as you think.*

And I was so grateful in that moment. When I tell this story now and people ask what I was thinking, it's this feeling of incongruous peace that I remember. It exists in my memory as the quick, satisfying sound of a zipper being hoisted. I never mention it, though—not because it seems so irrelevant compared to the details that come later, the juicy stuff that makes people cringe and cover their eyes. It's just that this is the moment of which I'm most ashamed. *Ziiiipppppp!* My pathetic gratitude. The wide-open door of it.

2

For the first five minutes of their walk, I just hovered at the top of the stairs, wondering if I should've double-checked Trevor's credentials before I let him whisk Kelli out the door. The responsible thing to do would have been to ask him to wait and then call Bestlife for a quick confirmation. As opposed to feeding the stranger fucking cookies, then standing off to one side with a stupid smile on my face as he zipped up Kelli's jacket. But, my mind babbled, surely Bestlife ran background checks, and surely your average sexual predator would not prioritize the 250-pound mentally handicapped woman with a skin condition his employer has placed in his care—or would he? Then I scolded myself: This mode of thinking was unfair, even sexist. I had not remotely entertained such dark notions about any of the female strangers who'd been alone with my naked sister in the downstairs bathroom throughout the week. But then I thought: Perhaps I should have.

You don't know what you're doing, said the robotic recorded-operator voice that had been playing in my head on repeat since I'd arrived. Whenever I felt myself flailing, I'd sit down, try to focus my brain, but all I ever got was the recorded operator. *We're sorry. Your call is important to us. But you don't know what you're doing.*

I spun around and went looking for my phone to call 911—but it took me so long to find it (why I was searching under my mother's bed and rifling through the basement cubby or why, for that matter, I didn't just think to pick up the landline, I couldn't tell you) that by the time I found it sitting in plain sight on the kitchen table, I had convinced myself that I was being irrational. I sat on the top step leading down into the foyer, clutching my phone, monitoring the front door. This was about fifteen minutes into Kelli and Trevor's walk.

Then I tried to distract myself by thinking about other things, but the things I started thinking about were a huddle of memories that had also been auto-replaying in my head for days, all revolving around the fight I had with my mother before she had to go into the hospital for her mastectomy, when I was thirty-five and she was sixty-seven. She had pleaded with me to come home and look after Kelli while she was in recovery. And I did as she asked, of course I did, but I wasn't exactly gracious in my acquiescence. The request had come at a bad time. My marriage was on the rocks—just entering the early stages of its slow, five-year implosion—and in a panicked and nonsensical attempt to distract myself from this inevitability, I was busy applying to law school. And I was angry at her, irrationally enough. That was my response to her diagnosis: I was mad at her for terrifying me by getting sick. But I told myself at the time it was for not being as troubled as I felt she should be by my failing marriage. Because my mother had never really taken my marriage seriously in the first place, since we didn't formalize it within, as she put it, "the sanctity of Catholic tradition." It had been formalized within the sanctity of a Caribbean all-inclusive package.

So, feeling betrayed by the world in general and her in particular, I had taken the opportunity to lecture my cancer-stricken mother. This was not the first time the idea of putting Kelli into care had been broached, but it was certainly the first time I, her adult daughter, had suggested it to her. It was, you have to understand, a cardinal sin within our family theology. Forbidden, like uttering the name of G_d. It was something doctors—foolish, soulless doctors—had suggested over the years as my mother aged. Also well-meaning but ultimately ignorant friends and relatives who, behind closed doors, my mother and the dutiful daughter I used to be had sadly laughed at and shaken our heads over. Imagine—day-to-day life without Kelli! Kelli's cartoon cackle, Kelli's placid physical presence. Kelli's needs, Kelli's routines. Kelli's helplessness, Kelli's bowel movements. Kelli's eczema and recurrent ear infections. Kelli's stubborn physical strength and increasingly unmanageable girth. Imagine not knowing the joy of what it was to care for Kelli, day in and day out, until the cancer, nibbling away at your edges for so many decades, finally crept its way into your center. And after a while, as my mother continued to shake her head and laugh sadly over the unimaginability of such things, I—as you can imagine—started to imagine them.

The screen door wheezed open. Kelli and Trevor were back, Kelli windswept and babbling as Trevor peeled the banana-yellow jacket sleeves from her arms before she could get tangled up in them in her hurry to move into the next phase of her day.

Kelli had a charming way of being "done" with her home care friends at the end of their visits. She was unsentimental about good-byes because Kelli was a creature of ritual, and she understood departures to be as essential to the visitation ritual as arrivals. After her baths, for example, she'd come charging out of the bathroom, trailing a flowery, girls' locker room cloud of shampoo and conditioner, and head to her upholstered stool by the window, muttering, *Bye-bye now, bye-bye now* without so much as a backward glance. "Oh, am I dismissed?" one woman had chuckled as she dried her hands and winked at me.

But Trevor had initiated a new ritual. And when I say *new*, I mean unprecedented. Before Kelli could charge up the stairs, Trevor inquired: "No hug for Trebie?"

Kelli does not hug. She has never hugged. She lets herself be hugged, certainly, although not for long. By way of physical demonstration, sometimes she used to put the back of her hand against my or my mother's forehead, but this was a game from childhood. She'd say, "Mumma got a fever?" and my mother would obligingly lean over so Kelli could pretend to check. She was also good at shaking hands, one of those straightforward social rituals she wholeheartedly endorsed. But hugging, like eye contact, was never Kelli's thing.

So I watched as Kelli hugged Trevor. As far as hugs went, it was definitely Kelli, meaning perfunctory, the way the back of the hand on the forehead was perfunctory—more of a performance of a fever check than an actual fever check. And this was more of a performance of a hug. She extended her arms straight out and kind of bopped them against Trevor's upper arms as Trevor put his hands about her soft, expansive waist and gave it a squeeze.

Bye-bye now, bye-bye Trebie, said Kelli, charging up the stairs, past me, to get to her stool by the window.

There was nothing troubling about the hug except for the fact that it meant Trevor was special. And for some reason, I didn't acknowledge that to him. I didn't want to let Trevor know how extraordinary the chaste physical rite he'd initiated with my sister actually was. I came down the steps and took the jacket from him and signed the bottom of his clipboard, as I had learned that I was supposed to do from Kelli's bathers.

"Same time next week," said Trevor in an inflectionless way, so that, perhaps, the statement would come across as neither question nor instruction. It left a blank spot for me to fill in, I realized, like the blank spaces on the form I was signing.

"So," I said. "I don't know for how long."

Trevor, looking down at his clipboard, now raised his eyes at me. He was one of those people who wrote with their mouths open, and his pale, pink lips had been parted as he filled in the sheet—they shone as if he'd glossed or just licked them. He was a ruddy, freckled Celtic type, a type that had always put me off a little, maybe because I'd grown up around so many of them. There was something about the barely there pigmentation, the delicate blue veins floating around beneath lacteal skin—his physiology felt too close to the surface somehow, as if it might come bursting forth.

"A lot of changes right now, I imagine."

"You imagine so," I answered, which was not really a coherent thing to say.

"Well, you know you can just call the office anytime, let them know what your needs are. And—" Trevor reached behind himself and started digging around in his back pocket. "You let me know what I can do, Miss Karie, all right?"

He gave me a business card. I looked at it, expecting to see his full name floating above the Bestlife address, but all that was on the card was one word:

TREV

And a cell phone number beneath it.

I was admiring the confidence of this, an all-caps personality asserting itself amid a small sea of undifferentiated white, when Trevor snapped me out of it with what he said next.

"Your mother was the best of women."

I raised my eyes at him, just as he had at me, realizing as I did that—yes—I'd been staring down at his card with my mouth open.

"Thank you."

"I'm not saying that to be nice. I really want you to *know* it."

"I do know it," I told him.

"I hope you do," said Trevor. "Because you have some tough decisions coming up, don't you, Karie?"

As he said this, he poked at the card in my hands.

After my divorce I sometimes used to tell myself, *It's just that I wasn't used to men.* Our father died when I was seven and Kelli was eleven, and our house became a girl world after that, a doll-strewn universe of floral-patterned curtains and panties flagrantly hung to dry in the living room because there was no father or brother around whose sensibilities needed to be sheltered from such things. I could shriek to my friends on the phone and, later, scream at cute boys on the television and nobody would wince or tell me to keep it down, or announce to me imperiously (as subsequent boyfriends did) that the actor I fawned over was known to be a "major fruit." My shrieking and screaming would often get Kelli started, and sometimes we'd spiral into gleeful, eardrum-piercing competitions.

But after my husband left, I would sit in our former home, now half-emptied of whatever furniture and *objets* he had deigned to take with him, and tell myself, like battalions of women had before me, that it was the fault of this thing called Men. But it was also my own fault, I thought, for not paying close enough attention to Men, for being cavalier, for not being as careful as other women I knew, women who made their painstaking efforts to understand and negotiate Men as creatures separate from themselves an ongoing project.

I'd never really wanted to believe in that—in Men as their own mass entity. I'd always scoffed at the Mars and Venus thing, the reductive, needless divisiveness of it, but now, sitting on my—formerly our—kitchen floor because frying an egg had proven a physical and emotional bridge too far, I considered that I had been cocky. I had been through the kind of wringer where I had thought I was an autonomous individual forging a happy, unencumbered partnership with a fellow, like-minded human being. Our deep friendship, loyalty, eschewal of antiquated boy-girl ritual (such as, say, a marriage formalized within the sanctity of Catholic tradition) placed us high above the fray, I thought, far beyond the clichés of, say, sexual jealousy. Or wandering eyes. Or arguments over dishes. Or the queasy intermingling of wrath and depression represented by a trail of soiled socks and underwear, where each item picked up—followed grimly like a trail of bread crumbs in one of the Grimms' fairy tales—leads to a kind of emotional oven in which one sits, and stews.

Anyway, years passed. I got over it, kind of, and after a while, Men became just men again. But I have to admit to a shift in my perception. It's like when you get an eye exam—through one lens, the optometrist shows you a rendering of a small, lonely farmhouse in a distant, empty landscape and, yeah, it looks okay to you. Solid. Distinct. But then a whole new lens gets slotted in and, Oh! How much sharper those lonely, distant farmhouse lines.

3

He came back on Saturday. The Bestlife workers didn't work on Saturday, had been my understanding. I was out mowing the lawn and Kelli was sitting on a plastic Muskoka chair, watching me, wearing her Halifax Mooseheads trucker hat to keep off the sun. She hadn't wanted to come outside at first—once Kelli's planted on her stool by the window after breakfast, it takes some cajoling to get her off it before lunch. Like I said, a creature of routine. So much so that even the unexpected sight of her boyfriend coming up the driveway didn't provoke the outburst of gleeful, repetitive *Trebie*s I would've expected.

"It's Trebie," I heard her remark, almost suspiciously, after I shut down the mower.

"How's my girlfriend?" called Trevor, and Kelli's suspicion immediately gave way to titters and happy rocking back and forth. It turned out my sister was a pushover. Trevor gave her a fake pinch on the cheek before sauntering over to me with a solemn half smile on his face, like a man holding a gift behind his back. He put his hand on the mower alongside mine.

"Let me do this," he said.

Suddenly my eye stung from a droplet of sweat mingled with sunscreen that had rolled into it. "I don't think," I replied, wincing, "this is in your job description."

Trevor waited for me to finish dabbing my streaming eye with a shirtsleeve. I wondered if he thought I'd abruptly started crying. If so, he didn't seem troubled. He struck me as the kind of guy who took a woman's sudden tears in stride, who waited for the storm to pass. I found that sort of admirable. "Can I tell you something?" said Trevor. "I got a buddy who works at Seaside. We had a couple ryes last night."

I blinked at Trevor with my one working eye. I had forgotten how smallish cities like this one worked, the way people found things out about one another—and Maritimers in particular had a knack for this. "Seaside" was Seaside Care Facility, which Kelli and I had toured the previous day. Irene had arranged for this squat, concrete sprawl of a building (which was out in Bedford and nowhere near the seaside, by the way) to become Kelli's new home on the occasion of our mother's death. It was my job to install my sister there by the end of the month. A bed was ready and waiting.

But the visit hadn't gone well. I may have made a small scene. I think it had something to do with facing, all in one afternoon, the quivering bundle of unimaginable outcomes I'd managed to push from my mind my entire adult life, telling myself that there was *simply no point in worrying about this now.* And that entire bundle had been wrapped up in one ultimately unthinkable question: *What happens when Mom dies?* Now that she had, the bundle of terrors had rapidly unfurled, right there at Seaside.

It hadn't been a house of horrors. It was simply the kind of place where people like my sister go to live. But I hadn't been to one of these places before. I'd been to Kelli's cheerful friendship circle at the community center and I'd been to various square dances and potlucks for Kelli and people like her, people functioning at the "severe" end of the spectrum—meaning not quite capable of, say, holding down a basic job, but not so disabled that they couldn't carry on, and enjoy, a simple game or conversation. I wasn't troubled by a roomful of the developmentally disabled, is what I'm saying.

I was troubled, if I'm honest, by the wheelchairs. The scrubs. The bedpans. There were people like Kelli, but there were also people at the outer reaches of the spectrum, people who couldn't hold a conversation, who had no language, who spent their days strapped to wheelchairs and beds, regularly fed and diapered. There was nothing wrong with that, I told myself, in fact it was good—it was a fine thing that Seaside provided care for these people. It was just that it gave the place a feeling of being somewhere between a home and a hospital. That's what I hadn't been expecting. That bringing Kelli here would mean turning her into a patient as opposed to just Kelli, the person she had always been. And the understanding that this had been my mother's horror all along; this had been her objection. And her objection had been justified.

So it was realizing that, plus wanting to turn to her and tell her so, plus discovering all over again the new, stupid, eternal fact of my mother's not being here anymore. What happens is, you throw a minor sobbing fit in the administrator's office.

"So I was thinking you could use some help," said Trevor. He put his other hand on the mower, crowding out mine. "Let me do this, then we'll have a cup of tea."

I sat beside Kelli in the other plastic Muskoka chair, watching Trevor push the mower in expert rows across the lawn, breathing in the smell of freshly slaughtered grass. Across the street, a white-haired neighbor pulled into his driveway and raised a hand to Trevor as he got out of his car—*I see you are mowing your lawn, sir; I salute you.* Trevor raised a hand right back. Who, I wondered, had done this for my mother when she was alive? Was there a neighborhood boy? Or some retired gent with a ride-on mower down the street? As the daughter who lacked a mental disability, it had been my responsibility to inquire about such things. *Who mows your lawn, Ma? How are you keeping yourself fed?* A responsibility I mostly shirked, and that my mother mostly encouraged me to shirk, right up until those awful, final days. Because my mother always insisted she was fine, and for the most part she always was. Over the decades the cancer would poke its head out, take a few experimental nibbles, before she would just seem to shoo it from her body, as if it were a horsefly. She didn't have time for such nonsense. So who was I to question such a woman's self-sufficiency? She had always been the force of nature, the monster of competence, the nice fuckin' lady—who harangued government agencies and spearheaded bake sales and dominated town council meetings.

And hadn't I always been the disappointment who would *never understand*? Who cared for *only your own comfort*? Who *would have to be a mother to even begin to grasp* et cetera? And we all knew that wasn't going to happen, didn't we? Because, let's face it, by the time I'd turned twenty I'd found that I'd done enough caregiving to last a lifetime. And let's just say I made that known.

Once the lawn was mowed, I made us all tea.

"What's the plan, Miss Karie?" Trevor asked after a few sips. He had flecks of green all across his bristly hairline, where flying grass particles had stuck to his perspiring brow as he mowed.

"I guess Seaside," I said, intuiting what he meant. "Did you like Seaside, Kelli?"

"Like Seaside," Kelli agreed absently. But I knew it wasn't a fair question. Kelli liked pretty much anywhere she was taken. She enjoyed outings, full stop. Be they to the mall, the doctor's, Tim Hortons. I might as well have asked her if she liked the ocean. She did, but that didn't mean she wanted to spend her life in it.

"It's not a bad place," said Trevor.

I glanced up at him. "But not great?"

"Well, there's other places I know," he said. "Some more expensive than others."

"I guess we should shop around." I flinched inwardly—and outwardly too, as far as I knew—at the words as I said them. Not just the soul-withering "shop around" but the stupid irony of "we."

"Well, yeah," said Trevor. "Why stop at Seaside?"

"That's the one my mother liked," I said. "I mean, she thought about all this a lot. She budgeted for it."

"Can't you kick in a little extra?" said Trevor. "Your mum said you were a lawyer."

"Um," I said. "I'm not practicing. I work as a legal consultant for a couple of—"

"Still," Trevor said, cutting me off. "Good money in that, I imagine." He blew on his tea.

This was a conversation from which my decorous mother would have found a way to excuse herself. Before I could imagine how, Trevor said, "I can call a couple of buddies of mine."

"You have so many *buddies,*" I remarked, stalling.

"Get you in to see a couple of places."

"Okay," I said after a moment. Because suddenly I was imagining an alternative to Seaside. For just a bit more money. For the rest of the day after visiting that facility, I hadn't been able to stop thinking about how all the women working there had messy hair—stray, random tresses falling from or poking out of their twisted buns and ponytails. It had upset me, stirred up a nameless, obsessive anxiety that I couldn't shake, that I decided to just lump in with all the other crappy feelings of the day. But thinking about it now, I realized my preoccupation with the hair at Seaside wasn't just a nitpick—it was a visual gauge of overwork. It meant these women went through their entire days with no time to check themselves in a mirror, to straighten their barrettes or retie their ponytails. So the hair just got crazier and crazier, the ponytails more cockeyed, with every frantic hour of their day.

Trevor said he would pick us up tomorrow. And I was lulled, drifting, imagining a professional bustle of sleek, shining ponytails when I agreed.

These days, when I tell this story to friends, it's always the moment Trevor lets himself in with his key the next day—a Sunday—that makes them kind of whoop in their seats. Or flop backward in a gesture of full-bodied incredulity. Or just stare at me like I'm an idiot. But, I explain, I just hadn't gotten around to opening the front door and leaving the screen unlocked—as I typically did before the home care people arrived. Trevor possessed a key, so clearly he was used to letting himself in. Apparently my mother had given it to him for the convenience of both of them. The key was sanctioned. She hadn't given it to any of the other care workers, but that was because, I assumed, they were on a rotation—you never knew who would be coming to bathe Kelli from week to week. Trevor, however, only covered walks, and he turned up like clockwork every Tuesday and Friday morning at ten on the dot.

But this was *Sunday,* some of my friends argue, and he wasn't working, he was visiting. Yes, I say, but why would he deviate from habit? This was a house he had a key for, and whenever he came over, he would open the door and come in. That was his routine. So it's understandable he'd do the same thing on Sunday he would've done on a Tuesday or Friday. Isn't it?

At the time, I thought nothing of it. Trevor said he'd come at ten on Sunday, just as he did on Tuesdays and Fridays, and it was ten on the dot when he inserted his key in the door. Kelli and I had our jackets on, ready to go.

I have to admit, everything about that day was off. It started with Trevor's insistence that we all cram into the cab of his pickup truck when there was a perfectly comfortable two-door sedan also parked in the driveway.

"No," said Trevor. "I'm more comfortable driving the truck." As if the question of who would drive had already been discussed and dispensed with.

So Kelli got in the middle, which she was not too happy about, especially when I had to root around beneath her thighs and buttocks to find the middle safety belt, which, it turned out, had been used so rarely it had been all but consumed by the tuck of the seat. Then I stuffed myself in beside her, which I was not happy about because being crammed against my sister was a lot like cuddling up against a lavishly padded space heater. And then, of course, there was Trevor, squeezing in behind the wheel, calling, "Suck in your guts, girls!" before he closed the door.

"Knee," said Kelli a moment after we pulled out of the driveway. Which meant her right knee was cramping up, as it often did when she sat in close quarters.

"Your knee sore, Kelli?" I asked.

"Knee sore."

"She's got arthritis," I explained to Trevor. "We should maybe get the sedan . . ."

Trevor glanced down at Kelli's thighs, like two massive, sweatpants-clad loaves of bread squashed together.

"Ah, you're good, darlin'."

"Knee sore."

"It's a short trip."

It was a thirty-minute trip out of town, the last five minutes of which took place along a winding dirt road that grew darker the deeper it took us into the woods.

This is like a fairy tale, I remember thinking. But the cautionary, old-world kind, the kind that never bothered with happy endings. Where parents take their innocent and trusting children to the forest and abandon them for hungry old ladies to entice into their ovens, for talking wolves to swallow whole.

"Kelli's knee," said Kelli.

"Almost there, Beaner."

And it was true. All at once the woods opened up—also like a fairy tale, but this time of the Disney variety. Because what stood before us was a mansion. An honest-to-god Regency-style mansion like something out of *Masterpiece Theatre*. Where was the horse and carriage? Where were Mr. Darcy and the Bennet sisters? It had a Doric portico and French windows and buttresses and balustrades.

"This is it," said Trevor. "Barnbarroch Manor."

I burst out into laughter. The angry kind.

It was a wasted thirty minutes touring a beautiful facility. The ponytails were impeccable—these ponytails could've been overseeing a spa in the south of France. There was no administrator to talk to, because we weren't supposed to be there, officially. One of Trevor's buddies who worked in food service had let us in, grunting at us to look around but be discreet—the staff would just assume we were visiting a resident.

So we wandered around. Inside, the floors were gleaming. There was a cavernous music and activities room where residents enjoyed joyful sing-alongs and studious yet leisurely craft making. There was an atrium with a pool where swimming and movement classes presumably took place, and the less active and less verbal of the residents could just cozy up and enjoy the humid, chlorine-scented sunshine. And speaking of sunshine, there was the unadulterated kind out in back, which residents soaked up as they strolled and lolled around the endless, impeccably manicured grounds.

There was no need to be annoyed at not being able to speak to an administrator or any of the employees, because there was no need to ask any questions. This was not something my dearly departed mother and I could afford in our wildest dreams.

"I just thought you'd like to see it," said Trevor once the three of us were re-stuffed into his pickup and plunging back into the green darkness of the dirt road, toward the highway.

"It was something," I said. I hadn't said much else during our self-directed tour.

"I know it would've been better to have an appointment so you could talk to someone in charge," admitted Trevor. "It's just that there's a waiting list. It takes forever. I figured, why wait when we've got an in with Finny?"

Finny was the name, first or last I didn't know, of Trevor's buddy in food service. He hadn't been much of an in, and he hadn't seemed like much of a buddy, for that matter. All he did was meet up with us at the front entrance and give us his grimacing, almost begrudging, warning not to talk to anyone.

"I just thought you should see what's out there," Trevor sounded a little defensive, even though I hadn't said anything. "There's a range of options I figured you might not even know about."

"It was gorgeous," I said, trying, for some reason, to mollify him. "But Barnbarroch"—I laughed lightly, deliberately—"isn't exactly a realistic option for us."

Trevor drove in silence for a while. His jaw flexed.

"Knee," mentioned Kelli.

"Just a couple more stops, Bean-o."

Kelli refused to get out of the truck. Her knee ached and walking might've helped, but she wasn't used to doing so much walking, let alone visiting so many strange and stimulating places, in the course of a single afternoon. After the god-awful Fenwick Centre downtown, where a hunched and overly familiar male resident tried to take hold of my sister's spare tire (and, when Kelli yelped in protest, shrieked rage into her face), Kelli decided she was officially done.

"Coming, Beaner?"

"Not coming," said Kelli. "Kelli's supper."

I looked at my phone. It was closing in on four o'clock. Not suppertime, but to Kelli's mind, I knew, supper meant going home. I was with her.

"She's getting hungry," I told Trevor across the hood of his pickup truck. We were in the parking lot of a place called Gorsebrook Residential Home. It didn't look bad—several steps up from the grimy bedlam that was Fenwick, and even a step or two up from Seaside. Seaside was brightly painted and spacious enough inside, but its industrial concrete exterior was the opposite of inviting. Gorsebrook was not as big, but it was a newer building with a light, welcoming exterior and large windows to let in sunlight. And I could see there was a pool.

"They got physio here on staff," said Trevor. "Just started with an acupuncturist a couple times a month, so I hear. If you believe in that bullshit."

"That's nice," I said.

"Let's go, Kelli-bean!" Trevor hollered, banging the flat of his hand against the hood.

"Not going. Kelli not going." Kelli began to rock back and forth. I felt a little like rocking back and forth myself.

"She's toast," I said. "I'll come back. I'll set up an appointment on Monday."

"She'll be okay in the truck, eh?" said Trevor.

"In the truck," said Kelli, rocking.

I glanced at her. Kelli had been left alone in the car before—her stubbornness had frequently won the day when my mother brought her along on errands. My mother would simply turn on the radio, open the window a crack, and lock the doors. Kelli was not the type to wander away. Kelli, an adult woman fully possessed of her faculties as far as any passersby could tell, would sit murmuring to herself and people-watching until my mother's return. But Trevor didn't know any of that. So on the one hand, I could claim, even mustering a faint air of outrage, that Kelli *by no means* could be left alone in the truck. And maybe even fabricate a story about how one time she had been left alone in a car with near-disastrous results.

On the other hand, we could leave Kelli in the truck. We could lock the doors and I could dart inside with Trevor for a couple of minutes. And then we could go home.

I looked at Trevor. He wasn't looking back at me; he was watching a teenager in a Nissan Sentra completely fail to parallel park nearby. He tapped two fingers on the hood of his truck in a steady *tick-tock-tick-tock* percussion. He wasn't waiting for me to decide, I realized. He was waiting for me to get a move on. And he felt he was being polite about it. Patient.

4

The barbecue hadn't been used in decades, as far as I knew. I recalled my mother covering it up decisively after my eighteenth birthday party, during which my boyfriend at the time had received a drunken faceful of propane flames that nearly sizzled away his eyebrows and his over-gelled bangs. But Trevor was determined to fire the thing up.

It was about five-thirty when we finally made it home, and he insisted, to apologize for keeping us out all day, on cooking us steaks— "My treat!" As Kelli and I climbed out of the truck, me making mild and inarticulate noises of dissent, Trevor instructed us to "get the fixin's ready" while he popped over to Superstore. Fifteen minutes later, he was back, a bag of steaks in one hand and a twelve-pack of beer in the other.

By "fixin's" I'd assumed he meant some kind of side dish, so I told him I had made a salad. Trevor shook his head. He never ate anything raw, he explained, so a salad would not do. Of everything I'd experienced that day, the revelation that Trevor had not consumed a piece of raw food in his entire lifetime threw me off the most. I stood there, rhyming off names of fruits and vegetables in disbelief.

"Apples?"

"Nothing raw."

"Bananas?"

"Nope."

"You never have, like, a raw carrot? Or berries?"

"S'gotta be cooked."

"Lettuce?"

"S'gotta be cooked."

"You cook lettuce?"

"I don't eat lettuce," said Trevor, patiently, as if he'd had this conversation with many a dumbfounded woman before me.

"So no salad?"

"No salad."

"What'll we have on the side?"

"Baked potato," said Trevor. It turned out he had purchased three, already wrapped in foil.

Trevor had also bought a fresh propane tank, and after only a few minutes of masculine fiddling he had the ancient barbecue up and running. I noticed he didn't bother to clean the grill, or ask me to do so, but at the same time there was no question that my mother would have allowed the barbecue to be covered up those near-thirty years ago without ensuring that the grill was spotless. My mother's standard of cleanliness was such that I could well imagine it enduring over decades. And if there were cobwebs, I thought listlessly, they'd burn up in the fire.

Kelli had claimed her perch by the window as soon as we got home, so Trevor and I were alone on the back patio, chatting about Gorsebrook, based on the brief look-around we took before I started to feel nervous about Kelli and insisted we go back to the truck. I'd been too anxious to really absorb much, but what I saw looked hopeful. The interior was clean, cheerful, and as sunlit as I'd predicted when I noticed the big windows outside. Because it was smaller, it seemed that Gorsebrook, unlike Seaside, didn't admit the more profoundly disabled, so the residents were all basically at Kelli's level—people she could talk to, play games with maybe. There were no wheelchairs parked in the hallways, and the beds, I noticed, were just regular beds—not hospital-issue. There was a common room with shelves haphazardly piled with board games and various musical instruments. It also had a Ping-Pong table, a pair of massive couches, and a TV for movie nights. Across the hall, the dining area had dollar-store vases with flowers on every table, and its walls were lined with splashily painted artwork courtesy of, I gathered, the residents.

The workers had seemed cheerful for the most part, and so had the residents—except for a girl who'd been hurrying down the hall in an open bathrobe, the sleeve of which got hooked on a railing and yanked her backward, causing her to yell *Bastard!,* which cracked Trevor up. Driving home, Trevor joked that it seemed like his kind of place. "But seriously," he said now. "It seemed nice. If you want to book a more official visit with them sometime, let me know."

I wondered why he thought I should let him know. Trevor hadn't mentioned that he had any kind of "in" at Gorsebrook, the way he had at Barnbarroch, some insider "buddy" who could speed the process or put in a good word for us. I let it slide, because he was talking about other things now. He stood at the barbecue and I sat in a plastic chair, watching the tendons in his forearms flex and contract as he manipulated the sizzling meat. He told me a little about his life. There was an ex-wife and a young son, who he saw only every other weekend, which broke his damn heart every day. And his wife was going to let the kid play soccer and not hockey, he said, even though Trevor had vowed to pay for all the equipment himself. "But will she listen to reason?" Trevor asked me. "No," he answered for me. "It's just: concussion, concussion, concussion. That's her only argument."

Also, Trevor said he was going to start a business of his own, soon, once he got the funds together. He and his brother had come very near to starting a business selling bodybuilding supplements, but his brother had ended up pulling, according to Trevor, "one dick move too many. So I decided basically fuck him." Now he and his brother didn't talk, but Trevor said he had learned much from the experience—enough to go it alone next time, he figured.

I sipped the beer he'd cracked open and handed me moments before. Every so often an alarmed yet muted part of my brain would sort of sit up, look around at what was going on, and demand an explanation. But then I'd just stare at Trevor's blond forearms with their tendons hypnotically flexing and contracting beneath the freckled skin and after a while that part of my brain would lie back down again.

Dinner was three identical plates containing nothing but a massive steak and a massive baked potato, steaming in its tinfoil. Kelli was stymied by this and afraid of burning herself, so I peeled the foil back on hers and discovered that Trevor had at some point dug into them and added mounds of cheddar cheese. I discreetly scraped out as much as I could and made a mental note to have Kelli drink a full glass of Metamucil before bed, which would add a good twenty minutes of cajoling to the bedtime ritual. Next came the job of cutting her steak up into tiny, choke-proof morsels, as Kelli's teeth were not the best and she had always shown a lot more enthusiasm for swallowing than for chewing, which in the past had led to the occasional purple-faced panic. I meditated on the infinitesimal bites of meat as Kelli huffed with impatience beside me.

If I'd been capable of being amazed—that is, if my emotional spectrum weren't at that point a pendulum that swung only between the states of *numb* versus *weepy*—it would have been amazing to me how easily I'd fallen back into all these routines I'd once disavowed with such vigor. Kelli's bad teeth. Kelli's obstructed windpipe. Kelli's blocked colon. I was not going to spend my life obsessing on these things day in and goddamn fucking day out, is what I said to my mother that angry summer when I was twenty years old.

To which, I recall, she had replied, the tips of her ears bright pink: *You* are the one who is obsessing on these things. *I* am not obsessing on these things. I am *dealing* with these things. This is called *life*. This is called *everyday life*.

There was not much else she could have said to get me out the door any faster.

When I looked up from Kelli's decimated steak, Trevor had already cleaned his plate and brought it to the sink, which he was now filling with lemon-scented suds.

"Don't do that," I admonished him.

"Hey," said Trevor. "This was my idea. I'm the one who brought this mess to town!"

It was not an expression I'd ever heard before.

———

Trevor left after the dishes and a final beer. ("See you Tuesday, girls. Same bat time, same bat channel!") And maybe I should have been lying awake in bed thinking about that, but I'd had three beers myself, and once I had started playing the old arguments with my mother on a loop, the loops circled faster and tighter into a compulsive, steady spiral that I couldn't pull myself out of. I lay there in the dark with my eyes wide open and every once in a while I'd realize my lips were moving as if I were back there—back *here,* that is—in this very house, furious and trapped and blaming her. Blaming them both, but mostly her, because she was my mother, she was supposed to take care of me, and all she seemed to want was for me to disappear into this life along with her. Plus, how could anyone blame Kelli for anything? Kelli was just there, through no fault of her own. Blaming her did no good. She was the stone idol, wordless and eternal, at whose feet you lay your sacrifice.

Oh, you and your life! *You and your precious young* life! These were the words my mother spat at me at one point during the angry summer's sweltering peak.

That sounds like an evil thing for her to have said. But it was also at the peak of one of our blowouts and I had been pushing her. We'd been standing outside on the same patio where Trevor had barbecued, the barbecue itself neatly covered, still early in the first decade of its disuse. We were out there so Kelli wouldn't hear us, because she cried when we argued (this being one of the less illustrious consequences of life in girl world—everyone was always bursting into tears). And, yes, I had pushed my mother. Oh god, had I ever, in all my young righteousness. *I* was ambitious, *I* had potential, *I* had big plans (unlike *you,* was the ongoing subtext), *I* needed expanded horizons, expansive vistas, freedom, Mother. Freedom to accomplish all the wonderful things the young, vivacious, ability-crammed me was so clearly capable of.

And oh, the grotesque understanding behind those words: *your precious young life.*

The awful, acerbic emphasis on *precious.*

Before then, I'd had no idea my mother was even capable of sarcasm itself, let alone vicious sarcasm.

And I had brought it out in her, this ugliness.

You'd think I would've been the one to burst into tears at that moment, but it was her.

Well, go, she'd said, turning toward the patio screen door and struggling with the magnet that held it in its frame.

To think I'd always considered that moment a victory.

Monday I called Gorsebrook to see if I could book what Trevor had called a "more official" visit, and was thrown off my moorings by the warm and caressing voice of a woman named Marlene. *Oh, Karen,* she said into the phone once I explained my situation. I was taken aback by the wincing sympathy of these words, as I'd practically been speaking in bullet points up until then, trying to keep things straightforward and unemotionally professional. And then Marlene bludgeoned me a second time with: *Karen, you poor dear.* And it was game over.

I never knew what was going to throw me off. There was no way to predict. I could spend a dry-eyed afternoon boxing up my mother's clothes and jewelry, breathing in the ghost of some decades-old perfume that inhabited the fibers of her turtlenecks and twinsets, thinking about nothing in particular, it seemed—nothing sad, nothing bad—for hours on end. Then an advertisement for life insurance—not even on TV but on the *radio,* for god's sake—might hit me like a truncheon. The tinkling music, the thoughtful, considerate words calculated to reassure. We *know.* We *understand.* The aural equivalent of a pat on the hand—not even a particularly *sincere* pat on the hand—could lay me out for hours.

And that's what Marlene at Gorsebrook's voice was like too—a hand on mine. I sat there sniffling on the phone, exasperated with myself. To be so randomly fragile when I had so much shit to figure out. I apologized to Marlene for all the time I was taking up with my blubbering and pausing to blow my nose every few minutes. But really

I wanted to tell her: This is *your* fault. Please stop talking that way you are talking. Can you please stop fucking *cradling* me with your voice.

Trevor stuck around for a while after Kelli's walk on Tuesday because there was baseball on TV. My mother had at some point purchased a massive flatscreen, and it turned out she had a subscription that included all the sports channels, which, Trevor explained, grinning like a naughty boy, "she was nice enough to let me peep at every now and then." I'd been surprised by the TV, and even more surprised when I'd discovered the Cadillac of a cable package she'd purchased to go with it, because my mother had taken a dim view of television when I was growing up. TV wasn't, as she used to say, "improving." Also it had too much "smut." But I supposed that as her mobility declined, and once she learned she could get BBC and curling on the upper channels, a lifetime of looking askance at "the idiot box" was out the window.

Trevor invited my sister and me to join him in the rec room, but Kelli was comfortably lodged in her spot at the window and daytime TV had never been part of her routine. So even though it was only a little after eleven in the morning, I grabbed two of the remaining beers and passed one to Trevor as I joined him in front of the looming screen.

He cracked the beer without missing a beat, tossing me a wink. "Playing hooky today, are we?"

Trevor had opted for Kelli's red recliner. He hoisted the footrest and sprawled comfortably backward as if the chair had been made for him. It had a cup holder Kelli never used, into which Trevor deposited his beer.

I remembered the Christmas my mother bought the chair for Kelli. It was probably the most expensive piece of furniture in the house except for a couple of inadvertent hand-me-down antiques. Kelli never required much at Christmas—she was happy to just rip paper off presents. Soft candy or stuffed animals that warbled a tune when their stomachs were pressed were always the biggest hits. But this one year my mother got it in her head that "Kelli deserves a good chair," and she shopped for the thing like I had never seen my frugal mother shop for anything in her life, going from showroom to showroom, depositing a no doubt grousing Kelli into one potential throne after another. At last a cranberry La-Z-Boy carried the day—massive and garish and completely out of place with the rest of the furniture. But also kind of glorious. To this day it took a combination of bribery and threats to pry Kelli off her window-perch stool with the balding upholstery and get her downstairs to sit in it.

I was gazing with incomprehension at the baseball when a commercial came on and Trevor inclined his head toward me and said, "Any decisions yet?"

"I called Gorsebrook," I told him. "The administrator was really nice. She said she can squeeze me in for a quick meeting Monday afternoon."

"Oh," said Trevor, still looking at the TV.

"You were right about the acupuncture," I said. Because I had a quick instinct, based on the tone of Trevor's *Oh,* that I should follow up by telling him he was right about something.

"If you believe in that bullshit," said Trevor. "Which I don't, personally."

"It seems like a pretty good facility."

"Yeah, on the surface," said Trevor. "But you gotta know what questions to ask."

I took a sip of beer. I had a feeling that if I said anything else positive about Gorsebrook, Trevor's opinions would entrench themselves against it.

"Look," said Trevor after a while. "Just let me know in advance. I'm happy to clear my schedule and come with you, you just need to let me know in advance next time."

The game came back on. Trevor watched a couple more innings in silence, jaw flexing. When the next commercial break arrived, he stood up, drained his beer, and told me good-bye.

I just sat in front of the baseball for a while, letting the weird tension of Trevor's leave-taking dissipate. I decided not to worry about it. The beer had made me passive, and passivity felt okay in that moment—better than the usual feeling of wanting to jump out of my skin as the recorded operator droned, *You don't know what you're doing* for the hundredth time. Kelli was silent at her window upstairs, likely dozing. The baseball game was the only sound and motion happening in the house. From the screen, disembodied male voices exclaimed to one another, exchanging boisterous theories about what might happen next. I was drawn by the urgency and anticipation in their voices and sat there watching and listening for quite some time. It was like when you sit by the ocean—noisy and unfathomable, offering the same kind of repetitive, raucous comfort.

Had the TV been turned off, I might've thought about the fact that I had only two and a half more weeks remaining of the five weeks leave I'd taken from work to get Kelli moved out of this house and into Seaside. I might have berated myself for the naïveté of having ever thought I could administrate my sister's future in a single month, when my mother—who was basically Superwoman in a salon perm—had made Kelli's world her lifelong project. But I wasn't thinking about that. I was aware of it, but not thinking about it, like a mist I was constantly having to peer through to make my way forward or a dirty windshield I couldn't be bothered to clean. Getting Kelli settled into Seaside was my entire reason for being here now that Irene was in the ground—her last request. Practically the only thing she'd asked of me in twenty years. And time was running out. I knew that. Yet I couldn't think about it—it was like focusing on the mist.

I was thinking, instead, about the word *life*—and the two particular occasions when my mother flung it at me in such angry exasperation that summer when I was twenty. And how, on those occasions, she managed to make it mean completely different things.

There was: This is called *life*!

And then there was: Your precious young *life*.

One representing reality, the other delusion.

Not that my life, at twenty, wasn't precious. It just wasn't *that* precious, was what she was saying—that is, not as precious as I thought. The young idealize things, they glamorize. They dream big. But then they leave home. They get student loans. They get minimum-wage jobs. They get incomprehensible charges on their cell phone bills. They get cold sores—massive, festering ones that no amount of makeup can obscure. They get greasy-headed landlords who walk into their apartments and poke around when they're not home. They get five-business-day holds put on their paychecks. They get drunk and throw up in public. They get refused service. They get yeast infections. They get groped on the subway. They get UTIs. They get obscenities yelled at them on the streets. They get plantar warts from the showers at their gyms. They get office jobs. They get tax audits. They get sexually harassed, but not enough to raise a fuss about. They get pregnancy scares. They have miscarriages. They get married, quickly, without romance, because to attempt to graft a sense of romance onto a life that has been pretty unromantic thus far, only to have it fall flat, would be worse than just adopting a wisecracking, cynical approach to romance from the get-go. They become pragmatic. They tell themselves, *This is pragmatism, not cynicism.* They get irritable bowel syndrome. They tell themselves, *So what if it is cynicism.* They get divorced. They go back to school. They feel too old to be going back to school. They get another office job with more responsibility and a pay bump, which they know should feel like a victory but does not. Their mother dies. They come home.

5

Marlene kept trying to follow up. She left bright, efficient messages on my cell phone every day at around the same time. "Hi, Karen! It's Marlene at Gorsebrook Residential? Just following up on our meeting of Monday, June twenty-fourth, regarding placement of your sister, Kelli."

I didn't know what to do because the less efficient administrator at Seaside had been following up with me too, but in a more haphazard kind of way, her inquiries punctuated by a lot of long *uhhhh*s and backgrounded by the sounds of rapidly shuffling papers as she scrambled to remind herself who I was and why she was getting in touch. This was Deanna. And while Deanna, when I'd met her, hadn't possessed Marlene's air of competency, nor her clear-eyed, strong, but empathetic gaze, what did bond Deanna and me was the fact that I'd sat weeping in her office on one end of her faux-leather couch while she perched at the other end, handing me tissue after tissue and looking around occasionally as if in hope some kindly and authoritative figure would usher me from the room.

The resulting problem being that, while I'd instinctively trusted and admired Marlene, I liked and sympathized more with Deanna. I'd liked the awkward and reluctant way she'd comforted me. I liked her clumsy inability to hide the fact that she was wishing it didn't have to be her—that someone else would take over. I liked that I could see her struggling. I couldn't quite believe that someone like Deanna was running a facility like Seaside, and I was pretty sure I didn't want my sister living there. But at the same time, my stronger inclination was the more irrational one—not to disappoint Deanna; not to let her down. So I was avoiding her calls too.

The other thing was, Seaside had an immediate opening; Gorsebrook didn't—this was what Marlene had told me Monday. Seaside had an immediate opening because my mother had claimed it in advance. It belonged to us. It had Kelli's name on it.

"But what we can do," said Marlene—on the afternoon she had so kindly "moved a few things around" in order to be able to squeeze me in for a chat "about your wonderful sister!"—"is have Kelli come in a few afternoons a week to spend time with the staff and other residents. She'll become used to the environment, and by the time we have an opening, she'll slot right in."

I had been surprised that a woman of Marlene's cultivated warmth and tact would use a term like "slot right in" when it came to a potential resident—it made me think of papers being slid into a file and the file being tucked away inside a drawer—but I forgave her when she added that there would be no charge for Kelli's trial afternoons.

"We just might ask you to contribute to supplies every so often," added Marlene. "We do crafts, baking. That sort of thing. We also encourage relatives to volunteer, if you'd like to sit in on a few afternoons and help your sister acclimatize."

I held up my hand in irritation, as if to say, God, shut *up,* as if Marlene had been haranguing me this whole time instead of potentially answering my prayers. Everything she was suggesting was ideal. Kelli loved to socialize. She loved having friends, a place to go, activities to look forward to. The idea of habituating Kelli to a facility before moving her there made so much sense I couldn't quite believe my mother hadn't come up with it herself. It was because, I figured, my mother had settled on Seaside long ago—maybe even before Gorsebrook, a much newer facility, had come into existence. Once my mother made a decision, it was inviolable. So I supposed she simply hadn't considered any alternatives, and she certainly wouldn't have considered consulting with me over them if she had. And I supposed, further, that Seaside had never offered her anything like this.

But then again, here was a thought. Here was a sudden thought I had, sitting across from Marlene's comely, competent face. Consider my mother, who had never been willing to even entertain the idea of putting Kelli in a home while she was alive. Who stood up from the dinner table mid-dinner and walked away the first time I'd mustered the gall to utter such blasphemy. Who went into her room and slammed the door and stayed there for an hour saying her rosary extra loud, with weird, angry emphasis on random words. (*Hail* Mary! *Full* of grace! The *Lord* is with thee!) Point being, this very same woman had arranged for Kelli to be put into a home upon her, my mother's, death. Summarily. Without so much as a how-do-you-do. Just— boom, Mother dies, Kelli goes to Seaside.

With all her careful administration of my sister's every potential need, her worry over any possible discomfort her daughter might suffer, you're telling me my mother gave no thought whatsoever to the agonies involved in un-wedging Kelli from the home she'd lived in since her girlhood? Into the bleach-fragrant hallways of what she'd always referred to as *One of Those Terrible Places*? A capital-*I* Institution? Because I don't believe it. I don't believe it. What I believe is that my mother thought about this eventuality deeply, compulsively. And what she envisioned, I can only conclude, is what is happening right now.

Which meant she'd left this specific agony to me. This was my inheritance. I was the one who suggested it in the first place, after all, in all my callousness. *I think it might be time, Mom.* I was the hardass. I was the proud, self-declared "realist." And now—look around, daughter—it's real. So deal with it. Deal with it the way you always wanted.

The only problem being, of course, that Gorsebrook did not have an immediate opening, and Marlene could not tell me when they would. And I had two and a half weeks left of the leave I had taken before my clients would expect me at my desk, dutifully pinging back responses to the daily slew of e-mails. My house, full of plants being watered by my downstairs tenant, was in a city eleven hundred miles away. And it wasn't that I couldn't get more time off work—working contract to contract and doing most of it from home made that easy. And it wasn't that my tenant wouldn't happily keep watering my plants and paying her rent by direct deposit.

If anything, it was how simple I knew it would be to remain. It had always felt easy, like falling into a hole or rolling over in bed and going back to sleep after the alarm goes off. That's why, I always told myself, I'd had to kick and claw so ruthlessly to get out in the first place.

Meanwhile, Marlene left messages. Deanna left messages. They were both being this diligent because of me—because I had made it clear to them that I was on a schedule, I was a busy career woman who needed to get my sister taken care of so I could get back to my life.

Trevor was still in a bit of a snit when he next showed up to walk Kelli. The screen door wheezed open and he called to her from the foyer as per usual, but this time he was all business, addressing most of his remarks to her, instead of me, while I negotiated my sister's arms into her jacket.

"Lookin' good, hot stuff! You working out?"

"Working out," Kelli tittered.

"You are not," I said, poking her gently in the gut. "Look at that tummy!"

"Kelli's tummy," agreed Kelli, liking the teasing.

"Abs of steel!" declared Trevor, glancing at me with a tight smile. "Let's get your sneaks on, Beaner."

Trevor kept up this banter, studiously ignoring me, right up to the moment he ushered her out the door—only then calling over his shoulder, "I'll have her home before midnight, Mother!"

While they were gone, I went to the kitchen and dug through the cupboards to assess the cookie situation. There was still half a tin of oatcakes (because nobody in the world ate these sugarless horrors except my mother—even Kelli would hesitate if they were put before her), and a handful of Irene's shortbreads, and there was the bag of store-bought chocolate-chip that were Kelli's reward when she was being well behaved. Otherwise things were few and far between on the homemade front, so after I'd scattered the remaining shortbreads and a couple of oatcakes for ballast onto one of the good china plates, I sat and browsed my mother's recipe books, waiting for Trevor and my sister to return.

The screen door wheezed open about twenty minutes later. "We're back from the pub!" hollered Trevor. "Had to drag this one off the dance floor!"

I came to the top of the stairs and saw that Trevor, for all his bluster, was gazing out the window at his truck while Kelli kicked off her shoes. He saw me in his peripheral vision but didn't turn his head.

"Kettle's on," I said.

Trevor looked up and waved his clipboard at me. "If I can just get your John Hancock, madam?"

"Kelli," I said. "Wanna have a cup of tea with Trebie?"

It didn't take much. It took very little, in fact. But what was strange was how instinctual it all was—I knew exactly what to say and do for Trevor to forgive me. It was like a script we'd both memorized in advance.

It's not that I was even thinking in these terms at the time—none of my behavior was strategic; I couldn't have plotted a strategy at that moment if I'd tried. I was a creature of compulsion and nerve endings in those days, boneless. I felt like a jellyfish, blobbing along in the ocean—a cow flop of protoplasm that recoiled when touched but otherwise veered wherever unseen currents propelled it.

I knew through my nerve endings that when Trevor, in all his chilly reluctance, climbed the stairs, he would be receptive to the sight of me in my mother's sunny kitchen, going over her cookbooks, planning to replenish her obligatory nice-lady stocks of shortbreads and sugar cookies. I had left the books out on the kitchen table for that reason.

I knew, also, that Trevor was not a man who could turn down a proffered cup of tea. That was the traditionalist in him, the slavish follower of Maritime social etiquette—he could no more turn his nose up at tea than he could a rye or two with a buddy after work.

And I knew that confessing to Trevor, as I did midway through the tea, that I had no one else to discuss my sister's future with would be the coup de grâce, would thaw him out once and for all.

Because Trevor, I intuited, needed to feel like he was someone's one and only.

"Gorsebrook could be okay," he allowed after a long, sagacious slurp from his mug. "I mean, I *have* heard good things. That's why I wanted you to see it in the first place."

"Well, I really appreciate you bringing it to my attention," I assured him.

Because at this point in the script, if Trevor was to come back onside, it was required that we reestablish and acknowledge that Gorsebrook had been his idea. It was almost as if Trevor were relaying these instructions to me psychically.

"But," I fretted, "they were so nice to me at Seaside."

Trevor leaned forward. He was responding to this side of me—flailing and a little irrational.

"Miss Karie, you gotta be tough. If Seaside's not the place for Beaner here, you can't worry about how nice they were. They want your money—of course they're gonna be nice."

"But it's also," I said, "the logistics of the thing."

Trevor leaned back in his chair again and crossed his arms. "Logistics," he repeated.

He didn't know what the word meant. The thing to do here was forge ahead, pretend the moment had never happened, kick dirt over it like a dog after a squat.

"Yeah," I said quickly, "I mean, the fact that Seaside could take Kelli now, today. And Gorsebrook is one big question mark on that front. Plus—"

"Plus Seaside was Rini's choice."

I nearly dropped my mug into my lap. Trevor was referring to my mother—*Rini*. But my mother's name was Irene. There were only a handful of people on the planet who'd ever called her Rini. One was no longer on the planet—my father, and only when he teased her, or had been drinking rum toddies. The others consisted of a cadre of little old ladies, scattered across the country, with whom she'd done her nursing training in her twenties. When I was a kid and the phone would ring and some distant, female voice would ask for "Rini," I'd call out to my mother, "It's one of the girls!"

And I'd watch as Irene grabbed the phone and squealed into it like a teenager.

Now Trevor was watching me, smiling slightly, as I took my time replacing my mug on the coffee table.

"Yes," I said at last. "Seaside was my mother's choice."

We both understood that this moment, this weird trump card Trevor had been keeping up his sleeve, meant that all was forgiven. By him, that is, with respect to me. All of what, I still didn't really know. I just knew the card had been thrown down and Trevor was, somehow, victorious. It reminded me of family games of Auction at my grandparents' kitchen table when I was a kid—how merciless and competitive Grandma Gillis used to get. Her eyes would glint behind her bifocals moments before she slammed the trump card down, knuckles connecting resoundingly with the table. *You've lost!* she'd crow as the rest of us threw our cards down in disgust—not *I win* but *You've lost.* The same sweet-faced old lady we'd had to beg to sit down and stop getting food for everyone just moments ago.

But Trevor's victory, such as it was, meant he was back on board. His smile loosened up, and he leaned forward again, arms on his knees. He was invested in our lives once more, just as he'd been the moment he'd placed his hand on my mother's lawn mower and taken it over from me.

What was *wrong* with you, friends always ask when I get to this part of the story.

6

I *hate this house.*

The feeling sat there in the background of my morning like a burgeoning fever. Like when you wake up just a little bit sick, and you decide *I'm not sick* and get up like nothing's wrong and just keep going about your business. But as the day ticks on you start to understand you're doomed—that the infection is about to boil over. I'd been ignoring this feeling, this sickness, I realized later, from the moment I'd arrived.

I'd ignored it throughout my nonproductive weekend. I had been fully intending to undertake the dreary obligation of cataloging my mother's stuff over those two days—mentally separating what could be hauled away versus what could be put aside for the eventual, inevitable yard sale. But before I could even get started, I got hung up sifting through old photo albums and shoeboxes also filled with photographs—photographs my mother had deemed unworthy of the album but still worth keeping, for some reason. I'd gone through the shoeboxes figuring I'd decide what pictures to throw away, but instead I spent the entire weekend poring over them, gazing at them, showing them to Kelli. Blurred faces and awkward expressions. Half-shut eyes, hanging-open mouths. Each photo held an ugly, imperfect fascination. They weren't exactly us, but neither were the pictures in the album us—the smiling, perfectly posed versions. We were somewhere in the middle, between the shoeboxes and the album, the grotesque and the ideal. I could see why my mother couldn't bring herself to throw the shoebox snaps away.

At the end of the process, during which Kelli and I barely went outside, I put all the photographs back and returned the shoeboxes to the closet where Irene had kept them stacked for decades.

Maybe I should've been taking Kelli for walks or drives down to the waterfront. But the fact was, there was something about my mother's subdivision that discouraged going out. There were barely any sidewalks, for one thing. There was a small lake at the bottom of the hill, ringed by a boardwalk, and I had, in the past, taken Kelli down there once or twice, but the hill was so steep that the prospect of walking back up it after a stroll around the lake with Kelli and her bad knee made the whole thing a nonstarter. Plus, the entrance to the path was at a busy street across from the Superstore—you had to dart across it, dodging traffic, to get to the lake. And Kelli had never been much for darting.

Driving somewhere was the other option, but any kind of road trip with Kelli always felt like an ordeal. The entire trip, she would nag you about how long it took the traffic lights to change from red to green, complain about her knee, and ten minutes in she would usually have to go to the bathroom.

In short, staying put was easier. That's what I remembered about my upbringing too, my life with Irene and Kelli. It always seemed easier to stay home. So easy, it got to the point where I couldn't stand to be there another minute.

And so it hit me that morning, around the time I was getting breakfast together. It blossomed to life in my gut, insistent and rude, like a menstrual cramp too early in the month. *I hate this house.* I hated, I realized, the white-glare fluorescent lighting in the kitchen and I hated the cream-colored, spill-something-on-me-I-dare-you carpet in the living room and I hated the "guest" bathroom in the hallway with its teeny-tiny hand towels trimmed with eyelet that were too delicate and pristine to actually sully with grimy hands and I hated the deck with the barbecue that had sat unused till Trevor—and here I will stop and tell you why that was.

Because on the occasion of my eighteenth birthday, when we used it and my boyfriend almost burned his face off, we were barbecuing because I had insisted. I had insisted on a lot of things in relation to that day. My mother had innocently asked what I wanted for my eighteenth birthday and I'd launched into a litany that went something like: I want to be able to pretend for at least one day that we are normal human beings. I want to have my friends over to the house. I want us to barbecue hamburgers and hot dogs. I want you to take Kelli downstairs in front of the TV and keep her there. I don't want you to bring her upstairs to meet everyone and get her to shake everyone's fucking hand the way you always do, she doesn't have to shake everyone's hand, she doesn't have to meet everybody, Kelli's happy one way or the other, you're the one who wants that, I don't want it, my friends don't want it, and Kelli doesn't want it. I want to have a thing that is for me, just this once. I am turning eighteen. I don't want to share it. I don't want to be considerate. I don't want to *include* her. I don't want to be the girl with the retarded sister, okay, for just this one day *please*.

I maybe didn't say it exactly like that, in fact I'm certain I would never have uttered that final sentence, but that final sentence was entirely the gist of whatever my selfish teenage monologue consisted of, and Irene got that message loud and clear.

My mother refused to come upstairs and show us how the barbecue worked. She insisted that poor banished Kelli needed to be kept company in the rec room and heaven forbid anyone should contaminate my sacred, sister-free celebration.

It hadn't even occurred to me that the barbecue would be a problem to figure out. I had assumed, in my blithe eighteen-year-old way, that it would be simple. I had assumed that in the way that an eighteen-year-old who has never even attempted a given task, but has seen lots of other people do it lots of other times, always will. Just think of all the confidence we start out with, all the certainty. And then we embark and we fail, much to our surprise. And then we fail at something else, and something else, and gradually the surprise dwindles and soon we are surprised by nothing and thus are made adults.

So I cranked up the propane and my boyfriend leaned in, weaving a little from the illicit beer he'd smuggled in at my request, lighter in hand.

And everything I've listed above, everything I disliked about my mother's house, had a story behind it like that. Except maybe the fluorescent lighting in the kitchen. I hated the fluorescent lighting just because I hated the fluorescent lighting and I never understood why my mother did not. The pitiless white glare never bothered her. *It's because I need to see,* she would always argue, a reasonable enough argument, I guess. *It's the kitchen and I need to see.*

The problem wasn't Kelli. That is, the problem *was* Kelli, Kelli was always the baseline problem, but in this case she wasn't the immediate problem. Kelli had, in fact, been a dream to live with these last few days, something I was grateful for, not knowing what kind of emotional state I'd be walking into in the aftermath of our mother's death, or how it might manifest itself with respect to Kelli's ever-changing moods. Because you never did know with Kelli. She could be sanguine in the face of utter turmoil, as she had been at our mother's wake—smiling and rocking at all the old friends and relatives coming up to say a tearful hello to her—yet you could walk into the living room and find her inconsolable for no apparent reason, tears puddling onto her lap. But ever since I'd come home, Kelli had been on a fairly even keel. I didn't take that for granted. There'd been times, in the past, when Kelli would wake me or my mother up several times a night for no other reason than to tell us she wasn't asleep, and there had been times when Kelli's digestion went completely offline, requiring the copious use of adult diapers and the washing machine running twenty-four/seven, and there had been times when Kelli got mulish and sullen and would refuse to do anything you asked of her, including, always most alarmingly, to come to the table and eat.

But no, Kelli wasn't the immediate problem this time around. The problem was just that I woke up one morning and it felt like the house had grown teeth.

I decided I should go out, by myself, somehow. Just for an afternoon. But the moment I started applying my mind to that puzzle, by which I mean the Gordian knot of *what to do with Kelli,* the trapped feeling intensified and the fluorescent kitchen lighting seemed to crackle with fresh intensity, as if, somehow, it had been fed.

Stuck to the refrigerator door was the card that read TREV. The name was almost obscured by the novelty magnet holding it in place, which was a pair of tiny, colorful Dutch clogs. I focused on the clogs. I decided to think about them awhile in order to put off thinking about the card. One of my mother's world-traveler nursing friends had sent her the magnet from Amsterdam a couple of decades ago. Fridge magnets had been the globetrotting nurse's thing, her version of a postcard—they arrived over the years in the shape of London beefeaters, tuk-tuks from Thailand, sombreros, bullfighters, Eiffel Towers, and even a weensy, magnetized Mozart at his piano. *She's not married,* my mother used to tell me every time she unwrapped one of these exotic, tiny trophies, as if that was the only possible explanation for a woman who seemed to be having such a great time. And yet she'd say it like she was apologizing on her roving friend's behalf.

These days, only the clogs and one of the sombreros remained on the fridge, but there might have been a veritable magnet U.N. languishing somewhere underneath it, for all I knew—they were cheap and would clatter to the floor if you shut the door too hard. Yet my mother, who usually had no tolerance for plastic doodads and dust collectors, was always so pleased to receive them. *It makes me feel like I've been there myself,* she used to enrage me by saying.

Which brought me back to the card with Trevor's personal number on it. It was my ticket out, to an extent. If I reached out to him, asked him for help as he was always encouraging me to do, I wouldn't get to go to Amsterdam, exactly, but I could fake my freedom for an afternoon while Trevor kept an eye on Kelli. I could drive over the bridge and wander up and down Spring Garden Road for an hour or two, stop for coffee somewhere, maybe check out the fancy new library that had just opened. I could imagine myself at liberty, at least, the way my mother always said she could as she rolled the tiny clogs (or bullfighters or tuk-tuks) between her fingers.

I tried not to think too much about what I was doing by calling TREV. I was practicing self-care, I lectured myself, and that was a thing that was important for women to indulge in during times of stress. Women are bad at self-care, online articles had told me, because they are always so busy caring for everyone else. Of course, that had never really been my problem until now. Therefore, I told myself, I was *inexpert* at self-care, unpracticed. Yes, it felt a little dodgy to be relying on Trevor—a man I didn't really know, even though he seemed well-meaning enough and was, after all, a professional caregiver, for god's sake. And, yes, he sometimes took things weirdly personally and had kind of bullied my sister and me into accepting various acts of kindness on his part. Still, it felt like the healthy thing to do was to focus on the kindness, as opposed to those minor anxieties. There'd been too much focus on anxiety already, I decided. I couldn't let this fog of guilt and doubt dictate my every move, couldn't allow it to keep me stuck in this house all month, chewing my cuticles. I had to take a leap. Maybe, I thought, that was just the nature of self-care—that is, a risky proposition.

I put my mind to who I was going to go out and see. I needed to have an actual conversation with someone—some chatty shopgirl or indulgent barista wasn't going to cut it. But the only people I knew in town were people from high school and elderly relatives—and in both types of faces I would be forced to behold a reflection of my teenage self, which I felt like I'd done enough of in the past few days to last a lifetime.

Finally, after an hour or so of combing through Facebook, I remembered a person named Jessica Hendy.

Jessica was from childhood, not high school like the two or three other old acquaintances I had around town. She and I had been best friends between the ages of nine and ten, which seems like it would make for a tenuous connection, but ever since we had reconnected online, I'd been remembering her with more vividness than I did even the handful of people I'd spent every waking moment partying and studying and sleeping with at university.

This was the only friendship I ever had that I now recognize as being obsessive. I mean obsessive in the way of little girls, where one day your affinity for this knee-socked, pigtailed person, your desire to spend every waking hour with her, moving through the world as a kind of conjoined being, obliterates every other thing you may once have wanted to do. Other friends don't just fall away—they are actively pushed. You turn tail and run off, hand in hand, if they try to approach. Everything but being together becomes an inconvenience, something to begrudge. Piano lessons, swimming. Brownies, family time. I suppose the experience acts as a kind of hormone-free sneak peek, in the pre-sex world of childhood, at what falling in love will be like.

My memories of spending time with Jessie came closest of all my childhood memories to being that clichéd thing, *idyllic*. It was something about that quality of obsessiveness that made it so. Leaving the house in the morning with a backpack full of Barbies, being called in for dinner after what seemed like no more than a couple of hours. The gorgeous inconsequence of time. I could remember long, mesmerizing afternoons of skipping—the hypnotic *thip* as the plastic rope hit the pavement, one end tied to a utility pole so one of us could turn and the other could jump. And chalk on sidewalks. Enormous, elongated hopscotches, unfurling down the block, square after square after square, talking seriously about whether or not we should call Guinness and enter it into the *Book of World Records* because who would ever think to make a hopscotch this long? And going to my house and Jessica being happy to hang out with Kelli; going to her house and not liking her house and not knowing why. Her mother, I remember, just didn't seem as *good* as my mother, somehow (I didn't realize then how few mothers would). And also Jessica had men in her house—teenage brothers and a dad—who would bluster through the kitchen, sometimes shirtless, hair tufting from beneath armpits, ignoring us, barking for things, and the mother would bark back at them, and this was what I didn't like about the mother. Because why did the mother have to be like *them*? I didn't mind them being like them—they were supposed to be alien, big-voiced and intimidating. They came and went like traffic, roaring past, always on the move. But why couldn't the mother, who stayed put (as it seemed to me that mothers should), be more like *us*? I remember her bare legs in the summertime, varicose veins, in a kitchen that never seemed sunny to me, no matter what the weather was doing outside.

My friend's name then was Jessie Madatall, but on Facebook she calls herself Jessica Hendy. She sent me a friend request about a year ago. Her picture showed an impeccable blond woman with an aquiline nose. She didn't look like the kind of person I would know. She had the sort of face advertisers make use of in campaigns to sell bank mortgages—wholesome and responsible, reassuringly smiley. And as I was contemplating this unfamiliar face and name, Jessica Hendy sent me a message.

> Hi Karen! Thanks for accepting my friend request. This is Jessie Madatall, your old pal from childhood. Jessie Hendy now—that's right, I made the leap! I've been married for 14 years and am the doting mother of a sweet and rambunctious 11-year-old boy. Life is good! There's a lot of catching up to do between now and—wow—childhood, but the reason I am contacting you today is because after a great deal of therapy and working through the issues of my past, I am reaching out to the people in my life who may have been hurt in some way or at the very least made uncomfortable by what was happening within my family when I was between the ages of 6 and 14. This is not to say I take the blame for what was done to me, but just that I've come to understand how a betrayal and a violation of a child can ripple outward—like a stone dropped into a still, lovely pond on a summer's day. My wonderful therapist and I have talked about the way other people can get caught up in those ripples . . .

At the bottom of her note, Jessica told me there was no need to reply. I decided, self-servingly maybe, that this was Jessica's way of saying, *I would rather you didn't reply,* and so I never did. Instead, I called my mother and asked, Why did you make me stop playing with Jessie Madatall?

And my mother replied, in so many words, after quite a bit of hemming and hawing, that she walked in on the two of us staging a kind of stuffed-animal gang-rape scenario one day after school. We had gathered up whatever dolls were on hand and could remotely be considered male in gender—we'd had no problem finding a girl doll to be violated, but boy dolls were scarcer, so it turned out a lot of my bears got in on the action, I suppose because they were named Teddy and wore bow ties.

I burst out laughing at this awfulness. It was the *language* she used, my mother emphasized to me. I just heard this *language* coming through the door and my blood went cold.

Was it like . . . the eff word and stuff?

No, no, said my mother. Everyone says the eff word—children say that all the time. No, it was just . . . so *conversational.*

Conversational?

Offhand, said my mother. Like she'd been watching too many grown-up movies.

Like what? I prodded.

Oh, just, said my mother; I could hear how distressed she was becoming. Just . . . Get on your knees, baby. That kind of thing.

Get on your knees, baby? I repeated.

Yes! A ten-year-old! Get on your knees, baby!

Why didn't you call the police? I yelled.

My mother didn't answer. She was stupefied. She hadn't been expecting the conversation to take this kind of turn. She'd thought we were talking about a naughty girl—someone who'd been a bad influence on me.

To think that Jessie had been working all these years. Kneading and reshaping a fragment of her life from so long ago—a period that to me had come and gone like a dream. My memories were of hopscotch and all-day skipping, with the occasional dark cloud drifting in to obscure all that golden childhood sunshine pouring down. And what had been just a dark cloud to me—troubling but insubstantial— was the shadow of Jessie's concrete and inescapable suffering.

I did remember things. Besides the Madatall men and their armpit hair and the unsunny kitchen. I didn't remember the teddy bear orgy, but I remembered strange, specific things she used to tell me and suggest. I remember her encouraging me to put a belt between my legs and pull on it to see what it felt like. I told her it reminded me of in winter, when I wore a snowsuit. Whenever I lifted my arms, the snowsuit rode up, so sometimes I lifted my arms, wearing my snow-suit, more than was strictly necessary.

That is your *pussy,* Jessie told me, nodding in an approving-teacher kind of way, as if about to bestow a check mark.

The word made no sense to me in this context. She might as well have called it a teapot, a marshmallow.

What is my pussy? I said.

That feeling, said Jessie.

7

Trevor showed up, stepping into the foyer before I could get to the door to open it for him, holding a mere six-pack of Alexander Keith's—he was only staying the afternoon, after all—and a box of Tim Hortons Timbits with which to tempt Kelli down to the rec room to keep him company in front of the sports channel. He wasn't dressed in his usual pastel, faux-scrubs Bestlife uniform. He was comfortable enough with us now to dress, I assumed, like Trevor-off-the-clock. Jeans instead of khakis and a black Pittsburgh Penguins shirt with Sidney Crosby's number on the back.

"You go out," decreed Trevor, "and have a good time. You need this, Miss Karie. Good for you, taking a break."

"I really appreciate it, Trevor."

"Oh, listen!" said Trevor. "This is what I'm here for. You know you can always give me a ring when it comes to Beaner-time—me and my girl know how to party, don't we, Big Bean?"

"Timbits," agreed Kelli.

I turned to her, nervous. Why I should've been nervous, I didn't know—Kelli was happy as a clam and Trevor was clearly the closest thing she had to a BFF.

"You gonna be okay with Trevor, Kelli?"

Kelli stopped rocking, maybe picking up on my apprehension. "Where Karie going?"

"Just out to see a friend. I'll be back for supper, okay?"

"Kelli's supper."

"Yes," I said, smiling at Trevor, who had snorted. "You'll get your supper, Kell, don't worry."

"And if you're good for Trebie," added Trevor, "maybe he'll even stick around and eat with his two favorite girls, eh?"

It's funny how you find yourself living and looking like a stereotype so much more often, so inadvertently, as you get older. Or maybe it's more accurate to say you become more conscious of yourself as one. It had been so long, it seemed, since I'd been out in public, sitting down to socialize with a woman of my own age, that I felt hyperconscious of the way we came across. It's easy to forget about the variety of social categories you might conceivably slot into when you've spent weeks inhabiting only one, i.e., *my sister's keeper*. But now Jessica and I sat across from each other in a bright café like two nice women in their forties. Maybe business associates (but probably not, given my jeans and Lululemon hoodie), maybe sisters, smiling through old resentments, maybe two moms taking a bit of "me time" or gal pals planning to hit the spa for mani-pedis after lunch. The waiter called us "ladies" and was flirtatious when we ordered wine. Jessie engaged with the flirting in a practiced way, and I got the feeling this sort of thing must be a mindless, daily obligation for her, like an office worker who automatically affects a singsong voice whenever she answers the phone, to approximate good cheer.

Jessie looked like a real estate agent, because it turned out she was a real estate agent. Her makeup was light and impeccable. Her eyebrows were professionally groomed. An approving phrase of my mother's came to my mind, as I looked at Jessica: *put together.* A very well put-together woman. You imagined a torso assembling itself out of parts every morning, bit by bit.

We were here, sitting across from each other, friends from childhood, with no idea what to say. We ordered food and sort of winced a smile every time our eyes met.

"You should know," said Jessica after a while. "I sent that message to a lot of different people last year."

"What message?" I asked like an idiot.

"That Facebook message."

"Oh god, of course," I said.

"I just don't want you to think I had a weird obsession with you after all these years. Ha, ha! My therapist and I just spent a lot of time going over my past, those years between the ages of six and fourteen, the people who were around me at the time, the fallout from—"

"Jessica," I said quickly, "I'm really sorry that happened to you."

Jessie nodded and smiled in the same practiced way she had flirted with the waiter. She was putting me at ease.

"We don't have to talk about it," said Jessie. "I'm just so glad we had the opportunity to reconnect! Life is good now, and I'm very grateful for that. I'm grateful every day."

The waiter brought us small bowls of some kind of puréed soup. Jessica had chosen the café, and it was the kind of place my mother would have loved, where you had no option but to eat daintily, in three smallish, tasteful courses. You couldn't order french fries or club sandwiches. Instead, Jessica Hendy and I had our choice of airy salads, delicate soups, and fragrant entrées featuring line-caught rainbow trout and steamed something or other with just a hint of dill. It was the kind of restaurant that, if you were not a put-together woman like Jessica Hendy, made you feel ungainly, like your hands and feet had somehow grown two sizes.

"Are you living here now?" asked Jessica over the soup. "Have you moved back for good?"

I opened my mouth to reply, and by the time I was finished the waiter had placed two modest scoops of berry-sprinkled lemon and raspberry sorbet in front of each of us. We were on dessert and I had told her everything. My mother's death, and funeral, and expectations for what would happen after she had gone. Gorsebrook. Seaside. Kelli's question mark of a future. I somehow even managed to shoehorn my divorce in there; even though it had happened five years before and I should've been well over it, it felt, for some reason, part and parcel of everything I was dealing with now. Finally, I told Jessica about Trevor and the long, strange day Kelli and I had spent feeling kidnapped, squashed together with Trevor in his truck. Not to mention the meal he invited himself to afterward, his massive, cheesy baked potatoes and no-raw-food policy—I threw this in as a kind of comic coup de grâce to try to lighten things up. I had spoken as if possessed. The only thing I didn't mention about Trevor was that I had left my sister with him, that he was the sole reason I was able to be there, partaking of this dainty ladies' luncheon with Jessica Hendy.

It was only once I took a breath that I registered that Jessie had dabbed her eyes with her napkin a couple of times during my monologue.

"Oh no," I said now. "Does it all sound that terrible? I made you cry."

"I cry at everything," Jessica assured me. "Learning to cry has been important. I'm grateful for it. I never try to fight it anymore—I just let 'er rip."

"Oh."

"I was mostly crying about your mother. I loved your mother!"

"Everybody loved my mother."

"You can't imagine what spending time at your house meant to me—it was so clean, so quiet. So normal."

"So normal," I repeated.

"It always smelled so good!" Jessie rhapsodized. "Fresh bread and lavender!"

"Did it?"

"The smell was just baked into the walls or something."

I couldn't meet Jessica's eye. I was thinking about my childhood compared to hers. How my mother had summarily pushed her out, and how I had barely shrugged over the loss of the friendship that had once been my obsession. I had, after *that is your pussy,* instinctively understood and agreed with my mother's judgment.

"And she was so beautiful," continued Jessie. "She just seemed so decent and good."

"I know," I said.

"I think I was kind of in love with her," said Jessica.

"I know," I said again. "And what did you think of Kelli?"

"I loved Kelli!" I knew she would say this. "Kelli seemed so cool to me! Oh my god, I would've killed for a sister."

"Well, Kelli wasn't a sister in the traditional sense."

"Well, I would've killed for a *Kelli,*" said Jessica. "I used to ask my mother if you and Kelli could stay overnight . . ." Jessica stopped smiling at this memory and looked up at me. "Anyway, I know it's been hard. I don't mean to idealize you. I'm just saying I did when I was a kid. You and your family. It was important, that time I spent with you guys. You gave me a model of how it was supposed to be. I'm very grateful for that."

Jessica Hendy spoke about gratitude a lot, almost compulsively, like an OCD person who keeps glancing at the stove. As I gazed at Jessica and her groomed eyebrows, her clear-varnished fingernails—inhaling her floral, lighter-than-air perfume—a bizarre thought occurred to me. That Jessica Hendy, after a childhood of nightmares, had built herself a persona—put herself together, as it were—in an unconscious, or maybe conscious, replication of my mother. My mother and her ordered, tasteful world. She had idealized it to such an extent that even Kelli, rocking in her perch by the window, seemed part and parcel with the magic, a grace note in the midst of Irene Petrie's lovely composition.

"And how is Kelli?" said Jessica.

"Kelli," I said, "is eternal. She hasn't changed."

"Does she still like to feel your forehead for fever?"

"She still does that," I said, and Jessica bared her news anchor's teeth in a smile, loving to hear it.

"She still does all the things she used to do," I said. "Every day for the last forty years."

"Karen," said Jessie. "It's going to be so hard for you to let her go!"

She was talking about Seaside. Or Gorsebrook. I hadn't decided yet. Which was crazy, because I should have had Kelli tucked into Seaside well before now. I was supposed to be wrapping things up and heading home in just a few days. Obviously that wasn't going to happen. Obviously I would have to call my expectant clients and let them know I'd need more time. But I hadn't even done that yet. I'd done nothing. The end of the month felt like the outer limits of an ancient map, where the uncharted world was unthinkable, a vague place of vague monsters. I couldn't seem to get my head around what had to happen next, couldn't rouse myself to action.

Deanna at Seaside had been leaving me weary, exasperated voice mails, whereas Marlene at Gorsebrook kept patiently, breezily "checking in" via e-mail every now and then. My affinities were slowly shifting. It was hard not to like Marlene better for the simple psychology of the fact that she seemed so much less desperate than Deanna—playing hard to get, the aloof popular girl. Yet intellectually I knew it was all very well for Marlene—she didn't even have a bed for Kelli, she was just lining us up for the future, whereas Deanna was likely besieged by inquiries about her available spot and couldn't keep it open indefinitely.

So I needed to decide, or else Deanna would decide for me. But I hadn't decided.

As I sat across from Jessica, all these thoughts flashed through my head in a single, panicked blaze, like the instant you light a match when it flares, then settles. And then I pushed the panic aside, as I'd been doing all month long.

"I let Kelli go a long time ago," I told Jessica. "I visited her and Mom, like, once a year. I haven't been involved in her life to this extent since I was a teenager. My mother and I fought about Kelli all the time and I told her I didn't want Kelli to take over my whole life, because when you care for Kelli, she just *does*. I love her, but I can't—I've just never been able to imagine giving my existence over to Kelli the way my mother did. Disappearing myself the way she did."

Jessica squinted. "I never thought of your mother as disappeared. She always seemed larger than life to me."

"But she was a larger-than-life *mother*. A larger-than-life caregiver. Whoever she was before that—I don't even know. She got rid of that person."

"Maybe that was her choice."

I studied Jessica a moment. Either she was understanding me completely or not understanding me at all. "It *was*," I said. "It was a hundred percent her choice. But I'm not her. I don't have it in me."

Jessica shook her head and smiled like I was being ridiculous. "Stop beating up on yourself."

I was startled. I didn't think I'd been beating up on myself. I'd thought I was being sort of blandly honest. Maybe Jessica's misconception had to do with the fact that I was still grief-stricken. Maybe every word I uttered about my mother was coming across with a sad, despairing cast that I wasn't even aware of.

"I'm just telling you the truth," I said.

"You are *self-flagellating*," said Jessica. "That's my therapist's word," she added with an air of apology. "I mean, we're both Catholic girls, right, you and me? He sees the Catholic stuff coming out in me all the time and points it out. So I'm super-aware of it now. In myself and others. I know what self-flagellation looks like, believe me."

"What Catholic stuff?" I said.

"You know, *guilt*," said Jessica. "The cosmic kind, the storm cloud hanging over your head everywhere you go. The, the . . . looking for penance in all the wrong places, if you know what I mean. Denying our own needs. Seeking to suffer."

"But I've *never* done that," I said. "That's my point. That's what my mother wanted me to do—deny myself—and I refused."

Jessica opened her mouth to argue, but that was when the waiter brought our bill on a small china saucer decorated with apple blossoms. She snatched it away before I could.

"I'm the one who invited you out," I protested. "I'm the one who did all the talking."

"Let me treat you," said Jessica. "It's so good to reconnect."

"I feel like we should have been talking more about you," I said.

"We have been," said Jessica. "This whole time."

I didn't contradict her. It seemed possible that, to Jessica, all conversation felt that way—as if the purgatory of her childhood was an eternal subtext, undergirding every human exchange.

———————

My afternoon with Jessica had done its work. Spilling my guts had left me feeling lighter, better, clearheaded yet sort of intoxicated, like I'd taken a hit of oxygen. This, I thought, strolling down the sidewalk to where my car was parked, was what I'd needed all along. Just a bit of human contact. An afternoon out; a sympathetic ear. It was a gorgeous, breezy summer afternoon and I realized how little time I'd spent outside since I'd been here. I'd barely even caught a glimpse of the ocean, something I usually made a point of the moment I was on this coast. The restaurant had been near the water, and now I could smell salt air, could see the harbor glittering in the distance. Tomorrow, I promised myself, I would call my clients and let them know I'd need more time. Some of the work I could likely do from here, so I'd offer them that as a way of softening the news that I'd be absent another month. A month might be excessive, but it was better to be on the safe side. Give myself lots of time to make a decision, to get Kelli nicely settled, to feel confident and good about wherever she ended up. That was what mattered, however long it took.

I was feeling positive for the first time in ages—and so grateful. Something nice had been done for me that day. I found myself wanting to do something nice for someone else.

8

He had hinted that he'd like to eat with us, after all. Actually, it was more that he had offered to eat with us, as a kind of reward—a reward for Kelli being good, he said, but also, I intuited, a reward for me as well. Because I had done the right thing and called him when I was in need.

I went to the grocery store figuring I'd pick up some chicken and potatoes for baking. I pulled out my phone as I lingered in the vegetable aisle, wondering what sort of green thing Trevor might find acceptable—and, without thinking, called the landline at my mother's house (as opposed to the number named TREV). It was lucky the line still worked, as I'd called to cancel it just a couple of days ago, after a bill had arrived in Irene's name.

I was not so much startled by the fact that Trevor answered, which of course I'd been expecting, but, rather, by the *way* he answered, which was: "This is Irene Petrie's residence." He sounded practiced and professional, like he'd been taking my mother's calls his whole life.

"Hello there?" called Trevor.

"Hi, uh, Trevor, it's Karen."

"Karie-on-my-wayward-son!" Trevor bellowed. "Ya have a nice time with your pal?"

"I did! Listen, I thought I'd bring home a couple of chicken breasts for supper. Are you up for some chicken?"

"Oh, now, you don't have to go cooking me supper!"

"No, it's the least I can do to thank you for giving me the afternoon off," I insisted. I decided to follow Trevor's lead in pretending he hadn't hinted that I should do this very thing.

"Well, chicken sounds great. Why don't I fire up the barbecue again, and that way I can earn my vittles?"

"You shouldn't have to lift a finger," I argued. "You've been earning your keep all afternoon."

"Spending time with my best girl is hardly earning my keep!"

I laughed a little, as if Trevor's whole Kelli-as-girlfriend shtick was something novel at this point. "How's she been?"

Trevor paused. I didn't like that pause, coming after all the breezy banter.

"Well, now," said Trevor. "At the moment, we seem to be having a bit of an issue."

"What issue?"

"Let's say, a slight bathroom issue."

I closed my eyes. Kelli's digestion. Kelli's colon.

"What's happening?"

"Well, she's been in there for a while."

"How long?"

"Maybe ten minutes. Says she's got a tummy ache."

"Oh god." I racked my brain. What did my mother do when this stuff happened? I had a memory of castor oil being massaged into Kelli's cushiony abdomen, mine too every so often, but had that been for diarrhea? Or constipation? I couldn't remember. With Trevor still in my ear, I headed to the pharmacy section of the store.

"Trevor, sorry to have to ask this, but do you have a sense of what the problem is?"

"Oh yeah," said Trevor. "I definitely have a sense. The whole neighborhood has a sense by now."

I went up and down the aisle, searching for Imodium. Would my mother give Kelli Imodium? She wasn't big on pharmaceuticals. She liked her home remedies for this kind of thing. Castor oil, yogurt, black tea with sugar. But it seemed to me natural products wouldn't be of much use if this was a full-on case of the shits. We'd been down that road before, my mother and I, and it had not been pretty.

"Oh no," said Trevor, "I'm sure it's just a little bout of something or the other."

I'd been thinking out loud, I realized as I scoured the aisles. Out loud to Trevor. I'd located the Imodium, the Pepto-Bismol. Now I found myself standing in front of a display of adult diapers. I reached out and batted one of the packages, labeled LARGE, off the shelf and into my basket. I stood there another moment, scowling at the display—the cheerful and relaxed senior citizens depicted on the packaging, the brand names like Prevail and Serenity—and batted in a second one.

"I hope you're right," I said.

"I'm sure she'll be all settled down by the time you get home," said Trevor. "But you might wanna grab a can of Febreze or two while you're there—ha, ha."

"Ha, ha," I said, heading into the Household Products section.

She was not all settled down by the time I got home. She was on the toilet, rocking and moaning. Her face was pink and sweaty. Her pants were around her ankles, and I saw that they'd been soiled.

"Oh, Kelli," I said, crouching down beside her.

"Kelli's tummy!"

"I'm so sorry, dear." I held my nose with one hand and flushed the toilet with the other. The smell had hit me the second I'd stepped into the foyer, despite the fact that Trevor had propped the door open, along with every window in the house.

I felt her forehead using my whole palm. It was hard to tell if she had a fever—the exertion itself could've been making her hot. She glanced up at me with desperate, glassy eyes.

The only window Trevor had not opened, it seemed, was the one in the bathroom, so I went over and cranked it. Trevor hadn't come in here with Kelli; he'd simply kept the bathroom door open a crack to speak soothingly to her as she struggled. The women from Bestlife were the ones who gave Kelli baths and dealt, when required, with bathroom issues, but Trevor's role in Kelli's care had always been more about exercise and socializing. This was new territory for him.

I told Kelli to hang tight and went back to the foyer for my bags of diapers and Imodium, which I had dropped when I heard my sister moaning. Trevor was waiting for me outside the door.

"Looks bad, eh?"

"Yup. I think she'll be missing dinner tonight."

"Tragedy!" joked Trevor solemnly. "You know it's bad when."

"I see she messed her pants a little."

"Sorry about that," said Trevor. "I didn't realize the gravity of the situation—didn't get her to the toilet quite in time."

"At least . . . is her chair okay?" In all my mother's life as Kelli's parent, she'd never, as far as I knew, permitted shit or vomit to get anywhere other than on clothes (which was rare enough) or in the toilet, where both bodily effusions belonged. I couldn't stand the idea that in under just a month of my care, Kelli's actual excrement might have been permitted to sully an actual piece of furniture in my mother's eternally pristine living room. *Fresh bread and lavender,* those were supposed to be the smells. The only smells. So that a wrecked child like Jessie Madatall could step across the threshold feeling she had entered a sun-drenched sanctuary of decency and light. Not a place of shit-smeared furniture, in other words.

Trevor placed both hands on my shoulders.

"Hey, now," he said. "The chair's just dandy. Fresh as a daisy."

This was the first Kelli emergency in the aftermath of my mother's death. And I'd thought I'd been braced for it to happen any day. But here I was, tearing up over a bout of diarrhea.

"Tell me what I can do," said Trevor.

"Um," I said. "You should go. I'm just gonna give her some Imodium, and once, you know, the tap turns off, I'll get her into a diaper and put her to bed."

"You'll need something to eat."

I laughed. "Oh god, who's gonna eat after this!"

"You'll need a bite later," insisted Trevor. "And let's face it, you may need some help getting her up off the toilet if she's feeling weak."

I couldn't argue with this, even though I hated the thought of it. Once when Kelli had a fever, I'd had to help her out of bed to the bathroom and she'd fallen on top of me and I'd barely been able to wriggle out from underneath her.

"I'll go upstairs and barbecue that chicken," said Trevor. "Keep out of your way while you get her looked after. I'll cover it in tinfoil for later. But that way I'll be nearby. Give me a shout when you're ready to get her off the toilet and I'll stand by, okay? Eyes averted, but ready with a helping hand!"

I nodded and Trevor gave me another stabilizing pat before heading upstairs, nabbing the grocery bag of chicken on his way. When I returned to the bathroom I removed the diapers and Imodium from the plastic bag and used it to gather up Kelli's soiled pants and underwear, carefully lifting up one Kelli foot and then the next, trying and not quite succeeding not to smear any on her feet and ankles.

As I was running a warm washcloth down her shins afterward, Kelli gave me another glassy-eyed glance, which she held longer than was typical for her. I put it down to her exhaustion at first—thinking she was too worn out to follow her usual eye-contact avoidance protocol. But no. It was just that she had a question for me.

She wanted to know when our mother was coming home.

9

I sat laughing across the kitchen table from Trevor. Trevor didn't laugh along with me. He was the kind of guy, I was discovering, who liked his own jokes, but when other people joked he just sat waiting for their mirth to wear off so he could get back to the conversation at hand.

Or maybe my joke wasn't all that funny. It hadn't actually even been a joke—more of a gut-busting (to me) turn of phrase relating to what I had to do next when it came to Kelli's future.

That phrase being: *Shit or get off the pot.*

I gasped and pressed my eyes with Kleenex. Sometimes, when something strikes me as being as funny as *shit or get off the pot* did at this particular moment, I lose all control. My eyes swell shut and start to pour tears and I hyperventilate and sometimes even hiccups come, which make me laugh all the harder. I could see Trevor becoming impatient, so I struggled to get myself under control. It wasn't hard. There is nothing that kills a laughing jag more efficiently than a strained, testy smile from the person sitting across from you.

Kelli had a diaper on and was in bed. There was a plate of cold barbecued chicken in front of me that I hadn't touched, and a plate that had been quickly polished off and wiped clean with a bun in front of Trevor. All that remained were a few graceful swirls of barbecue sauce, as if from an artist's brush across the white of the plate.

"I can't," I wheezed, indicating the chicken. I took a few head-clearing breaths and blew my nose as Trevor cleared away my plate and covered it with the tinfoil he'd been using to keep the chicken warm in the oven while I dealt with my sister's misery downstairs.

She had some misery downstairs, all right!

Trevor shoved my covered plate into the fridge with a clatter, sounding like he was displacing various other dishes and jars when he did. I was getting on his nerves. I tried to take another deep breath without chuckling. I rubbed my face. I did everything but slap myself.

"Sorry, sorry," I said to Trevor.

"Goddamnit, Miss Karie! How long you gonna go on like this?"

The question sobered me. "I know . . ."

"Yeah, but you don't know, I don't think! You just waltz in here after I don't know how many years, trying to do everything by yourself, taking care of your sister twenty-four/seven, trying to organize her life—not to mention your poor mother's affairs—in under a month, all on your own! You need help, for the love of god!"

"I have help," I said. "I have you guys at Bestlife. I mean, I have access to all the same resources my mother did, so I should be able to—"

"Rini was doing this her whole g.d. life! She was a trained nurse! Now, you tell me: What would you have done today if I wasn't here?"

"About Kelli? I would've—done the same stuff, I guess—"

"No you wouldn't've, because you wouldn't have been able to get out to the store to buy that medicine or diapers because you wouldn't've been able to leave her."

I thought about this. It was true: I couldn't have just left Kelli moaning on the toilet to drive to the store. But my mother had used a grocery delivery service. That number too was on the fridge, on a list pinned beneath the sombrero magnet. I probably could've called it and had the items brought right over.

"You can't do everything on your own!" ranted Trevor. "How long can this continue?"

That was the question, though, wasn't it. That was where the *shit vs. pot* dilemma made itself known. I'd chosen neither, deliberately keeping myself in limbo. Even my so-called decision that afternoon to call my clients and take an extra month had been a cop-out, I realized. A delay tactic. All I was doing was kicking the can down the road— the can of Kelli's future. And, let's face it, my future too. Because our futures were entwined precisely in the way I'd vowed they never would be when I left this house at twenty years of age.

"You gotta make some decisions," said Trevor.

I nodded. "I do."

"But most of all," said Trevor, "you gotta ask for help when you need it! That's what that number on the goddamn effing fridge is for."

I nodded some more. Trevor sat down across from me again. He'd been pacing from the moment he'd rammed my plate into the fridge and slammed the door.

"It's not that I don't think you can do this," he told me.

I looked up at him. "Do what?"

"Look after your sister. You got it in ya, Miss Karie."

"Thank you," I said after a moment.

It seemed Trevor believed that I doubted that about myself. He thought my anxiety was wrapped up in the fear that I was not capable of caring for Kelli, when I knew full well that I was. I'd spent my entire childhood and teenage years in training for it—trained impeccably by the mother of all experts. True, I might never be in Irene Petrie's league, but it wasn't that I thought I couldn't do it. That was not the fear at all.

"You girls had a scare tonight," said Trevor. "But we got through it, eh?" He reached over and put his hand on my forearm. I was startled by its size—his freckled pinkie was at the crease of my elbow and his hairy blond thumb was at my wrist. "All you needed was a little bit of help."

But Trevor didn't know as much as he thought he did. Yes, it had been my first Kelli emergency without my mother, but on the grand scale of Kelli emergencies, it was pretty small potatoes. There had been shit, and shit was unpleasant, but shit wiped off. It was nothing compared to the terror of her nearly burst appendix at twelve, or the second-degree burns on both palms at fifteen (she'd thought she could pick up the boiling kettle by the sides instead of the handle), the blocked windpipe, the ear infections, the soaring fevers, and so on.

Now Kelli was in bed, emptied out, but obediently drinking tea and replenishing her fluids. She'd be okay. We'd been through worse, my sister and I.

Trevor gave my forearm a final squeeze with his massive pink hand and apologized for, as he called it, the "tough love."

"I should get a move on." He stood up and stretched. "I'll just poke my head in and say good night to Beaner." But he didn't move. He was waiting for me to say the thing I was supposed to say.

"Thanks so much, Trevor," I told him. "I don't know what we would've done without you."

Kelli was in her bedroom as I had left her, sipping sweet black tea with a bendy straw out of the largest mug in the house. My mother had kept a stash of these straws in one of the lower cupboards, precisely for occasions such as this, because just as Kelli gulped her food, she also gulped her liquids. The bendy straw was a way to encourage little sips, and even though Kelli was perfectly capable of hoovering up her tea with it, she seemed to grasp that the straw required a more delicate approach.

Kelli looked up at me when I came in, lips closed around her straw—and, for the moment she kept her eyes on mine, it was like she was ten years old. The truth was—and this was something I'd forgotten—Kelli could be kind of a sweetheart when she was sick. Her usual mulishness left her, and after whatever convulsions and agonies had passed, she'd lie docile in her bed, uncharacteristically willing to follow orders.

"Feeling better, Kelli?"

"Feel better."

"How you doing with that tea?"

"More tea," Kelli said, handing me the mug.

"That's probably enough for now."

"Nuffer now," Kelli agreed.

"If you have to go to the bathroom again," I told her, "you call me, okay? Don't go by yourself." Kelli was capable of going to the bathroom herself, but she was not so capable—as far as I knew—of maneuvering her way out of an adult diaper.

I felt her forehead. It was cool. Was it a stomach bug? Food poisoning? Could there be such a thing as a bad Timbit? They probably made them with eggs, and eggs could go bad. But Trevor hadn't had a problem, and he had eaten most of them himself. Trevor had reported to me that Kelli had only had about four of the Timbits in addition to half of a beer. Beer usually gave Kelli no problems—it was just another liquid she had to be stopped from gulping down too fast, which was why she was permitted only half.

"Were those Timbits good, Kelli?"

"Good," said Kelli, uninterested. She didn't want to talk about food.

"They tasted good?"

"Timbits," said Kelli.

This wasn't really getting us anywhere. I felt her forehead again and Kelli made quick eye contact as I did.

"Mumma comin' home," she said. It was almost as if she were being deliberately casual, throwing it out as a quick gambit, perhaps hoping I'd forgotten our conversation in the bathroom and would just absently agree.

"No, she's not coming home, dear," I said, taking my hand away. "It's like I told you in the bathroom."

"Trebie home," said Kelli after a moment.

"Trevor's gone home, yes," I told her.

"Coming back," said Kelli.

This was sort of interesting, because I'd never seen Kelli make this kind of intellectual leap before. It seemed as if she were comparing two different absences in her life—Trevor's versus my mother's. Trevor's version of gone was the kind that got allayed every once in a while—he came and went, like the tide going in and out. Whereas my mother's gone was unadulterated, like a lake drying into a crater.

"Yes," I said. "Trevor's coming back. But Mumma's gone now."

"Gone. She gone now," said Kelli.

Kelli got it. She didn't like it, but she got it. There was no point in hedging or being euphemistic. I couldn't have her mooning in her perch by the window, expecting that any moment our mother might stroll up the walk, and it wasn't as if Kelli could conjure up pictures of angels and pearly gates if I were to tell her our mother had gone to heaven. My sister understood the basics, *here* and *gone,* and in this case that was all she needed to understand. But I believed that Kelli understood death too—she had accompanied my mother to innumerable funerals over the years. She was intimate with caskets, priests, black clothes, weepy aunts, stiff uncles in somber suits. She had to know that funerals meant the axis around which *here* and *gone* revolved.

"Remember the funeral?" I said. "Remember when everyone came to the house? Uncle Danny and Francie and Leo and the Cape Breton cousins? That was for Mumma. To say good-bye."

"Leo," said Kelli, perking up, because she'd always had a thing for our young cousin Leo, who'd flown up from Boston.

"That's right, Leo was there."

"Beard," said Kelli. Kelli wasn't big on beards, and Leo had morphed into a textbook hipster at some point, sporting a gloriously oiled beast to go with his forearm tattoos and stiff, rolled-bottom jeans.

"You didn't like Leo's beard?"

"Don't like that beard," she confirmed.

"We'll tell him to shave it off next time, eh?"

"Shave that beard," said Kelli, imagining it. "Shave that beard, Leo." She smiled, liking the sound of what she was saying, and repeated it rapidly a few times to herself, testing out its rhythms. *Shaydatbeard, Leo, shaydatbeard.* This kind of singsong, staccato repetition of whatever collection of words happened to appeal to her at a given moment was a pastime of Kelli's and it meant that she was feeling better. She tried whispering it awhile and even started rocking slightly. I said it a few times with her, which Kelli also seemed to like. I kept pace with her, following her distinctive Kelli rhythm, whispering when she whispered, and soon the words meant nothing. That is, nothing but their original sense of play and teasing remained—the sounds just meant pleasure for Kelli now. They soothed her. They soothed us both. It was very much as if we were praying together. And I left her bedroom knowing what I had to do.

I had to stay.

10

It's hard for me to admit this now, but the euphoria I experienced the moment I made this decision—the weird endorphin-releasing cascade of revelation and sense of having shaken off, little by little, a kind of psychic hair shirt—made me feel giddy, and I badly wanted to call someone with my amazing news. It genuinely did seem like amazing news, at the time—a downright epiphany. *I can give up! I am giving up!* So the first thing I did was go to the fridge and reach beneath the Dutch-shoes magnet for the card that read TREV.

But I didn't call Trevor. I almost did, but something stopped me. I knew, of course, that Trevor would approve—his pep talk over my uneaten chicken earlier that evening had made it clear what he felt my course of action should be. To stay and care for my sister, naturally. And in a way, it made sense that he would be the one I called, because, for better or for worse, Trevor was the one who knew, most intimately, of my dilemma these past few weeks. So it was tempting. I knew that Trevor would not only understand my decision, he would laud it. He would congratulate me.

At the same time, though, I had to admit: I didn't really know Trevor that well. And furthermore, the face smack of endorphins had had a clarifying effect on my brain; the fog that had settled into it from the moment I'd stepped back into this house to preside over the end of my mother's life had finally lifted, or so it felt. And I knew at last that I would have to draw some boundaries.

Trevor was amusing in his corny, boisterous way. And he was great with Kelli. But he was also, it had to be said, a little pushy. He could be bossy, and moody when he didn't get his way. But most of all, he was presumptuous. It was the presumption, I realized, that I couldn't encourage. He had been a good friend, going above and beyond his designated role—somewhat inappropriately above and beyond, but in a way that was well-meaning and helpful. And he could continue to be our friend, certainly. But if I was going to live here, if I was going to move back (and here I experienced another woozy jolt of exhilaration—*Am I really going to live here? Am I actually going to move back?*)—if I was going to live here, we would have to establish some ground rules. I pulled my hand back from the card that read TREV. In my grief about my mother and my panic over what to do with Kelli this past month, I'd let Trevor stray a little too far into my life. Our lives. I couldn't just call him up like he was one of my girlfriends, to crow about my latest life decision. But if not Trevor, who?

"Do you know," I said to Jessica Hendy, after apologizing for calling her so late, and so soon after our lunch. And after telling her my news, and after apologizing again and laughing like a semi-hysteric when she told me to stop apologizing. "I almost called the home care guy! I had no one else to tell, so I almost called the guy who takes Kelli for a walk every week!"

"You mean the guy you said kidnapped you?" said Jessica.

I laughed. I'd forgotten having described the day with Trevor in the truck that way. "Yeah, yeah, yeah," I said. "The guy who mowed the lawn for us that time."

"Ugh," said Jessica. "I'm glad you called me instead."

"Oh, he's fine," I said. "And ultimately I wouldn't have found Gorsebrook without the guy."

Gorsebrook, I had explained to Jessica in a rush, was the answer to all our problems. Gorsebrook would make it easy. If I moved here, I could take care of Kelli for as long as it took for a bed to open up. I could work from home, find new clients, maybe keep some of my old ones if they were amenable to a long-distance telecommute. As far as my house in Toronto went, I'd simply rent it out—so even if work slowed down, I'd have a supplementary income to keep me going. I'd sell this house, move somewhere smaller and cheaper near Gorsebrook, and get Kelli started in the day program. I could walk her there every day, volunteer from time to time. Kelli would get to know the place and the people and eventually it would come to feel like a second home. When the time came for her to move in, it would be seamless, and I'd be right down the street, able to visit as often as I liked.

It was the perfect compromise. I wasn't giving my entire life over to my sister's care, but nor was I abandoning her. It didn't have to be one or the other—that was the big revelation of the evening for me. I wanted to shout it up at the fluorescent rectangle glaring down from the kitchen ceiling, as if that was where my mother's ghost resided. *Mom! It doesn't have to be one or the other!*

"So you're going with Gorsebrook for sure?" said Jessica.

I swooned a little, still jangling with elation, at the words *for sure.*

"Well, nothing's for sure," I babbled. "But that's the decision I've come to. I'm gonna call Marlene in the morning. Then I'll call Deanna at Seaside and let her down easy."

"But you said Kelli can't get into Gorsebrook right away?"

"No," I said. "So it'll be me and Kelli for a while longer but, I mean, it's nothing I can't handle. And then I'll buy a place downtown and—oh! You can help me! You can help me get a place, that's your job! And you can help me sell *this* one!" I felt my voice starting to climb in pitch.

"Of course!" said Jessica. "But one thing at a—"

"It seems so obvious now," I marveled. "I don't know what I was so afraid of! I don't know why this whole thing felt like such a big, god-awful ordeal . . ."

"Because you lost your mother," said Jessica. "And you had to put your life on hold to come home and take care of your sister. And it was hard."

"Yeah, but that's what I'm realizing. I put my life on hold. And I can just, I can just . . . keep it there."

"Oh, Karen," said Jessica.

"What?"

"But how long until the spot opens up at Gorsebrook?"

"They can't tell me," I said. "I guess it's a—well, this is kind of grim, but maybe it's a waiting-for-someone-to-kick-off kind of situation."

"But did she give you any idea when that would be? Because you could end up looking after Kelli a pretty long time, if that's the case."

I tried to appreciate what Jessica was saying instead of feeling annoyed. She was only being pragmatic. And, after all, she had spent the entire afternoon listening to me moan about my ongoing terror of ending up as Kelli's caregiver-for-life. Now here I was on the other end of the phone, sounding crazy, announcing myself all in.

"I know," I said, trying to sound sobered up. "I know, but after tonight with the—the sudden-onset diarrhea and everything. It was. I just realized. I can do this!"

"I mean, that's great, Karen," said Jessica. And I could hear in her voice, in that hesitant *I mean,* a decision to bite her tongue. She had pushed, ever so slightly, but now she was backing off. It made me feel defensive.

"And I'll have help. I have my mother's folder, everything she's set up."

"Kelli's World!" remembered Jessica. It was like I had emptied out the entire contents of my head onto Jessica's plate that afternoon.

"Yes, *Kelli's World!* And I'll have Bestlife in the meantime—they've been great. And, you know, in emergencies, there's always Trevor."

"Who's Trevor again?" said Jessica.

"The kidnapping guy."

"Promise me," said Jessica, "you will not call the kidnapping guy."

"I knew you had it in ya!" Trevor shook my hand in the foyer and clapped me on the back like we were a pair of businessmen congratulating each other on the deal of the century.

I told him a few days later, during one of his official home care visits. (I'd started to think of him, on those days, as "Clipboard Trevor," as opposed to jeans and T-shirt "Trevor off the Clock.") I had called my clients that same morning to let them know I wasn't coming back. Family issues, I'd explained. That phrase—the somber hand wave it represented—had been a masterstroke. It deflected questions, discouraged demands for explanations. Thrown off, they murmured their regret and wished me the best. I offered my services long-distance. One told me that would not be tenable, which I'd been expecting. The other said that they'd think about it, which I thought they actually might.

But I found I didn't care one way or another. I was still rippling with self-amazed glee. I'd done it. I'd just picked up the phone, had a couple of five-minute conversations, and changed the future. So it was fun, telling Trevor. I had even been looking forward to it, basking in the hearty approval I knew I had coming. But at the same time there was an off quality to that heartiness—a quality that made me glad I hadn't given in to my instincts and called Trevor, instead of Jessica, to spill my news.

Maybe it had to do with the convoluted way I told the story, standing there with him in the foyer—trying to capture the crazy elation of the moment, of hugging myself in the kitchen after I'd left Kelli's room, the future cracking open in front of me, spilling forth a giddy cascade of revelations and game plans. (*Quit my contracts. Rent my house. Sell this house . . . !*) At the same time as I was trying to get my euphoria across, I was careful not to let Trevor know how close I'd been to calling him. I had almost crossed a line, in all my heedless exhilaration, and for some reason I felt like it was important not to let him know how close I'd come.

I told Trevor I had called Jessica—as if she were a dear, close friend, as opposed to someone I hadn't spoken to since I was ten. After all, Trevor didn't know that she wasn't. I described how I'd snatched up the phone and, laughing like a hysteric, babbled my news at poor, bewildered Jessica. And Trevor's wide smile stayed in place but his eyes grew vague, fixed at some point on the wall behind me. The effect was like when you pause a movie and the expression on the actor's face—unremarkable just seconds before—seems monstrous in the frozen moment. But then his eyes refocused and the smile widened further, and he followed up his slap on the back with a corny, congratulatory pumping of my hand.

What I wasn't expecting was for Trevor to show up again the very next day, this time accompanied by an eight-year-old boy. It was not one of his home care days. On this day, Kelli was booked for a bath, so we had been expecting a short, pillowy thirty-something woman named Brenna, who always smelled like a perfect fifty-fifty combination of spearmint and tobacco, to arrive at any minute. I headed to the foyer when I heard the rap at the screen door, ready to usher Brenna across the threshold, but then I heard the metallic wheeze of the screen door opening and when I got there Trevor had already stepped inside with the boy.

He was small for his age and seemed introverted. He wasn't gazing around at this new environment, the way you'd expect a curious child might. He looked down at the rubber mat, where Kelli and I kept our shoes.

"I brought you girls a visitor!" said Trevor.

"Hey there," I said. The kid flinched and didn't look up.

"Introduce yourself, bud," said Trevor to the kid.

"Mike," said the kid.

"Hey, Mikey," I said.

"Not Mikey," said Trevor. "He was named so there wouldn't be any of that nickname crap. You know, Bobb-y, Tedd-y, Kenn-y. None of that shit. Just plain Mike. Right, Mike?"

Mike didn't answer.

"This your little boy?" I asked, even though it was obvious.

"The fruit of my loins," affirmed Trevor. I blinked at him and wondered where a guy like Mr. No-Nickname-Crap had come across such a florid phrase. "Thought you and Beaner'd like to see the little dude. We'll all have tea and celebrate your big news!"

So that's what this visit was meant to be—a kind of sprinkling of confetti in honor of my decision to move home. He had brought his child over as a celebratory gesture, as if Mike were a cake or a bunch of balloons.

"He looks like you," I said, even though he did not at all. The kid was dark-haired beneath his Penguins ball cap, with a heartbreaking pair of brown eyes.

Trevor slipped off his shoes and bent down to help Mike do the same.

"I don't wanna take off my shoes," protested Mike.

"Well, you wanna go upstairs and meet my two best girls, maybe have a couple of cookies"—Trevor winked at me—"that's what's gotta happen!"

Mike relented just as Kelli appeared beside me at the top of the stairs. She loved children, and when she'd heard the squeaking voice in the foyer, she hadn't been able to wait for Mike to come to her. Meanwhile, the momentum the idea of cookies had seemed to spark in Mike came to a halt when he spotted Kelli.

It was always interesting to me how children responded to my sister. They saw immediately that something was different with her, but they were usually more fascinated than scared. When I was eleven, my mother substitute-taught my Wednesday-morning religion class for a few weeks (all my classmates adored her, of course, and complained when depressive and shiny-faced Sister Claire returned after her hysterectomy). But my mother had been a volunteer who knew nothing about teaching, and so she usually just spent the hour presiding over vague theological discussions on issues like what it meant to be a Good Samaritan or why Jesus was mean to his mother and told her to go away that time. One day, at loose ends for a lesson plan and because the babysitter got hung up, my mother decided she would bring Kelli to class. It would be a class about Kelli! I begged her not to, but she insisted this was a great idea. It would teach my classmates about "unusual people." So the kids all pulled up their chairs around my sister like she was the winning display at a science fair and Kelli sat rocking and sneaking shy, smiling glances at everyone from beneath her bangs. Even as a child herself, she'd loved children.

"When you all came into the classroom today and saw Kelli for the first time," said my mother after everyone had settled and gaped, "what was your impression of her?"

"There's something different about her," one tactful girl responded. The children had already been infected by my mother's air of benevolence—they knew not to come out with an indiscreet word like *wrong*.

"She's *special*!" said a triumphant boy. He knew this word because there was a group of students known as the "special" class in our school—more functional than Kelli, able to learn a few academic basics. We only saw them coming and going in the hallways, though— they weren't permitted to linger in the playground at recess with the rest of us. I knew, from watching kids following behind them in the hallways, limping and slobbering in comic exaggeration, that they would've been mocked to death if they were.

"She *is* special," said my mother. "We're all special, because God made every one of us. But Kelli is special in a different way. You might say *extra* special."

And if I had not been eleven years old at the time, I would've been thinking words along the lines of *Oh, for fuck's sake*.

"And how did you *know* she was special?" asked my mother. "How could you tell?"

Why was she doing this? Making my classmates itemize all the ways Kelli was different? Did my mother not know that children were shits? Did she have no idea that all those Kelli qualities she was forcing them to scrutinize would be thrown, viciously distorted, into my face at recess?

The kids respectfully answered my mother. They cited the rocking, the humming. The whispering to herself. One kid attempted to reference the fact that Kelli was fat by calling it "her, kinda, squishiness," which made my mother laugh. To me it felt like they were stockpiling ammo.

Then: "Why did God make Kelli the way she is, do you think?" my mother asked, silencing everyone. I looked up, interested at last. It was not a question my mother had ever brought up before. My mother was an ours-is-not-to-reason-why kind of gal, or so I'd always thought. The idea that over the years she might actually have been formulating an answer to such an unfathomable question, without my knowledge, was tantalizing.

One brave child, the class keener, tried to answer. "Maybe . . . for us to help?"

I knew my mother, and I knew this was the wrong answer. On some level I was surprised she didn't take umbrage and overturn the table, because imagine if *I* had said such a thing. That Kelli had been put on earth for *others,* as a kind of pet, a creature of need and dependence offered up by the Almighty the way a parent gives a child a hamster in order to impart responsibility: No. My mother had always maintained that Kelli was her own person, of and for herself, just like anyone else. She always stopped short of saying *independent,* because that, of course, was clearly not the case. Kelli could never be independent. Yet I knew, weirdly, that this was what she meant. In her mind, somehow, Kelli stood on her own.

But instead of overturning the table, my mother told the keener in her gentle, lilting voice, "I think that's lovely. But aren't we *all* here to help one another?"

The kids nodded in drugged, cultish unison.

"So just as we help Kelli, doesn't Kelli help us?"

The kids nodded some more, marionette heads at the ends of bobbing strings.

"And *how* does Kelli help us?" prompted my mother. A few jaws went slack. They didn't know. But they were waiting to hear. And so was I.

"By teaching us," said my mother, "to be *selfless.*"

"Selfless," a few of the kids repeated. They were struggling with the unfamiliar word. It was not a word your average eleven-year-old would have had much use for up to this point.

"To *give of* ourselves," said my mother. "To be kind."

Now the nodding started up again. *Kind,* they understood. I even heard a few quietly exclaimed *ah*s around the room.

At the end of the class, to Kelli's delight, my mother encouraged everyone to go up to my sister and shake her hand.

And how about this: There was no exaggerated rocking and gibbering directed at me over recess. No mockery, no drooling-idiot faces pushed into mine.

My mother's magic had made my classmates, briefly, kind.

11

W hat grade you in?" Kelli was asking Mike as she snuck quick, almost flirtatious glances at him. This was the stock question she had for every child she encountered. "What grade you in? What grade you in?"

Mike didn't understand Kelli's cadences, so I acted as interpreter.

"She'd like to know what grade you're in, Mike."

"Just graduated from the big three, didn't ya, buddy?" answered Trevor.

"Nice job," I said. "Way to go."

"What grade you in?" repeated Kelli. It wasn't that she cared about the answer. She, like me, had just been trying to draw the kid out.

"He's in third grade, Kell."

Mike looked offended. "I'm *finished* third grade!"

"Heading into grade four," I amended. Mike, it seemed, was quick to irritate, like his father. "Up for some cookies?" I suggested, looking to make peace, and because Mike had remained frozen in his spot since Kelli had arrived.

"What's the holdup?" said Trevor to Mike, who still had a sneaker dangling from one foot. "Get your g.d. shoes off."

There was a rap on the screen door and Trevor paused, peering out at who was there, before he pushed it open to let pillowy Brenna step inside. Brenna looked him up and down. The smell of tobacco wafted up to where Kelli and I were standing, overpowering the spearmint, which meant she must've just finished a cigarette—I imagined the only opportunity Brenna had to do her smoking was in the close quarters of her car, driving from one client to the next.

"Hey, Brenna," I said.

"Hullo," said Brenna, still looking at Trevor. "And if it isn't Mr. Trebie."

These words, parodying Kelli as they did, should've come across as playful or teasing; but the unsmiling, inflectionless way Brenna uttered them threw everybody off. I was waiting for Trevor to reply with his usual cheery bluster—maybe he had a nickname for Brenna like he did for me and Kelli; maybe Brenna was yet another of his "best girls." But no—Trevor was, to my surprise, at a loss for words.

"The boys just stopped in for a visit," I explained.

"Oh, a visit?" said Brenna.

"Shit," said Trevor. "Is it bath time? Sorry, ladies, usually I'm up on the schedule. Brain fart! Mike, get those shoes back on." Mike looked up at Trevor with exasperation.

"You don't have to go," I protested.

"No, no, Beaner needs her bath. We just stopped in to say a quick hello. We're on our way to the Dairy Queen up the street."

Mike looked startled to hear this.

"Well, I promised Mike a cookie. Let me grab you guys a couple for the road." I dashed into the kitchen.

Kelli, meanwhile, was alternately babbling greetings to Brenna and whispering gleefully to herself in anticipation of her bath.

"Why don't you head down to the bathroom and get yourself ready for Brenna, Kell?" I called as I yanked open the cookie tin. That was all Kelli needed, and she plunged down the stairs, for all I know stampeding poor, forgotten Mike in the process.

All that was left in the tin were shortbreads, but then I remembered Kelli's good-behavior stash of chocolate-chip, which I suspected Mike would prefer. I wandered back to the top of the stairs to ask him.

Mike, I saw, already had his shoes back on. He was at the door, fidgeting with impatience but being ignored because Brenna was standing close and speaking quiet words to Trevor, who stood rigid, his hands bulging in his pockets. Bulging because they were balled into fists—I could tell from the way the tendons in his forearms flexed, like they had when he was barbecuing.

"Mike?" I said. "Shortbreads or chocolate-chip?" And that's when Brenna stepped away from Trevor and went without a word to join Kelli in the bathroom downstairs.

Mike said chocolate-chip, so I went back to root through the cupboards for Kelli's secret stash. When I turned around, Trevor was standing in the kitchen with me, a half smile on his face and his fists still bulging in his pockets.

My instinct was, for some reason, to apologize.

"Sorry about the mix-up with Brenna," I said.

Trevor shook his head tightly, trying to smirk as if he were relaxed. "The ladies at Bestlife," he said. "They can get a little territorial."

"Can they?" I said.

"Yeah. Because they got no fuckin' lives of their own, if you wanna know the truth, pardon my French."

I turned away to tear off a couple of squares of paper towel. I took two cookies out of the bag and wrapped the towel around them. I even dug around in a drawer to find a rubber band to wrap around the cookies and keep the towel in place. All this activity made ample time for Trevor to say whatever it was he wanted to say. But he wasn't saying anything. I handed him the cookies.

"It was really nice to meet Mike."

"We'll have another visit sometime," said Trevor. "Maybe on the weekend."

Now we were just standing across from each other. For something to do, I turned away from him again and flicked on the dishwasher. I had just finished loading it when Trevor and Mike arrived. On some level, I expected the electric hum to be reassuring, but just underneath the hum there was a steady grinding noise that made me tense.

"Listen," said Trevor. "I have a buddy who sells real estate. You wanna look at condos sometime, he can get you a good deal. I'll let him know you're a friend."

"Oh—thanks!" I said. "I'll keep it in mind. My friend Jessica said she'd help me out—she's a real estate agent too."

Trevor nodded, but it was an indulgent, parental kind of nod, the kind of nod you give when you're waiting for someone to stop talking nonsense. "You're gonna want someone you can trust."

I tried to remember exactly what I had told Trevor about Jessica, the day I'd called to ask if he would babysit Kelli. Had I mentioned our out-of-the-blue Facebook reconnection after thirty-plus years? Our mutual girlhood obsession with each other? Who knew what I might've told him in passing. I might've even—and I hoped I hadn't, but I might've—touched upon Jessica's abusive past. *She just got in touch one day—her therapist suggested it, believe it or not. She had a pretty awful childhood, apparently . . .* Jessica had still seemed like an imaginary figure to me at that point—a dream I might have had— and it hadn't seemed to matter what I told Trevor about her, any more than if I'd told him the plot of a movie I'd recently seen.

"No—totally," I said now, nodding. This was unintelligible—it felt like I was trying to give him every possible answer in just a few words and gestures—*yes, no, absolutely, never.* "Jessica's great. I trust her. But thanks."

Trevor stopped nodding and frowned. Being indulgent and parental was not having the desired effect. He lowered his head to look me in the eye. "I mean, does she even know the neighborhoods? Because I know the neighborhoods. I lived here my whole life."

Trevor's fists, which had relaxed briefly in his pockets, now bunched themselves up again, and I could see the outlines of his knuckles pushing against the fabric of his jeans. The dishwasher kept grinding away in the background.

"I'm sure she knows the neighborhoods," I said. I made a jerky shrugging gesture—an easygoing pantomime to let Trevor know how confident and in control of my life I was.

"Okay," said Trevor. "But what I'm telling you, Miss Karie, is, you don't know this town as well as you used to. You don't know the people here. You don't know the people coming and going in your *house,* for that matter. In your *bathroom downstairs.*"

He bobbed his head significantly, indicating the floor beneath us with his chin.

Through the floorboards I heard Kelli's muted, blissful *heh-heh-heh-heh-heh*. And a murmuring, indistinct remark from Brenna before the water turned on and started thundering through the pipes, drowning them both out.

This was stupid, I decided, irritated. This weird, apelike display of dominance in the kitchen. It was all about Trevor feeling he had lost face in some indistinct way with Brenna. And he was trying to get it back by undermining me. Brenna had torn a strip off him for some reason, and he didn't like it. His masculine pride had made him all fist-bunchy, and now he hoped to drag me into it, get me on his side, make me suspicious of the very people who'd been holding my and my sister's lives together these past few weeks.

"Trevor," I said. "Thank you. But I can't go through life distrusting everyone just because I don't know them—"

"I'm not saying distrust everyone," insisted Trevor. "I'm just saying you need to be careful. And you need to be smart."

"Trevor—"

"You're all by yourself now, Miss Karie. And you need to be *careful*."

He said this last thing with a certainty that somehow knocked the fight out of me. I stood there feeling almost winded.

Trevor saw what was happening to my face—that it was getting blotchy, that I had started blinking rapidly—and his own face softened and relaxed. He wasn't upset with me anymore, and his demeanor became almost fatherly.

"Just remember you got friends," he said. "Real friends you can count on. Not people you pay money to for services fuckin' rendered. Pardon my French."

Trevor made a gesture then. To this day, I don't know how to describe this gesture. That is, I don't know how to describe the intention behind it. He took his hands out of his pockets, finally, and exposed his palms to me—they were shiny and disconcertingly smooth, as if he'd sanded them like pieces of wood. Then he raised them and let them hover before my eyes a moment, as if he were a saint displaying his stigmata. Finally he took another step toward me and extended them. I stepped back and felt my ass bump against the counter.

"Dad!" yelled Mike from the foyer. He barked it like the word had been sitting there swelling in his throat and he'd had to yell to keep it from asphyxiating him.

"Coming, goddamnit!" Trevor bawled. He smiled at me. "We'll have a proper visit soon."

12

H i, Miz Petrie dear, and how are you today?" The question came out, despite the *dear,* as clipped, impatient, too busy for the usual social niceties. I'd never met Margot in person, but over the phone, at least, it struck me that she had a personality similar to Brenna's—terse and no-nonsense—and I wondered if the ladies of Bestlife were all versions of one another, an assembly line of short, squarish-yet-pillowy women who, despite their soft exteriors and the occasional *dear,* were tough enough to step to a guy like Trevor and look him up and down.

Margot was the senior administrator at Bestlife, my point person when it came to Kelli's care. She had walked me through my mother's schedule and expressed her condolences in the same harassed tones that she was using now. I had appreciated this about her—I'd been on the receiving end of a lot of syrupy consolation the week of my mother's funeral, but Margot hadn't a drop of syrup in her. She was, if anything, vinegary. I hadn't doubted that her sympathy was genuine; it was just that she'd made it very clear that my problems were my own, and very sad, and meanwhile the important business of seeing to the needs of my sister would be supervised and competently handled. It was nice to hear from her again.

"Hi, Margot! I'm good, thanks. How are you?"

"I'm fine, dear," Margot huffed. I think she had been hoping I wouldn't bother to reciprocate the time-wasting inquiry into her well-being. "I'm just calling to check in with you about the workers we currently have coming out to see Kelli. How has everyone been working out?"

"The workers? Everyone's been great."

"You're happy with them?"

"We're really happy."

"Miz Petrie, I'd like you to know that you are welcome to request that a worker be taken out of Kelli's rotation at any time, for any reason."

I hesitated.

"Okay," I said. "That's good to know."

"If a worker," continued Margot, "makes any requests or demands of you not relating to the care of your loved one, you should feel under no obligation whatsoever and you should feel free to call me to discuss these matters."

I laughed a bit. "You sound like you're reading off a form, Margot."

"I assure you I am not reading off a form," said Margot, sounding offended.

"No, I just mean," I said, "what's this all about?"

Margot sighed briefly. Even her sighs were clipped and efficient. "We encourage our workers to be friendly. And sometimes people come to think of them as friends."

"I understand."

"But we've occasionally had issues where—oh, say, for example, just recently. We have a client who's an older gentleman. We send a worker out to administer his medication every day. But one day this gentleman decides he needs his gutters cleaned. So when his caregiver arrives, he offers him fifty dollars, maybe, to get up on a ladder and clean his gutters while he's there."

"I see," I said.

"You're new to all this, Miz Petrie."

"Yes," I said, "I am."

"And God bless you, your mother dying was such a shock, I hope you are doing all right."

"Oh," I said, flustered by this abrupt, officious expression of sympathy. "Thank you. I'm okay."

"And I am not saying that you are offering anybody fifty dollars to clean your gutters. I am just saying that it is inappropriate for a worker to be crossing those lines."

"I get it," I said.

"It's because," said Margot, "we come into your homes. We prepare your food. We give you medicine. We give you baths. We help you exercise. Sometimes we even go to the *bathroom* with you."

"Yes," I said. "You do."

"Those lines are so easily blurred."

"It's the intimacy," I suggested.

"Yes!" said Margot. "That's exactly right. The care we give is intimate. It's very personal. And so people start to feel they have a personal relationship with their caregivers. You see? But it's a professional relationship, Miz Petrie, with parameters. That's what we need to keep in mind."

"Am I being scolded?"

"Dear god!" exclaimed Margot. "Oh my dear god, no!"

I started to laugh. It was the extremity of Margot's reaction—I'd felt like I'd insulted her earlier, but now it was as if I'd slapped her with a glove.

Margot waited for me to finish laughing.

"Now, Miz Petrie—"

"Please call me Karen."

"Yes, okay. Now, Karen? Do you have any concerns or questions for me at this time?"

Was I going to be the one to say the word *Trevor,* or would Margot? Did she want me to or not?

"I think you're saying," I began, "the workers shouldn't overstep, no matter how much we might rely on them. Yes?"

"Yes."

"And I guess," I continued, "that we shouldn't encourage them to overstep."

"By asking them to clean out your gutters or whathaveyou."

I decided to try something.

"Or say, you know . . . say we want to give one of the workers a key to the house so it'll be easier for them to—"

"Good god!" Margot exclaimed again. "By no means should a worker ever be given a key to the house! Nor should he ever accept it. Or she. That would be a fireable offense right there."

"I see."

Margot sounded shaken. "I hope that's a hypothetical."

"Yes," I said, "that's a hypothetical. Can I ask another question?"

"Of course," said Margot, recovered and back to sounding impatient.

"Did my mother ever have any issues with any of the workers? Did she ever report any problems or ask for someone to be taken out of rotation or anything like that?"

"Oh, Miz Petrie," said Margot, relaxing at the mention of my mother and forgetting to use my first name. "Your dear mother, god love her. Your mother never gave us any trouble at all. Your mother was just a *dream*."

Of course. Of course my mother was.

I decided, in that moment, that it was time to get this phase of things over with. For Kelli and me to move forward with our lives.

Really, I'd been imagining this all along, from the moment I'd decided to stay—the moving forward, that is. Once we sold the house, I imagined, once Kelli was enrolled in the Gorsebrook day program, we'd both be free—or free-ish. We'd rid ourselves of this place and its stifling routines—the tedium of Kelli and me stuck together, eating every meal beneath the fluorescent kitchen glare day in and day out. Not just the house but this whole winding rabbit warren of suburbs my mother had inexplicably chosen to settle into after my father died, for no reason other than, as she said, it was "close to a hospital," which struck me as not a very optimistic motivation although maybe understandable following her husband's untimely death at the breakfast table from cardiac arrest (an arrest so sudden, so absolute, the paramedics said he had likely died in the millisecond between putting his coffee down with a startled look and slumping face-first onto the linoleum). So Kelli and I spent the second part of our childhoods, the post-father part, in this neighborhood, if it could be called that, a neighborhood surrounded by glittering traffic and glassy car dealerships and squatting strip malls.

But soon we would leave that behind. A fantasy I'd been only half-conscious of in the past few days blossomed full-blown in my mind as I sat there on the phone with Margot. Kelli and me in a sleek, bright condo on the fashionable side of the bridge, maybe overlooking the harbor, but still within walking distance of Gorsebrook. We would walk there together in the mornings; there'd be no more driving just to get to the grocery store or buy a cup of coffee, no more negotiating four lanes of traffic just to get across the street to the stupid Starbucks. We'd find somewhere leafy, with amenities and parks and small, local shops and friendly, waving neighbors. We'd go for strolls. Kelli's bad knee would get the exercise she could never get enough of here, especially with an aging, cancer-ridden mother unable to take her anywhere, not even in a car at the end.

Would we even require home care in this new life? Not for walks, clearly. Kelli would be getting all the exercise she needed once we established ourselves in our new neighborhood. And what about baths? Surely I could handle baths! My mother had managed them herself for years, right up until the cancer kept her from being able to stand for long stretches of time. *I,* on the other hand, was perfectly healthy. Why hadn't it occurred to me before that I could handle baths? It struck me all at once that the standard of care Kelli was receiving, the daily comings and goings of the workers, had been tailored to assist a woman who'd been old, sick, and growing weaker every day.

All these thoughts went through my head, it seemed, during an intake of breath—not even a particularly long or measured one. And that was when I told Margot I wanted to cut back. I said we would only need someone to come by twice a week, for Kelli's baths. And that I would like to assist with those baths, to learn the ropes, as it were. And after a couple more weeks, perhaps we'd cut it back again.

"So no more walks?" asked Margot lightly.

"I think I can manage the walks," I assured her.

"Whatever you need, dear," she murmured, and her voice faded out briefly, as if she had tilted her head away from the phone. Even more distantly, I could hear the sound of a pen tip dragging itself in a long, deliberate line across a page.

13

After that random bout, Kelli's diarrhea didn't return, didn't turn out to be a bellwether for some subsequent, more serious ailment, to my relief. But just to be on the safe side, I was extra careful about her diet in the following days, plying her with yogurt and probiotics and turning the kitchen into an assembly line of various muffins and cakes held together with nothing but psyllium husks and flax—my mother, I recalled, had always sworn by both, and it was easier to get Kelli to eat a muffin than swallow a pill.

The diapers were now tucked away under the downstairs bathroom sink, ready to be deployed for future emergencies, and I was feeling pretty good about getting Kelli's intestinal trains running on time when an entirely different issue arose.

She started getting up at night.

This was extremely bad news. When Kelli started getting up at night, you never knew why and you never knew how to stop it and you never knew how long it would go on. All you knew was that Kelli had murdered sleep—not just her own, but yours. Because Kelli didn't like to be up alone.

"Oh god, it's just like when you were babies," I remember my mother moaning at the breakfast table, the two of us peering red-eyed at each other over our tea as Kelli snoozed into the afternoon. She never had any trouble getting back to sleep after the sun came up, unlike my mother and me. "It's exactly like having a newborn. They wake up, they cry, you don't know what they want, all you can do is pace and sing, give them something to eat, but it just goes on and on night after night until you turn into a zombie."

That's how Kelli's bouts of sleeplessness went: they were cycles, so you knew they would abate eventually, but after a couple of weeks you felt like you'd been dipped into a vortex of blurring days and nights, of clocks without meaning. You stopped believing it would ever end.

I felt the hot, chubby knuckles dabbing at my forehead. Kelli produced heat unlike anyone I'd ever met; her knuckles felt like two warm little pixie feet tiptoeing across my brow.

"Karie sleepin'?"

"Oh, Kelli!"

I exclaimed *Oh, Kelli!* as opposed to *What's wrong?* because the experience was so viscerally familiar—it took me right back to the last time this had happened, when I was about sixteen and I felt those chubby knuckles dabbing at my head every night for two weeks straight, sometimes multiple times a night—and my sleep-deprived instinct after a certain point was to leap out of my bed and fasten my hands around her throat.

I sat up and tried to pull myself back to the present. I wasn't sixteen. This hadn't been going on for days on end. I didn't want to kill my sister.

"What's up, Kell?"

"Sleepin'."

"No, I'm not sleeping anymore. Are you okay?"

"Gettin' up."

I rubbed my hands across my face.

"Yeah, I'm up. You're up. We're both up."

"Who up, Karie, who up?"

I flung the covers off and sat on the side of the bed. I wasn't sure, but I interpreted this question to mean that Kelli wanted clearer proof that I was indeed "up."

"Karie's up," I assured her. "Now what's the problem?"

Kelli hummed and whispered to herself briefly, looking at the floor. I waited.

"Baffroom," said Kelli.

"Kelli, you know how to go to the bathroom yourself!"

"Baffroom self," Kelli agreed, turning to go.

I wanted to flop back into bed in exasperation, but I made myself get up and follow her, just to ensure that she wasn't sick again, that there would be no repeats of the previous week's disaster.

And there wasn't. Kelli peed. She emerged. She announced, in her way of announcing these things, that she was going back to bed.

"Good stuff," I said, as if sarcasm would ever get me anywhere with Kelli. "Thanks for keeping me in the loop there, Kell."

"No one up," Kelli remarked as she shuffled back into her room.

Instead of feeling annoyed, I knew I should be grateful. This seemed like it could be just a blip—it hadn't been anything like when we were teenagers. There had been no getting Kelli back to bed in those days. She wanted something to eat, wanted to linger interminably, humming and whispering, on the second step of the foyer, she wanted to sit on her threadbare stool and gaze out the window as if she could see anything out there but her own reflection. It struck my mother and me that she simply wanted the night to be as day during those strange periods—she wanted to defy the natural order of things, and she wanted us to keep her company on this obstinate ride.

It kept happening, though. Not the way it used to, in endless stretches between midnight and dawn, but quick, random dabbings at my forehead followed by *Karie sleepin'?* and the insistence that I get up. I started to acclimate to this new pattern, eventually understanding that all I had to do was basically open my eyes and say hi, and Kelli would shuffle around, ask a few questions about who was up, and whether or not we were up, then hit the bathroom before heading back to bed.

Still, it was infuriating to be woken from a deep sleep with such regularity. It made me tense and moody because it brought me back to the end times of my marriage, the beginning of the end, when he wanted to leave but could not bring himself to say it, when neither of us could really bring ourselves to say much of anything. So instead he would stay up drinking, feeling resentful of my oblivious slumber in the next room—even though I was far from oblivious; I was merely escaping into unconsciousness at the first possible opportunity—until at last he roused himself to fling open the bedroom door and poke me awake with incoherent, hostile questions and demands. Once, when I wouldn't wake up, he slipped one of his earbuds into my ear and started blasting a band we'd both been listening to a lot around that time—a gleeful, screamy band with a name like Total Annihilation or Massive Carnage or something.

There's something about knowing you are not safe in sleep that gives a person bad dreams. The expectation of being woken every night—that feeling of insecurity and dread I remembered carrying around with me as my marriage was drawing to a close, like a rotting smell I couldn't find the source of, shit I didn't know I'd stepped in—was unnerving. The subconscious starts sending messages: Be vigilant. Don't relax. Here's a bogeyman or two to keep your nerves on edge.

I started dreaming about my mother a lot as a result of Kelli's nightly up-and-down. They weren't sad dreams. That is, I knew she had died, in the dreams, but somehow it was incidental, it wasn't a big deal. My reaction when I saw her was strangely casual. I thought: *Oh, there she is.*

So it wasn't my mother's presence itself that made the dreams bad. It was more the activities I found her engaged in, and even then, I couldn't necessarily tell you why. In one, she was barbecuing a whole pig on a spit on the back patio. She wasn't using the barbecue; she had constructed an actual fire pit somehow. I didn't know how the wooden boards beneath it could be standing up to the heat, but I figured my mother must know what she was doing. I asked her, *Who's going to eat all that?* And she said, *Kelli will eat whatever's left over.* Somehow I knew she was talking about the gross parts, the ears and brain and snout and feet. But I knew that if I argued, my mother would insist that these parts were actually considered delicacies in certain culinary circles. So I stood there mute as my mother slathered the pig in sauce, feeling paralyzed, muzzled by logic that she hadn't even articulated.

In another dream, I knew my mother wasn't dead, that she was just living downstairs in the laundry room. I was impatient with her about this dumb, irrational decision; I could hear her bumping around down there and got up to confront her about being stubborn and not just coming back upstairs to resume her normal life. In the dream, my mother being noisy in the laundry room was the reason Kelli kept getting up in the middle of the night; I suppose I had gone to bed knowing I would be knuckle-dabbed awake in only a few hours and drifted off in a state of consternation, turning over the puzzle of Kelli's wakefulness in my mind, and this was the fun-house mirror of an explanation my subconscious came up with.

I explained to her with what I felt was more patience than she deserved: *Mom, it's great you're not dead, but for Christ's sake, come upstairs. You can't have it both ways. Either die or come upstairs.*

My mother said, *All right, I'll come up in a minute.* And then I watched as she put a load of laundry in. And I realized she was full of shit. She was stalling me. She would never do what I wanted—she'd just agree to whatever I said and then do as she pleased.

Maybe these don't sound like particularly bad dreams. All I can say is that they made my heart pound in such a way that I could hear it in my ears, and I always woke up from them with this sound like a washing machine in the spin cycle thumping in my head—I never simply drifted into other dreams.

In fact, the morning of the laundry dream, I couldn't help myself—I climbed out of bed and went down to the laundry room. I flicked on the overhead light; the stark, sudden glare of it in contrast to the soft morning light coming in from the window made me flinch. The overhead—another long, fluorescent rectangle, like the one in Irene's kitchen—gave out a steady humming noise, a sound that made my eyes water whenever I noticed it upstairs but that I found sort of companionable and soothing down here. Maybe it was the mundanity of it—a humming overhead light precisely as you'd find in all of the most boring places in the world. Waiting rooms. School hallways. Queues at government offices. Nothing strange or uncanny could take place in a room lit like this. It was neat, certainly, and well organized in accordance with Irene's usual standards, but except for some eyelet curtains she'd installed on the lone window, it was the one room in the house she hadn't bothered to make cozy.

I took a step toward the window and saw something I hadn't noticed before. It had a small shelf installed below it, a shelf that had always held, as far as I could remember, scrub brushes and special laundry products like Shout for getting out tough stains. But the shelf didn't have that stuff anymore. Instead, it held a small array of framed family photographs.

I'd seen these pictures before. They were snapshots Irene had taken and stuck into miniature frames at various points over the years. The house was full of such pictures. For as long as I could remember, Irene's end tables and shelves had always been littered with these small, framed, concentrated hits of memory. But I'd never seen them in the laundry room before. I picked each of them up in turn to get a good look. Grandma Gillis holding me as a baby while toddler Kelli looked on from our mother's lap. Then one of me at sixteen, dressed for a formal dance and looking sort of inappropriately sexy. I was wearing a low-cut dress I'd bought for myself at the mall as a kind of punishment of my mother because she had been too busy to shop for it with me. I remembered being surprised by the resigned way she had accepted this punishment at the time—she'd sighed, dutifully taken my picture, and given me a shawl to "keep warm," and that had been the extent of it. But what I could not remember her ever doing was framing this photo and leaving it out on display. The last time I'd seen it, it had been tucked safely away in a photo album chronicling my teen years.

Then there was a photo of Irene alone that I had seen many times before, because she used to keep it by her bed—Irene in her forties, around the age I was now, standing up in front of her choir at midnight Mass, hair curled, earrings twinkling, warbling the solo. She was backgrounded by a wall of lit candles, and her mouth was wide with song. Her eyes sparkled heavenward, and it was a beautiful, triumphant portrait—one of those photographs that were so rare in the days before digital, where, as if by magic, you were captured precisely as you'd always hoped to see yourself.

And finally there was a fourth, lone photograph, of Kelli sitting on her stool, looking out the window. It had been taken about twenty years ago, and thirty-year-old Kelli sat in precisely the same posture and attitude with which she had sat on that stool every day since. She weighed less then. Her hair was more blond than silvery, and her shoulders had less of a hunch to them. But the essential Kelli hadn't changed.

My eyes shifted back and forth between the photographs as the light hummed overhead. But the humming didn't reassure me anymore. Seeing the pictures in this new context made them seem alien. Here was Irene looking perfect, here was me looking a way I never looked, here was Kelli looking, as always, like Kelli. Why would Irene have plucked these particular photos from the album, the end tables, the knickknack shelves and placed them here? They were lined up side by side, in a bit of a semicircle. Place a candle before them and you'd have a shrine.

14

Even though I had cut back on home care at maybe the stupidest time possible—the time when things were genuinely about to get busy after weeks of numbness and inertia—I was slowly starting to realize that I was doing okay. I didn't feel nearly as oppressed and put upon as I had during those endless post-funeral days, when the care workers dutifully arrived to take Kelli down for baths—and out for walks, in Trevor's case—and therefore off my hands for an hour or so every afternoon. That brief, daily reprieve was a freedom I had, at the time, insisted to myself I needed. But now I didn't seem to need that freedom after all. Why, I wondered, had I placed such stock in it for so long? In being alone, unhindered? Hadn't I had my fill of unhindered solitude these past few years? It turned out that I had.

I was entering a new phase. Instead of feeling burdened by my role as Kelli's keeper, now I felt energized and dynamic. Kelli was a situation to be daily grappled with, and every day that I grappled with her—to whatever degree of success—gave me a sense of purpose and accomplishment. For one thing, I started taking Kelli everywhere with me, the way my mother used to do—wrestling her into her jacket and prodding her into her shoes and nagging her into the car to come with me on errands and anything else I felt like doing. Kelli and I went to the bank. We went grocery shopping. We met Jessica for coffee to sign paperwork for the sale of the house. When we were feeling cooped up, we drove down to the waterfront and rode the commuter ferry across the harbor and back. When we didn't feel like cooking, we took ourselves out to Boston Pizza or down the hill to the Brass Rail—a favorite special-occasions restaurant of my mother's—where you could order a slab of pan-fried haddock so large it hung off either side of the plate.

These outings didn't always go a hundred percent smoothly. I'm thinking in particular of the moment in the grocery store when the button on Kelli's pants went flying after she bent over to pick up an avocado I'd unknowingly nudged out of the bin. As she straightened, the pants slid to her ankles and, since I was distracted by the grocery list, Kelli determined that the best thing to do was to step out of them and continue on her way. I was learning to take this sort of thing in stride. People staring was not the end of the world. Teenagers pulling out their phones and managers approaching to ask if they could "help" were easily dispatched, especially once I learned to apply my mother's ice-queen imperiousness—a persona she reserved especially for this kind of incident. As a kid, I called it my mother's "good day to you, sir" because everything she uttered in that tone sounded like it should be followed up by those five words. Now I found myself rocking a frosty "good day to you, sir" all my own ("Put the phone away *right now,* young man. I'm not going to tell you again"). I had rolled my eyes whenever she affected it back when I was growing up—I'd found it so theatrical and needlessly bitchy. But now I saw that it was a secret weapon.

It was all this running around that probably kept Kelli from noticing that she was no longer being taken for her walks two days a week. Or if she did notice, she didn't complain about it to me. Kelli was wonderfully low-maintenance during this period—except for her bouts of wakefulness, which lately had developed a new wrinkle. Every so often, I realized, after a couple of restful, undisturbed nights, Kelli would get up without waking me. Which sounds like it should have been great, but those were the occasions it turned out I had to watch out for. Because Kelli seemed to be moving stuff. One morning I got up and the kitchen chairs were all over the place—one in the doorway of the kitchen, one turned facing away from the table, another in the living room. Another time I got up and found the blue recycling bin my mother always kept in a corner of the kitchen on its side at the top of the stairs.

"You can't put stuff there, Kell," I told her. "One of us could trip."

"Trip fall down," acknowledged Kelli.

"That's right," I said. "Don't move stuff around when you get up, okay? It's just going to make you more awake."

"Don't move stuff, no," Kelli agreed. But it kept happening. One afternoon I opened the hallway closet and found everything on the floor. All the coats and jackets had been pulled off their hangers.

The strangest thing about all this was that it seemed so uncharacteristically energetic of Kelli. In her waking hours, Kelli never even roused herself to so much as open the closet door, let alone rifle through the coats or rearrange furniture. Could it be, I wondered, that she was sleepwalking? And, in sleepwalking, was she a completely different kind of Kelli?

I decided not to worry about it. Whatever was prodding her out of bed those nights didn't seem to cast a shadow on her daylight hours, and that was all that mattered. She was cheerful and easygoing company lately, seeming to enjoy all our errand running, not to mention the treats I bought her afterward for being good—and she liked seeing Jessica. Getting her off her stool and into the car wasn't nearly the pitched battle it used to be. It occurred to me that maybe keeping Kelli busy had been the key to keeping Kelli happy and compliant this whole time. I'll admit it. I was starting to think I had a real handle on things. Right up until the afternoon Jessica took us condo shopping.

They were always tickled in equal measure to see each other. When I first reintroduced them, Kelli remembered Jessica at once—or not quite at once, but as soon as Jessica reminded her of a game they used to play together. "Kelli," she had said, "Do you remember Round and Round the Garden?" And Kelli, who hadn't yet made eye contact, but who'd been smiling to herself and rocking slightly to the sound of Jessica's pleasing voice, had abruptly stuck out one pudgy hand, palm facing up.

Jessica took the hand in both of hers and started marching two glossy fingernails across my sister's palm, incanting, "Round and round the garden, like a teddy bear. . . . One step, two step . . . tickle under there!" At which point Jessica pretended to tickle Kelli under the armpit—remembering or perhaps intuiting that Kelli wasn't wild about abrupt or intimate touching.

Kelli's smile grew big and she erupted in *heh-heh-heh*s. And then she spoke the words *Jenny Mad-tall*. Which, I only then remembered, had been her pronunciation of Jessie's name back when we were all children together.

So that was how the afternoon began—like all our other Jessica meet-ups, with some kind of elaborate coffee confection for Kelli and one or two games of Round and Round punctuated by multiple eruptions of *heh-heh-heh* (especially once all that sugar and caffeine hit Kelli's bloodstream), which always got Jessica and me chuckling too. Good feelings all around. So I had no reason to anticipate Kelli giving me any trouble during the condo hunt, and she didn't—not for the first couple of viewings, anyway. She gamely accompanied us into one generic, freshly painted living space after another, annoyed if there were too many stairs or by the fact that there wasn't any place to sit down once we got there, but otherwise agreeable, strolling from room to room with us and even offering opinions when they were solicited.

"Think you'd like to live here, Kelli?"

"Live here," said Kelli.

"This would work for us okay, don't you think?"

Kelli glanced with disapproval at the empty kitchen. "Eat," she remarked.

"No, there's nothing here to eat yet, is there? But we can fix that if we have to."

"Fix that," agreed Kelli.

The mood shifted when it came time to check out a couple of high-rises. I'd forgotten that Kelli had an issue with elevators. Kelli did not often have occasion to ride an elevator—usually only when my mother took her for various medical or dental appointments. She would if she had to, but she would never do so happily, and she would always be vocal about her feelings. I remember being driven crazy by my mother's patience with Kelli on those occasions, how she stood, holding the door open, even as other people, strangers, entered and stared daggers at her and Kelli, wondering what the holdup was. But my mother just stood there, holding the door, calling sweetly to Kelli as Kelli paced and muttered and shook her stubborn head.

Getting her in hadn't been a problem. At that point in the afternoon, it felt as if Kelli would've followed Jessica over a ledge. But the moment the elevator started to move, all Kelli's disinclination came flooding back. "Agh!" she yelled as we began to lurch upward. "Broken! Floor bro-ken!"

"It's just an elevator," I told her. "You've been in elevators before, Kelli."

"El-vaer," said Kelli, the way someone else might say "maggots" or "sex offender."

Jessica glanced over at us. "She okay?"

"No," said Kelli.

"She's fine," I said.

"If it's an issue," said Jessica, "we can cross the high-rises off the list."

"No, no," I said. "That's gotta be like eighty percent of the buildings. It won't kill her."

"Kill her," said Kelli.

The doors slid open and Kelli flung herself into the hallway.

It just got worse from there. The condo, with its granite countertops, vertiginous view, and energy-efficient fridge, was looked over, and soon enough it was time to get back into the elevator again. This time, Kelli kicked up a major stink.

"No el-vaer. Not."

"Kelli," I said. "You gotta get in."

"No el-vaer, no!" Kelli stared at the floor and began rocking in place.

"Rocking's not going to help!" I said, losing my patience. "We're fifteen stories up! Do you wanna go home?"

"Home," said Kelli.

"Then you have to get in the elevator."

I was already in, mashing the button to keep the door open while Jessica stood in the hallway, looking back and forth between Kelli and me.

"Get in," I said to Jessica.

"Are you sure?" said Jessica.

"We need to show her we're serious. Come on, Kelli," I said. "Jessica and I are leaving now. We have to leave."

Jessica stepped into the elevator with me. Kelli hadn't raised her head to witness this, but I knew she had registered it. She stood there rocking and whispering furiously to herself, maybe cursing me, maybe psyching herself up.

"*Kelli!*" I yelled. "Get in here!"

Kelli started yelling back at me, her furious whispering becoming abruptly loud and audible—a lot of *no*s and *el-vaer*s and *home*s and *Karie*s and proclamations that *Kelli don't want to, she don't want to!*

"Now!"

"*No Karie no Karie no Karie no Karie—*"

"Get the fuck in here!"

Without lowering the volume on her protests, Kelli finally lurched into the elevator—and hollered all the way to the ground floor, despite the presence of an apprehensive mother and bug-eyed daughter who had joined us a couple of floors down.

When it came time to see the next condo, Kelli wasn't budging. I'd had every reason to expect that this would be the case, but still it made me furious. The rage that overtook me in the previous building was still simmering as we drove to the next viewing. Jessica could feel it. She suggested a coffee break, but I said no, we'd already had enough coffee and we'd already wasted enough time.

I knew I should've calmed down by now. A person couldn't propose to spend her life with someone like my sister and be a grudge holder. Because the sister in question literally cannot be reasoned with, and the person who is capable of reason needs to grasp that. A person needs to have, therefore—as her mother was always said to have—the patience of a saint. At the very least, a person needs to accept that she'll experience the occasional eruptions of anger and then, saintlike, let them go.

But I couldn't let it go. Things had been going so smoothly and Kelli had been such an easygoing delight and the two of us had been *moving forward* with such momentum and now, just as we were taking our first shaky, newborn-foal steps into the future, *now* she digs in her heels? *Now* the old, familiar Kelli reasserts herself? By *old* and *familiar,* what I really meant, I suppose, was adolescent. Kelli's mulishness had reminded me, viscerally, of our adolescence together—had transported me back into it, it felt like. As Jessica negotiated the traffic to the next condo, I sat in the seat beside her, seething with what felt like a downright hormonal wash of irrationality and outrage. Because *of course* it was ridiculous to get mad at Kelli for being Kelli. I'd known that then as well as I knew it now. But, my angry teenage brain kept shrieking, *why* does Kelli *always* have to be *so* Kelli? My angry teenage brain felt righteous, convinced it had a point. It refused to back down.

"Are you coming, Kelli?" I said. Jessica had parked, and the three of us sat tensely in the quiet car.

"Not coming," said Kelli.

"We're going to see another condo. Would you like to come with us or not?" My voice, I could hear, was ridiculous. I was spitting out each syllable like a toxin.

"Stay the car," said Kelli.

"Last chance," I said. "Jessica and I are going to go look at another place. Do you want us to go without you?"

"Not coming," said Kelli. Her voice rose. *"Not coming, no Karie, not coming, no, Kelli stay the car, Karie, no—"*

"Fine!" I yelled.

I got out and slammed the door. Jessica got out a moment later but kept the door open.

"Will she be okay?"

"She'll be fine," I said. "We'll all be the better for it."

Jessica bent down to talk to Kelli. "Gonna be okay, Kell?"

Kelli rocked and whispered sullenly to herself for a moment or two. "Car," she said finally.

"Let her cool off," I said.

"Let's all cool off," said Jessica.

The individual in question, as the police later described him, was only remarkable, appearance-wise anyway, in his unremarkability. If he had looked explicitly homeless, or mentally ill, or some combination of both—wild-haired, pants on backward, filthy-bearded—Jessica and I might've reacted with less confusion. I was angry at myself, afterward, for my muted instincts, the way my first thought was to assume the man had made some kind of innocent mistake. I was witnessing something wrong, something threatening and out of the ordinary, and my mind had gone immediately to an assumption of safety, of *surely everything's okay. Perhaps the gentleman is confused; perhaps he just needs help.* My instincts, I realized, had failed me, and they had failed Kelli. They had simply leaped over the possibility of real danger in order to scuttle to the side of reassurance. And what kind of instincts were those?

Leaving the building and walking toward the parking lot, we could see that he was leaning on the hood of the car, bashing the windshield with the flats of his hands and yelling what sounded like "Eh? *Eh?*"

"Oh," said Jessica. "Is that guy—?"

"*Bitch?*" I thought I heard the man say. I dismissed it in the next instant. Certainly he didn't say *bitch.*

"That's *your* car, isn't it?" I said to Jessica. I knew full well it was Jessica's car. The fact of the matter was, I didn't accept what I was seeing. I didn't trust what I was hearing. I was waiting for someone to come along and clear the matter up.

Jessica broke into a wobbly run before I did, clacking across the parking lot in her high heels.

Kelli has swallowed her tongue, a businesslike voice announced in my mind. It solemnly began to tick off numbered points: (1) You left her alone; (2) She swallowed her tongue; (3) The nice man can't get into the car to assist her, much as he would like to, because (4) Kelli doesn't know how to work the locks. And (5) You will not get there in time to save her.

I started running as well.

"Hey!" Jessica was yelling.

"Do you need help?" I called. Because surely the man meant well, and surely the right thing to do was to offer assistance.

"Fuck YOU!" yelled the man, ignoring Jessica and me. So he was yelling this at Kelli. He kicked the side of Jessica's car. "Cunt!"

In the car, I could see Kelli rocking to save her life, eyes closed, hands jammed against her ears, lips moving rapidly.

"Whoa, whoa, whoa!" Jessica was saying. The man whirled to face her, teeth bared, and suddenly I wanted to tackle her, pull her down behind the safety of another car, where we could crouch together and figure out what to do.

"Fuck you too!" yelled the man.

"Get away from my car!" shrieked Jessica.

"Fuck this rude bitch!" yelled the man, referring to Kelli, kicking Jessica's car door again.

Jessica had skidded to a halt the moment the man turned to bare his teeth at her, losing her balance briefly as she went over on one high heel. She yanked out her phone and waved it lopsidedly at him.

"I'm calling the police!"

"Go ahead and call them! We live in a *society*!"

I stood blinking at the man, trying to figure out what this meant, and how to get to Kelli, and if Kelli was hurt, and how any of this could be happening. I couldn't make sense of the person in front of me, the *individual in question,* couldn't put him into any kind of context. He was, as I said, ordinary except for the snarling red face, the vicious bulge of his eyes. As I later described him to the police, he was not particularly large—around five-eleven, bearded, cropped hair. I didn't say so to the cops, but he also struck me as familiar—later I put this down to his physical type being so generic. Just a man in his late thirties, a little heavy but not exactly fat—a *dad bod,* as I'd heard his kind of build described. A man who's discovered he can't necessarily drink and eat anything he wants to anymore without developing love handles—and decided he's okay with that. He wore a short-sleeved plaid shirt over a T-shirt with some faded, innocuous slogan emblazoned on it. Jeans. He could've worked in a hardware store; he could've been a dentist or financial analyst off the clock. He could've been anybody. He was just a guy.

"She's retarded!" I screamed at the man. This was not a word I often used when it came to Kelli. But this was the one word people unambiguously understood.

"Fuck you!" the man yelled back at me, assuming an affront. *"You're* retarded!"

"Not *you,* her!"

"You're *both* fuckin' retarded!"

He slammed his hand against the window close to Kelli's head. He kicked the door again for good measure.

"The police are coming," said Jessica. She was holding up her phone. "And I'm recording you now. You're on video."

The man glared at her and seemed to be gathering words in his mouth, some poisonous retort. But then he turned, spat hugely on the car, and jogged away.

What If a Man

15

Once, when I was around sixteen, my mother and I had this theological discussion in the House and Home section of Woolworth's. Kelli must've been at her friendship circle or home with the sitter, because Irene and I were by ourselves, arguing over a bin of cushions printed with inspirational sayings. The cushion Irene was there to purchase was, of course, for Kelli. Irene was concerned about Kelli's stool by the window—it did not have sufficient padding, as far as my mother was concerned, not when you considered the vast stretches of time Kelli was prepared to spend on it watching the comings and goings of the street.

The cushions in the bin were emblazoned with sparkly, silk-screened messages: *Every day may not be GOOD, but there is something GOOD every day. A DIAMOND is a chunk of coal that did well under PRESSURE. Difficult ROADS lead to beautiful PLACES.* They depressed me—*Ah, you're miserable, aren't you?,* they all seemed to be saying. *That's good. That's as it should be.* Irene kept picking up and reading out one cushion adage after another and asking me if I liked it. And I, being sixteen and impossible, kept saying no. Sometimes when you're young and in a situation you feel will never change, everything takes on a swoony, cosmic significance. This was one of those moments for me. Objectively viewed by any reasonable person, I was just being a moody brat. But in the moment, as my mother recited one listless platitude after another, all of which seemed to be extolling, in one way or another, the virtue of suffering—of just sitting and waiting suffering out, and patting yourself on the back for it—I felt like I might go crazy.

Pretty soon Irene got fed up with my monosyllabism and started lobbing the cushions at me the instant I rejected them. I refused to flinch or protest as they bounced off my chest and face and back into the bin. I had a feeling that Irene and I were now trapped in some kind of vortex, that we would spend eternity in the purgatory that was Woolworth's, fluorescent-lit with a Muzak version of Sheila E.'s "The Glamorous Life" playing above our heads, Irene pulling cushions from the bottomless bin, chucking them forever, me rooted there, unflinching, to receive them.

Only then my mother read a cushion that gave me pause.

It's not about the DESTINATION but the JOURNEY, she read.

She bunched the cushion in one hand and raised her arm to throw it at me. "Wait," I said.

She raised her eyebrows.

"That one's okay," I said.

She turned the cushion around to read the silk-screened lettering again. "Really? You like this one?"

"Yes," I said, "because it's the opposite of what you said before at Boston Pizza."

Irene peered at me. We had gone to Boston Pizza for lunch and ordered ribs. Without acknowledging it to each other, we had taken advantage of the cushion expedition, and our time away from Kelli, to make an afternoon of it.

"What did I say at Boston Pizza?" asked Irene.

"You basically said what all those other pillows said," I told her. "You said, 'I'll get my reward in the next life.'"

To be fair to Irene, what she actually had said was that having "happy, healthy girls" was her reward. And the only other reward she needed was, as she put it, "waiting for me on the other side." I have no idea how this came up over baby back ribs and a side salad, but I'd been gritting my teeth over it for the remainder of the afternoon. Irene often got a little philosophical when it was just the two of us—I suspected it was the only opportunity she had to reflect on her life. And perhaps there was something about me—about my attitude toward everything at the time—that brought such musings on.

"Oh," said Irene. She read the saying on the pillow again. "Well, this is a nice idea too, isn't it? Let's get this one."

"No," I said. "Because you don't believe that. You don't believe it's about the journey."

Any other parent at that point would probably have told me to go wait in the goddamn car, but Irene understood exactly what I was getting at, that this was an assault on her worldview that could by no means go unchallenged. She clutched the cushion in both hands, her cheeks blazing.

"Every moment of every day," she said, "cannot simply be about *you*. Who are you if you're not doing good? Who are you if you're not doing what's right? What is the good of the journey if you're alone?"

"But you're alone at the end of the journey anyway," I argued. I was being very much a teenage girl now and crying, standing there over the cushion bin.

"You are *not* alone at the end of the journey," said my mother, sounding appalled, a "good day to you, sir" creeping into her tone.

"You don't know that," I said.

"I do know that," said Irene. "Faith is knowing that. Faith is giving of yourself. Faith is doing so and expecting no reward."

"Great—so now there's *no* reward!" I yelled. "There's nothing!"

"Faith is its own reward!" Irene yelled back.

We went home empty-handed. And after a couple of days, Irene reflected out loud that Kelli seemed perfectly comfortable on her stool. Perhaps she didn't need a cushion after all.

I was ashamed by how blithely I'd decided to move home and assume my sister's care—how blithe I'd been about it ever since. Just because it had been going well, just because I'd been so lucky these past couple weeks, I'd assumed I was nailing it. What a fool I felt now, remembering the smug way I'd grinned up at the fluorescent kitchen light, where I for some dumb reason imagined my mother's ghost resided, declaring, *Mom! It doesn't have to be one or the other!*

I'd thought that life with Kelli could be balanced, mitigated. That Irene had just been doing it wrong all these years. I'd thought we could hang out like normal sisters, run errands, go for lattes with Jessica Hendy, and every now and then I could just go off and have a little temper tantrum if Kelli got on my nerves—leave her in the car, assume she'd be fine. I'd assumed I could indulge myself if need be, that there could be some kind of fulfillment beyond my sister's care—that I didn't have to give myself over to it completely. But here's what I needed to understand—what Irene understood. Either you were all in with Kelli, or you were not. But if you were, Kelli had to become your joy. Kelli would be where you went for meaning. Kelli was what it was all about. And Irene was right about this too—it *was* like faith. It was exactly like faith in that you had to stop futzing around and let it take you over. No more hemming and hawing. No more trying to have it both ways. And once you put your petty shit aside—your petty ego and your petty needs and your petty ambitions—that was when at last the world would open up. The world that was Kelli. It was a small world, a circumscribed world, but it was your world and you did what you could to make it beautiful. You focused on hygiene, nourishing meals, a pleasing home that always smelled good. That was your achievement and, more important, that was *you*. Once you accepted that, you were—and this was strange to think, but the moment I thought it, I realized I had put my finger on the savagely beating heart of my mother's philosophy—free.

When I was a kid, my mother had a lavishly illustrated encyclopedia of the saints she would sometimes flip through with me, and I remember how she always made a point of skipping over Saint Teresa of Ávila. She didn't want to talk about the illustration that went with it. It was a photograph of the sculpture *The Ecstasy of Saint Teresa,* and it was pretty obvious to me even as a child why my mother disapproved. It was a sexy sculpture. The smirking angel prepares to pierce Teresa's heart with his holy spear, and boy oh boy is Saint Teresa ready. Her eyes are closed, her lips are parted, and somehow everything about her marble body, swathed in marble clothing, looks to be in motion. Saint Teresa is *writhing*.

She's writhing because this is what it is to be a Catholic saint. This is your fulfillment. The giving over. The letting go. The disappearance.

This is what it takes.

16

We sat taking in the weekend sunshine as neighbors came and went, picking through my mother's possessions spread out on the lawn. I was only nominally presiding over the yard sale, because Jessica's twelve-year-old son, Martin, had taken it over within minutes of arriving. Martin had stood by during the first sale of the day, watching me haggle listlessly with a neighbor over a technically "vintage" but unquestionably hideous desk lamp, and when he could stand it no more, he interjected with the ease of a natural-born salesman. Before I knew what was happening, Martin had talked the neighbor up by fifty cents on the grounds of "they don't make lamps like this anymore," and thereafter made himself the Monty Hall of the yard sale, rushing from one potential mark to the next, albeit only after negotiating a "cut" of the day's earnings from me.

So Jessica and Kelli and I sipped beer while Martin ran the shop, and it was the best thing that could've happened that day. I sat at a distance as my mother's old belongings were subtracted from the lawn piece by piece. Padded-shoulder jackets from the eighties; dishes of the variety no one used anymore (saucers, ornate dessert plates, the small utilitarian bowls my mother used to call "fruit nappies"); hardcover books bought or given as presents and never read; the bookshelves they dutifully lived in, neglected, for so many decades; endless end tables; unused linens, as stiff as when they were first purchased, because they were always set aside for some nebulous occasion described only as "good"—and good, somehow, never came around.

When we had hauled all this stuff out the front door that morning,

I couldn't shake the feeling of being a kind of executioner, dragging one item after another, each a physical representation of my mother's existence on earth, out into the sunshine to be sacrificed. I had forced myself not to think about the crass next stage—the bartering, the transactions. Some ruthless, practiced picker nickel-and-diming me across a table of my mother's clothes, my mother's jewelry, my mother's dishes. I wasn't sure I could handle it.

But now, thanks to twelve-year-old Martin Hendy, who I believe discovered his calling that day, I didn't have to. All I had to do was nurse my beer and make inconsequential chitchat with the neighbors as Jessica and Kelli entertained each other.

"Round and round the garden—"

After the tenth or so rounding of the garden, I decided to get another beer. "Okay," I said to Jessica. "So you realize that's basically going to be your job for the rest of the afternoon?"

Jessica smiled at me. "We'll see who gets tired of it first."

I went inside thinking about how content Kelli and Jessica made each other. When she wasn't driving you crazy, Kelli's presence could have a calming effect. It wasn't just her rhythmic whispering and murmuring, although that could be very soothing. It was a quality I could only think to describe as her companionability. She comforted you with her presence. My mother had the power to make people feel *kind*—reassured that the world was a decent place and that they, therefore, must be decent too. But Kelli could make you feel less alone.

When I came out with the beer, Trevor was with them, standing very close to Kelli's chair, as if he had just stood up after leaning over to kiss her on the cheek. Jessica was squinting up at Trevor, shielding her eyes from the sunlight, smiling in the vague, expectant way you do when you meet a friendly person who acts like they belong but you haven't yet learned how.

"Karie-that-weight!" he announced when he spotted me.

It was nice to see him again, even though I had been vaguely hoping I wouldn't after our conversation in the kitchen. Kelli, needless to say, was rocking with happiness and muttering a stream of blissful *Trebies*. She had missed him, I knew then—of course she had. Impulsively, I handed Trevor the beer I had brought out for myself.

"Ah, now it's a yard sale," said Trevor, cracking it.

He told us he'd seen one of the flyers I'd tacked up at Superstore and thought he'd swing by to say hello. He seemed cheerful, if a bit reserved, but he stood chatting with us after I'd introduced him, like any other friendly neighbor. It had been a week since I'd cut back home care, and to my relief there didn't seem to be any hard feelings that I could discern. Trevor, after all, had never been one to disguise his feelings. There were a couple of folding deck chairs nearby, and I offered to unfold one so Trevor could join us, but he declined. He was standing spread-legged with a hand on his hip, and I got the impression that he was enjoying being on display like that, fully unfurled for our benefit. He was, he said, "Having a Saturday on the town with the boyo," and gestured across the lawn to where Mike was lingering at a table of books and porcelain knickknacks, watching with undisguised awe as Martin Hendy worked a customer.

"Oh, that's your son?" said Jessica, and Trevor rolled out his patented "fruit of my loins" line.

"That's *Jessica's* son," I told him, pointing out Martin's blond head. "Working at the table."

"Well, now, that's something we have in common," said Trevor, winking at her. "We should set up a double date."

Jessica's mouth fell open at this abrupt flirtation, and her neat eyebrows flexed upward but she didn't say anything.

"Trevor!" I said, laughing.

"I mean for the boys," said Trevor. He grinned and swigged his beer. "Mike doesn't have too many buds. Your boy play soccer, Miss Jessie?"

"He's crazy about it," said Jessica, turning her gaze back to Martin and keeping it there. By now I had a sense of the persona Jessica typically put forward to strangers—and this was not it. I remembered her competent, inconsequential way of flirting with the waiter, when she and I first reconnected—her dutiful charisma, like Marilyn Monroe stopping to sign an autograph for a fan. And since then I'd kept noticing this effortless, almost reflexive way she had of charming the pants off whoever crossed her transom.

But this was the first time I had ever seen Jessica's vivacity switch to the off position. It wasn't Trevor's flirting that had done it. It was the other thing—*Miss Jessie*. The same thing he'd done to my mother, and to me, that I'd never really given a second thought to. That is, changed our names, from the moment we first met.

Or, more accurately, he simply took our secret names—the name Kelli called me, the name my mother's nursing friends called her—and made them his own. Jessica's secret name was from her childhood, which made it taboo.

For the first time, it occurred to me to wonder if Trevor had also called my mother "Miss," the way he did me, and Jessica just now. *Miss Karie. Miss Jessie.* If he'd also tacked that prissy title onto "Rini," like a fussy little bow.

"Yeah, they're all crazy about the soccer," Trevor was saying. "Running and kicking, and that's about all there is to it. I tell Mike, you want a summertime sport, you play baseball. That's what we do in this country, at least. But no, he wants to do what his friends are doing." Trevor raised a hand to his face and scratched his stubble philosophically. "No helping that, I s'pose."

Jessica glanced at me as if to say, *What am I supposed to do here?*

"Trevor," I said. "You sure you don't want to sit down? Have another beer?"

From her look, I could tell that this was not how Jessica had hoped I'd intervene. But Trevor shook his head and drained his beer.

"Nope, me and Mike gotta be getting along. Weekends are all I get with him. Single father, don't know if I mentioned that."

He winked elaborately at Jessica again, mugging like an actor in a silent movie.

"If I could just use the facilities," he added.

"Sure," I said, trying not to smile. I had never seen Trevor on the make before. I couldn't wait for him to go so that Jessica and I could marvel together at his audacity.

But as Trevor moved past me toward the house, she gave me a look like I'd taken out a pistol and started twirling it around on one finger.

"Get in there," she said.

"What?"

"Don't let him be alone in the house."

"Jessica," I said. "There's nothing in there. It's all spread out on the lawn."

Jessica leaned toward me and hissed: "Get the fuck in there."

I stood for a moment, then went inside.

And what was I supposed to do? Trevor had gone into the downstairs bathroom. There was no reason for me to go downstairs—the place had been cleared out. But going up into the kitchen didn't make sense either, if I was supposed to be monitoring him. Was that what I was supposed to be doing? But I couldn't monitor him while he was in the bathroom anyway.

I stood there in the foyer, halfway between upstairs and downstairs, feeling silly. But I was also a little freaked out, my heart fluttering. It had to do with Jessica's urgency—the way she'd hissed at me. But Jessica, I told myself, was being irrational—maybe because of the scare we'd had in the parking lot the week before with the man who'd screamed at Kelli. Maybe the encounter had left her feeling vulnerable, defensive. Jessica had been, I thought, heroic in the moment, brandishing her phone and taking one slow, wobbling step after another toward the man until he'd been successfully warded off. But afterward she'd been withdrawn. We'd sat in the parking lot a long time, even after the cops had come and gone. The officers, a man and a woman, both of whom looked to me like teenagers playing dress-up, had watched Jessica's video avidly, like children studying a turtle on its back. They had her e-mail them a copy and said they'd be in touch. Afterward, we just sat in the car as Jessica took long breaths and I murmured things I thought would reassure her. That the man was probably drunk, that he was maybe having a particularly bad day, that he had probably wanted to ask Kelli for directions or something and became confused and then incensed by her refusal to meet his eye or roll down the window.

At last Kelli had announced that she needed to pee. And that, rather than all my murmured reassurances, was what seemed to snap Jessica back to her practical self. Someone had to pee. Someone had an immediate, functional issue, a basic problem to be solved. That had been the tonic Jessica needed.

Perhaps Jessica, I thought now, as I waited for Trevor in the foyer, was more readily freaked out by men in general—more than your average woman, I mean, given her past. Which I certainly couldn't blame her for. But the fact was, she didn't know Trevor, and I did. Soon he would emerge from downstairs and find me standing there, at which point I would tell him—what?

Then I remembered his previous visit—the cookie gambit—and dashed upstairs to wrap a couple in a paper towel, just as I had done to fend him off the day he first brought Mike over. The downstairs toilet flushed and I darted back down to the foyer just in time to intercept Trevor before the screen door could wheeze open again.

"Hey," I said, handing him the paper bundle. "For you and Mike. For the road."

"Well, thank you kindly," said Trevor, taking the cookies. He went to stuff them into the pocket of his cargo pants, where they were sure to get crushed, but that pocket was already bulging with something or another, so he stuffed them into his opposite pocket.

He wasn't meeting my eye. He seemed almost embarrassed to be alone with me. It was very different from our moment together in the kitchen, when he'd been so patronizing about how I couldn't trust anyone, how I needed to be careful, showing me his palms, lowering his head to make me look him in the eye, to make sure that I was seeing him, understanding him. But now Trevor seemed, of all things, shy.

I realized that this would likely be the last time I saw him.

"I guess you must've noticed," I said after a moment. "We sort of cut back on home care a couple of weeks ago." For some reason I was shielding myself with the words *we* and *sort of*—as if there were someone else involved in the decision, as if the thing "we" had cut back on hadn't been, specifically, Trevor.

He crossed his arms. They were sunburned, and the gingerish hair of his forearms had turned a platinum blond that made me think of the beach. He smelled like the beach too, or beach food, anyway, the salty, deep-fried smell of the concession stand—maybe he and Mike had stopped for french fries on the way over. "Goin' it alone, eh?"

"Yeah. You know, I'm not working right now. I just realized I can handle things on my own until Kelli and I get settled into our new place. It's less complicated that way."

"Good for you, Miss Karie," said Trevor, nodding with pursed lips. "Like I said, I always knew you had it in you."

As a leave-taking, I felt like this was going pretty well. Trevor seemed—not anxious to go, exactly, but certainly more than ready to. Perversely, it made me want him to linger.

"We had kind of a scare the other day," I confessed.

Trevor's brow puckered. "A scare?"

"Some crazy guy," I told him. "In a parking lot. We'd left Kelli in the car while we were looking at condos—Jessica and I—and some nut started screaming at her and beating on the car."

Trevor frowned with every muscle in his face. "Jesus Christ!"

"I know," I said.

"Police come?"

"Oh yeah. And Jessica got a video of the guy. So, you know, I hope they catch him. I don't know what they'd charge him with, but I hope they give him a talking-to at least."

Trevor stared, grimacing, at the floor.

"Miss Karie," he said a second later. "I was a bit of a dick the other day when I came by with Mike. Pardon my French."

This change of subject blindsided me. "Oh—no you weren't!"

"I was being a big know-it-all, telling you your business. You shoulda just told me to shut up."

"It's fine," I reassured him. "You were just—"

"But listen—please," he said. "If something like that happens again—some asshole gives you trouble—for the love of god, don't be afraid to give me a call."

"I will," I said. "I promise."

Trevor cleared his throat and shifted, looking up from the floor at last. A blush had begun to creep up his neck, pinkening his freckled cheeks.

"Your mother and the Beaner out there—" Trevor began, actually gulping with the difficulty of getting the words out. "Well, I never told you, I guess, how good your mom was to me when I was going through my divorce. And all the custody BS that went with it."

"Really?" This threw me. I thought about how indifferent my mother had been about my own divorce. Imagine if our divorces had been going on concurrently: me, a desolate puddle on my kitchen floor in a city many miles away as my mother offered tea and matronly wisdom to Trevor, musing sympathetically on the ancient, imperishable struggles of men and women trying to live together—wisdom I wasn't sure she could even credibly claim, having been married so young to a man who died so early, and having never married again.

"So what I'm saying is—" continued Trevor, rubbing abruptly at his neck as if it had started to itch. His eyes were darting around the foyer. I could see that talking about my mother—his *feelings* for her—had put Trevor in a kind of masculine panic. He roughened his voice and forced the rest of his words out in a rush. "For a long time my motto's been: Whatever Rini needs. Period, the end. And after she died, I guess I just automatically figured . . . if Rini's daughters need help, I gotta be there for them too. I'm just sorry as all shit if I was pushy about it."

At which point Trevor actually hung his head.

"You've been *great*," I assured him. "Really. We really appreciated all your help."

"Well," he sighed. "You just hold on to that card of mine, all right?"

"I will," I promised. And in the moment I absolutely meant it.

Trevor looked relieved. Not by what I'd promised, but by the simple fact that the conversation was almost over. "Good, good," he muttered, heading for the door.

"Trevor," I called. "Do you want the TV?"

Because I had been standing there feeling like an asshole. Chasing him into the house like that. Not to mention the bloodless way I'd cut him out of our lives, impulsively, at the tail of my call with Margot, after all he had done for me and Kelli. Also the stiffness of his ruddy, blushing face when he spoke about my mother. How his expression tightened, blankening, betraying nothing in a way that betrayed everything. It broke my heart. Trevor the tough guy, the guy's guy, all hockey jerseys and lawn mowers and barbecues, traditional in the most stifling sense of the word, with no one but my mother—in her soothing, soft-voiced sanctuary of pastels and throw pillows, potpourri and china saucers—to whom he could confide his secret pain.

The more he protested, the more I insisted. We didn't need it. Kelli would rather gaze out the window any day, and I watched stuff on my laptop more than I did on my mother's monolithic screen, because I found it depressing to sit in the basement gawking at the thing by myself. It was huge and ungainly and by no means condo-friendly. It was an albatross. Furthermore, it was—I didn't say this, but to me it was—a man thing. It was men who craved giant TVs in basements, because men liked massive screens and high-def resolution and surround-sound speakers—the kind of all-consuming technology that permitted nothing from the real world to creep in and distract them. It made sense that he should have it. I would not take no for an answer. The TV belonged with him.

We came out of the house arguing and stood there for several minutes as Jessica and Kelli watched us curiously. Trevor waved his arm and shook his head, but what he didn't do, I noticed, was walk away.

Finally things progressed to the point where Trevor said yes, okay, he would be willing to accept the television—but only if I would let him pay me something for it. This was reasonable, but for some reason I told him no.

Trevor protested that for god's sake, the TV should be out on the lawn, included in the yard sale—one of the pickers was sure to pay a good price for it. And, yes, I had considered including it in the yard sale but had ultimately decided not to because the TV was so obviously new and top-of-the-line. I figured Kelli and I could watch it until it came time to move, then sell it on Craigslist or something for a decent price. I remember thinking, at the time, how singular the TV was among my mother's possessions. It had to be the newest item in the entire house, and it didn't fit with anything else—the doilies, the flowered upholstery, the eyelet-trimmed towels. It was flat and huge and black and rectangular. An austere extravagance. What had prompted her to go all out on such an item, considering her prognosis? Then again, maybe it was her prognosis that had prompted it. Maybe she'd thought to herself, *Why the hell not?*

Someone was poking me in the hip. I looked down to see Martin Hendy peering up at me through his blond lashes. "This man would like to buy the microwave," he said.

Trevor turned to the man in question before I could, drawing him into our argument in all his frustration. "Maybe you'd like a big-screen TV to go with it, eh? Going cheap!"

Martin was standing with a man who lived across the street. Mr. . . . Something. He had introduced himself to me at my mother's wake, and either his first or his last name was, I recalled, Gill. I remembered that when he and his family had moved into this suburb, my mother had kept referring to them, in her tolerant, broad-minded voice, as "the new Mediterranean family." But when I visited and got a glimpse of these neighbors, I realized she had meant Middle Eastern—she sometimes got the two confused. And *Middle Eastern* was her blanket term for any number of non-white ethnicities.

Before I could say anything, Martin had dashed off to make his next deal and Mr. Gill and Trevor had already clasped hands in quick, wary greeting, as if they knew they'd once been introduced but could not remember when or where.

"Oh, hello," Mr. Gill was saying.

"How's it going," said Trevor, looking around as if this were already a conversation he wanted out of.

"I haven't seen you about," said Mr. Gill.

"Nope," said Trevor. "And I'm just on my way now, so it happens."

"Trevor, no," I said. "You are taking the TV."

He held up his hands again, this time in surrender instead of resistance. "All right, all right," he said. "Jesus. Let me just go back the truck in. *Mike!*" he bawled at Mike, who had been trying on a pair of my mother's clip-on earrings and whipped his head around at the sound of his father's voice.

"Stay put," Trevor hollered, striding down the driveway. "I'm just getting the truck."

Mr. Gill and I watched him go, both of us a little stunned by the noise and abruptness of this departure, and me in particular by how suddenly Trevor had given way about the television.

After a moment, Mr. Gill and I shook hands.

"I was your mother's neighbor," said Mr. Gill. "Arun."

"Yes, hi," I said. "I remember."

"I was very sorry to hear about her passing."

"Thank you," I said.

He was a slight, balding man with long lashes fringing a pair of liquid eyes—expressive to the point of being cartoonish. "She had a difficult time of it."

"She did," I said, nodding rapidly. "It wasn't easy." I wanted to get this part of the conversation over with, because gazing into the warm, commiserating eyes of Arun Gill while sharing memories of my mother as the surrounding neighbors carried pieces of her away was a recipe for precisely the kind of emotional breakdown I'd been congratulating myself for having avoided this entire day. It was time to talk microwave.

Mr. Gill glanced over at the driveway as Trevor backed his truck in. "It must have been a comfort to you, though," he reflected, nodding at the truck.

"Yes," I replied to be agreeable. Then I realized I didn't understand. "Sorry," I said. "What was a comfort?"

"To have your brother here," said Mr. Gill.

17

Downstairs, footsteps and voices now echoed, because there was no more furniture to absorb these noises. Only Kelli's thronelike chair remained, sitting nobly and alone like a banished emperor.

I had yet to figure out what I would do with the upstairs furniture. It was nice, and my mother had kept it pristine, but it was not our style, Kelli's and mine. The idea of stuffing my mother's unfashionable, many-times-reupholstered chairs into a condo—the type of insolently sleek, modern condo I had in mind for us, anyway—depressed me. But it seemed extravagant to buy everything new—especially for a woman who was currently between jobs.

I was sweeping up dust bunnies in the basement, muttering about all this, listening to my own voice and the dry rasp of the broom echoing in the empty corners as Jessica stood nearby, looking around, with her hands on her hips. She was getting ready to go. Martin had received his cut of the yard-sale takings and was counting it obsessively upstairs as Kelli pelted him with repeated questions about what grade he was in and if he liked school and how old he was. I could hear Martin answering dutifully. Kids, I had found, adapted to Kelli's patterns more easily than adults. Martin had intuited that the pleasure of conversation for Kelli wasn't in the details, it was in the repetition. I could hear that he had made it a bit of an absentminded game, started leavening the tedium of the conversation by singsonging his replies, which I had no doubt made Kelli love him all the more.

Grade-six, grade-six, gradey-gradey grade-six, Martin was singing above my head.

Heh-heh-heh-heh-heh-heh-heh, went Kelli. Then: *What grade you in?*

"So I don't know," I was saying to Jessica but mostly to myself, still muttering in a stream-of-consciousness way about the furniture. "I guess it depends on the condo. How big it is, the style. Maybe if I reupholster everything, it won't bother me so much, but, god, if I'm going to pay for that, maybe it *does* make sense to just start fresh with a whole new slew—"

"Okay, so you will get the key back from that guy," interrupted Jessica.

I stopped sweeping and looked up at her. This was a conversation I thought we'd already finished.

"I just want to make sure," she said. "You will get the key back from the kidnapping guy."

Jessica thought I was crazy, and she'd spent the remainder of the afternoon, once Trevor had blustered off with the TV, making that known. I'd let it slip about the key not long after he left, flopping down into the Muskoka chair beside her and chuckling about his abrupt, almost pissed-off departure with perhaps the most expensive item in the house. I'd explained, in response to Jessica's incredulous look, how it had broken my heart to hear Trevor talk about my mother and everything he'd done for her—and her for him. I'd needed to give him something for his trouble. And besides, I'd added, smirking, I'd just found out that the guy was my brother.

Arun Gill had blushed and apologized profusely once I'd corrected him, flapping his Bambi-like eyelashes in confusion. After he hurried off across the street, hoisting the microwave in his arms, I told myself it had been an easy enough mistake for him to have made. After all, this was the kind of thing neighbors did all the time—observe a person's life in a half-assed way from across the street and make the attendant half-assed assumptions. And I supposed Trevor had been around a lot in the last few months of Irene's life and likely very visible, standing out as the lone man among the home care ladies, helping Irene out like any good, devoted son should and would. While I, her actual daughter, had been in another city, doing nothing. If that made me feel weird or uncomfortable, it was really no surprise. It was my guilty conscience twinging.

I'd expected Jessica to smirk along with me at the idea of someone taking Trevor for my sibling, but when I told her what Mr. Gill had assumed, she just seemed befuddled by it. "Ugh, Karen," she said.

"Trevor and my mother clearly had a little deal going on," I explained. "I think he was helping her out around the house, going above and beyond. Mowing her lawn, cleaning out her gutters, that sort of thing. I mean, she gave him a key. Which you're not supposed to do with home care, but I think it's fairly common with the less able-bodied clients."

Jessica looked over at me then, and I was not able to get her off the subject of the key for the rest of the afternoon.

"He's not," I said to Jessica now, as I swept, "the kidnapping guy. You know what he is? He's lonely. He's just a lonely person. Hence the flirting," I added. I threw a wink at Jessica, cocking my head with a quick, actorly flourish, the way Trevor had, as if he'd been mugging for a TV audience.

"That wasn't flirting," said Jessica. "I don't know what that was."

"He's one of those guys who just needs to feel useful to someone," I explained. "He wants to help. He wants to be able to swoop in and save the day, like . . . Superman."

Jessica absorbed this comparison. "Okay, but get the key back," she said.

"We kind of said good-bye," I told her. "I don't think we'll be seeing him again. And we're selling the house anyway."

"Karen," said Jessica, "it might take months to sell the house."

"You know, I think he hated taking the TV," I reflected. "He, like, *hated* it. He was angry about it."

"Because," said Jessica—and I knew what was coming because she'd said it a few times already—"it was nuts of you to give it to him."

"But that's not why," I said. "It's because he doesn't want to feel like he's been paid back. He doesn't want to be recompensed."

"Then why did he take it?" said Jessica.

"*Ew!*" yelped Martin, above our heads. "*Ew, agh! Mom!*"

We'd enjoyed, earlier that afternoon, a summery, childlike lunch of hot dogs, coleslaw, and a potato salad Jessica had brought, and now a large portion of that had been chewed up, semi-digested, and regurgitated onto Kelli's lap, not to mention my mother's spill-something-on-me-I-dare-you carpet. We had almost made it, Kelli and I. We had almost gotten free of this place without defiling my mother's domestic temple, without violating her impeccable standards of cleanliness and caretaking. *Oh well,* I thought. We were selling the place anyway. Soon we would leave it all behind, all these violations, all the infractions and trespasses I'd accumulated over the years. All my big and little incidents of falling short.

"Kelli puked," said Kelli, with a weary air similar to what I was feeling.

Jessica was already in the kitchen, yanking open cupboards in search of a bucket, and Martin had followed her in order to be in a different room. "Thank god," she called, "she didn't have the Kool-Aid!"

"But the ketchup," I said glumly, standing and staring at the defiled carpet.

"It'll be all right," said Jessica, rushing back into the room and throwing an armful of paper towels on top of the not-quite-liquid puddle between Kelli's feet.

Kelli burped. It came from somewhere very deep within her, and her face looked as if someone invisible had just spoken in her ear.

"Bucket," whispered Jessica, just as Kelli leaned over and let 'er rip. She didn't intend to get any on her lap this time.

I created a little sanctuary around the downstairs bathroom toilet for Kelli, laying a quilt across the cold tile and grabbing some pillows from the spare bedroom for her to kneel on as she retched. Jessica suggested lighting a scented candle and placing it on the sink to help dispel the vomit smell and generally give my sister comfort. Jessica said lavender would be ideal. Did I happen to have a lavender candle lying around?

I almost laughed at this. Whose house did she think she was in?

There was an entire unopened package of votives in the cupboard above the fridge that I'd specifically kept out of the yard sale and put aside for whenever Kelli and I were in need of a whiff of mother memory.

The retching was violent and continuous for the first hour, and after Jessica had called her husband to say she would be late and handed Martin her phone to play with, we conferred. Kelli kept heaving long after there was nothing left to bring up, and it pained me to see her shuddering through these futile contractions. She and I had the same shellfish allergy, and it had always manifested in precisely this way—heaving emptily, over and over again, well into the wee hours of the morning—so I knew what she was going through. Her stomach was seizing up, so violently that it required nearly every other muscle in her body to contract along with it, flinging bile upward into her esophagus, forcing everything out. In the morning, she would feel like she'd spent a whole day at the gym, doing abdominal crunches from every possible angle.

"It has to have been the hot dogs," I said to Jessica. "This is exactly like her shellfish reaction."

"But *you* ate the hot dogs," said Jessica.

We yanked the hot dogs out of the freezer anyway and pored over the ingredients, looking up some of the more exotic-sounding ones online to see if they happened to have anything in common with the composition of shellfish, but they didn't. We talked about the coleslaw, store-bought—nothing but cabbage, carrots, and mayonnaise. Jessica's potato salad. Only we'd all eaten that together.

In the bathroom, Kelli gasped and heaved.

"Maybe you should take her to Emergency," said Jessica.

I couldn't explain it, but I was confident I didn't need to. There was something about this puking jag that was so familiar to me—so utterly on the nose—that I felt sure of its cause. It *had* to have been something she'd eaten. I'd experienced this reaction myself, and I'd experienced my sister experiencing it on enough vividly god-awful occasions in the past: the night of the puréed seafood bisque at our cousin Tamara's wedding reception (me), the weekend of the battered scallops at the

Claybourne Society for Developmentally Disabled Children's annual fish fry (Kelli). So there was no question in my mind. I knew what our shared shellfish reaction looked like, and it was this. And just as I knew precisely what kind of misery Kelli was going through now, I was equally certain that after a few hours she'd puke herself out and would, ultimately, be okay.

"I'm going to try and get a Gravol down her," I told Jessica. "Once she's gotten everything out. That usually does the trick."

Jessica looked dubious, stymied by my certainty. She was still holding the package of hot dogs in her hand and kept glancing at it, as if waiting for an explanation to materialize on the plastic wrapping. (*Now with shellfish!*) We stood together in the foyer, listening to Kelli moan and retch. The acoustics of the bathroom made it sound particularly operatic.

"I'll go down and be with her," I assured Jessica. "I'll put a heating pad on her back."

"And keep her hydrated," said Jessica. "If she doesn't stop, if she can't keep anything down, you've got to take her to the ER."

"I will," I promised.

"Will you be okay?" said Jessica. "Do you want us to stay?"

"You've done more than enough already," I told her. Jessica had taken care of the vomit on the carpet herself after I'd rushed Kelli downstairs and set her up in the bathroom. Once I knew she was okay, I came back up to face the music in the living room, only to discover nothing but a damp spot on the carpet and another of my mother's candles burning nearby, filling the room with a smell like sweet summer hay.

"I only wish," I joked to Jessica, "I had a TV I could give you."

She grimaced at that. She didn't think it was funny.

18

Noise," said Kelli.

It was pitch-black outside. Two hours from sunrise, I'd soon find out, and I couldn't believe she was out of bed after the night she'd just had. We'd spent nearly five hours together on the bathroom floor as I'd rubbed my sister's back and talked softly about subjects I knew would comfort her—our mother, our splendidly bearded cousin Leo, Jessica Hendy and her little boy. It was only around hour three that the intervals between spasms of retching eventually began to space themselves out long enough, like pregnancy contractions in reverse, for Kelli to raise her head from the toilet, shoot me a miserable look, and make the inevitable inquiry as to when our mother was coming home. Soon after that, I was able to pop a Gravol into Kelli's mouth and coax it down with a sip of water. It was approaching midnight by the time the bilious desperation in her eyes began finally to fade. She even allowed herself to lean back from the toilet and rest against the wall. The toilet paper roll was directly behind her head, and it made for an impromptu cushion.

Twenty minutes later I had her in her nightgown and in bed, with a big plastic tumbler of water and a bendy straw on her nightstand and a bucket from the laundry room positioned well in reach. But she closed her eyes the moment I pulled the covers up over her, griped sleepily when I insisted she take a final sip of water, and then conked out, exhausted.

Which was why it was so alarming that she was out of bed and standing over me now. I went to pick up my phone to check the time, but it wasn't on the nightstand.

"Did you puke?" I asked, scrambling out from under the covers. "Do you have to puke? Where's your bucket, Kelli?" For a moment, I was convinced that Kelli had climbed out of her own bed just to stumble down the hall and vomit all over mine.

"Broke," said Kelli. "Brok-en."

"What's broken?"

Kelli abruptly sat down on my bed. She was still weak, I realized, from her night of vomiting.

"Kelli, you need to go back to your own bed." She looked ready to sink down onto my pillow and start snoring any moment.

"Bed," Kelli agreed, but looked irritated, as if to say, *What's wrong with this one?* I heaved her up and steered her into the hall. "What broke, Karie, what brok-en?"

"I don't know what's broken. That's what I'm asking you."

"Outside."

"Outside?" I maneuvered Kelli back into bed and went to her window. The street was silent and dark except for the stretch of mellow golden pools cast along the sidewalks by the streetlights. Framed in Kelli's window, the street looked like a stage or a movie set—waiting for a show to start. I imagined Fred Astaire materializing out of the darkness, tuxedo tails flying, tap-dancing his way into one of the golden pools and bowing deeply.

"Nothing out there, Kell," I told her.

"Noise," said Kelli. And, as if she'd evoked them, that was when I heard the sirens.

Vandals, the police determined. Not robbers. Probably just teenagers. Later that morning, an officer came to the door to reassure me on this front. He was visiting everyone on the block to let us know, even though we had all come to our own conclusions the night before. I'd stood in my bathrobe, part of a loose clutch of similarly bathrobed and pajama-bottomed neighbors—blinking and murmuring at each other—many of whom I'd met for the first time at the yard sale that day. Now we were all united in the crisis, we were like a single entity, and information and speculation rippled through us like dual electrical currents. How many houses had been broken into? Had anyone been hurt? Did anyone see the guy? Or was it guys?

They broke into a garage, the cop told me that morning. Threw some stuff around, spray-painted profanities. The home alarm system was triggered, he said, and the little buggers fled. Garden-variety mischief. But I'd already gathered this information in the dark of night. A woman named Marilyn, wearing blue rubber gloves (she'd been giving her hands an overnight beauty treatment, she explained), lived next door to the vandalized house and told me that in fact *she* was the one who had heard all the crashing first—her bedroom being just a few feet away from her neighbor's garage. *So really,* I *was his alarm system!* she bragged, pointing at herself with one rubbery hand. *I phoned Arun, and that's when he activated the house alarm to call the cops!*

"But how do you know," I said to the cop on my doorstep, "they didn't intend to rob the place? And the alarm didn't just scare them off?"

"The garage was *vandalized,*" the cop repeated. "All the effort just went into making a big mess."

"So you think it was targeted?"

The cop tilted his head at this word—and the official mask of benign patience he was wearing briefly slipped. He knew now that I was being coy. He knew that I knew, and I was just waiting to see if he would tell me.

"We do have reason to believe it was targeted, yes."

He had reason to believe it was targeted because the vandals had spray-painted PAKI GO HOME and similar epithets on the walls of the garage. Noel had told me that. Noel was the excitable, high-voiced retiree who lived on the opposite side of the vandalized house from Marilyn. Noel had heard the husband and wife next door babbling fearfully to each other out on their front step and, intuiting in his gut the sound of crisis, he'd jumped out of bed and rushed down to the basement to get his Remington 870. But the shotgun was locked away in its cabinet and he couldn't remember where he had hidden the key—all he could remember was patting himself on the back, the day he hid it, for coming up with such an ingenious spot, one he knew his grandkids would have no chance of ever finding.

By that point, the first police car was already pulling up, so Noel went outside to gawk along with the rest of the neighbors. The garage door had been rolled open, and that's when Noel saw the message that had been scrawled across the wall of Arun Gill's garage. In the o of the word HOME, Noel noted, the vandals had scrawled a happy face.

"Ignorant bastards," Noel remarked at the end of this story, and hawked onto the sidewalk as if for punctuation. He lamented his lost key for the fifth or so time since I'd been talking to him. A couple of shots in the air, he reflected mournfully, would've lit a fire under those bastards' asses—*but good*.

It was only once I went back inside after the police cars had pulled away and the excitement had died down that I found my phone. It was lying on the floor of the foyer, facedown, where I could only suppose it had fallen from my pocket or purse or something. When I picked it up, I saw that its face was cracked.

Kelli stayed in bed all morning, but by dinnertime her appetite was back. It was as I'd predicted: a minor, inexplicable bout, just as her attack of diarrhea had been a few weeks before. Just another mystery in the overall mystery of Kelli.

To keep occupied while we waited for the house to sell, I decided to do as much of the cleaning as I could myself. It was a big house and a big job, and I planned my days around which rooms I would tackle. I went to the store and bought scrub brushes and sponges and high-tech, environmentally unfriendly cleansers like Comet and Scrubbing Bubbles and Mr. Clean Magic Erasers, in defiance of my mother's insisting, throughout my childhood and adolescence, that nothing worked like a little vinegar, lemon juice, and baking soda, thereby making every cleaning job about a hundred times more arduous than it needed to be.

I learned things about Irene as I cleaned, spending entire afternoons with Oceanview FM playing songs from every possible era as I knelt on the kitchen floor as if at prayer, half my body consumed by an emptied-out cupboard. For one thing, I learned that Irene was not the meticulous neat freak I'd always believed her to be. In the backs of those cupboards, I found casserole dishes stuck together with grease and dust, a cast-iron pan that had rusted into a crusty, red shadow of its former self, and ancient, stiffened rags that had been tossed in, for some reason, and forgotten about—almost as if my mother had been involved in this very task, that is, cleaning the cupboards, and decided in the middle of it: *Fuck this.*

Then I shoved aside the fridge and discovered the veritable U.N. of refrigerator magnets I had always imagined dwelled beneath it. There, blackened with grease, was tiny Mozart at his piano. There was the Thailand tuk-tuk, the Eiffel Tower, and more, all swimming in a dried, dust-fuzzed puddle of blackish-brown who-knows-what. After I'd heaved the fridge aside, I just stood there for a while, taking in this vile, decades-old stew of plastic doodads and hardened gunk—grappling with it. *My mother never looked behind the fridge.* Irene Petrie. Not once. Not in a very long time. There had been spills. Clearly, there had been spills over the years. A fumbled bottle of soy sauce. A jar of pickles slipping from wet fingers, pooling brine. And my mother, Irene Petrie, had mopped up what she saw, knowing full well that a good portion of the liquid would have seeped beneath the fridge, for that's what liquid does. It tends to seep.

And what did my mother do?

She left it there.

For decades.

I knelt before it, and scrubbed.

Jessica called when I was cleaning out the fridge. I was sitting cross-legged on the floor, surrounded by condiments, feeling like Gulliver among the Lilliputians or an eccentric child holding court with her toys, if her toys were Worcestershire sauce and French's mustard and a jar of homemade tomato relish and a jumbo bottle of No Name barbecue sauce. These were my assembled friends. This was my community.

"Hey," said Jessica. "Just checking in. How's Kelli?"

Kelli's puking fit seemed like ages ago to me but, I realized, it had only been a couple days. But they were days that had been consumed by cleaning. It felt like I'd spent the past forty-eight hours in a kind of trance, a communion with the house and with my mother's memory. Or maybe something more than her memory. For the most part, the experience had been meditative, although now and then the house-work took an unexpected turn of the sort that made me feel almost under attack. For example, I opened a high cupboard I had forgotten to clean before the yard sale, one that had held, for as long as I could remember, Irene's recipe books. But the cupboard turned out to be crammed haphazardly full of pots. They tumbled out as if they'd been lying in wait the moment I opened the cupboard door. I covered my head with my arms, and now my arms were bruised.

"Kelli's great," I told Jessica. Then I remembered that she didn't know about the vandalism of Arun Gill's garage the night of the yard sale, so I told her about that—and how Kelli had woken me up complaining about noise.

"God," said Jessica. "What a night you had!"

I reached into the fridge, yanked out one of the crisper drawers, and carried it over to the counter to empty it out. I wanted badly to keep cleaning.

"Yeah, it's been pretty eventful lately," I agreed. "Talking to the cops twice in the same week. First the crazy guy in the parking lot, now apparently the KKK's at large in our neighborhood."

"You doing okay?"

"Also there's a ghost," I added, laughing. This was the first time I'd said it out loud—that I had acknowledged the thought to myself at all.

"A ghost?" repeated Jessica.

"Yeah. I'm thinking we have a ghost, moving the furniture around at night, putting stuff in weird places. Your basic poltergeist MO."

I laughed again, to reassure Jessica that I wasn't really serious. "I mean—it's Kelli. She's been getting up at night a lot lately."

"Oh," said Jessica.

"It's just—moving stuff around has never really been her thing. So it's weird."

"Okay, but you know it's not a ghost," said Jessica. Jessica was the kind of person, I had noticed during our reacquaintance, who never quite got a joke. Or that wasn't it exactly. It was more like she never quite accepted jokes or flip remarks for what they were. Whenever I made a flip remark, instead of laughing, she always just peered closely at me. It could be discomfiting. That's what it felt like she was doing now, on the phone. I had given her an out, a "just kidding" about the ghost, so we could laugh. But she wasn't laughing. She was peering.

"I haven't left the house in a couple of days," I told her. "My imagination might be working overtime."

The dishwasher, which had been running this whole time, switched cycles at that moment and emitted a grinding sort of whine. It was an old Sunbeam and had been doing this off and on for the past couple of weeks. I'd been ignoring it, hoping it was one of those minor mechanical issues that would work itself out. I knew I should probably replace it for the incoming homeowners, but I also knew I probably wouldn't, as long as the dishes kept turning out okay.

"Anyway," I said, moving away from the grinding dishwasher. "I've started the cleaning."

"Oh, Karen," said Jessica, accepting the change of subject. "You should hire someone to do that. With everything else you have going on right now."

"No, it's good. I mean, I will if it gets too much. But right now, it's therapeutic."

"You didn't tell me how Kelli was," said Jessica after a moment.

"Yes I did."

"You said she's great."

"She is! She's in her spot by the window, rocking up a happy storm as we speak. Jessica says hi, Kelli!" I called into the living room.

"Jenny Mad-tall," came the reply. "Heh-heh-heh."

"Kelli says hi back," I told her.

"But how'd she do after all the vomiting? Did you ever figure out what caused it?"

"No. It had to have been food poisoning. Kelli was just more sensitive to something or another—something in the coleslaw maybe—than we were."

"I don't get it," said Jessica.

"The mystery that is Kelli!" I said, picking dried vegetable matter out of the corners of the crisper.

"Maybe you should take her to the doctor," said Jessica.

I stopped scrubbing for a moment. "Yeah," I said. "Of course. I mean, she seems fine. But definitely, once things have settled down—"

"You know, house hunting doesn't need to be the priority right now—"

"Oh, it's very much the priority," I told her. "You have no idea how desperate we are to get out of here."

"I do," said Jessica. "I'm just saying, you sound a little frazzled."

I stopped scrubbing altogether. Was I frazzled? I didn't think I felt frazzled, exactly. Busy, maybe. But mostly I felt focused, and motivated.

"Did you get the key back from that guy yet?"

Jessica now knew Trevor's name, but for some reason she never said it. It was always "that guy" or "the kidnapping guy." It was as if she could ward him off that way—keep him at a distance.

"Jessica!" I said. "I haven't even seen him."

"He's going to be back," said Jessica. "Guys like that always come back."

"Guys like what?" I said.

"Guys that can't stand for you not to be thinking about them," said Jessica.

I was applying steel wool to the corner of the crisper and didn't really think about the thing I said next. "You know, you're actually reminding me a bit of him right now."

Jessica was silent for a few seconds. "Don't say that." She sounded distant, like she was holding the phone away from her face. She understood what I meant. She'd heard me complain about Trevor, in particular the benign way he had of bullying Kelli and me, enough to understand. I could hear how the very idea of having something in common with Trevor had cooled Jessica several degrees, made her want to end the conversation. We exchanged a chilly good-bye. I felt bad, briefly, but then I emptied out the second crisper, filled it with sudsy water, and resumed my work.

19

After I finished with the crispers, I decided to go back to sorting through the little village of condiments I had left on the floor in front of the fridge. Some of them were downright ancient, I saw at once, and had to be tossed. The Worcestershire sauce, for example, I was certain had been there since my teen years. The tomato relish was fizzing with biological activity, turning itself into alcohol. But then there were the condiments I wasn't sure of, that felt somehow eternal, like the French's mustard. How did you know if mustard went bad? It was already a sickly yellow.

After a while, I developed a nice rhythm of tossing and keeping condiments, making instantaneous decisions about their fates the moment I weighed them in my hands. *Toss, keep. Toss, keep.* But I stopped when I got to the barbecue sauce.

I knew it was still perfectly good because we'd eaten it with Trevor just the other day. But I couldn't bring myself to put it back in the fridge. There was something wrong with it that I couldn't put my finger on. Its bland yellow label stared back at me. *No Name barbecue sauce.* The bottle was about a third full.

After a moment I reached into the fridge and placed it on the shelf with my mother's other condiments, along with the few I'd bought myself since I'd been here. I looked at them, gathered together, and then I removed the ones I'd bought—the fish sauce for stir-frys and balsamic vinegar for salads—and placed them back on the floor. I wanted to see only my mother's condiments, congregated there on the shelf.

And then it made sense. There was the Grey Poupon and the sauerkraut in red wine sauce and a variety of artisanal jams, jellies, and pickled veg with handwritten labels bought from craft markets or the like. Some of these jars were tiny and still had decorative ribbons tied around them.

And this was the problem: The No Name barbecue sauce loomed over my mother's dainty jars and bottles as if a giant yellow gorilla had lumbered into a village of unassuming pygmies.

NO NAME BARBECUE SAUCE, it bellowed.

Apple-Ginger Preserves, peeped one of the tiny, beribboned jars in a decorative, feminine script. *Madeline's Bread and Butter Pickles.*

NO NAME BARBECUE SAUCE.

Bumbleberry Compote. Sweet Baby Dills.

I picked the sauce up again. As I've said, the massive bottle was about a third full.

And it had been—I remembered this from the day Trevor hauled it out after our drive out to Barnbarroch Manor, after he'd pulled the cover off the barbecue and I'd been surprised to find it so pristine—it had been about half full on that day. Just a week and a half after my mother's death.

We'd only used it twice since then, after all.

I looked at the expiration date—almost a full year from now. So the massive bottle, now only a third full, had not been purchased forever ago, like the Worcestershire sauce and the tomato relish had, left to languish indefinitely in the back of my mother's fridge.

It had been bought fairly recently. By a woman who at the time would have been inching her way toward death's door. Bought, and very promptly eaten up.

Arun Gill stood in his still-defiled garage, just arrived home from work. The mess the vandals had left had been hastily, partially cleaned up—tools and other items they'd flung around had since been shoved into neatish piles, to be replaced on shelves and in cupboards later.

The racist graffiti remained. I could see that there were other scrawls in addition to the PAKI GO HOME that Noel had told me about.

There was a more formal, policy-minded DEPORT ALL MUSLIMS and, on the opposite wall, almost as an afterthought, F.U. ISIS SCUMBAGS.

I'd been waiting for him, sitting at the window alongside Kelli and gazing at his house. From the street, the sight of the two of us framed in the window like that, side by side, staring vacantly, probably made it look as if she and I had finally synced up in some creepy, sisterly way like the twins in *The Shining,* become two halves of the same person. But when I saw Mr. Gill pull into his garage, I told Kelli to stay put and hurried across the street.

It was only once I got there, once Mr. Gill got out of his car and saw me lingering in his driveway, that I noticed I was still holding the jumbo bottle of No Name barbecue sauce. I had, I realized, taken a seat at the window beside Kelli with it in my hands after I'd finished replacing all the other condiments in the fridge.

I gestured with it by way of greeting. "Hi."

He invited me in, but I explained that Kelli was alone in the house and I felt I should stay where I could keep an eye on her in her window and she could keep an eye on me. We both turned and waved at her, and Kelli's rocking become a little more pronounced. Kelli had been not exactly alarmed but certainly curious when I'd told her I was going across the street. Now she was likely getting a kick out of seeing me on the other side of the window, experiencing it as a performance put on for her benefit.

"So," I said, not sure where to begin. "Really sorry about the break-in yesterday."

"You didn't see anything, did you?" asked Mr. Gill. "Did the police talk to you?"

"No. I mean, they did, but I didn't. Kelli heard something. She woke me up. She said she heard something breaking."

"Yes," said Mr. Gill. "It's good to have alert neighbors, I can tell you that. Marilyn"—he inclined his head toward the house next door—"was on the phone to the police before I was!"

"It's a great neighborhood," I said. "Good people."

"Very good," said Mr. Gill. "You and Kelli will be missed. As your mother is missed."

It was kind of him to include me in that list, I thought, even though I had only really met most of the neighbors yesterday. Mr. Gill had an understated courtliness to him—everything he said seemed to extend a certain generosity, seemed to be inquiring what he could do to make you more comfortable.

"Um," I said, glancing down at the barbecue sauce in my hands. Mr. Gill watched me expectantly, probably assuming that any moment I'd explain why I had brought it with me. "Speaking of my mother," I began. "You know that guy, yesterday? Trevor? The care worker? You thought he was my brother?"

"I'm so sorry for that mistake," said Mr. Gill.

"No, no, no," I said. "It's no big deal. It's just, I was wondering. What exactly gave you that impression?"

Mr. Gill began to flutter his Bambi-like eyelashes again, abashed. "It was entirely my misapprehension," he said. "I saw him mowing the lawn from time to time. Working on the house—"

"Working on the house?" I repeated. *Cleaning out the gutters?*

"Yes. And the car—"

"The car?"

"And spending time with your sister, of course. I often saw them out for walks on the weekends."

"On the weekends," I repeated after a pause.

"I suppose your mother relied on him quite a bit," said Mr. Gill.

I looked down at the barbecue sauce again. Mr. Gill did too.

"May I ask—" he began delicately.

"I think that's right," I said. "I think she did. Quite a bit. So you're saying—based on all those things—you just assumed?"

Mr. Gill blushed. He opened his mouth and began to stammer. "My dear Miss Petrie," he began.

"Karen," I said.

"Karen, I don't wish to—I'm not sure . . . Well, it's awkward, rather."

I watched him carefully. It was not, I realized, that he had just assumed.

It was that he had been told.

So let's say you are Irene Petrie and you are dying of cancer. Scratch that—you are not dying of cancer. You will be, but not yet. When you are, it will overtake you all of a sudden, in a very un-cancerlike fashion. More like a heart attack really, or a stroke. Pouncing on you not out of the blue, exactly, because it's always been there—like a moody but up-till-now relatively docile cat. A cat who scratched and nipped every once in a while but mostly slept. A cat who will later, out of nowhere, launch itself at you, spitting poison, spiky-furred and claws extended.

That cancer—a vicious, sudden, angry metastatic cancer of the liver—will lay you out, yes. And the doctor will call your semi-estranged daughter and tell her she must come now. You'll see her briefly, exchange a few words, and that will be that. But before that, you, Irene Petrie, are not dying of cancer. You are *living* with cancer. As you have for the past decade, give or take, since your mastectomy. And you have always done a bang-up job of it, if you do say so yourself.

The fact is, however, that you are now in your seventies and you're not as spry as you used to be. This annoys you, because you are busy. There are doctors' appointments to be kept—for both you and your disabled daughter, Kelli. Every appointment means bundling Kelli into the car, coaxing her into a given office building, performing a series of negotiations to get on the elevator, once going up and once (always the worst of the two trips, now that she's been reminded of her loathing for these contraptions) going down. Between the two of you—an old lady living with cancer, an intellectually disabled woman with chronic ear infections—there are a lot of doctors' appointments.

Then there is the house. It's big, a lot for a lone septuagenarian to take care of by herself—especially a septuagenarian who was brought up with the impeccable domestic standards of Irene Petrie, a trained nurse who came up in an era where nurses, especially those who did their training in Catholic hospitals, were taught to think of themselves not as medical professionals but as priestesses of a sort. Priestesses of the bedpan, of cleanliness and efficiency. Priestesses not because they wielded any sort of authority but because what they were doing was considered a sacred vocation—a calling. They served a higher purpose. ("This is not about *you*," Irene often recalled her glowering supervisor announcing to the fidgeting assembly of white-wearing, vestal virgin–like student nurses their first day on the ward. "Get that out of your heads, ladies. You're not special. You're not saintly. You do not *heal*. You create the *environment* for healing. You have been called to serve. To soothe. To care for the sick. And what does that make you? *What does that make you?*" The students knew the answer because the instructor had told them already, at the beginning of her speech. *"Grateful,"* they murmured in unison.)

You, Irene Petrie, have never not had someone to look after, even long after you retired from nursing, and it has never occurred to you to be anything *but* grateful for that particular burden. Dutifully, therefore, you spend your days creating the environment for healing, even though your daughter, of course, can never be healed of her particular malady. Maybe that's why every so often, in those last few years anyway, you fall down a little on the job. Once, maybe, one day in the middle of cleaning out the bottom cupboard, a cushion from the living room placed as a buffer between the hard linoleum and your old-lady knees, it occurs to you that there is no head nurse, no instructor or supervisor lingering around the corner to assess your work. There hasn't been in multiple decades. Not only is there no head nurse, there is, for that matter, no *one*. No one who exists, anywhere on the planet, who will give a good goddamn whether or not the insides of your bottom cupboards are clean.

And maybe that's when you toss the rags you've been using to scour the cupboard into its semi-scrubbed darkness and shut the door on it. And forget about it for, literally, the rest of your life. Maybe that is the first concession, Irene's first *fuck it*. An acknowledgment. *I'm alone and old and for god's sake, I can't keep this up.*

And when your daughter calls, your daughter who was born with all her faculties intact, she will ask how things are going, and you will speak as if nothing has changed. Because, really, what has? As long as the rags are in the darkness, unseen, there's no reason you should have to think about them. So your daughter will ask all the dutiful-daughter questions she always asks and you will hear, as you often hear, the tapping keys of her computer in the background every time you open your mouth to reply. And you will briskly swat her questions away just as you have a hundred times in the past. It has always been vital for you to demonstrate to your daughter, during these conversations, that what you do every day is not hard, is certainly no *chore*. It is work, yes. But it is a joy to do it. This life has been a gift, and you are *grateful*. This is your side of a very old argument you and she are having. The argument, it seems, is the subtext of every conversation you ever have.

How's your health? Fine. How's Kelli doing? Fine. Do you need anything? No.

Maybe that's how it goes. It gets difficult, but you are not going to tell her that. Maybe you don't even tell it to yourself. The doctors' appointments, the groceries, the house, the garden. The knee gives out. Going up and down the stairs is fraught. The back stiffens. The garden becomes impossible. A jar of pickles slips—the brine seeps beneath the fridge, where no one can see it.

Fuck it.

How are you? Fine.

Kelli gets you up five nights in a row.

How's Kelli? Fine.

The gutters are overflowing. Now the roof is leaking. The ladder's in the garage, but what is creaky-kneed, stiff-backed, old-boned Irene Petrie going to do with a ladder? Meanwhile, the home care worker has just brought Kelli back from her walk.

Normally, you, Irene, are a stickler for the rules. You have the utmost respect for the home care workers—the no-nonsense Margot, for example—because she is of your ilk. Competent and efficient, tirelessly working, being remunerated little to nothing for her efforts. This is *care* as you have always understood it. Selfless. Obedient. Obedience is key, your nursing school instructor always used to say. *Because we don't have time for any nonsense around here, ladies. A hospital is no place for foolish girls who think they know best.*

But as the strapping, friendly home care worker (a *man*—so vital and useful and strong) ushers Kelli into the foyer, you, Irene, remember again that the nursing school instructor is long dead. There hasn't been an instructor, or supervisor or head nurse, looming over you for many years. The rags are in the cupboard, unseen, and you need your gutters cleaned. Or your garden weeded. Or your back deck painted. Who knows what you needed that day, Irene. You could've tried to do what you'd always done: take care of everything yourself. But you would have failed at that eventually, and you knew that day was drawing close. You must've felt it in your water, in your swollen septuagenarian joints—how close you were to falling short.

So you did what came next, what came, almost, naturally. You said fuck it. And you asked the nice man standing in your foyer for his help.

For lack of a daughter, then—a proper daughter, a daughter who called more than once every couple of months, a daughter who visited more than once a year, a daughter willing to shoulder her way past the slammed-shut door of "Fine" every time she asked her mother, "How are things?"—Irene had managed to recruit herself a son.

A son nothing like the daughter. Willing to apply his shoulder to any and every shut door you put before him. Trevor was all about muscling open doors, because Trevor lived to give. Unlike some people. Trevor was doting to the point of being pushy. Trevor got angry if his opinions were not heeded, because he was trying to help, goddamnit. Trevor took the initiative. He put his hand on the mower— *Let me do this*—and took it from you before you could argue. He got up on the ladder to clean the gutters and noticed, perhaps, that some of the shingles had come loose up there. He promised to be back on Saturday to deal with that little issue; then maybe he'd see about the lawn.

—*Oh no, Trevor dear, I couldn't ask you to—*
—*Not another word, Rini, not another word.*

—*Well, at least let me*—(reaching for her purse)

—*Goddamnit, I'm gonna stop you right there, Rini—pardon my French—before you insult us both.*

It was just what Irene needed but had never had. Someone to take over. Someone to insist that she could not do it all, and to ignore her when she insisted that she could. Someone to steamroll that iron will of hers and take things upon himself, someone who didn't ask permission first, who matched Irene's yin of passive, uncomplaining selflessness with a yang of brash, assertive selflessness all his own.

—*I hope you'll stay for dinner, at least, Trevor?*

—*Dinner with my two best girls? Now, that I won't fight you on, Rini.*

—*Shall we barbecue? I bought steaks!*

Meanwhile, thanks to this collaboration, the illusions of a semi-estranged daughter were permitted to remain intact. Irene Petrie remained a superhuman specimen of competent womanhood, cancer and all. Irene could do it all herself; she needed no one. She was *fine*. Until she wasn't.

But up until that moment, it had certainly been a convenient arrangement for all concerned.

Kelli found me in the basement, staring at where the big-screen TV used to be. I'd been sitting in her chair, remembering the easy way Trevor had reclined in it like it was the throne to which he'd been born, sliding his beer into the cup holder without having to look to see where it was. And I was thinking about my mother's giant television, how puzzling its existence was to me, and how the certainty just overtook me on the afternoon of the yard sale that it belonged with Trevor. Because it *did*. Because, in fact, it *was* Trevor's television. Just as, I assumed, the outsized cable package that went with it, that offered all the sports channels, was Trevor's cable package.

Earlier, I'd been upstairs, on the balcony, gazing at the barbecue. I'd pulled off the cover—it was a new cover; why hadn't I seen this before? Not discolored from decades of sitting out all year but a vibrant, shiny blue, still with creases and the smell of plastic on it, freshly bought, maybe only a season old.

And the barbecue itself? How could I have ever thought it was the same as the one that had belched flames into the face of my drunken boyfriend on the occasion of my eighteenth birthday? This one was obviously not almost thirty years old. The chrome still shone. The grill had not even been adequately blackened from the repeated, fiery intermingling of animal fat and caramelizing sugar courtesy of the liberal application of No Name barbecue sauce.

She had bought it for him. All of it. The barbecue. The TV set. The cable package.

In gratitude for all he'd done.

Kelli lingered in the doorway, watching me.

"Karie don't cry," she said after a moment. "Not cryin'."

"Sorry, Kell."

"No," said Kelli, going back upstairs.

That, I thought, was our family in a nutshell.

20

It was late summer and the heat had become tropical, without even a breeze off the Atlantic to offer relief. Kelli and I had to be ready to bolt at the drop of a hat now that the house was on the market, but it was by no means drop-of-a-hat kind of weather; nor had my sister ever been a drop-of-a-hat kind of girl. Kelli's thing was to dawdle. She liked a few hours' advance notice of any potential outing, to sit in her chair and think about the proposed destination, perhaps issue a few inquiries, before she would agree to heave herself to her feet and be helped on with her shoes. It wasn't that Kelli didn't like going out—in fact, the magic words *Tim Hortons* could get her very excited indeed at the prospect—it was simply that Kelli would not be rushed. Especially not in this weather, and definitely not more than once a day. One outing was enough for Kelli—more than enough. But Jessica had people coming over twice, sometimes three times, in a single sultry afternoon.

I did my best to develop a system that would expedite removal of Kelli from the house whenever I got the call from Jessica, a gone-in-sixty-seconds game plan. Gradually I had realized that the best way to deal with Kelli was to work with and not against her idiosyncrasies. I bought her a new pair of comfy outdoor shoes that could double as slippers and made her wear them around the house and—voilà—no interminable process of battling to get her shoes on at the last minute. I kept Kelli's sunscreen in the car so she'd have no excuse to hem and haw and argue with me in the foyer, twisting this way and that as I tried to slather her face with it. But that—the shoe gambit and the sunscreen maneuver—was about all I could do other than paint gorgeous, evocative word-pictures of the delights that awaited her at Tim Hortons or, if we needed to mix it up a little, Starbucks. Still, Kelli kept to her own pace, and more than once we'd just be coming out of the house—usually hollering at each other—as Jessica pulled up with her latest fresh-faced carload of prospective buyers.

It was around this time that I started thinking again about the day-away program that the competent and comely Marlene at Gorsebrook Residential had told me about, wondering if it might not be a good idea to get Kelli started on it sooner rather than later. I'd barely thought about Marlene since I'd made the decision to move home and told Deanna at Seaside, in so many words, that she could take her empty bed and shove it. But now I remembered how central Gorsebrook's day program had been in my plans to manage life with Kelli, not to mention how useful it might be in particular now that I had would-be homeowners tromping into the house at all hours of the day. If I could get Kelli installed at Gorsebrook a few afternoons a week, I thought, I could give her schedule to Jessica and have Jessica book viewings of the house around it.

"Hello, Marlene," I said into the phone. "It's Karen Petrie?"

"Oh, Karen!" said Marlene, and I was thrown off. Because the *Oh, Karen* wasn't the warm bear hug of an *Oh, Karen* I'd come to expect from Marlene. I had been looking forward to speaking with her again, remembering how, when I'd called to confirm that, yes, I wanted to officially put Kelli on the waiting list for a bed at Gorsebrook, Marlene had practically cooed into my ear how *thrilled* they would be to have my sister, how *happy* they were to have us both "as part of our community," and I'd hung up feeling warm and buzzy, comforted, like I'd just been sitting by a fireplace, drinking mulled wine, instead of on the phone with the administrator of a residential care facility. There was no question in my mind that I had made the right decision. Such were Marlene's interpersonal gifts.

But now Marlene sounded distracted.

"How are you?" was all I could think to say. Usually Marlene asked this question first.

"I'm fine, Karen. Thank you. How are you?" The words came out rapidly, like a script or a perfunctory prayer.

"I'm calling," I said, "because I was thinking I'd like to get Kelli started in the day program."

There was a strange hiccup of silence.

"Oh, Karen," said Marlene again.

"Is everything okay?" I asked.

She heard the alarm in my voice and I, in turn, heard her draw a breath. She was doing everything she could, it struck me, to muster a reassuring whiff of the old Marlene with what she said next.

"I'm so sorry, Karen, you have to forgive me, I'm a little distracted today. Listen, of course, of *course* we would love to get Kelli started in the program, absolutely."

"That's great," I said.

"We're having a bit of a crisis here today," Marlene confessed.

"Oh no," I said. "Would you like me to call you back?"

"I would," said Marlene. And then came that strange hiccup of silence again. "We've been talking about how to address . . ." She trailed off, and with that "we," I started to get the feeling that these beats of silence actually indicated brief, whispered conversations with someone else in the room, during which Marlene perhaps covered the receiver with her hand. "You know what, I should just tell you what's going on right now," she said.

A chorus line of imagined catastrophes high-kicked in my head. Gorsebrook was closing—after I had given away our bed at Seaside. They were ending their day program—after I had given home care the heave-ho and organized the entire upcoming year around it. They'd gone bankrupt—their accountant had absconded to the Canary Islands. They were awash in scandal—one of their hulking, hairy-fingered orderlies had been discovered in a resident's room engaging in—

"A resident," she told me, "has gone missing today."

"Oh my god," I said after a moment.

"We discovered the absence this morning, quite promptly. He *was* at breakfast, so it *was* only about an hour before we realized he was gone."

Marlene was hitting those self-justifying *was*es pretty hard. She was using me, this unexpected phone call from a potential but as yet unconfirmed client, to practice her spiel—what she'd say to other families, to her board members, to whomever else she was accountable to. I was the first to hear this little speech, and all the kinks had clearly not yet been worked out.

"The police were notified immediately. We are speaking with everyone who would have had contact with the resident, retracing his steps . . ."

"How—um . . ." I said.

"I beg your pardon, Karen?"

"What is the extent of . . ." I swallowed. I'd lost all sense of the acceptable terminology and had to stop myself from yelling, *How retarded is he?* into the phone. ". . . of his impairment?"

"Do you mean is he—"

"Is he like Kelli, basically, is what I'm asking. Does he—like, for example . . ." I was struggling to get the words out again. Because my heart had started to pound as soon as I'd said *Kelli*. "Can he ask and answer questions?"

"Jeremy," said Marlene, "loves to walk, and he's very friendly. But he—no, if you're asking could he find his way home by himself, if he could ask for directions or tell someone that he's lost, I'm afraid the answer is no."

"How could this happen?" I asked.

"Oh, Karen," said Marlene again. And this was the least reassuring *Oh, Karen* I'd heard from Marlene yet. An *Oh, Karen* near tears.

There was no getting the bed back from Seaside. We would have to go on their waiting list, Deanna told me when I called. And, she stressed, we'd be starting from the bottom. The *very* bottom.

I called other places I had not been nearly as enthusiastic about as I had been about Gorsebrook—even the grisly Fenwick Centre—and they all told me a version of the same thing. Bottom of the waiting list—the *very* bottom. An indefinite wait. And none of them offered Gorsebrook's day program. The only place with a bed immediately available was, no surprise, the opulent Barnbarroch Manor, which I called out of desperation just to confirm that the fees were as entirely out of my range as I'd suspected. They were. And when I asked if there were any kind of government subsidies available, I could hear the administrator I was speaking to swallow what I guessed was a guffaw.

This is what happens, a voice in my head kept saying. *This is what happens at One of Those Terrible Places.* Hadn't Gorsebrook sounded too good to be true from the start? Hadn't that always been in my gut? But I had denied my gut, hadn't I? Because the skilled and Machiavellian Marlene had told me exactly what I'd wanted to hear. That I could tuck my sister away somewhere, out of my keeping, and she would be perfectly happy and safe.

"You're awful-izing," said Jessica, who I'd called soon after getting off the phone with Marlene. "That's my therapist's word. You're letting your imagination run away with you."

"But maybe Marlene doesn't actually know what she's doing," I babbled, continuing to awful-ize. "And all that ... *professionalism* of hers, what if that's her only skill? Putting on a reassuring face? Making people feel like she's got a handle on things? But really it's a facade and she's barely keeping it together? I've known people like that. People who know how to say all the right things, and meanwhile, just beneath the surface, they're completely inept."

"But that's a worst-case scenario," said Jessica. "It's more likely this is just a terrible oversight—"

"Losing a resident—that's a worst-case scenario," I said.

"Just wait and see," said Jessica. "You weren't going to move Kelli into Gorsebrook tomorrow."

"Yeah, but I would've liked to have gotten her started in the day program. And—like, god . . ." Something occurred to me then that started my heart pounding again, like when I'd imagined Kelli in the lost resident's—Jeremy's—place, alone on the sidewalks of downtown, pacing, hands over her ears, whispering frantically to herself. (And what if a man came up to her then? A man who wanted something? Who didn't understand, and got angry? Like the man who kicked and pounded Jessica's car that day? *Fuck this rude bitch!*) "I'm just realizing," I told Jessica—and I could hear that my voice now had a yelping quality to it—"I've bet our future on this place! This whole upcoming move has been organized around Gorsebrook. I've been basing all our decisions on it. Where we're going to live. The neighborhoods where we've been looking at condos . . ."

"We're looking downtown," said Jessica. "It's a good place to be, no matter what. Everything is close."

"I can't put my faith in these people," I muttered. Now I was stuck on the memory of the man in the parking lot screaming at my sister; I kept imagining what would have happened if a locked car door had not separated them. If something like that—worse than that—were to happen to Kelli again just because I'd let myself be lulled into the idea that she'd be fine under the care of strangers, I would literally not be able to live with myself.

"Karen," said Jessica, "just wait and see."

"Wait and see what?"

"What happens to Jeremy. How Gorsebrook handles it. Just give them a chance."

"Okay," I said after a moment. "I'll wait and see." I said it, but I wasn't convinced that I meant it. I said it because Jessica wanted to hear it, and I felt like I was done speaking to Jessica for the time being. She wasn't giving me, somehow, what I had wanted from the phone call. I had wanted reassurance, and I suppose she thought that she was giving it to me, but the more she tried to calm me down about Gorsebrook, the more my gut roiled against her efforts. I thought of the pots tumbling out of the cupboard onto my head, the coats yanked off their hangers in an act of what felt like frustration. Someone was becoming increasingly fed up with me, and I couldn't blame that someone. The message was: *Stop kidding yourself and do what you know is right.*

Jessica was talking about real estate now—she'd sensed that I wanted to bring the call to a close and had switched over to business.

"I'll be bringing around some people tomorrow afternoon, about three," she was saying. "Will that work for you guys?"

I looked around. The house was clean—impeccably so, worthy of Irene Petrie in her prime.

"Yes," I said. "Is there anything I should do before they come? Maybe some fresh flowers."

"That'd be nice," said Jessica. "And you could bake some cookies if you have time. Smell is really evocative for buyers, and cookies smell like home."

"Okay," I said quickly, hoping to segue into a seamless good-bye.

But I knew what was coming. Jessica had to get her question in— the question she'd asked me practically every day since the yard sale. Whenever we spoke on the phone, she used it almost as a means of signing off, the way someone else might say, " 'Kay, love you."

"Get the key back from that guy yet?"

"Um," I said. "I'm going to. I will."

This threw Jessica off. She'd been poised to scold me briefly, as she always did, in response to my routine of scoffing, assuring her that the key was no big deal and that Kelli and I would be out of the house soon enough that it wouldn't ultimately matter either way.

"Really?" said Jessica after a moment.

"Yeah," I said. Then: "I called him, actually."

"You *did*?"

"I did," I said. "I'm seeing him later today."

Jessica puffed a breath of astonishment into the receiver. "Good for you, Karen. Wow. You're taking action!"

"Yes," I agreed. "I'm taking action."

It was a white lie. The truth was, I'd been intending to call earlier but had gotten distracted in all my Marlene panic. Jessica's inquiry about the key, however, reminded me of my game plan concerning Trevor. It was time to get it under way.

I'd let a few days go by since the Revelation of the Barbecue Sauce, as I'd come to think of it. And I had considered letting the days flicker past indefinitely, one by one, until Kelli and I were out of this house, on to different things, and Trevor was well and truly out of our lives. But I knew I wouldn't do that. I'd already given away so much of Irene. The yard sale had picked the house almost clean of her— subtracting the lamps, the jewelry, the heavy stacks of hardbound-only books (because Irene always thought paperbacks looked "junky" on her shelves). We still had the house itself, Kelli and I, but soon that would be gone too. And it wasn't that I wasn't willing to give all this up—clearly I knew it needed to be done, and was doing it—it was just that Kelli and I had *had* these things already, these pieces of Irene. We'd soaked them up. We could rest assured that we hadn't over-looked, or missed out on, any of them. But what we'd never had—or *I* hadn't, at least—was a proper introduction to our mother's son.

"Karie-me-back-to-old-Virginny!" he exclaimed when he picked up his phone.

I'd had a little script in my head that I was poised to begin reciting after we'd exchanged hellos, but his greeting threw me off so much I burst out laughing.

"That's a—that's a deep cut!" I told him.

"Yeah, I'm pretty proud of that one," said Trevor.

After that, the conversation was easy. We caught up like old friends. Could it be, I asked myself at one point, that I actually missed Trevor? This point came when I was telling him about the catastrophe at Gorsebrook. His reaction was completely opposed to the one I'd gotten from Jessica—and I realized that Trevor's brand of reassurance was the kind I'd been craving all along.

"What kinda fuckwit operation are they running over there?" yelled Trevor. "Pardon my French!"

"Right?" I knew, intellectually, that Jessica's advice to reserve judgment about Gorsebrook was level-headed and logical. But at this particular moment, it felt good to finally have my panic validated, to hear someone be appalled on my and Kelli's behalf. I needed to be reassured that what had happened at Gorsebrook was outrageous and that I had every right to feel as freaked out as I did.

"Jesus Christ—these people gotta get their shit together!" Trevor bellowed.

"Well, I'm really hoping this isn't the norm."

"If it is, better to find out now than a couple of months after you got the Beaner settled in there."

"Yeah," I agreed.

"I can talk to—" Trevor began, but then he stopped himself. "You need any help looking around for other options, you just let me know, Miss Karie."

"So, Trevor," I said. "Kelli and I were thinking we might fire up the barbecue tonight."

Trevor insisted that he could pick up the steaks, but I told him no—the steaks were bought. In that case, he said, he'd do the grilling, and again I told him no. He would do nothing. He would be, I said, a hundred percent our guest for a change. I could sense Trevor mentally fidgeting on the other end of the line, tormented at the idea of simply sitting back and being waited on, and I was ready for a fight. But after a moment of silent struggle, Trevor told me, simply, thank you, that dinner sounded great and he would be there "with rings on my fingers and bells on my toes."

"I look forward to *that*," I said.

"Oh, I got all kindsa tricks up my sleeve," said Trevor.

21

He arrived with a twelve-pack of beer and—this was new—a forty of Captain Morgan rum paired with a large bottle of diet cola. The combination reminded me of drinking in high school, buying pop at some fast food place, then two or three of us ducking into the women's bathroom to pour half of it down the sink to be replaced with whatever happened to be in the pint one of us had hidden in her parka. I was pretty sure I hadn't touched rum—or at least not rum and Coke—since puking myself inside out behind the vice principal's car outside a grade ten formal dance. I planned to not go near Trevor's Captain Morgan. I shoved it into a corner of the counter where it wouldn't get in the way of my food prep.

Not that there was a lot of prep to be done. Trevor liked things basic, and I'd decided to make what I knew he'd like: steaks done medium, baked potatoes slashed down the middle with cheddar shredded and left to melt inside the gash. I'd even bought some sour cream and chives because I had a feeling that Trevor would find those touches fancy—not in a pretentious, highfalutin way, which was always a no-no, but more of a genuine gesture of having gone the extra mile to make the meal special. I steamed some broccoli for about three minutes longer than I normally would have, remembering Trevor's feelings about raw vegetables.

At last we all sat down to eat. I don't suppose I need to tell you that Kelli was over the moon. Since Trevor had been forbidden from helping with the meal, he'd taken one of his beers into the living room to sit with her while I cooked, teasing her and telling her stories. Over the sound of my chopping, I'd hear a steady stream of *heh-heh-heh-*

*heh-heh*s coming from the next room. Now, as Trevor held her chair out and bowed deeply, playing the obsequious waiter, Kelli took a seat, smiling and whispering to herself with pleasure, almost voluptuously. She had her friend back.

I couldn't tell if Trevor was waiting, wondering what this was, or if he was simply happy to be back, enjoying, as he said, "a night in with my two best girls." He seemed as Trevor as ever—blustery, full of jokes and bullshit—but with slightly less of an edge. Ever since we'd spoken on the phone, I could tell he was making an effort to rein in his dictatorial tendencies. When he'd arrived at the house, he'd looked around, frowning at its freshly staged, newly blank interior, scrubbed of any trace of Irene Petrie, but said nothing. He'd shaken his head soberly when I told him about the vandalism of Mr. Gill's garage, tut-tutting about how unsafe the neighborhood had become, how lax the police were when it came to "juvenile delinquency," suggesting that Kelli and I might think about having an alarm system installed—he'd be happy to do the work for free. Then, over dinner, when we spoke again about Gorsebrook and Trevor began to get fired up (*Buncha g.d. incompetents!*), I could sense he was struggling with a desire to jump to his feet and deliver a lecture on how, precisely, Kelli and I should handle this abrupt, dismaying glitch in our once-seamless plan for the future. But instead of telling us what to do, he took a breath—the most deliberate, self-conscious breath I'd ever seen him take. Then he picked up his napkin and belched into it thoughtfully.

"You'll do," he recited, like a mantra, like he'd been practicing it in a mirror, "whatever you think is best, Miss Karie."

The meal was over, and we looked around the table at its wreckage. Stripped bones, potato-skin carcasses, crumpled foil, red-stained napkins.

"Trevor," I began.

Trevor lurched out of his chair, and that's when I knew he *had* been waiting. He went straight to the cupboard, grabbed two tiny glasses—the juice glasses my mother had used to serve herself a shot of health-giving V8 juice every morning—and then turned and retrieved the bottle of Captain Morgan from the corner of the countertop. He sat down at the table again, placed one of the juice glasses in front of me, one near him, then twisted the cap on the rum. It broke open with a loud crack.

Trevor was as nervous as I was.

"Are we celebrating?" I said.

"I don't know, Miss Karie," said Trevor. "But whatever we're doing, thought this might help smooth things along."

He poured us both a shot. The sweet holiday fumes wafted up at me.

"This isn't going to work for me," I said. I stood up and got the cola out of the fridge, along with some ice.

"I'm sorry," said Trevor, flushing. "This is a problem I have, so I've been told. I *presume*."

I plunked an ice cube into my juice glass of rum and tipped some cola on top of it; the cube exploded somewhere within its depths, jumping in the glass like a piece of popcorn, and Trevor and I jumped slightly too. Then I offered the cola to Trevor.

"Yeah," said Trevor, reaching for it. "Let's be civilized, hey?" He splashed an obligatory amount into his glass, just enough to turn the amber liquid brown.

"Kelli pop," said Kelli with a note of impatience.

"Sorry, Kell," I said. "Feeling left out?" But Trevor was already on his feet, getting down a glass for her.

And then he started talking before I could.

It had not begun like I thought it had. It had not begun with my mother gazing helplessly up at a gutter overflowing with autumn leaves that had been left to rot over the winter and congeal in the drainpipes like cholesterol clotting an artery. It hadn't begun with a blown fuse needing to be replaced or a loose step crying out to be nailed down before a heedless Kelli, lumbering her way toward the car in anticipation of whatever treat she'd been promised to get her moving, could be tripped and sent sprawling, ass over teakettle. There hadn't even been so much as an especially stubborn jar lid that required twisting into submission by a muscular pair of hands. Irene hadn't needed Trevor, not at first. Trevor had needed Irene.

Oh, the good-son shtick came later, no question. There was the lawn mowing, the yard work Mr. Gill had witnessed. The extracurricular weekend walks with Kelli. And then, finally, the big ask: a late-night trip to the ER when my mother lost her voice and was convinced that the cancer had abruptly colonized her throat. (It turned out that her preparation for her church choir's Christmas concert—which, of course, she was solely responsible for organizing—had merely been too exacting, i.e., performed to Irene's usual standards, i.e., she had been belting out high-pitched *O come let us adore him*s every other night, multiple times a night, for weeks on end and blown her vocal cords to shit.) But this incident—the rush to the ER—had been the first time Irene called on Trevor to go above and beyond for her. Because she was scared and she had no one else to call. "Took her long enough," smirked Trevor. He'd been offering himself up to her for months, he said—for grocery runs, Kelli-sitting, whatever Rini needed—but Irene always insisted she was "fine." Which rang familiar. She resisted him, Trevor implied, as long as she could before finally picking up the phone and croaking out a request for help.

It killed her to have to do it, he told me. She kept rasping out apologies for bothering him, until he practically had to clamp a hand over her mouth to make her stop talking before her voice choked off completely. At first, Trevor told me, shaking his head as if reliving the exasperation he'd felt, Irene had wanted him to simply stay at the house with Kelli while she drove to the hospital *herself*. Trevor had vociferously nixed that idea, and convinced her they should all go together. Yes, they all might be waiting in the ER for hours on end and, no, Kelli wouldn't love the experience, but at least Trevor would be there to keep her entertained and distracted while they waited for Irene to get checked out. And so it was this night, Trevor told me, their night together huddled in the ER waiting area, Kelli between them, with screaming people occasionally rolling by on stretchers, and moaning people abruptly interrupting themselves with a hiccup and then vomiting onto the floor from their pain, that brought Trevor and Irene's relationship to the next level. This was when—he didn't say, but didn't have to—the three became as family.

"But even before that, Miss Karie," Trevor assured me, "I was *all* about your mum. I woulda done anything for that woman—I was just grateful she finally gave me a chance to prove it."

Because, a few months before the late-night trip to the ER, Irene came upon Trevor parked in the driveway of her house, his big shoulders trembling beneath his golf shirt as he sat weeping behind the wheel of his truck. His wife had moved out earlier that day and taken Mike. You can be sure Trevor was not thrilled to be describing this incident to me. He was on his third juice glass of rum, taking it in regular, compulsive hits, like a smoker with a cigarette. After the first glass, he'd accepted my offer of an ice cube, but he wasn't bothering anymore to dilute the rum with cola. The cola had been brought along, I now understood, merely as a nod to decorum—although I certainly was making good use of it. I'd noticed that every time my drink began to dwindle, Trevor would reach over and top me off with the Captain Morgan before I could raise a hand in protest. So, to counter this, I'd started preemptively topping myself off with the cola in order to keep my glass full. But I couldn't let my concentration wander from this task; otherwise Trevor would swoop in again with the Captain Morgan. So after a while I was practically replacing every sip I took with cola. It got so the whole process came to feel like a slight, unspoken argument we were having in the background of our actual conversation. Conversationally, we were being open with each other—openhanded and openhearted, rolling a ball gently back and forth between us. But in the background, in this small way, we were doing battle.

Anyway—yes—Trevor had been weeping. That was even the word he used, and uttering it made his freckled face and neck flush pink. Irene had been waiting to greet him in the foyer, because she had seen the truck pull in, but when he didn't come inside, she went outside to find him. He'd spent the previous week in what he called "talks" with his wife. The talks had started Saturday night after Trevor had gone out of his way to set up a "date night" because he felt like things had not been so romantic with them lately. But when the hour approached and he started prodding her to get ready to go, Leanne said she didn't want to. She was tired, she'd been working extra shifts, and she said that going out with Trevor to try to be romantic just felt like more shift work piled on top of everything else she had to do. He apologized sarcastically for how she found him "a chore." She said she didn't find him a chore, but lately she found being *married* a chore. Trevor said he was *trying* to make marriage fun, goddamnit, that's what this entire fucking date night was about, and if she would come out on the goddamn fucking date she would see just how much fun they could have. Leanne said why didn't Trevor go out and have fun by himself, and she would stay home and rest because that was all she wanted, really, was some rest. Trevor barked, *Good then!* And went out, as Leanne had suggested, but he did not have fun.

He sat in a bar and stared, unblinking, at a curling game (which, he interrupted himself agitatedly to insist, was not even a *real* sport, because real sports did not use *brooms*) on the bar's big-screen TV. He knew that something new had happened. Leanne had often been tired, she had often not wanted to do things with him, including having sex, but she had never come out and said a thing like their marriage was a chore. It sounded like a small thing, a nasty little throwaway line of the sort that so-called romantic partners have flicked, booger-like, at each other since the dawn of time. But this was not the sort of thing Trevor and Leanne ever said to each other. It represented a new frontier in their relationship—a definitive shift. Trevor sat there on his stool, one hand braced against the bar, face rigid, everything rigid, afraid to move a muscle. Because he knew that the floor was dropping out from underneath him. He knew that the future—the life he had and was supposed to have with Mike and Leanne—was in the process of going away. Becoming something else. He tried to tell himself that it was nothing—a minor argument. The husband hits the bar to blow off steam, the wife broods in front of the TV, and later they come together in bed, whisper apologies, however grudging, and life goes on. But life wasn't going to go on. Something had been set into motion, like when a few stray pebbles come sprinkling down from a mountaintop before the entire south face slides into the valley below. And maybe if Trevor just sat very still, alone at the bar, he could keep the trembling precipice from giving way.

A few days later, the side of the mountain had come down and he and Leanne were separating, although he still couldn't claim to understand why. No one had cheated. No one had maxed out the credit cards and tried to hide it. No one had any objections to the way anyone else had been parenting Mike. As far as Trevor could determine, Leanne was walking out because their marriage made her—for reasons she couldn't even properly articulate, no matter how late they stayed up talking and ranting and pacing and sitting with their heads in their hands—*sad*.

Trevor took a big slurp from his glass and blinked up at the ceiling a few times. His freckles seemed to glow under the fluorescent light. He looked worn out, like a tired little boy.

"My biggest regret," he said after a moment. "I never introduced your mom to Mike."

"You never brought him over?"

"I can't explain it," said Trevor. "For the longest time, I didn't want to. I didn't want—you know. The two worlds to collide. Mike was part of everything that was going on with Leanne. Not that any of it was his fault. But your mom. And this house . . ."

"I get it," I said. To teenage me, the house had been a steel trap. But to Trevor, like Jessica before him, it was a sanctuary. Fresh bread and lavender. Tea and sympathy. Kelli and Irene.

"Your mom told me," said Trevor, looking down at the table, "you had a pretty bad breakup yourself."

It was as if he had reached out and pressed a button on my body—or a bruise. It made me wince but it didn't exactly make me feel defensive.

"She said she wished you were around for me to talk to," he continued. "Guess she figured we could compare notes."

I opened my mouth and closed it again, because I was worried I'd

say something that sounded disparaging of Irene in that moment—
for example, *She knew? She cared?* We only spoke a handful of times
during my breakup period, and I couldn't remember much about
it except for a flurry of exchanged *fine*s. I also remember feeling
shamed, braced for an *I told you so,* even though *I told you so*s had
never really been my mother's style. Still, I felt like I could hear it in
her every inconsequential word about Kelli's latest doctor's appointment or what St. Joseph's had in store for their annual Easter pageant
that year.

But maybe I had been hearing something else. As much as
I tried to keep it to myself during those phone calls, how desolate
and unmoored I felt, perhaps Irene had understood. What I remember most is a fuzzy, panicked feeling of not knowing where I stood
anymore. A dream I had stands out in my mind—and dreams and
days were hard to differentiate back then, but this had to be a dream,
because I walked into a room of our house that he had used for an
office and found it flooded with summer daylight. The roof had blown
off. I figured it must have happened in a storm—a storm I must have
slept through, because I'd never noticed it raging. On the one hand,
I considered, this couldn't be a good thing, the roof blowing off the
house. I didn't know how to deal with it, logistically—whom to call,
where to begin. On the other hand, it was a beautiful day. Birds and
treetops overhead.

It had to do, I think now, with freedom's sudden anarchy—the
way freedom can descend upon your life, out of nowhere, a tornado
touching down. Abrupt, unasked for, but freedom nonetheless and
therefore accompanied by, even in the holy mess it leaves behind, a
germ of exhilaration.

It was so unexpected, maybe, because I'd always thought of getting
married as the thing that gave me freedom, not the thing from which
I would one day be emancipated. A husband was a get-out-of-jail-
free card, I thought on some level, a fail-safe, because how could I be
dragged into the mire of Kelli servitude alongside my mother if I had
a husband? ("To look after" seems like it should be the final clause of

that sentence but, of course, the idea was not to have to look after any-one. It was more about attaching myself to a legally binding anchor of sorts. Securely lodged. Immovable.)

And maybe Irene knew all this. In fact, it occurred to me as I sat blinking across from Trevor: of course she did. She knew I'd lost my get-out-of-jail-free card. And likely she'd known from the beginning what idiocy it was to think of a marriage—of all things—as such. My stomach clenched miserably with fresh bereavement. It felt as if Irene had died all over again, right there in the kitchen, in my arms. My mother had known what I was going through, I realized, the entire time. Because my mother was no fool. She felt it. She got it. And I could have come home. I could have spoken with her. I could have asked for her comfort, and she would have given it to me. She would have. But now she was not here. Only Trevor was here now—her ruddy, big-shouldered avatar. Her chosen son.

22

The dishes still were not cleared, and Kelli had long ago left the table to sit at her perch by the window. But it was late now, going on ten. I knew this because I could hear Kelli making the soft, inquisitive noises she always made when it was time for her before-bed snack of toast and peanut butter (a bit of chuckling and *Kelli toas'*, whispered intermittently). It felt to me like a good time to take a breather, as talking with Trevor about our mutual end-of-marriage crucibles had left me feeling raw, like I was being peeled open one strip of flesh at a time.

After Kelli was in bed, we carried our juice glasses into the living room and flopped down into seats opposite each other. It felt like we both should be exhausted by this point in the conversation, but there was something about having laid ourselves so emotionally bare that was sort of exciting. More than exciting, actually—thrilling. Thrilling because it was so dangerous, I think now.

So finally I understood why Trevor had been so weird and why Trevor had been so pushy and why Trevor had so much trouble negotiating boundaries when it came to Kelli and me. I had been a stranger. A stranger Trevor had nonetheless loved, because he loved Irene. But at the same time, a stranger who'd arrived at Irene's deathbed and swiftly taken over the house and the care of Kelli once Irene was in the ground. It had been disorienting for Trevor. After over a year of cozy nights in front of Irene's big-screen TV, of family barbecues on Irene's back deck and afternoons of yard work and plates of cookies and intimacies exchanged over multiple mugs of tea, Trevor was yanked back into the role of Professional Caregiver, for whom an overly familiar relationship with his clients would be a Fireable Offense. It made his head spin. Trevor now had to back off from the family that had become his family and pretend like the previous year had never happened. And who knew what the daughter from the city would turn out to be like? The moment she caught a whiff of his relationship with Rini, she could report him, and he would lose his job. And never see Kelli again.

Trevor had been so weird because Trevor had been pretending he wasn't grieving.

It was midnight before I could ask the question. I was curled up in the love seat near Kelli's perch, which allowed me to gaze occasionally out the window at the golden pools the streetlights cast along the sidewalk. The street was very quiet, as it had been—or at least as it had appeared to me to be—the night Mr. Gill's garage was vandalized. From where I sat I had a perfect view of his house. He'd installed a large, bright spotlight above his garage—an eye-watering LED that glared, unblinking, throughout the night.

We held our drinks in our laps and I was relieved to be able to nurse mine now. Trevor was too far away, seated in my mother's rocking chair on the opposite side of the coffee table, to swoop in and top me off. He'd brought the rum and cola along and, efficiently, had even filled a cereal bowl with ice cubes so we wouldn't have to get up and go to the kitchen when it came time to freshen our drinks.

I'd been sipping, but now I took a gulp and felt the fizz and liquor burn a slow trail down my throat and sit glowing in the pit of my stomach.

"Did my mother," I said, "ever talk to you about me?"

Trevor leaned back, and the springs of the old cushioned rocking chair he was sitting in thrummed. He sipped his drink and for a few seconds seemed to be looking around for a cup holder in the armrest. When he couldn't find it, he cradled the drink in front of his crotch.

"Well, Miss Karie—"

"Could you start calling me Karen?"

Trevor's face went blank. "I don't know if I *could,*" he said, startled.

"It's my *name,*" I said. "To be honest, the 'Miss' thing drives me a little . . . I don't like it."

"It's just—" said Trevor. "I always feel a bit strange calling ladies by their first name. Feels a little . . . informal."

This made me smile. Trevor, whose problem was that he presumed too much, gave the women in his life these twee little nicknames because he didn't want to be presumptuous.

"You can be informal with me," I said. "I just found out you're basically my secret brother—you can call me by my name."

"Karen," said Trevor, frowning. I knew what he was thinking, and he was right. It didn't work.

"Or," I said, "why don't you just keep calling me Karie. Like Kelli does."

Trevor nodded. He still looked uneasy, but *Karie* was clearly better. "Good, good," he said, then tried it out: "Karie."

And then he said it a different way. "Karie," he began. I looked up from my drink. He was leaning forward in the chair now, holding his juice glass between his knees, face somber, about to tell me what I'd asked to know.

At first, Irene's daughter Karen was something of a stock character in Trevor's mind. Not a villain, exactly, but definitely a variety of jerk. Rini would mention her from time to time, and Trevor, unconsciously, built himself a picture based on his own assumptions intermingled with the vague details Irene sometimes passed along. For example, the daughter lived in Toronto, so that was pretty much a strike against her right there. Toronto, as every east coast Canadian is raised to understand, is where the nation's arseholes congregate. It is a place for people who care only about work—but not even real work. Not construction or the fisheries but some vague, glad-handy business that takes place in office towers and requires the wearing of suits and a lot of insincere smiling and shaking of hands. Such people live in towers identical to the towers in which they work. They spend what little free time they have shuttling themselves from one tower to the next, existing at the gloomy heart of a cluster of such towers, where the rays of the sun can never reach them. They don't have fields or backyards, because fields and backyards are places for picnics and barbecues, friends and families. And these people may have friends—insincerely grinning, glad-handy friends exactly like themselves—but they don't have families. And they don't have families, one supposes, because they don't have souls.

Not that Irene described her city-dwelling daughter in such terms, but Trevor, as we know, had a habit of presumption. From Irene he gleaned merely: A City Person. Work That Kept Her Busy. No Kids and Over Forty. And so a picture developed in Trevor's mind.

And speaking of pictures, Trevor got to see a few. This was once things got cozy between him and Irene, once he found himself coming over fairly regularly for dinner, spending an hour or two in Kelli's recliner-throne downstairs afterward to catch the occasional hockey game. (And some nights, I learned, if he'd had more than a couple of beers, Irene would even insist that he stay the night in the spare room downstairs.) One such evening, Irene was keeping him company, working on her photo albums as Trevor watched the game. When "Coach's Corner" came on, he muted it and wandered over to the couch where Irene was sitting to peer at the snapshots she'd been chuckling over. He remembered two in particular.

There was the snapshot from Kelli's twentieth birthday party—me with my arms wrapped tightly around Kelli as she laughed but, being Kelli, simultaneously pulled away. I was wearing two party hats, one on either side of my head, like colorful conical horns. "You looked like fun," said Trevor. "You didn't look like the person I'd been imagining." I had been drunk, I remembered. I'd been taking nips of something in my room in anticipation of the dance I was planning to meet my friends at once I'd finished having cake with Kelli and Irene.

The other photo Trevor remembered was one from Halloween, ten years earlier, the two of us scowling in the kitchen, side by side, about to tear each other's heads off. I had insisted, despite my mother's warnings, that Kelli and I go trick-or-treating as Siamese twins—and this, of course, had been a disaster. Five minutes after Irene had wrestled us into our shared costume and snapped the photo, we were screaming at each other and Kelli was dragging me across the room—she in one leg of our oversized pair of twin pants, me helpless in the other—so she could sit at the window and rock her aggravation away. I ended up going out trick-or-treating myself, wearing the giant costume, one empty pant leg flying in my wake, explaining to people that I was a Siamese twin whose sibling had just been surgically cut away—and that I was "so much happier now."

"You were cute kids," offered Trevor. "The two of you standing there, all pissed off." He was being kind, softening me up for what was to come.

"But you must've thought," I blurted, "I was such a bad daughter to Irene."

Trevor leaned back and considered his words. "I just wondered where you were. Your mother—"

I jerked forward. "My mother never told me *anything*." I knew I sounded like I was pleading. "I checked in with her every month . . . or so. She never told me what was going on. I asked. But, I mean, she was so shut down. I didn't push. I should've. We were both shut down. We had this fight when I was twenty and we never really—"

"She told me about the fight," said Trevor.

I leaned back. "She did?"

"And I said to her, Rini, for Jesus's sake, pardon my French. The girl was twenty years old when you had that spat. Do you know how much stupid shit I was going around spouting when I was twenty?"

"And you said that because," I said slowly, "she still hadn't forgiven me for what I said back then."

Trevor leaned over to place his drink on the coffee table.

"Miss—sorry. Karie. *Karie.* You two—okay, I'm gonna tell you what I said to her. You just forgot how to talk to each other after that. You hurt each other's feelings so bad you spent the rest of your lives trying not to do it again. So you both ended up just not saying any-thing for the next twenty years."

"Twenty years," I repeated, "is such a long—such a *stupidly* long fucking time."

Neither of us had to add: *especially when one of you has cancer.*

I slurped my drink and realized, as I did, that at some point I'd switched from carefully measuring out my sips to make sure I stayed in control to taking a gulp whenever I felt like I needed a dose of strength, of courage. And that, I fuzzily concluded, had been a flawed policy, the upside-down logic of someone becoming drunk, because, the more I drank, the more limp and tremulous I felt—not strong. Not courageous. My strength was draining away, not shoring itself up, with every sip I took.

Trevor stood up, the decades-old springs of Irene's cushioned rocking chair thrumming as he shifted forward. I didn't look up, as I was busy sort of gasping softly to myself in an attempt not to cry. At that moment, I probably looked a little like Kelli whenever she put her head down, mouth moving, whispering whatever it was she always whispered to soothe herself. The next thing I knew, Trevor had plopped down beside me on the love seat. I'd been curled up with my feet underneath me but now, to make room for him, I automati-cally straightened and placed my feet on the floor. When I did, Trevor took advantage of the shift in my posture to slip his arm around my shoulders. Now my face was sort of tucked into the warm crook of Trevor's armpit, my head resting on his shoulder. I could smell the spicy perfume of his deodorant, which was not unpleasant. It had an artificial, beachy undertone that was nothing like the ocean, and yet somehow evoked it. It was the smell, I thought, of *blue.*

"Poor Karie," said Trevor.

I tried to relax against him, as it seemed the thing to do. I could feel the muscle of his shoulder shift beneath my cheek. A sober voice spoke up from somewhere inside me then—some distant cerebral outpost the Captain Morgan hadn't been able to reach. *The idea,* this voice observed bemusedly, *is for you to cry against him now. To let it all out. That's what this is about.* And the second that voice spoke up, as ready as I'd been to cry right up until this moment, everything seemed to go dry. My head cleared, my sinuses emptied, and I was parched. I was going to stand up, I decided. I'd maneuver my way out from under Trevor's heavy biceps and go to the kitchen, drink a full glass of water, and maybe splash some on my eyes while I was in there.

As I was thinking this, Trevor patted me on the shoulder and then drew me to him a little tighter. Squeezing, as if to prime my internal emotional pump, as if to say, *You can do it. Let it all out.*

So we sat in silence for a few moments.

"Thank you for being there for her," I said eventually. "I'm glad you were. I feel like shit that I wasn't, but I'm glad you were."

"Do you know what she used to say about you?" asked Trevor. I tensed against him, and he gave my shoulder another squeeze.

"She used to say, *I mustn't bother Karen with any of this.*"

"'Any of this?'" I repeated.

"Her health stuff. If something scary showed up on the scan or what have you."

"But she'd tell you?"

"She'd tell me."

I shuddered, and Trevor squeezed me again. "But why wouldn't she want to tell me?"

"She used to say it would make you upset. I told her, *Goddamnit, Rini, if this shit gets serious, you have to call her!* And she'd say, *Yes, yes, but in the meantime, no point getting her all worked up.*"

"I would have come," I fretted into Trevor's armpit. "I would've helped her if she asked."

"She seemed to think," said Trevor slowly, "you couldn't handle it. She used to say, *You know, I've never met anyone so in terror of*—um. Lemme just think how she put it."

I sat there rigid against Trevor, waiting to hear what it was I was so in terror of.

"Oh, just . . . being *needed,* I guess."

That was when I gave in and cried against Trevor. I could feel his warm body relax and soften against mine as I did. After a moment or two, he turned his head and, with a firm, grandmotherly smack, kissed me on the temple.

"Ah, Karie," he said. "You and I are just two lonely people."

I sat with that. With the *you and I* of it.

"Just like the song says, eh?" And then he turned his head again to croon into my ear, quavering and tuneless.

"Where dooooo we all belong?"

The Enchanted Coach

23

I woke to sunshine streaming through my curtains and checked the time on the cracked face of my phone. It was ten in the morning. I lay back, stunned but grateful that Kelli had permitted me to sleep in so late. Not only that, but she hadn't gotten up the night before.

As for me, I was hungover and wrung out, but as I sat up I realized that I was feeling good—better than I had since Irene's death. Unburdened. Like a curse had been removed.

And the whole house smelled of bacon.

It turned out Trevor had been up since eight and had already cleaned the dishes from last night, made Kelli breakfast, and was now methodically pouring her tea out of one mug and into another to cool it enough for her to comfortably gulp down. A maneuver I recognized as being straight out of Irene Petrie's Big Book of Kelli Care. He winked at me as I sat down. "Rough night, Mother?"

As good as everything smelled, I was in no condition to face the mess of eggs Trevor had produced, but I nibbled some bacon and admonished him for going to so much trouble. Trevor—who, I realized, had been waiting for me to eat—sat down and scarfed up the eggs himself while I sat across from him, blowing on my own mug of tea. Kelli was still in her pajamas and had finished eating long ago, but she didn't seem to want to leave the table. I knew why. Because it was comfortable, all three of us together like this. And I knew, for Kelli, that it was also familiar—breakfast with Trebie. When I had told Trevor at around one in the morning that he was welcome to sleep in the spare room downstairs, he got to his feet, went to the linen closet without having to be told where it was, and shooed me off to my room, insisting that he would make the bed himself—as, it was clear, he had done many times before.

We chatted about nothing in particular for a lazy hour or so until Kelli, finally bored with our bleary conversation, wandered off to the other room to stare out the window, which signaled to Trevor and me that it was time he and I haul ourselves up "off our hungover arses" and clear the dishes.

I was wiping down the counter, grimacing at the grinding noise the dishwasher was making, when I remembered Jessica. She was bringing potential buyers to see the house this afternoon. I turned to Trevor in a panic. I still needed to tidy up, vacuum, bake cookies, and buy flowers.

"Number one, fuck the cookies," pronounced Trevor. "Pardon my French. That's above and beyond on a day like today. *You* clean up, *I'll* run out and get the flowers. And I'll grab a can of Glade or whatever from the drugstore."

"Okay, but can you get one that smells like cookies or baking something?" I said. "And then I gotta figure out what I'm gonna do with Kelli for an hour."

"What time did you say they were coming?"

"Around three," I said.

"We'll go for fish and chips," said Trevor without missing a beat, as if this were the most obvious of solutions.

"Fit-chip," echoed Kelli from the next room. You'd almost think she had been sitting there waiting for someone to make this suggestion.

Trevor winked at me. "Me and Beaner got a place we like."

It was unnerving to realize how blind I'd been to this sort of thing all along. Trevor and Kelli's shorthand. Their obvious intimacy. Now that the scales had fallen from my eyes, I saw it constantly. I kept having to remind myself to be happy for Kelli, that things were back to a kind of normal for her now—as normal as they could be without my mother, anyway. Trevor had told me last night after my crying jag, as I was pulling the collar of my shirt up over my puffy face and stanching my tears with it: *Don't feel sad about then. Just be happy about now.*

So that's how I decided to feel. I would be happy I was here for

Kelli now. And I would make amends to her and to Irene as best I could.

Trevor drove us out to a fish joint in Eastern Passage that he told me was a favorite of Irene's when she didn't want to cook and she felt like she deserved "a treat." Normally, I knew, my mother took care to avoid any food of the deep-fried variety, but fish and chips were her kryptonite, reminding her of her beach-centric childhood on Cape Breton Island. It made her think of tourists and miniature golf and ice cream and salt-stiffened towels spread out across the picnic table to dry. Whereas Kelli liked anything involving french fries.

My sister swaggered into the restaurant, its walls festooned with buoys, plastic lobsters, and nautical ropes in various artful knots, as if she owned the place. She barreled past the PLEASE WAIT TO BE SEATED sign to a table overlooking the boat-cluttered harbor, which, Trevor explained to me, was her favorite spot. I didn't think the servers would mind, it being the middle of the afternoon—the place was practically deserted. A matronly waitress called a greeting to Kelli as she strode by.

"How you doing, dear?"

She recognized Kelli. For some reason, I felt grateful that she had at least not called her by name. There were people in the world who knew my sister, yes, who I didn't know, but at least they weren't on a first-name basis with her. There would have been something extra shameful in that, somehow. Trevor raised a hand to the waitress.

"Ready for a feed, that's how!"

"That's our girl," the waitress answered.

Trevor ordered for all of us. Kelli would have "the usual," and I would have what Kelli had.

We were up to our elbows in deep-fried everything, promising one another we'd have a healthier dinner later that evening—in fact, maybe the healthiest thing would be to have no dinner at all—when the call came. I looked at my phone—HEALTH AND WELLNESS, the caller ID announced, the coincidence of which gave me a weird feeling, like the phone had become sentient and was chiming in on the conversation.

I figured the call had something to do with Kelli. About her benefits, maybe. Which meant I'd better answer. I grabbed a bunch of napkins and wiped the excess grease off my hands.

The woman on the other end sounded bright and autopilot friendly. She asked me if I was who I was, and, once that was established, *how* I was, and, finally, what kind of day was I having today? I got comfortable—it was factory-standard Maritime preamble; Nova Scotians could go on all day with this kind of excessively informal back-and-forth. It didn't matter who you were talking to—it could be your next-door neighbor or a bill collector, and you'd still find yourself swapping anecdotes about sick relatives or your recent car trouble. Inevitably, we even talked a bit about the weather, how the temperature had dropped in the last couple of days and there was a feeling of impending autumn in the air now, wasn't there? Yes there was, and wasn't it sad that summer had to end? She told me she'd already seen some leaves that had turned when she was out for a walk in the Public Gardens and, Oh! It gave her a sinking feeling. *Tch, tch, tch,* another summer past. I said *Mm-hm* to this and was flailing around for what to say next when she asked when might be a good time to visit me and Kelli.

"Sorry?" I said.

"I was wondering when I might stop by and have a visit with you and your sister. I tried to drop in a few minutes ago, but no one seemed to be home."

I processed this, or tried to. Finally I repeated, "You tried to drop in?" In my dulled, hungover mind, I struggled to rearrange the pieces of information I had—or thought I had—on hand about this caller. Some government worker, whose name I hadn't caught, contacting me about Kelli's benefits, wanting to . . .

"What is this actually about?" I asked, interrupting my own train of thought. "You're calling about Kelli, right?"

Across from me, Trevor put down his fork and, frowning, began to wipe his hands.

"Yes!" said the cheerful civil servant. "I thought it might be best if we could set an appointment for me to come by and see how you two are getting on."

"Okay, wait," I said. "Who are you again?"

"My name's Eleanor Mallon and I'm with the Department of Health and Wellness."

"Health and Wellness," I repeated. I glanced up at Trevor then. The look on his face turned the greasy meal that had moments ago been warmly nestled in my stomach into a cold yet somehow burning clump.

"I don't understand what this is about, though," I said.

"Karen," said Eleanor Mallon. At the same time, Trevor leaned forward and whispered to me, "Karie!"

"As I think I mentioned," began Eleanor Mallon, "we've had a report."

Someone had called Eleanor Mallon, or Eleanor Mallon's office, perhaps even some kind of hotline, some kind of *emergency* hotline, and informed her, Eleanor, or whatever civil service flunky happened to receive the call, of a developmentally handicapped woman—a client, receiving benefits—whose care had been newly entrusted to her sister after their mother's recent death. The sister had been away for many years and was perhaps not as familiar as she could be with the client's needs. There were a number of concerning incidents. The client had been severely ill on two occasions in the past month, but on neither occasion was she taken to a doctor. There was also an incident in a public parking lot. The police had to be called. The client had been left alone in the car, and—

Will she be okay?

Bending to inquire over the back seat, blond hair curtaining her face.

Gonna be okay, Kell?

My vision had begun to pulsate—I was aware of the pulsating, even if I was only distantly aware of anything I was seeing in front of me, anything but the sound of Eleanor Mallon in my ear. Beside me, Kelli was obviously mopping up ketchup from her plate with a fistful of french fries. Many of them had split open, and their fluffy white potato guts were oozing up from between Kelli's knuckles. Trevor sat with his hands braced against the table, watching me. He had pushed his plate away. About halfway through my conversation with Eleanor Mallon, he pushed my plate away too, and I saw him signal to the waitress.

"I also understand you've discontinued some of Kelli's home care visits," chirped Eleanor Mallon.

"I've cut back on them, yes—" I began. "Because . . ." I glanced up at Trevor.

"Not to worry—we can certainly discuss it when I stop by!" said Eleanor Mallon with an air of generosity, like she was talking about dropping off a casserole and, oh no, it was no trouble at all. "But, of course, these visits are a service covered by your sister's benefits—they're meant to make things easier for you."

"It's just," I said, "we're getting ready to move house, and things have been a little chaotic . . ."

Trevor started shaking his head at me. *Don't justify*, he seemed to be saying.

"Oh gosh, well, I can just imagine what a busy time it must be. Why don't we have a big chat about that when we get together. We'll talk about what kind of assistance would be most helpful for you and Kelli. How's tomorrow morning?"

"Tomorrow morning," I repeated into the phone, with zero inflection. I was staring pleadingly at Trevor. He locked his eyes with mine and nodded.

He spoke in a low, soothing voice the entire drive home. I'd always thought I was the one with ESP in my relationship with Trevor—being able to anticipate and intuit his likes and dislikes, what he approved of and what he would disparage. But in this moment, Trevor seemed to be the one with ESP. He knew what I was thinking and what I needed to hear. He spoke steadily, to dilute the tension and as if replying to every panicked thought that the conversation with Eleanor Mallon was giving rise to in my head.

"You're thinking," he said, "this is the worst thing that can happen. But it isn't, Karie. It's bad news, yes, and it's a pain in the fuckin' ass, pardon my French. But these people don't want to take Beaner away. That's not what they wanna do, and if that's what you think is gonna happen, get it out of your head right now. They just wanna be sure she's okay, and as soon as they see that she is, they're gonna be happy as pigs in shit. Me and you just have to show them that she is."

"But," I said.

"That time she was sick with the squirts," said Trevor sagely.

"And she was sick the night of the yard sale too. She was puking."

"Okay, so we tell 'em people get sick. You and me get sick, Beaner gets sick, everyone gets sick. But she didn't *stay* sick, right?"

"I think it's because she got so sick *twice*," I fretted. "So close together. They feel like I should've gotten her checked out. Maybe I should've."

"Okay, so this is what happens when you get a call from these people, Karie. They psych you the fuck out. You gotta get a grip before you start second-guessing everything about your life. You start to feel like a dirtbag. 'Cause only dirtbags get visits from social workers, right? I'll tell you a story. Social workers came to my house when I was a kid. There was a picture I drew at school. We were supposed to draw pictures about what our families did at Christmas, right? So I guess I drew something about how on Christmas Eve my old man opened all his presents and thanked us for each of them and gave us big hugs and kisses and told us how much he loved us—he even cried a little, you'd think the soppy bastard was going off to war the next day. Anyway, then he went to bed, and then the next morning he got up, looked around all red-faced at the mess of paper and open boxes, and hollered, "Who the fuck opened all my presents?" Okay, so, turned out he'd been in a blackout the night before, only I didn't know what that was, I just thought he had a really bad memory. So anyway, the old man throws a fit, kicking presents around and yelling that the bunch of us ruined his Christmas morning. Then he storms out of the house and he's gone all day. My old man was always a bit of a sook, you wanna know the truth, you couldn't do enough for the fuckin' guy, pardon my French. So anyway, dumb kid that I am, I draw a picture of this at school—two panels, my dad on Christmas Eve and my dad Christmas Day, kind of a before-and-after sort of thing. And *knock-knock-knock,* if it isn't social services at our door the very next day.

"My point, Karie, is that my old man was a drunk and a big fuckin' baby but he didn't hit us, he didn't abuse us, and he didn't neglect us, and as soon as the social workers got that confirmed, they were over the moon. You could practically see them wipin' themselves down they were so relieved. They don't wanna take people away. It's a pain in the ass and a major expense. 'Cause if you're not looking after Kelli-bean, guess who is? Them. And that costs."

We drove in grim silence for a good five minutes or so as my mind raced. It was obvious to me how this had happened—the dots were easy enough to connect. It even made a kind of sense. I'd explained it to Trevor back at the restaurant, in the shell-shocked moments after I'd put down the phone. But I couldn't get over how callous it was, how unfair. Not to mention out of character. "How could she do it?" I muttered now.

"Because," said Trevor, setting his jaw. "She's a rich bitch who's had everything served up on a silver platter and she has *no fucking idea* what people like us have had to go through."

I wanted to feel it, what Trevor was saying about Jessica. Of course, I knew that the opposite was true. Jessica had, in fact, experienced the *knock-knock-knock,* the social workers at the door, and—unlike young Trevor with his damning Christmas drawings—the upheaval that came after. He and I were the ones who had no idea. But I didn't tell Trevor that—I didn't contradict him. I couldn't, because I needed him on my side now that I knew I had an enemy.

24

She was waiting for me, because I'd called to make sure she stayed put once she'd finished showing the house. I told her I wouldn't keep her long. I tried to keep my tone light as we spoke on the phone, almost singsong, as if it was important to deceive her about how I was feeling—as if I were laying a trap.

When we pulled into the driveway, Jessica was sitting in her car with a pair of potential home buyers—two middle-aged men, one blond, with a buzz cut, the other with a striking shoulder-length mane of silver hair. Even though I could only see the backs of their heads, it was pretty clear that the three of them had become buddies in the time they'd spent wandering around my mother's blank slate of a house. Now the men were leaning toward her and waving their hands around, telling the same story simultaneously, it looked like, as Jessica laughed hugely, flashing her excellent teeth.

Jessica said something as we pulled into the driveway that prompted the silver-haired man to turn and wave at me. I climbed out of Trevor's truck and—even though it felt forbidden to be interacting with him, somehow, like I was violating some kind of real estate taboo—raised a hand in return. In further defiance of the taboo, he pointed at the house and gave me a thumbs-up, as if to say, *Good house!* By now, Jessica had climbed out of the car and was walking toward me, her bright real estate agent's smile fading as she caught sight of Trevor, taking Kelli's hand with an exaggerated air of courtliness, to help her down from the truck. He looked like one of Cinderella's footmen, helping the princess from her enchanted coach. It was a performance for Jessica's benefit, just like when he'd stood with his legs spread and hand on his hip at the yard sale, putting himself on display.

"I'll get Beaner inside and get her settled," Trevor murmured to me. He turned, without greeting Jessica, and clapped his hands at Kelli. "Shake that booty, Big Bean! Maybe we'll get some cookies happening, eh?"

Jessica watched as he hustled Kelli away. She had stopped walking about halfway up the driveway and was now simply standing there, taking the three of us in. It was only after Kelli and Trevor had disappeared inside and the screen door wheezed shut behind them that she started moving toward me again.

"What's up?" she said. The question contained multitudes but was, I knew, mostly about what she had just seen. Only I didn't want to talk about Trevor.

"Did you," I began. And I had opened my mouth with every intention of uttering a complete sentence. It was going to be straightforward and inflectionless and I would keep my emotions under control. But just a few words in, I felt my face begin to throb. Blood whooshed like the ocean in my ears, making me forget what I wanted to say. Jessica's eyes widened as she looked at me.

"Karen, what's—"

And I slapped her.

The only person I'd ever slapped previous to this was a weedy, drunken architecture student at a Halloween party, back in university—I'd been dressed as Elvira, Mistress of the Dark, and he'd taken my low-cut costume as an invitation to plunge his hand deep into my cleavage. I couldn't tell if I had hit Jessica hard or not, and I was immediately worried about it. I stared at my palm and clenched my hand, thinking that if I had really smacked Jessica a good one, my palm would be stinging from the impact, like it had with the architecture student—but I was so adrenalized I couldn't tell what my hand felt like exactly. I peered at Jessica's cheek to see if any kind of welt was forming. I could hear myself apologizing, as if from another room. Jessica was holding her face just as the drunk boy had, gaping at me, and I wished she would take her hand away so I could see if there was a mark or not.

"Did it hurt?" I asked.

"What is happening?" said Jessica.

The back door of Jessica's car flung itself open, and now the man who had given me the *Good house* thumbs-up came rushing toward us, scowling like Beethoven, his silver hair flowing behind him.

"Excuse me," he said. "Excuse me. Oh my god."

"It's all right, Nate," called Jessica, holding out her arm as if to keep him at bay. Nate stopped and seemed to hover in the driveway, vibrating like a hummingbird.

"Do you want me to call the police." This was a question, but said like a statement, a very emphatic statement, loud, slow, and deliberate, as if every word were followed, in his mind, by a period. He stared straight at me. Jessica turned to him.

"It's okay, Nate. Please wait for me in the car with Jason and I'll be right there." Jessica had been holding a kind of glazed eye contact with me, but now she blinked a bunch of times and jerked her head toward Nate. He walked backward a few steps, still scowling. He had been holding his phone in his hand, I realized, and now he pocketed it and went back to the car.

Jessica turned to me, and we looked at each other.

"You have been talking to people about me," I said.

Jessica did a thing with her body then. I could see her sort of settle into herself as she faced me—becoming more aware of her physical self. It was as if she were tightening her core muscles yet keeping everything else loose—making her body taut and soft all at once—ready, as it were, to rumble. I thought of the last yoga class I took, how the instructor had told us to ground ourselves, to imagine roots growing out of our feet and into the earth. That's what it seemed to me that Jessica was doing. She was grounding herself.

"I have been talking to people about you," Jessica repeated. And I noticed that she didn't repeat these words as if in disbelief, as if to dismiss them as nonsense. She wasn't denying it. I experienced another oceanic whoosh of blood into my face, and my hands twitched, but I had the feeling from Jessica's new posture that if I tried to slap her again she would step deftly to the side and maybe flip me over her shoulder.

"You admit it?" I said.

"I am trying to sell your house. So yes, I have been talking to people about you."

"About me and Kelli!" I shouted. "You think I can't take care of Kelli!"

"I think you can't take care of Kelli," Jessica repeated. On some level, even though I couldn't really appreciate it in the moment, it was fascinating how Jessica was negotiating with me. She was employing strategies—strategies she had obviously learned well via a lifetime of therapy, and that she'd had occasion to use in the past. She'd rooted herself to the pavement of my mother's driveway and was now taking measured breaths, repeating my words back to me, taking her time, refusing to be drawn into the blood-whooshing current of my anger. It intimidated me. I was not grounded, I knew. I was all over the place. I was overhead, swooping among the treetops, grasping at branches.

"That's not true, Karen. I *do* think you can take care of Kelli. But I also think you could use some help."

"So you blow the whistle on me? You report us to social services?"

"No!" said Jessica, looking more stunned than she'd been by the slap. "I wouldn't do that."

"Then why were you acting so weird the day we left Kelli in the car? You went home after that and you called them, didn't you?"

"Are you kidding?" said Jessica. "I was acting weird because that day was insane."

"Well, she asked me about that day—the Adult Protection worker who called."

Jessica's face lost its tension all at once. "Oh, Karen," she said. "Oh no."

"Yes!" I said, almost in triumph. "Someone reported it, and that someone also told them about the night Kelli got sick. *Both* times she got sick. And you were there."

"I *wasn't* there both times," said Jessica. "The first time she got sick was the first time we got together, remember? For lunch. You—"

"Yes, but I told you about it. And you were there the night she puked." I was furious that she would even be arguing with me, that she wouldn't just admit what we both knew to be true. "You wanted me to take her to the ER. And it was the same thing the day we left her in the car—you were questioning me and judging me the whole time."

"I wasn't judging." Jessica looked steadily into my eyes and spoke low, as if I were some skittish, flailing animal she was attempting to coax into a pen. "I just genuinely wasn't sure what was best. And I promise you, I didn't report anything to anyone. But, Karen, I did talk to some people."

"Who?" I demanded. "And why are you talking about us at all?"

"Friends," said Jessica. "Just—people who know about home care and disability services around town—"

"Well, thanks a lot. One of your *friends* called Adult Protection, and they're coming over tomorrow to decide whether or not to take Kelli away."

Rather than deny it, Jessica glanced away from me and took a breath. In that moment, I could see her make the decision to stop playing defense. "What are you going to do?" she asked, turning back to me.

"We'll deal with it," I said, crossing my arms. "Trevor is helping me."

Jessica glanced uneasily at the house. "Karen, why is this guy still around?"

"Because," I said, "he was good to my mother. And he's good to Kelli."

"Did you get the key back?"

The question sent the blood surging into my face all over again.

"I already told you I was getting the key back! Trevor's not the issue here!"

I watched as Jessica attempted to reground. She squared her shoulders. "I've been meaning to tell you—I heard some stuff about the outfit this guy works for."

I stared at her. "What stuff?"

"Did you know these companies aren't regulated?"

"Of course they're regulated. They're government—"

"No, they're *not* government. They're *contracted* by the government. And some are more aboveboard than others."

"I can't believe this!" I shouted. What I actually couldn't believe was all the shouting I was doing. I hadn't even shouted when my marriage broke up—not once that I could remember. There'd been muttering, whispering, gasping, and sometimes sloppy, quiet sobbing. Hissing too, when things got heated. But I couldn't remember ever raising my voice. Basically the entire experience had been funereal. Now, however, I was wishing I'd done some shouting after all over those long, gray months of negotiating his departure. There was something exhilarating about it—so much so that I was a little worried that I wouldn't be able to stop. The idea of having to stop—of the adrenaline draining away as I knew eventually it must, leaving me spent and sad at Jessica's betrayal, as opposed to raging and self-righteous like a Valkyrie—was too depressing to think about. *Maybe this will just be who I am from now on,* I thought distantly. I tried for a second to imagine what the rest of my days would be like—gleefully, furiously biting the heads off friends and strangers alike.

"You actually reported me for using home care?" I shouted.

"I didn't report you, Karen!" said Jessica, losing her composure enough to shout back. "I'm explaining to you why I was asking around. And what I found out. Apparently each company sets its own standards. Some do background checks and some don't—"

"Background checks?"

"It's really odd that the company you're using would pair a male worker with a female client. It's *really* unusual. Most aboveboard places would never do that."

We glared at each other for a long moment. I could feel the Valkyrie draining out of me. The conversation was becoming about something else.

"He just takes her for walks," I said at last. "Outside. In public. It's not like they're ever left alone together."

"They're alone right now," said Jessica, glancing again at the house. I turned and looked at it too, more as a performance of disbelief and exasperation than to actually take it in. But when I did I saw Kelli riveted at the window and a blurry, big-shouldered shadow looming behind her.

"He's her best friend," I said, turning back to Jessica.

"I thought he was her *worker*," said Jessica. "I thought that's what he was supposed to be. He's supposed to be one or the other. He's not supposed to be both. It's against the rules."

"I know that," I said, remembering my phone call with Margot. *Those lines are so easily blurred.* "But people break the rules. Even my mother. She was human. Sometimes human beings just need each other and they just—reach out. She trusted him."

"Karen," said Jessica. She was saying my name a lot. It felt to me like another one of her therapy strategies, and I had to admit, it was sort of effective. I kept flying off in all directions, propelled by a combustive mix of guilt and fear and fury, and she just kept reeling me back to earth with her patient, low-voiced *Karen*s. "There are *so* many services your mother could have accessed. As a senior? With serious medical issues? As Kelli's primary caregiver? I looked into it. She had every right to that care."

"My mother knew what she was entitled to," I said. "She'd been negotiating that system for years—"

"But she was *elderly*," Jessica interrupted. "Maybe it got hard for her, maybe she couldn't stand the thought of going through a whole bureaucratic rigmarole just for a bit of extra help." And my mind flashed on the stiffened cleaning rags I'd found in the darkness of Irene's bottom cupboard, the gunky stain left to congeal and harden beneath the fridge. *Fuck it.* "My point is," continued Jessica, "Trevor is a front-line care worker." This was the first time she had ever deigned to mention Trevor by name, and I could tell, as she spat out the two syllables, that she wasn't happy about it. "If she reached out to him for help—which, sure, why wouldn't she, he's there, it's convenient—his *job* was to report that need back to the agency. That would be his training. What he's *not* supposed to do is become her personal handyman! The agency could've gotten her the help she needed. Instead, he just ended up isolating her."

"She didn't just need *help*," I argued. "She needed family. Trevor was there when my mother needed him. He wasn't just helping around the house—it went so much deeper than that."

"What does that mean?" said Jessica.

"He was like a son to her," I said. "The neighbors assumed he was, because that's what she told them. That's what she *wanted* him to be."

Jessica stared at me, and I realized how high-pitched and strangled my voice was now. I wasn't angry anymore, but I was shaking.

"Karen," said Jessica. This had to be the ninth or tenth *Karen*. "Don't yoke yourself to this guy just because you feel guilty about your mother."

"I don't feel guilty," I told her. "I feel *grateful*."

25

I made a soup for dinner, and for the first time, Trevor didn't offer to help with the meal. He didn't exactly argue with me, but I could tell he wasn't thrilled about the idea of soup in general, remarking that he was "not really a soup guy." As far as Trevor was concerned, if you couldn't barbecue it, it didn't qualify as cooking. I pointed out that if salads were out of the question, we'd just have to figure out new and innovative ways to serve vegetables. That got Trevor off on a somewhat passive-aggressive rant about how soup was really just salad in disguise—it was *boiled* salad, he joked—which, if you thought about it, was actually pretty disgusting.

Despite Trevor's disapproval, making the soup soothed me. For one thing, it canceled out the cloying smell of the Vanilla Vroom air freshener Trevor had picked up from the drugstore earlier and blasted all throughout the house in anticipation of Jessica bringing Jason and silver-maned Nate over for the viewing. (Given Nate's *Good house* thumbs-up, he must not have minded the Vanilla Vroom, but the sight of the homeowner assaulting his real estate agent had likely soured him on a bid.) For another thing, Trevor talked to me as I stood meditatively chopping vegetables in the kitchen, reassuring me about Jessica and going out of his way, it seemed to me, not to ask too many questions about what our post-slap conversation in the driveway had consisted of. "Good for you" was all he'd said when I came inside after our confrontation. His voice was serious and low, even though I sensed that he'd been delighted by the slap. But Trevor kept his demeanor somber, as if in respect for what I'd accomplished out there. He'd given my shoulder a big-brotherly pat as I came up the stairs from the foyer.

It was clear that Trevor felt that Jessica had been adequately dealt with. And now the priority was mapping out a game plan for our upcoming visit with Eleanor Mallon.

The game plan was to make the place immaculate, one, which was no difficult task considering I'd been keeping it neat as a pin for potential home buyers all month long. But Trevor thought I should also consider hauling some of Irene's personal touches out from the basement cubby where I'd stored them—her tasseled rugs, her family photographs. A doily or two. Basically, he wanted me to reapply my mother's personality to the freshly blank decor.

"Because you gotta get it feeling homey again," he explained.

"But . . . this woman knows that we're moving soon. I told her, so she'd understand . . ."

"It's not about what she knows, though," said Trevor. "It's about what she *feels*. Walking into this place. In her gut. You want to give her that nice feeling when she walks in the door—like: Oh, yeah, this is a good, cozy place to live."

"It's about creating an impression," I suggested.

"Exactly," said Trevor. "Right now, the impression is that you basically got Beaner living in a goddamn hotel lobby."

"It's *staged*," I protested. "When you're selling a house, you want it to look like—"

"I don't buy that staging bullshit," said Trevor, stretching in his kitchen chair. He was sitting with a juice glass of rum in front of him, rum I assumed must be left over from the night before, even though I'd been surprised to learn that we hadn't worked our way completely through the bottle. He'd offered me a shot after I came in from speaking to Jessica, but I'd shuddered at the idea, so he'd cracked a beer for me instead. I nursed it as I chopped. "You ask me," he went on, "people wanna buy a house that looks like human beings live there. Not fuckin' *robots*."

I stopped chopping, irritated. "It doesn't look like . . . a robot hotel. It just looks like a house that—"

"I'm just saying, for tomorrow," said Trevor. "Homey touches. That's what you want when this lady shows up. You want her to feel you've made a nice home for Beaner. Your mum was all about the homey touches."

After the soup—which Trevor ate, though he made a point of leaving a soggy collection of carrot coins in the bottom of his bowl, on the grounds that they weren't quite cooked enough for his taste—we went down to the basement cubby. We hauled out a couple of my mother's rugs, the single box of doilies and knickknacks I'd held back from the yard sale because I couldn't quite stand to part with them, and another box, this one of framed photographs, which held the wedding photo, my long-gone dad riding a horse in Bermuda (on his honeymoon, his and Irene's one and only trip outside the country), and my mother's nursing graduation photo—her old-fashioned cap affixed miraculously to her styled coif, her armful of roses, her eyes shining, gazing away from the camera as if so transfixed by the future she couldn't even be bothered to acknowledge the current moment being captured for posterity. Photos of me and Kelli. As babies. As children. As adolescents. As young women. And that's where the photos of me stopped—at my own graduation photo, to be precise. (I was staring directly into the camera, unlike my mother, and for some reason had clenched my jaw instead of smiling. It was like a passport photo, utilitarian, saying nothing but *Get me out of here.*) And although Kelli had no graduation photo, the pictures of her—at birthdays, at picnics, at outdoor concerts, getting bigger and older as she tore open Christmas presents by the tree—went on and on. A documentary in stills of an endless childhood. Trevor hung the photos up precisely where they'd been before.

Kelli watched all this activity with approval. My mother had always kept an eyelet-handkerchief thing spread out as a kind of mat beneath a lamp that sat on one of the end tables in the living room. As I was replacing it, I caught Kelli's eye. She'd been watching me from her stool by the window.

"Mumma," she remarked.

"Remember this stuff, Kell?" I said.

"Mumma stuff," said Kelli, smiling at her lap.

When this activity was finished, I accepted a rum and Coke with ice that Trevor produced out of nowhere for "a job well done" and we sat in the re-doilied living room with Kelli. I had to admit, the space felt comfortable again—or at least familiar. Like we belonged in it, or to it. Like we had gathered a beloved old blanket around ourselves and were snuggling in.

Something about unboxing and replacing all those old photographs had put me in the mood to talk about Irene. I wanted to talk about how we first began to fight with each other. Because, it seemed to me, we hadn't always fought. There was a time when Irene and I were two peas in pod. We liked the same things. We both liked the beach—just lying around on it in the summer, reading magazines, soaking up the sun, as everyone did so heedlessly back then. Irene used to slather me in coconut suntan lotion to help "brown me up," because that's what you did—no one had a notion about things like UV rays and SPF back then—and together we'd loll on towels as Kelli sat nearby in a floppy hat (unlike my mother and me, Kelli turned into a boiled lobster the moment sunlight hit her), rocking and running her hands through the sand. And my mother would always tell me how wonderful it was that I, a child, just liked to *sit*. I didn't need to be up and shrieking with the other kids, frantically expending energy, hurling myself into the waves, heedless of the undertow and prompting her to have to chase after me, squawking warnings, like the beleaguered, undignified parents on all sides of us. It became a point of pride with me, much as I sometimes craved to do exactly what she was describing. If I wanted to go into the water, I strolled casually down to the surf, like a woman in no hurry, as opposed to the eager, vivacious kid I was. When I dove beneath the surface, I kicked and flailed with abandon, tiring myself out, so that afterward I could amble composedly back up the beach to flop down at my mother's side for another languorous, coconut-scented hour or so. She told me I was the ideal companion.

I was the ideal companion at church for a while too. My mother and I both loved to sing; we'd share a hymnal and belt out whatever song had been chosen by the choir that day, which you were not really supposed to do—belt, that is. At least, that was the impression I got from the side-eye of the surrounding parishioners. After all, there was already a choir there to do the singing—the congregation was just expected to sort of murmur and sigh along, staying more or less in tune, not joyously raise our voices to the heavens. We were Catholics, after all, not Southern Baptists or evangelicals, which is just a way of saying that in our tradition, pleasure taking and churchgoing were two things that were not supposed to go together. But my mother and I didn't care. We sang our hearts out, pushing our mutually thin, quavering voices to their limits. We sang "Yahweh, You Are Near" and "I Am the Bread of Life" and my favorite, the weird, drony-then-triumphant "God's Spirit Is in My Heart," the chorus of which was too high-pitched for my single-octave voice, strictly speaking, but I shrieked it out anyway. My mother and I always sang the abrupt, exuberant chorus with exclamation points.

> *He sent me to give the Good News to the poor!*
> *Tell prisoners that they are prisoners no more!*
> *Tell blind people that they can see!*
> *And set the downtrodden free!*

What I didn't realize the whole time we were belting out hymns that were clearly intended by their composers to be softly warbled was that my mother was dying to be in the choir. Of course she was. And, of course, she would have been if she hadn't had two little girls—one disabled and the other too young to look after the first if left alone with her in the pew. I hadn't understood that, however. I had just assumed that my mother was huddled over the hymnal with me every Sunday, yodeling songs loud enough for the choir leader to take note of her, because that was her favorite place to be. So when I was twelve or so, and Irene finally decreed that I was old enough to sit alone with Kelli in the pew while she sang up front with the choir, I experienced it as a betrayal. And that's when, much to my mother's dismay, I began to whine. As of that moment, I was no longer the ideal companion—Irene made that clear. But I couldn't do anything about it. I didn't want to be stuck in the pew, alone with Kelli. I tried to imagine belting those hymns out all by myself—a gawky twelve-year-old with a terrible voice, Kelli rocking and humming at my side—how I would look to everybody, how I would sound, and it made me never want to go to church again.

Of course, I had to keep going to church, at least for a few years longer; my mother never gave me any choice. But after that, I refused to sing.

"You ladies," said Trevor, shaking his head.

"What?" I said. Trevor was grinning and leaning forward, like my story had tickled him. He swished the rum around in his juice glass, and I realized that for the last hour or so the amount of liquid in there hadn't dwindled. Meaning not that he wasn't drinking it, but that he had been topping himself off intermittently from the bottomless bottle of Captain Morgan without my noticing.

"You *ladies*," he repeated. "Always at each other's throats."

"But we weren't always at each other's throats," I said. "We barely spoke, in fact, for years."

"That's what I mean, though," said Trevor. "You don't *settle* things. You don't get past it. You just let it all stew."

Trevor wasn't just talking about me and my mother, I realized. He was talking about all of us—my entire side of the human equation.

"Men settle things," said Trevor. "Take me and my brother, with our business. I find out he's giving creatine powder away to his buddies before we even get the storefront set up, I head on over to his apartment, he opens the door—I pop him one! *Pow!*" Trevor yelled this so loud it made Kelli look up, as he mimed a sudden punch. It was short and fast and his biceps bulged and contracted.

"You hit your brother?" I said.

"Oh, I asked for an explanation first—I'm a reasonable man. And when the explanation was clearly bullshit, as I was fully expecting, I let him have it." Trevor tapped his fist into his palm a few times, relishing the memory.

I sat up. "But that didn't clear the air," I said. "You told me you and your brother aren't on speaking terms anymore."

"*He* stopped speaking to *me*," said Trevor. "I told him I was through with the business, and he took that pretty hard. But as far as I was concerned, the air was cleared. He knows he can call me anytime and we'd have a nice chat."

"*I* just popped somebody!" I argued, pointing past Kelli out the window. "Just a few hours ago, out in front of the house! I hit a fellow woman! So, yeah, I wouldn't say I let anything *stew* in that case."

Trevor began to chortle. "Oh—*you* two girls," he said, rolling his eyes. "You two are just *beginning* to work all your shit out. You got a long ways to go yet."

"I don't know what that means," I said, sitting back.

Swirling his rum around some more, Trevor then unspooled an elaborate story—a narrative tapestry he'd clearly been embroidering in his mind for weeks. It was the story of me and Jessica and our relationship to each other, about which I was sure I'd told him basically nothing. I, he explained, was intimidated by Jessica, because she was so blond and well put together. Also because she had children and a husband and I did not. It ate away at me, he said.

Jessica, for those same reasons, looked down on me. She enjoyed spending time with me, however, because everything she possessed stood out in relief against everything I did not. And that made her feel amazing about herself. She went home after spending an hour or two with me, according to Trevor, preening with self-satisfaction. "Better than a trip to the goddamn spa," he reflected.

Meanwhile, I spent time with Jessica because being in her presence reflected so well on me. I "sucked up" to her and wanted to please her, apparently, in the hopes that some of her magic and good fortune might rub off on me. It was a little embarrassing to behold, Trevor hinted, how abject I became in Jessica's golden presence.

He was describing two natural-born hypocrites. Two people who had despised each other all along but pretended otherwise in pursuit of their own interests, their own vanities. A pair of vampires clawing away at each other, each trying to get the advantage, the better to suck the other's blood.

Trevor took a meditative sip of his drink before glancing up at me, concerned that he might've said too much.

"It's understandable, though," he said.

"What's understandable?" I said.

"You're still figuring out how to stand on your own two feet. Figuring out who you are. And you're gettin' there, Karie. You're doing great. You don't need that bitch. And you sure as hell let her know it today."

I shook my head, but for some reason my brain whirred as if stalled and I couldn't think of how to argue with what he was saying. There were a handful of things I could have said, though they only occurred to me later. That I was a woman in my mid-forties, the owner of two homes, the holder of two advanced degrees. That I had always been the primary breadwinner in my marriage and had even supported my husband during his two full years of grad school. But I knew that if I were to point out any of those facts (other than my age), they'd fall on Trevor's ears like the made-up tale he had just told me.

The evening dwindled, and the three of us sat in a companionable silence broken occasionally by the sounds of Kelli whispering and snickering to herself in her contentment. After a while, she started making her toast-and-peanut-butter noises, indicating, like vespers, that it was almost time for bed. Trevor heaved himself to his feet and supposed out loud that he should be getting along home. I looked up in surprise. It was not that I expected him to stay over every single night now that he had revealed himself to be my mother's secret son. But we'd just had a long day together of stewing over Jessica Hendy and panicking over Eleanor Mallon and re-Irene-ifying the house from top to bottom in preparation for the latter's visit. And despite the occasional way he had baited and irritated me, Trevor had mostly spent the last twelve hours propping me up. And now he was easing his way out from underneath me, leaving me to stand on my own to face the Adult Protection worker in the morning.

"You don't want some strange dude hanging around when the social workers come knocking on the door," Trevor explained, as if once again reading my thoughts. "Every single person they see, they're gonna have questions about."

"But you're a family friend," I protested. "People are allowed to have family friends."

"We just wanna give the lady as little to do as possible," said Trevor. "And get her out the door, back to her office, writing a report saying how everything's tickety-boo with the Petrie girls."

I stood up. Everything Trevor was saying was making sense, but I couldn't stop arguing about it. I wasn't ready for him to go.

"But isn't it *good* for her to see we have friends around? People we can turn to for support? Don't they want to know we have a community we can access? In case we . . ."

Trevor's hands landed on my shoulders like two weights. I wobbled briefly under them, and he steadied me.

"You just text me the minute she leaves," he said. "And I'll be back."

26

She was as pleasant and gracious in person as she'd been on the phone, and this annoyed the hell out of me at first. I'd woken up that morning primed for enemies, leaping out of bed like Rocky Balboa. I wanted someone to go up against and emerge victorious over. I opened the door to her and imagined Trevor's brother opening the door to him, except this time the person opening the door would be the one ready with the sucker punch. In my mind I saw Trevor's arm snap forward, the biceps bunching and contracting. *Pow!* That's how I wanted to handle this visit with Eleanor Mallon. Metaphorically speaking, of course. It was not really an appropriate mind-set to be going into the situation with, but I couldn't help myself—I wanted to win this thing, decisively. I wanted to be the fist, snapping forward.

"Karen! Hello!" She was only in her mid-thirties but had an older, housewifely air—one of those women who for whatever reason decide to get the jump on middle age in terms of their fashion choices and the cultivation of a generally dowdy demeanor. She struck me as a bake sale facilitator, a Brownie leader, an organizer of elaborate children's birthday parties featuring exotically and imaginatively curated loot bags. She wore unfashionable, owly glasses and had a smile too big for her face.

She started talking and didn't stop as she lingered in the foyer, removing her shoes, asking where she might place her jacket, noting again the new autumnal chill in the air, the changing leaves, pivoting seamlessly into: That's a lovely burning bush tree in your yard, by the way! And won't it just be spectacular come late September? And what a lovely neighborhood too! And are we sad to be leaving it? And did

Kelli and I grow up here? And so forth. In this way, Eleanor Mallon managed to fill any awkward conversational gaps completely during the time it took me to put her jacket aside and lead her up the stairs to the living room and introduce her to Kelli.

She leaned over and offered Kelli her hand, which Kelli was pleased to shake.

"Malla," Kelli repeated after Eleanor introduced herself.

"Eleanor Mallon," repeated Eleanor.

" 'Nor Malla," muttered Kelli.

"Kelli puts her own spin on people's names," I explained.

Eleanor straightened up, smiling. "You can certainly call me Nora if you like, Kelli. My hubby calls me Nora!"

"Kelli knows 'Nor," said Kelli.

Eleanor sat in the cushioned rocking chair with the noisy springs, playing it cool. I wondered how much experience she'd had with the developmentally handicapped. Kelli wasn't like a lot of other people in her situation—at least as far as I knew. She had her own way of handling conversation, for example. She might exchange a few words with you and then disappear into rocking and muttering whenever the spirit so moved her. It occurred to me that if Eleanor Mallon didn't understand this about Kelli, she might note it down as some kind of problem—she might assume Kelli was unduly upset or traumatized. As I took a seat across from the Adult Protection worker, I felt my face begin to perspire and I knew I was psyching myself out. I tried to remember Trevor's soothing monologue in the truck on the way back from the fish and chips place. *They don't wanna take people away.* I jumped up again to offer Eleanor Mallon a cup of tea, which she graciously accepted, although she insisted that she didn't *need* any, it was only if I had the tea already made and I would not go to any special trouble just for her.

"It's already made," I assured her, because of course it was. Just as the cookies were already sitting on the kitchen table, arrayed on a plate. The house was fragrant with their buttered-cinnamon smell, as I had risen early to ensure that they were freshly baked, remembering Jessica's advice. Of course, the cookie tactic was no longer about selling the house. It was about the same thing all the re-Irene-ification of the place the night before had been about. Selling, to Eleanor Mallon, the *home*.

While I was in the kitchen, pouring milk into my mother's china jug, I could hear Eleanor Mallon take a stab at making chitchat with my sister.

"So how've you been, Kelli?"

"Kelli-bean," said Kelli, maybe thinking of Trevor.

"How've you been feeling? I heard you were sick?"

"Kelli puked," said Kelli.

"Oh dear," said Eleanor Mallon.

"Right there in that chair," I said, placing a tray of tea and cookies on the coffee table in front of the social worker's crossed legs. She was wearing nutmeg pantyhose, and her toes looked sad and trapped behind the hosiery. "Just let 'er rip right onto the carpet, didn't you, Kell?"

Kelli actually smiled at the memory. She didn't recall the misery of the experience, only that she'd been naughty. "Kelli puked the carpet," she confirmed. "Kelli's tummy. Tummy hurt."

Eleanor Mallon turned to me. "What was it? A bug?"

"Okay, so here's the thing," I said. And as I said it, I knew I was about to start talking too much, too fast. "I'm pretty sure it was something she ate. Kelli has a shellfish allergy. Or, not so much an allergy, because people tell me it's only an allergy if you get hives and swell up, which she doesn't, she just pukes. It's a reaction. I have it too—we go anywhere near clams or mussels, bivalves basically. Everything just comes up. Lobster and shrimp are fine, for some reason. But it's—"

"So Kelli had shellfish?"

"No," I said. "We couldn't figure it out—"

"We?"

I tried not to give Eleanor Mallon a look of contempt. *Don't play dumb with me, 'Nor Malla,* I wanted to say. I took a breath.

"My friend Jessica Hendy," I said. "The one who called you, I assume. She was there the night Kelli got sick."

Eleanor Mallon gazed at me through her owly glasses. *Too-wit, too-woo,* I wanted to say. Where was that from? A children's show, I thought—there'd been a character named Wise Old Owl who knew all the answers. Just like Eleanor Mallon did. She knew, for example, who had called Adult Protection. She knew what was going to happen to me and Kelli next. She knew the kind of answers I should be giving to her questions and the kind I shouldn't. Which I did not. I could only guess. I, therefore, was at a disadvantage. The longer she stared, the more I wanted to say it. *Too-wit, too-woo. Too-wit, too-woo, Owlface.*

"And so," resumed Eleanor Mallon, "you and your friend Jessica tried to determine what Kelli might've eaten that made her sick?"

"Yes!" I said. "It was weird, because we'd all eaten the same thing. And I have the same seafood reaction that Kelli does, so if it made her sick, it should've made me sick too."

"So perhaps it wasn't something she'd eaten."

I deflated. Now came the indefensible part of my story. "I just really felt like it was," I told her. "I'd seen Kelli get sick like that a lot of times in the past. And I mean, *I've* been sick like that. It's a—it's a really distinctive way of getting sick."

"Vomiting?" said Eleanor Mallon. "Vomiting seems a fairly general way of getting sick to me!" She laughed in order to demonstrate that we were just two nice women, well disposed to each other, having a friendly and inconsequential conversation.

"I mean the *way* she was vomiting," I said tersely. I may have even snapped this. "I'd seen it before. Everything comes up in one big heave and then you're retching for the rest of the night—your stomach's basically in contractions, even though you've already brought everything up."

Eleanor glanced at Kelli. "Oh, poor Kelli. That must've been awful for you."

"Kelli puked the carpet," said Kelli. "Heh-heh-heh-heh-heh."

Eleanor Mallon broke into a grin, charmed, as people always were, at my sister's cartoonish chuckle. She glanced at me. "She doesn't seem that traumatized, does she?"

"No," I said. "She's actually pretty pleased with herself."

We were smiling at each other now. Good old icebreaker Kelli.

Eleanor Mallon went over everything with me a couple of times. How Jessica and I had scoured the ingredients list on the hot dogs, the store-bought coleslaw. How we had gone back and forth on the idea of taking her to the Emergency Room and, yes, Jessica had been pro and I had been con. But I had also, ultimately, been right. Once she'd had a Gravol, my sister's retching spasms had eased off, and she'd been back to her old self by the following day. Eleanor paused to scribble a sentence in the notebook she'd brought along—she carried a black, dog-eared Moleskine like some kind of undergrad Hemingway wannabe. It subtly altered her housewifely vibe into something a little more bohemian; perhaps beneath Eleanor Mallon's cardigan and rayon blouse there beat the heart of a poet.

"Well," she said, once she had finished writing. "Let's talk about the diarrhea."

We went over this too, and it was about halfway through the whole unpleasant story that I realized that I was, perversely, enjoying myself. It was *good,* even sort of exhilarating, to be talking about the past two months with Eleanor Mallon—an entirely new person, someone who wasn't Jessica or Trevor. I kept reminding myself to keep my guard up, but Eleanor Mallon, as she listened, kept blinking myopically and dribbling cookie crumbs onto her chest, and they were forming a little pile in the crease of her blouse, which made it impossible not to feel disarmed. As I spoke, I experienced a dawning sense of just how small my world had become since I'd arrived home in time to see my mother off into the afterlife and assume the care of Kelli. I once had friends, I realized as I spoke to Eleanor Mallon. In the other city where I used to live. A social circle, even. Sometimes we would go for coffee, or a yoga class, or one or two would drop by in the evenings for a glass of wine. Presumably, I still had these friends. I could call them, and they would talk to me, I was pretty sure. But over the last couple of months, it seemed I had forgotten about them. I'd forgotten about everything but where I was now and what I had to do. Or, it wasn't that I'd forgotten exactly—a couple of them had even e-mailed me, with subject lines like "Checking in" and "How's it going out there?" And I'd e-mailed back. But it had felt perfunctory. The fact was, these people felt impossible to me now—as if I'd traveled too far away. They might as well have been characters from a book, or a film I'd once enjoyed. At some point, without thinking about it, I'd given up on them, relinquished them, feeling as if I had no choice. I was like Shackleton now, stuck in a hut at the South Pole, surrounded by snow. It wasn't that the world of human souls had disappeared. I knew it was still out there. I had a few items from it—candles, canned goods, wool socks, boxes from London stamped BISCUITS—reminding me that it hadn't gone away. But knowing that didn't make a difference. I was too far gone. My world was now the hut.

"And this gentleman, Trevor," interrupted Eleanor Mallon. "Who you say you called that night to watch Kelli?" Which was when I knew I had slipped up.

I paused, then swallowed. "Yes?"

"So he's a friend?"

I gazed at Eleanor Mallon a moment, the same blank way she had at me through her glasses when I'd mentioned Jessica Hendy. I was thinking of the best, quickest way to dismiss Trevor from the conversation. *We just wanna give the lady as little to do as possible.* A family friend who helped my mother out from time to time—end of story. Maybe I'd say he was a cousin. A second cousin, just to be on the safe side. Did Adult Protection workers look into that kind of thing? What happened if they found out I was lying? How deep did they dig?

As I was pondering this, Eleanor Mallon became aware of the pile of cookie dust that had accumulated on her blouse and attempted to tip it into the open palm of her hand. But when she went to pull at the crease in which the crumbs were nestled, the elasticity of her blouse caused it to spring back, sending the cookie crumbs sprinkling up into her face like tiny fireworks before they settled into her lap.

"*Oh,*" Eleanor Mallon fretted. There was nothing to do but stand up from the cushioned rocking chair and brush the crumbs onto the carpet. But it was clear she didn't want to do that. So I saw poor Eleanor Mallon make the decision to simply remain seated in the chair, covered in crumbs for the duration of our interview.

That was the moment I stopped being afraid of Eleanor Mallon and decided I would let her help me.

27

Trevor turned up around five with a package of premade, pre-seasoned hamburgers, some cheddar slices for melting on top, a bag of buns, and Mike, who did not look happy about any of this. But having met Mike a few times now, I wondered if he ever looked happy about anything. Trevor had also brought ice cream, which reminded me that the first time he'd brought Mike over, it had come across as an obscure gesture of celebration. So likely Trevor thought we were celebrating today as well.

I had texted him after Eleanor Mallon left, as he'd instructed me to. I'd told him the visit had gone okay and I was feeling good about it. Hence, I supposed, Mike. And ice cream for dessert.

Trevor had not brought beer, as there was still a bunch left in the downstairs fridge, and it seemed as if lately he had made the switch to rum, in any case. He commandeered the barbecue, stationing a juice glass with a few fingers of Captain Morgan and some ice on the patio railing alongside him. Because Mike was there, we were able to convince Kelli to relinquish her perch by the love seat and sit outside with the rest of us as Trevor grilled. She kept sneaking smiles at Mike and asking the occasional question about how he liked school, but Mike didn't understand what she was asking and didn't seem interested in having me interpret for her. He held some kind of cheap electronic game at his crotch and kept glancing down at it, with an equal lack of interest, to press the occasional button. I thought that at any moment Trevor might bark at him to put it away, but he didn't seem to notice.

It was almost September now, but that autumnal chill in the air that Eleanor Mallon had kept going on about was nowhere to be had.

The evening sun blazed directly onto the four of us from its angle on the horizon, as if it had been trained on us like a spotlight, by stagehands. Trevor, however, was in his element—his happy place, you might even say—slathering the premade patties with No Name barbecue sauce, swirling his drink in his hand, and making enough conversation to compensate for the rest of us.

And Kelli, I had to admit, was in her happy place too. Her boyfriend Trebie chattering away at the barbecue, calling her Beaner, bringing her Mike, who, despite his singular lack of boyish charisma, she clearly adored. She and I were sharing a beer—that is, I had poured a little of mine into a juice glass for her and she had downed it in two gulps, causing Trevor to bellow, "Easy on the sauce, there, Drunky! We're gonna be picking this one up off the floor by the end of the night, Mother!" This last remark was directed at me, with a wink. Mike's game made a musical booping noise, and I glanced over at him. He was peering savagely down at it, burrowing his chin into his chest.

"Kelli music," ventured Kelli. Mike looked up, frowning.

"She likes things that make noises," I told him.

"Let her see it," said Trevor.

Mike tucked the game into his stomach like a football player ready to make a break. "She won't know how to play it."

"She doesn't goddamn need to know how to play it," decreed Trevor. "Just let her see it."

Mike stood up unhappily.

"If you show her how it works," I told him, "she'll really like that. She doesn't even have to hold it. She'd just like to see what it does."

Mike relaxed a little. He moved toward Kelli and held the game in front of her.

"You gotta try to get it in the net," he said. "With these buttons." He tapped a button rapidly with his thumb and the game emitted a triumphant series of boops.

"See, that's a goal," said Mike.

Kelli began to rock. "Heh-heh-heh-heh-heh," she said. Mike straightened up, smirking. Kelli didn't reach for the game, but I could tell she was waiting for him to do it again. I was about to explain to Mike that this was what she wanted, but something made me bite my tongue. I could see him looking at her carefully now, making the effort to understand for himself.

"You wanna see it again?"

" 'Gain," said Kelli.

Mike began rapidly tapping buttons again, leaning in so Kelli could have a good view. "It's kinda easy for me to score," he explained, "because I've been playing it for so long."

"That's a hint, if you didn't know," Trevor said to me. "That's a hint to Dad that someone wants a new game."

The contraption emitted another victorious series of boops and Kelli emitted another series of *heh*s, and this time Mike cracked a genuine smile.

"All right, enough of that electronic shit," said Trevor. "Everyone grab your plates."

To my surprise, Mike was aiming that smile at me.

"If I get a new one," he said, "I could show her that too. I bet she'd like it."

"Down, boy," said Trevor, cuffing Mike lightly on the back of the head.

Because we couldn't stand the burn of the evening sun in our eyes, we went into the kitchen and assembled our burgers beneath the glare of the fluorescent. Trevor started cutting Kelli's burger up into choke-proof, bite-sized chunks before I could. Mike was chattier now, and told us, at Trevor's urging, about how he had started grade four, about how his teacher was "fat but nice" and his favorite subject was still recess, just like last year. Trevor rolled his eyes and grunted something about the apple and the tree; then he admonished Kelli, who was cramming pieces of burger into her mouth like she was in some kind of competition, to slow down—that g.d. burger wasn't going to run away off her plate—and then he winked at me again and I didn't think I had ever seen him enjoying himself more. When all of us—

except Mike, who dawdled over his burger—were finished eating, Trevor topped himself off with more rum and brought me another beer from the fridge, since he was up.

"I shouldn't," I said.

Trevor cracked it for me. "After what you been through today? I don't know anyone who deserves it more."

"It really wasn't that bad," I said. Trevor sat back down. He looked at me with a slight, expectant smile on his face and said nothing, which was uncharacteristic—Trevor tended to be a rejoinderer. I realized he was waiting for me to elaborate on the visit with Eleanor Mallon.

"It was like you said," I told him. "She just wanted to help."

Trevor's smile widened. "How'd she like the house?"

"The house?" I repeated.

"After all our hard work gettin' it in shape for her," said Trevor.

"Oh!" I said. "I think she liked it. You know, she did the whole 'What a lovely home you have' thing when she first came in."

"Homey touches," said Trevor, nodding. "That's what makes the difference to these people. You know, I was thinking, after this whole dustup with the real estate agent, you may wanna actually hold off a bit on selling the place."

I took a swallow of beer, thinking about this. True enough, I'd been wondering how things were going to proceed between Jessica and me in terms of selling the house now that I'd *slapped* her. I knew that soon I was going to have to call and try to work things out. But it had never occurred to me that I could just take the place off the market.

"I think," I said slowly, "Jessica would be professional about the whole thing. I mean, I don't think she'd—"

"No, I just mean," said Trevor, "with Adult Protection breathing down your neck and everything. Maybe it's a sign. Maybe the thing to do is just hang fire for the time being while you and Beaner get settled. Show 'em you got things under control."

"I actually feel pretty good about the visit today," I told him. "I don't think they're going to be breathing down our necks."

"Well, that's good!" Trevor swished his Captain Morgan around in his glass and took a quick hit. "What'd she say? She ask about Beaner getting sick?"

"She did, yeah. And, you know, I was just honest with her. I told her I used my best judgment and Kelli seemed better the next day, and she seemed to accept that."

Trevor nodded. "She tell you who ratted you out?"

"No. I tried to draw her out about Jessica, but she just gave me a blank look."

"Those social worker types," said Trevor sagely. "They're good at that. What about when you left her in the car? She ask about that?"

I winced a little at the memory. "Yeah—basically, I put it on my mother. I told her Irene used to do it all the time and Kelli was always okay." I remembered how lame I'd felt when I explained this to Eleanor Mallon, knowing, as I said it, what an inadequate excuse it was. What I hadn't told her was how angry I had been, how I had left Kelli there as a punishment as much as a last resort. And leaving this part of the story out made me worry that maybe the person who'd reported me had left it in, which I knew would make me look even worse in Eleanor Mallon's eyes. I was not just a careless sister. I was a sister who let her emotions get the better of her. To the extent of putting Kelli in danger. Furthermore, I wouldn't even admit to it.

"So what'd she say about that?" said Trevor.

"Believe it or not, that's when the conversation became kind of great. I mean, you were so right: They *don't* want to take people away. They want to help you figure out how to take care of them so you don't get into those kinds of situations as much—you don't feel so alone."

Trevor frowned. "Well, you know you're not alone, Karie."

"No," I said, "I know I'm not alone. I just mean she was really great about going over Kelli's benefits with me and the kind of help that's available. There are all these services I didn't know about—Eleanor says they can set us up with a team, practically."

"Wait," said Trevor, holding up a hand. "I thought you'd decided you didn't even need home care—now you want a team?"

I had gotten to a point in the story where I felt I should start editing myself a little. Because the truth was, Eleanor Mallon and I had started talking about the need for "a team" after I'd asked her about what Jessica Hendy had told me in the driveway the day before. In particular, what Jessica had said about Bestlife, the home care service my mother used. I asked Eleanor Mallon if it was true that these companies weren't regulated, and that some were more aboveboard than others. Eleanor Mallon confirmed for me that, yes, this was so. And then, after I explained to her about Trevor (he was, I said, a home care worker my mother had befriended who occasionally broke the rules by helping her out around the house), I asked Eleanor Mallon if she thought it was out of the ordinary for a provider like Bestlife to pair up a male worker like Trevor with a female client like my sister. Eleanor Mallon blinked a few times behind her owly glasses and told me she wasn't entirely sure, but her instinct, she said, her *gut feeling* was that, yes, this was somewhat out of the ordinary. *Not exactly standard operating procedure* was how she put it.

She'd raised her eyebrows then. "Do you have concerns about this person?"

"Trevor?" I'd said. "Oh no—no, no, not at all! He's great with Kelli. Totally professional. I just heard it's an unusual setup, the boy-girl thing. It just got me wondering about Bestlife."

Eleanor had told me she would ask around just to make sure. She'd make a few inquiries about Bestlife and let me know what she found. She stood up at that point, glancing at her watch—I guessed the visit had gone longer than she'd expected it would—and carefully transferring the cookie crumbs sprinkled across her lap onto the tea tray. But that was when I realized, with a sudden jolt of adrenaline, that Eleanor Mallon might be in a position to advise me on Gorsebrook too. The next thing I knew, I was babbling about Jeremy going missing. I described to Eleanor, despairingly, how I had pinned all my hopes on Gorsebrook Residential. How I had planned my and Kelli's entire future around it. And now I had lost faith and I did not know what to do.

Eleanor sat back down. She assured me that she had heard nothing but good things about Gorsebrook. But if I was concerned, she encouraged me to start Kelli off in the day program as a trial run—just until I had a good sense of the facility. If I felt overwhelmed with Kelli's care in the meantime, Eleanor stressed that there were services I could access. Multiple services. And she took some brochures from her bag and went over them with me. *Meet Your Team* was the title of one. The brochure was glossy, soothing, full of gently smiling caregivers and their clients kicking back in sunlit rooms. "You don't have to do this alone," said Eleanor Mallon. "Please remember that, Karen. You should never feel alone in this, because that's a recipe for burnout. And burnout, when you're someone's sole caregiver, is natural, by the way. It's not a failing. It's what happens when you don't have the help you need."

I didn't tell Trevor about that—how I'd gone from being petrified of Eleanor Mallon one moment to realizing her utility the next and grasping at her as if she were a life preserver. I also didn't tell him about the feeling I had once she left the house. A feeling like it had been winter these last couple of months instead of summer. But now it was abruptly spring, the world was waking up, and I had flung open all the windows and fragrant air and sunlight were flooding every room.

Trevor peered at me from his end of the table as I delivered the edited version of all this. "Not so much a team," I said. "Just, like, people we can call on. I mean, Irene was using Bestlife for years, even back when I was kid, for just a few services—the baths and the walks. Eleanor says she could've had help with groceries, cleaning, babysitting—I don't think she ever really bothered exploring the options that were out there. And there's tons!"

I jumped up and went to the cupboard above the fridge, where I'd stashed the brochures Eleanor had left for me, and brought them over to show Trevor. *Meet Your Team* was at the top of the pile, and I put them on the table beside his empty plate. He stared down at them.

"I thought the plan," said Trevor, "was you wanted to get off home care completely, pretty much. I mean, as far as I'm concerned, you've been knocking this whole deal out of the park all on your own. That's what Health and Wellness needs to know. You and Beaner been doing great!"

"Thanks," I said. "I know. And we are. But I guess—I realized, talking to Eleanor, that I need to have a game plan. For the unexpected stuff, moments of crisis. Like, say we give Gorsebrook a try but it doesn't work out, I might need to—"

Trevor snorted at the mention of Gorsebrook. "You're not still thinking about that shithole?"

"Well, I was thinking I might still want to give the day program a try for now . . ."

Trevor widened his eyes as if appalled and I found myself talking faster, trying to make him understand. "Or, you know, with incidents like the guy in the parking lot," I said. "This kind of stuff happens, and when it does—"

"No, no, no," said Trevor, waving a hand. "That guy was crazy. It's not like he's coming back anytime soon."

I was startled that he'd be so dismissive of the angry lunatic screaming at my sister as she hunched and rocked in Jessica's back seat—he'd seemed so outraged by the incident after I'd first described it to him.

"Yeah," I said. "But still, I need to be ready for those times—when Kelli's being stubborn and won't get out of the car. I can't just leave her there like Irene did—I need backup. And Kelli's going to get sick sometimes, and I might need help. This is the thing—I just need to acknowledge that I need help."

"Well, that's what I been sayin' all along," huffed Trevor. "And you got—"

"Like, I can't isolate myself," I continued. "Or I'll end up like Irene."

It was only many hours later, going over this conversation as I lay awake in bed, that I realized I'd been practically parroting some of the things Jessica had said to me in the driveway the day before. I had thought, as I was talking to Trevor, that I had come to all these conclusions on my own, in the course of my conversation with Eleanor Mallon. But, going over it in bed, I understood that despite my fury and my certainty that Jessica had betrayed me, I had actually absorbed everything she'd said. And when I met Eleanor Mallon, I knew intuitively that she would be the perfect person to confirm what Jessica had told me.

Trevor downed his rum and got to his feet and began collecting our plates off the table.

"Should I get the ice cream going?" I asked.

"Ice cream," murmured Kelli in agreement.

Mike dropped the remains of his burger onto his plate as if it had scalded him. "I want some ice cream."

"I don't know if we're in the mood for ice cream anymore," said Trevor, yanking open the dishwasher.

Kelli and Mike uttered a simultaneous protest at this, which was not quite drowned out by the noise of Trevor clattering plates.

"Sounds like these two are definitely in the mood," I said.

"You," said Trevor, whirling on Mike. "I don't wanna hear a word about ice cream till you finish that fuckin' burger."

Mike did a thing that upset me then, for reasons I couldn't quite pin down in the moment. It reminded me a little of when Jessica Hendy had grounded herself out in the driveway. Mike underwent a similar kind of physical transformation—but his seemed more instinctual than deliberate. Like a reflex. His features flattened out as if he were an android unplugged from its power source. His whole body went still. It was like watching a boy turn himself to stone.

Then he pushed his plate away.

"I'm done," he said.

Trevor strode over to the table, picked up Mike's plate, and slammed it back down in front of him. Our glasses vibrated in unison, and the nearly empty bottle of No Name barbecue sauce toppled over onto its side. Kelli put her hands over her ears and began to hum.

"Trevor," I said after a moment. He turned to me.

"Do you know," said Trevor, "how ashamed your mother was of you?"

I told myself: *This feels like a punch in the gut because it was meant to be a punch in the gut. It was wielded like a punch in the gut. But you don't have to respond to it like a punch in the gut. You don't have to agree. That is, don't crumple—don't cave in.* I glanced over at Mike to see if he was still made of stone, but he'd relaxed a little now that Trevor was addressing me. I was already beginning to understand Trevor's rhythms via Mike's instinctive strategies. You keep your shield up until the adversary's back is turned. And then you take your breather.

"Hey," I said. "I'm sorry I said Irene was isolated. Obviously she wasn't. I just meant—"

"She *was* fuckin' isolated," said Trevor. "She was the loneliest woman I ever fuckin' met, if you wanna know the truth!"

I shook my head, because this wasn't true. The choir. The committees. The bake sales.

"She had friends," I said.

"She was *sick*!" said Trevor. "You know what happens to friends when friends get sick? Friends fuckin' leave! And who's left then? Family! Only Rini didn't have that, did she? She was lucky if she got a lousy fuckin' phone call every other month!"

The kitchen was reverberating with the noise of Trevor's voice. It disoriented me—this was not Irene Petrie's kitchen as I had ever experienced it before. And neither had my sister. Kelli was actively trying to drown Trevor out as she rocked with her hands over her ears, muttering, *NoTrebie No.* Mike, to my surprise, had resumed eating his burger. It was like he had sidestepped this reality and gone back to the more peaceful one from a few moments before—the reality where I hadn't angered Trevor and all was well.

"She always told me she was fine!" I felt a damp heat begin to prickle from my armpits, and I knew I was rising to Trevor's anger despite myself.

"And that was great fuckin' news for you, wasn't it? Because you never had to lift a finger! She didn't need some goddamn 'team,' she needed her daughter! But you were too busy seeing to your own needs, I guess. You were too busy being selfish and getting massages and manicures and hitting the bars and god knows what else!"

I almost began to laugh. Trevor, it seemed to me, was veering off the rails.

"Hitting the bars," I repeated.

"Once you became the gay divorcée over there in Toronto," Trevor pronounced. "Oh, Rini told me all about it, don't you worry!"

"All about what?" I said. Now the heat had invaded my face, the same the way it had with Jessica in the driveway. "I got divorced, it sucked! That's all my mother knew, and that's all she wanted to know. She didn't give a shit!"

A moment ago, Trevor had seemed on the verge of foaming at the mouth, but now he grew still and folded his arms.

"Maybe she didn't give a shit," he said, "because she had no sympathy for a woman who'd walk out on her husband."

I reeled. "I didn't walk out on him!" Was this what Irene had told Trevor? Had my mother just assumed it must be all my fault? "He walked out on me!"

"No, Karie," Kelli muttered at the other end of the table.

"Horse. *Shit,*" said Trevor, bending at the waist, toward me, to give special emphasis to the second word. An air of glee had overtaken him. "He walked out on you because you didn't give a shit about anyone but yourself. That's what's always been your problem—Rini said as much. You were working all the time, leaving him to his own devices—"

"I was *working?*" I sputtered. *Working* had been my spousal trespass?

"You never made him a priority. You never made anyone a priority. It was always about you, your own needs. That's been you from day one. And you're still fuckin' doing it! And *then!*"

"And then *what?*" I shouted. I was surprised to hear myself shout, because a dull voice inside me this whole time had been mumbling something along the lines of: *Fair enough. That's what Irene said? Well, no surprise. Wasn't that the subtext of all those fines over the years?* That was my internal monologue. But the external effect of hearing all this was that my face was on fire and I was white-knuckling the edge of the table and barking in panicked response to Trevor's *And then.* And then what? What was coming next? Maybe something worse. Something I didn't even have the advantage of already knowing.

"And then—you wonder why the guy has to get shit-faced every night just to put up with you! You wonder why he's off chasing co-eds!"

I rolled my eyes. Was this the best he had? "'Co-eds'?" I tried to infuse my voice with as much big-city disdain as I could. If Trevor was going to press my buttons, I could press his. "Nobody's called them co-eds since, like, the sixties." I hoped to convey in my tone the unspoken final part of that sentence, which to my mind was: *you ignorant fucking redneck.*

But Trevor didn't even seem to hear me, let alone register my subtext.

"Christ, I feel sorry for the poor guy. Sending you signals right and left. But they just go sailing over your head because you got it so far up your own arse. 'You resent my relationship with young people.'" Trevor bobbled his head, quoting this line in a plummily accented, cartoon-pompous voice meant to evoke effeminacy, among other undesirable, to Trevor's mind, male qualities. He was sketching a quick impression of what he imagined a man who was married to me would be like. "And you standing there acting like you have no idea what he's talking about!"

Now I understood what was happening. Trevor was strip-mining our conversation from a few nights ago. I had told him about my marriage breakup in an almost semiconscious state, but Trevor, it turned out, had been on high alert the whole time, hoarding all the jagged little details. Only how many of these details had he gotten from me, and how many from Irene? I couldn't remember all the things I'd said to Trevor that night. I knew, however, that I would never have used a word like *co-eds.*

"He was *fucking* them co-eds!" Trevor crowed. "Six ways from Sunday! And no wonder!"

A glass went soaring across the room. We all watched as it sailed past the fridge, where I had more or less aimed, and instead flew through the entryway, down into the foyer, shattering in the place where all of us had taken off our shoes.

Trevor looked at me with satisfaction. "Gonna be a mess," he said.

I said he should leave.

"I'm not the one flinging dishes around." Trevor seemed calmer, pleased now that I had acted out, as if I'd ceded the moral high ground altogether, leaving him king of that particular mountain.

"It's getting late," I said. "You should probably be getting Mike home."

Trevor, who'd been leaning against the counter, now straightened up and clapped his hands at Mike.

"Let's go, buddy," he said. "Damn right I'm not exposing my kid to *this* bullshit."

"I want ice cream, though," said Mike after a moment.

"We got it at home."

"No we *don't*," said Mike.

"Jesus Christ!" bellowed Trevor.

"Take it!" I jumped up and went to the freezer. "Just take it with you." I grabbed the ice cream and tucked it, for some reason, under my arm. Trevor watched as I moved around him to get a plastic bag from beneath the sink. Even though he was standing in my way, he didn't give any ground, so I had to maneuver carefully in order not to come into physical contact with him. This whole time the tub of ice cream was turning my right breast into a block of ice. Finally I stuffed the ice cream into the plastic bag and held it out to him, but Trevor didn't take it. So I put it on the table in front of Mike. Neither Mike nor Trevor moved. Mike was watching Trevor, and Trevor was watching me with an expression like I'd just finished performing some kind of filthy, degenerate act in front of him and his son.

"Thank you for the barbecue," I said.

"What more do you want me to do?" said Trevor.

"I don't want you to do anything," I said.

"Oh, *that's* fuckin' hilarious. If it wasn't for me, someone woulda carted ol' Beaner off to the group home long ago. Before her sister got her fuckin' killed."

I wasn't going to rise to this. Something about my maneuver with the tub of ice cream, radiating coldness into my boob and armpit, had brought me back to myself—settled me in a way I hadn't been able to settle myself when I'd been in the driveway hollering at Jessica Hendy. Trevor was still spoiling for more of a fight, but I wasn't going to give it to him.

"Kelli and I are fine," I said.

"Fine!" repeated Trevor. "Just like your poor ol' mum was fine, eh? She's sick and dying and alone but, sure! As long as everything's *fine*." Trevor's face transformed in the short time it took him to speak these last two sentences. At the evocation of Irene, his jaw squared and his lips whitened and his face became a mask of aggrieved nobility. His voice even trembled on cue at the words *dying and alone.* It was building to something, this abrupt and ersatz show of emotion. I thought Trevor might actually be preparing to squeeze out a couple of tears, just to demonstrate, once and for all, who cared about our mother most.

But that's not what he did. He turned toward the counter and, with his forearm, swept the dishpan, which had a few plates and some cutlery in it, into the sink and onto the floor. Nothing broke, but the clatter of the dishes and silverware against stainless steel was tremendous. It caused Kelli, who'd only just removed her hands from her ears, to start hollering—an affronted jumble of *Trebie*s punctuated by loud, emphatic *no*s. Trevor glanced over at her, startled. He'd never been yelled at by Kelli before.

"*You* get to break the dishes," Trevor argued with me, even though I was not the one who had reproached him. "Why don't I get to break dishes? Eh? I'm the wounded party over here. Why don't I get to break a few dishes?" He picked up a heavy glass water jug from the table and weighed it in his hands. He shook his head, lips still pursed, as if to convey how unfortunate he found this situation, this sad circumstance that had come to pass through no fault of his own.

I glanced again at Mike, hoping for some kind of guidance. But Mike was no help. He was still in his stone-boy alternative reality. He'd even taken his game out from the pocket of his hoodie, and although he hadn't turned it on, he was scrutinizing its every angle as if it were some kind of alien artifact that had just dropped into his hands.

All I could do, I realized, was wait to see what Trevor would decide to do with the jug.

He'd been watching me the whole time, and the moment I resigned myself to this—that the situation was entirely in his hands—was the moment he grinned and put the jug back down on the table.

"Ah well," said Trevor. "I guess someone has to be the grown-up." He clapped his hands again at Mike, who stuffed his game into the pocket of his hoodie and stood up.

Tomorrow I would call and change the locks.

28

I was young enough when my father died that I remember him mostly as a series of haphazard, blown-out snapshots—as if there'd been a monkey with a Polaroid camera running around the house back then, snapping photos from behind the couch or under the table, or else unbearably close, while perched on his subject's chest or shoulders, maybe—and those became my memories. Stubbled face, rosy with broken blood vessels, argyle socks, shoes like boats. Hairy chest in summer, white then pink then, finally, a peeling, late-August red. Flat and bald on top, like a landing pad for a mini-helicopter to alight on. And then there were the noises he brought into the room, minor masculine earthquakes marking emotional atmospheric shifts—his noises were always bigger than anyone else's, demanding more attention. The clichéd Daddy-laugh—that is, the booming laugh, the vibrations of which you could feel in your tiny chest, as if your body were being invaded by it. And anger too, sometimes, the resonant shouts, coming usually from the kitchen, from the bedroom—almost never occurring in the same room as my sister and me, but somewhere just off to the side. My mother never yelled in response, because yelling was vulgar. She was a snapper, though, and occasionally a hisser. She would snap at him to keep it down. She would not, she often told me, be *drawn* by my father's outbursts. As far as she was concerned, he was like a toddler throwing a fit on these occasions, and she treated him that way—maybe infuriating him all the more, or maybe giving him what he wanted—until he'd hollered himself out.

But, she said, he would be sweet afterward, also like a toddler. He'd be worn out and a little abashed and always wanted to do something to make it up. Often he'd dash down to the store to pick us up "treats"—a rainbow pack of freezies for me and Kelli, maybe an Arctic Bar for Irene. Or sometimes he'd load us into the car to go with him, making an excursion of it. I have a sense of my father's desperation in those days; I associate it with a smell: the blue splash of Aqua Velva he'd pat on his cheeks before leaving the house. To me it was the smell of urgency—the urgency with which he called us to the car, and the forced ceremony of it, like he was performing an impulsive ritual, a warding off of something, similar to how my mother crossed herself every time she passed a church or graveyard. Having herded us into the small, sacred space of the family hatchback—mother and father in front, the two little girls safely belted into the back—he'd give us a shared destination involving the joyful consumption of sugary treats, have us sing songs, exchange knock-knock jokes, forget the world outside awhile. Forget, even, the house, the family home—leave behind the place where we'd been off in separate rooms, listening to his shouts muffled by the walls between us. Just be in the car, be the family unit, on the move and inescapably together.

My mother always said that she never took Dad's temper "amiss." You should always forgive men's anger, she told me once, because they "don't know any other way. It's part of how they love." When they're boys, they pull your pigtails. When they're men, they yell and break things. But then they calm themselves, feel stupid, and life goes back to normal. My father's occasional temper tantrums were, she said, his way of staying "healthy." Although it had always seemed to me that his heart attack at forty-nine stood in opposition to this theory.

I thought about my father's anger that night as I lay awake in bed, trying to intellectualize why Trevor's anger in the kitchen had disturbed me so much. Trying to come up with a reason for my unease that was anything but the most obvious reason of all, I think now. I told myself it had to do with my father. It had reminded me of him, had tweaked a deeply submerged and perhaps upsetting childhood memory of shouts in a nearby room. This was perhaps my way of telling myself that everything would be okay. Because things were always okay after my father got mad. But, of course, Trevor's anger had been nothing like my father's. His anger wasn't of the wholesome, shouty variety, where the experience is akin to an emotional orgasm and the shouter feels flushed and almost pleasant afterward, having dislodged something from deep within himself. No, Trevor's anger had been flat and steady, and to me he seemed in perfect control of it, which, according to my mother, my father never was. It didn't feel like Trevor's anger had surprised or blindsided him, or had been building to a climax. It felt like it had been there all along beneath the surface, like buried cables, humming with information.

First thing the next morning, I tried Jessica, but there was no answer. It was too early to be calling, clearly. That was why she didn't pick up. Jessica was probably mad at me, yes. Undoubtedly. But I didn't think she'd just avoid my calls. I was pretty sure she wouldn't. She would have been entirely within her rights to turn on her heel and abandon me in the driveway the moment I'd slapped her. To never talk to me again. But she hadn't. She'd stayed and grounded herself and tried to reel me back to earth with her steady eye contact and low-voiced *Karen*s. *Hey, I'm sane now,* I wanted to tell her. *Sorry about all that.* I wanted to explain that I'd been caught up in having a secret brother these last few days, how it had felt like a last grasp at Irene—I understood this now. I had been crazy in the way of grief-maddened people, devoting themselves and their every last dollar to charlatan psychics who claim to bring messages back from the grave. I had been hoping for the same thing, perhaps. A final message. A benediction. I thought Trevor would be the one to give it to me. But something had gone wrong and things had taken a strange and ugly turn and what I really wanted now was Jessica. My need for Jessica to forgive me was almost physical, like a hunger. I didn't think I could go on without it. I felt monstrous, the way a werewolf must feel after a night of rampaging, waking up bewildered and horrified, blood under his fingernails, human shreds between his teeth.

I picked up my phone to try her again a couple of hours later, but it rang in my hand before I could call up her number. The display told me: GORSEBROOK RESIDENTIAL.

"Karen, hello!" Marlene sounded like she had gotten her mojo back since last we'd spoken—her voice was back to being warm and caressing. She said she had good news. "I've been calling all our clients to let them know. Jeremy was returned to us safely approximately eight hours after he went missing."

"Eight hours?"

"We would've let you know sooner, but first we wanted to conduct a thorough investigation as to what went wrong. It turns out a relative had taken him out on a day pass, but the information wasn't logged."

"So he was safe the whole time?"

"Yes!" said Marlene. I could hear the relieved smile in her voice. "We still don't have a satisfying explanation for how the documentation disappeared—we're very meticulous about that. It was an unforgivable oversight, and the person responsible has been let go."

"Where did Jeremy go?" I asked.

"Where?" said Marlene, surprised by the question. "Well, apparently his sister took him to IKEA. And then to eat at Swiss Chalet. Two of his favorite destinations, from what I understand."

I laughed a little. I wondered if Kelli would like to go to IKEA sometime.

"Karen, I hope you'll still consider us for your sister. I want you to know that a bed has come up, if you're interested. It should be ready in about a month. A couple have come available, actually."

"Oh," I said. Marlene's tone had darkened when she'd said *a couple,* and I intuited why. "Because of what happened with Jeremy?"

"Yes, I'm afraid. But if you'd like to stake a clai—"

"What I'd like," I interrupted, "is to sign Kelli up for your day program. And then let's just see how we do."

I hung up with the same exhilarated feeling I'd had after Eleanor Mallon had come to visit. Like I'd gone from room to room, throwing open the windows of the house, flooding it with clean, oxygenated air. Things were moving again. Gorsebrook was back on. This time, I vowed, I wouldn't let myself get mired down; I would ride the momentum downhill, out of this house, into our condo on the other side of the harbor and the accompanying new stage of life.

It had been easy to turn down Marlene's offer of a bed for Kelli. I stood there holding my phone after the conversation, trying to remember why I'd ever thought I needed a bed in the first place. The decision to move here, to give up my house and job, had seemed monumental enough at the time—the idea of taking Kelli on full-time in addition to all that had been too much to get my head around. But now I had the day program. I had Eleanor Mallon's brochures—*Meet Your Team*. I was equipped, and, for all my earlier screwups, I knew that I was capable. But all that wasn't really why I changed my mind. What changed my mind was the simple fact that at some point over the past few weeks, the idea of placing Kelli in a home had become unthinkable.

Unthinkable in the way it had always been to my mother, I realized. Here I was at last, after all those years at odds with Irene, standing in her shoes, in her house, understanding her completely. By no means could Kelli be put into *One of Those Terrible Places,* no matter how un-terrible Gorsebrook might actually be. It was terrible enough to think of her apart from me. Not that I was capitulating entirely to my mother's martyrlike approach to caregiving—Irene had been far too stubborn in taking all of it on herself. If only she had reached for the competent, professional help that could have eased her burden. If only she had looked beyond Trevor. Then again, who could blame her? Trevor had had the advantage of being there precisely when my mother's need for help arose—filling up the doorframe, blocking out the light. Shooing her back inside.

But I wasn't going to think about Trevor today. Today I would focus, at last, on the future.

Later on, in the afternoon, I figured Jessica was apt to pick up if I called, but at the last moment my nerve failed me and I decided to send her a Facebook message instead. Facebook was the place where we'd first rekindled our childhood acquaintance, after all. The impulse was kind of like that of a spurned boyfriend, taking his girl to the park bench where they'd had their first kiss.

"Jessica," the message began, "this is my official apology for being an insane idiot."

After an hour of composing and deleting multiple drafts, some terse and weirdly legalistic, others self-consciously informal and filled with lame parenthetical asides—"Things have been stressful (as you well know, haha)" and "I overreacted in the driveway (understatement of the year!!)"—I just deleted everything but the first line and asked her to forgive me.

Then I told her I was taking Kelli to Gorsebrook tomorrow and could she meet me for coffee nearby? And I said I understood if she didn't want to see me again.

Moments later, bobbing dots appeared in the message window beneath what I had typed. I watched them rise and fall for an approximate eternity, until finally a two-word message arrived.

"Of course," it read.

And then another came: "I'll pick you up at Gorsebrook."

I put my laptop aside and stood up from the couch. I paced a little, full of energy. Kelli glanced up, as if expecting me to make some kind of announcement. And then I did. I told her I was taking her to Swiss Chalet for supper that night.

DEAR KARIE, it began, (AND DEAR KELLI). The folded note had been stuck to the door with a ragged piece of duct tape that looked as if it'd been chewed off the roll.

SORRY I GOT ALL UPSET. MY TEMPER IS WHAT I LIKE LEAST
ABOUT MYSELF AND SOMETIMES THE PEOPLE I LOVE DON'T
LIKE IT MUCH EITHER. ANYHOW I APOLOGIZE. YOU GUYS
WILL ALWAYS BE MY TWO FAVORITE PEOPLE. I KNOW RINI
WOULD WANT ME TO DO EVERYTHING I CAN FOR YOU GUYS.

SHE TOLD ME THAT A LOT BEFORE SHE DIED SO IF IT SEEMS
LIKE I PUSH TOO HARD SOMETIMES THAT IS WHY.

BUT LISTEN I AM HERE NO MATTER WHAT. PERIOD THE
END. YOU CAN CALL ME ANYTIME AND I HOPE YOU WILL
OK.

TREV

Underneath the TREV, he'd drawn a happy face. He'd also stuck a
couple of happy faces, maybe as an afterthought, to lighten the tone, in
two of the o's of the final sentence. In the HOPE and the OK.

I stood on the step and read it a couple of times, until Kelli, standing beside me and wanting to be let inside, began to get huffy. I'd
gone the whole day not thinking about Trevor—looking forward
into the sunny new beginning represented by Gorsebrook tomorrow,
as opposed to backward into the upsetting past of yesterday's barbecue. It had felt like a psychologically healthy decision in the moment,
but now, standing at our front door, I realized that this decision had
meant that in putting Trevor out of my mind, I'd done the same thing
with my plan of changing the locks. And now it was too late in the
day for that.

As I unlocked the door to let Kelli barrel past me into the house,
a high-voiced *Hullo!* sounded somewhere behind me. I turned to see
Noel from across the street hurrying up the driveway. He wobbled
with a slight old-man limp, indicating a bad knee or maybe a touch
of bursitis.

"Noel," he said, as if I wouldn't have remembered him from the
night Arun Gill's garage was broken into, when he'd bemoaned his
inability to defend the street with his locked-away Remington.

"Yes, hi, Noel," I said.

My neighbor's face was stern and officious, like a G-man's. "Some
asshole poking around your house this afternoon," he said. "Thought
I should let you know."

I smiled and waved the note at him. "Yes—the asshole left a note.
That's okay—we know him."

"Oh, I know him too," said Noel, continuing to grimace. "Never liked the look of the prick, between you and me."

I figured it must've been Noel's hypervigilance when it came to neighborhood safety that colored his perception of Trevor—commingled with maybe just a hint of middle-class disdain. Trevor, he knew, didn't live here. And didn't look like he would live here. Therefore Trevor did not belong.

"He's my sister's care worker," I explained.

"Well—" said Noel, dialing down the pugnacity a notch or two when he saw I wasn't about to get up in arms with him. "I just thought you should know he was poking around when you weren't here. I used to tell your mother the same thing."

"You told my mother he was poking around?"

"Oh, he was in and out like he owned the place," griped Noel. "My dad had workers looking in on him for years—he'd had a stroke in his sixties, made it hard to get around—but none of them had a key. No one was letting themselves in when he wasn't around. She shouldn't have allowed that."

"Wait," I said. "Did Trevor let himself in today?"

"No, no," said Noel, "I didn't see that if he did. Just irritates me, seeing him back here. Your poor mother."

"Why my poor mother?"

"The way he was always hanging off her. Never giving her a moment's peace. I think she made the mistake of slipping him a few extra dollars one time, and after that he never left her alone."

I had a sudden feeling like the surrounding houses of my mother's neighborhood constituted magic portals of a sort, the door to each leading to an alternate reality. Mr. Gill's door led you into the reality where Trevor and Irene were a blissful, bonded, mutually appointed mother and son. But now I had just peeked beyond Noel's door to the world as he saw it. And Noel's take was something altogether different. As Noel kept talking, face pinkening, winding himself up again, I got the feeling he'd been wanting to vent on this subject for a while now.

"Walking her to the goddamn car, walking her into the house," said Noel. "Never letting anyone say a word to her—"

"He wouldn't let you talk to her?"

"Acted like a goddamn prison guard," complained Noel. "I got my snow blower out last winter after the first big dump—I do everyone's driveways. Your mom comes running out of the house, 'Oh, no, Noel, you better not. He won't like it.' 'He won't like it,' I say. 'What won't he like about me taking five minutes to clear out your goddamn driveway?' 'He likes to do it himself,' she says. 'Jesus Christ,' I tell her, 'whose driveway is it, yours or his?'"

"Did she ever," I said, glancing down the street toward Mr. Gill's house, "talk about Trevor to you? Like, did she tell you who he was?"

"I knew he helped looking after your sister," said Noel. "I saw them out for a walk the first time he started coming over—had no idea who he was, and let me tell you, I was out the door like a shot. Thought she was being kidnapped."

I smiled at the thought of this. Imagine Trevor's reaction to this high-voiced old man stumping over to him from across the street, demanding to know what he thought he was doing with my sister. Noel, it struck me now, was the quintessential nosy neighbor. He had the real scoop on Trevor because he'd demanded it from the very second he'd clapped eyes on this invader. Mr. Gill, on the other hand, had been newer to the neighborhood, and clearly more of a minder-of-his-own-business. Unlike Noel, he'd never asked who Trevor was to my mother—he had, at some point, been told. And told a lie. And I had just assumed that the person doing the telling was Irene.

29

The genius of the Gorsebrook day program was that it commenced with the distribution of snacks. The atmosphere in the common room was a clamorous free-for-all at first, and I couldn't imagine how the workers planned to get everyone under control. The participants were rushing to and fro, poking at one another, shouting and shrieking laughter—it was a cacophony, and I could tell my sister found it overwhelming. But Marlene kept us at the outskirts of the action, explaining that this was just the usual pre-program blowing off of steam and very soon things would become orderly and structured. She introduced us to the two coordinators, a short, plushy woman named Lina who would've looked like a librarian if it wasn't for her hair, which was a nicely faded seapunk blue, and a gangly young man called Ian with a ponytail and a South Shore accent. Seeing them side by side, it was hard to not think of Jack Sprat and his wife. In fact, they did have the air of being versions of each other, the way husbands and wives sometimes did—they were both soft-voiced, smiling, and held their eye contact to a near-uncomfortable extent as they shook my hand, as if to ensure that I understood that they were *seeing* me. Kelli shook their hands as well but didn't have much use for the eye contact.

I was worried. The crowd and clamor made Kelli turn in on herself, and she'd been staring at the tiled floor and covering her ears intermittently since we'd arrived. Additionally, a stocky boy had barreled up to us like a speedy little tank almost as soon as we arrived, causing Kelli to rear like a horse. He'd only meant to greet Marlene, but he had been pleased to be introduced to me and Kelli and insisted on giving us both hugs.

"Kelli's not so much into hugs," I told Marlene. The moment I said it I realized I was doing the thing that most annoyed me whenever strangers did it to Kelli. I was talking over and not to the boy, taking it for granted that he wouldn't understand.

"Kelli doesn't like hugs, I'm afraid, Arthur," said Marlene.

"But I'd like one, please," I said.

The boy—who I call a boy because that's how he seemed to me, with his shy grin and the excited way he bounced from foot to foot, but who, I should note, had an older man's bald spot—smiled and flung his arms around me. Someone had doused his hair in some kind of spicy pomade that morning and combed it flat over his bald spot, which I was now observing and inhaling up close because it was directly under my nose.

"Wekkome," said Arthur, releasing me. "I wekkome you. Wekkome you too, Kewwi."

"No," said Kelli peevishly as Arthur vroomed off to welcome someone else.

On the other side of the room, Ian started clapping his hands. "Snack, folks! Snack time! Get in your chairs!"

Lina approached Kelli and spoke directly to her. "Kelli? Would you like to sit and have a snack with us? Then maybe we can play some games afterward."

"Snack," said Kelli suspiciously. She shot a quick glance up at Lina.

I turned to her and spoke with all the heartiness I could muster: "That sounds great, eh, Kell?"

Marlene came too, and we all settled in at the long worktable with the other "program participants," as they were referred to at Gorsebrook. Lina chatted with Kelli, introducing her to some of the people nearby as everyone studiously unpeeled the parchment from their morning glory muffins. Marlene, meanwhile, continued to murmur to me about how the program worked and what to expect. The snacks were a way to get everyone settled and at the table, and then the plastic plates and juice glasses would be cleared and craft supplies would be distributed. Later there might be a bit of exercise (simple yoga or rudimentary calisthenics of the head-and-shoulders-knees-and-toes variety, which I could not for the life of me imagine Kelli taking part in), something called a "drum and rhythm circle," and then the day finished off with a variety of easygoing games. Marlene suggested that the best time for me to slip away might be shortly after Kelli became immersed in the post-snack craft portion of the day (assuming, I thought, that she *did* become immersed, as opposed to closing her eyes and covering her ears in protest of the noise and strangeness).

I checked the time on my cracked phone. Jessica was picking me up in about twenty minutes, so hopefully that would be just enough time to get my sister settled.

A young man appeared by Marlene's chair and stood weaving beside her. His manner was similar to Kelli's, in that he was a rocker and a ground-looker-at-er, his head cocked off to the side as if it had been wrenched into that position by some malevolent chiropractor. He clearly wanted something from Marlene, but his stratagem was to assert it with his presence, as opposed to beseeching her with his eyes or voice. He just rocked and waited and wiped his wet mouth on his sleeve.

"Hello, you," said Marlene, taking his hand.

"Finny comin'," said the boy, looking off to the side.

"No, sweetie," said Marlene. "Finny's had to go away, remember? He got a new job."

"Wan' Finny."

"I know, Jeremy. But Finny can't be here today. But Ian's here. And Lina's here. It's going to be a really fun afternoon."

The boy rocked awhile, his expression unchanging. "Huck," he said, and leaned abruptly toward Marlene, still not looking at her.

"Okay, honey," said Marlene, and hugged him. After which, Jeremy toddled away.

"That was Jeremy?" I said. "*The* Jeremy?"

"That was him, our lost little lamb. You can imagine how frantic we were."

"Yeah," I said. "I wouldn't be thrilled at the thought of him wandering the streets on his own."

Marlene grimaced. "Oh, we were far from thrilled. But now he's wondering where Stephen is—they all are. It's always an upheaval when we have to let someone go."

"Stephen?"

"The Finny Jeremy was talking about. Stephen Finn. He only worked half-time in reception, but the residents get very attached. They don't like change."

"He's the one who screwed up the day Jeremy went missing?"

Marlene shook her head, not to indicate "no," but in a kind of an agitated spasm. "He was there when Jeremy's sister checked him out. And then somehow managed to clock off without logging it."

"Did you ever find out what happened? I mean, how the mistake came about?"

Marlene shook her head again. "It was unforgivable. Checking residents in and out was eighty percent of Stephen's job. We had no choice but to let him go." Marlene, to my fascination, was almost scowling—it was the first time she had ever really dropped her PR mask with me. The welcoming and agreeable persona that made her so good at her job slipped in that moment, just enough to show me how completely fucking furious she was at this idiot who had nearly brought the whole place crashing down around her ears.

"It was my own fault," Marlene muttered.

"No, no," I said. "You can't blame yourself."

"I was never crazy about him," she confessed, glancing at me. "But he had a reference from Barnbarroch Manor—so. I don't know if you know that facility—it's swanky."

"I do know Barnbarroch," I said after a moment.

And I knew Finny.

As soon as we were seated with our Americanos, Jessica hauled out the tablet she carried around everywhere for calling up real estate listings. I thought for a second we were about to dive right back into the condo hunt—maybe as a way of avoiding the elephant in the room that was the recollection of my open palm whomping her across the face—but instead, when I leaned over, I saw that she had typed the name "Stephen Finn" into her browser's search bar. Several photos of a soap-star-handsome cricket player popped up, his toothy smile multiplied across the page.

"He's a residential care worker," I said. "I don't know how much of an online presence he would have."

Jessica went back to the search bar and added the name of the city we were in. She had a miniature keyboard for her tablet and hunched over it, tapping away. She hadn't said much since we sat down.

"What are you looking for, exactly?" I asked.

"I want to see what this guy looks like," said Jessica.

I'd started relaying the story of Stephen Finn almost the moment I'd climbed into Jessica's car, figuring it would make for the ideal ice-breaker, which I felt we were in need of. Also because I was still mulling over the weird coincidence of what I'd learned from Marlene—how this person I'd encountered during the pointless field trip with Trevor out to Barnbarroch should be the person whose incompetence had almost derailed my sister's Gorsebrook adventure.

"I met him," I reminded her. She raised her eyes from the screen.

"So what did he look like?"

I tried to remember. "Grumpy," I said. "He wasn't pleased about letting us in. It was a favor to Trevor."

"Physically, though," said Jessica.

I thought about it. I tried to conjure up an image of Finny the man, the physical specimen. I remembered forearms bristling with dark hair, holding the door open for us. He'd addressed Trevor briskly, in monosyllables, but not Kelli and me. I remembered looking past him, trying to see into the impressive foyer. There'd been no time for introductions, because he had to get back to work.

I shrugged. "Just kind of . . . medium build, I guess. A little stocky, maybe."

Jessica turned back to the screen and resumed pecking. I looked around. We were at a coffeeshop on Argyle, surrounded by people doing more or less the exact same thing Jessica was on their various devices. I was starting to feel impatient. I wanted her to put away the tablet and look at me, to get on with the post-slap conversation, to make sure she and I were okay. To apologize as many more times as might be necessary and have her reassure me that all was forgiven and our friendship was intact. It felt like maybe all the intensive googling was Jessica's way of circumnavigating that. Maybe she was less willing to forgive and forget than I'd been counting on.

"Why do you want to *see* him?" I asked finally.

"This guy," said Jessica, turning the tablet toward me. I squinted at the picture on the screen. It was a group photo, taken outdoors, of what looked to be a softball team. The photo was featured on the website for a facility called Arborville Advanced Care—a nursing home, apparently. The team was co-ed, of all ages and shapes—staff members, clearly. They called themselves, the caption informed me, the Arborville Anteaters, which I thought was rather playful. The photo, the caption also mentioned, was three years old.

Below the caption, the names of the teammates were listed, and I saw from a glance that one of those names was Stephen Finn.

Jessica tapped a fingernail against the screen, at a spot where a man was standing in the front, at the very end of the row. He was posed in a way that stood out from all the other members of his team, facing forward, toward the camera, instead of inward, as everyone else had clearly been instructed to do. Everyone else had also been instructed to "squeeze in," it looked to me, their bodies packed cozily together, and Stephen Finn was the only one who had refused. As a result, he stood distinctly apart from his teammates, as if he'd arrived late or had been standing there minding his own business when a softball team decided to congregate for a photo and he just happened to be caught in the frame. His nonconforming attitude toward the camera struck me as almost belligerent. And it was the belligerence I recognized before anything else.

I looked up at Jessica. "That's the guy from the fucking parking lot," she said.

I wasn't sure. I had been sure a moment ago, when I'd had that flash of recognition, but now, scrutinizing pixelated Stephen Finn, I wasn't sure.

"It's him," said Jessica.

I squinted at her tablet's screen. Stephen Finn had the dad bod of the parking lot screamer, yes, and the goatee grown to cover a babyish pair of cheeks, but his expression in the photo was slack and vague, whereas the face of the man in the parking lot had been taut and pulsating. It was hard to compare the two.

"I don't know," I said.

"It's him," said Jessica. "Do you realize what that means?"

I looked up at her. She could see I realized what that meant, but she said it anyway.

"Trevor is friends with the guy from the parking lot."

I flashed on what Noel had said. How Trevor never gave my mother a moment's peace.

"Please tell me," said Jessica, "he hasn't been coming around anymore."

I thought about the note on the door. I AM HERE NO MATTER WHAT.

"He's not," I assured her. "We had a parting of ways."

"But you've said that before," said Jessica.

This surprised me. "I did?"

"At the yard sale. You said, 'We kind of said good-bye' after you gave him the TV. And the next thing I know, he's alone in the house with Kelli and you're slapping me in the face in your driveway."

I winced. There it was at last, plopped down onto the table between us. "I know," I said. "I'm sorry. I don't know what was going on with me." Of course, I did know what had been going on with me—I knew precisely. I remembered Trevor's shouldery silhouette looming behind Kelli in the window on the day I slapped Jessica. I had turned to glance at the house and there they were, Kelli and her protective shadow. I'd spent the previous half hour in a cold panic about Eleanor

Mallon and, in spite of everything that happened afterward, I couldn't deny the feeling that his silhouette had given me in the moment. That things would be handled and we were not alone.

"Anyway," I went on, "we kind of had a fight the other night. He started acting like a tool and I told him to get out."

Jessica went still and looked at me. "What did he do?"

"Nothing," I said. "Just started acting snotty. He gets mad when anyone disagrees with him."

"What did he do?" she asked again.

"Nothing," I said again. "He left."

Jessica frowned. "I had a friend," she blurted. Then she stopped. "Okay, actually, no. This is a story my psychiatrist told me about one of his patients. This woman kept getting into accidents. She was in her seventies, a grandma. And all her life she'd been accident-prone. She tripped coming down the stairs and twisted her ankle. She knocked her head with the cupboard doors practically every other day, so that her husband duct-taped sponges all along the edges. She broke glassware in the dishpan and cut her hands to shreds, that kind of thing. Her kids thought she shouldn't drive, but she was a perfect driver—never had a ticket in her life. Anyway, one of her daughters finally noticed that this was happening whenever her mother got upset about something, whenever there was upheaval. For example, when one of her kids announced out of the blue that he was getting married, she got up from the table, tripped over the open dishwasher door, and went sprawling. Sprained her wrist."

"So it was like an unconscious manipulation," I said. "To get people to look after her."

Jessica shook her head. "No! She never let anyone raise a finger for her. She was a woman of our mothers' generation, you know? The grin-and-bear-it generation, the women who were raised not to cause a ruckus. So she just kept her feelings inside and compulsively bashed the crap out of herself whenever something made her feel bad. It was a pathology."

"I don't do that," I said after a moment.

"What you do is worse," said Jessica. "You stand there as the roof is falling in, and when the pieces land on your head you're like, 'Oh well—serves me right for letting the roof fall in, I guess.'"

I decided not to let this hurt my feelings. "Okay, but I'm not like that anymore. I know I was stuck in that house for a while—"

"I'm not talking about the house," said Jessica.

"—but I'm moving forward now," I insisted.

"You keep giving him all this leeway," said Jessica.

"No," I said, becoming defensive. "It was my mother. My mother's the one who gave him all the leeway. I took my cues from her—"

I broke off, sounding whiny even to my own ears. I wasn't just arguing with Jessica anymore. I was arguing with the droning voice in my head that had been low-key jeering at me ever since I'd talked to Noel. Right now it was saying: *But you didn't actually take your cues from Irene, did you? You took your cues from someone else, a stranger. Someone who told you stories of Irene. Which you decided, for some reason, to believe.*

"Did it ever occur to you," said Jessica, "that Trevor might've been the one who called Adult Protection on you?"

I kept my face neutral. It felt a little awkward for her to be broaching this topic, because I'd thought we'd both basically accepted the idea that it had been Jessica's—let's face it—meddling that had led to Eleanor Mallon arriving at my doorstep.

"It wouldn't make sense for him to do that," I said at length.

"If he got Finny to scare you in the parking lot, it would," said Jessica. "If he did that, what wouldn't he do to scare you? He'd do anything."

"But why would he want to scare us? He loves—Kelli. He loved my mother."

"Oh, for fuck's sake!" yelled Jessica, causing the surrounding keyboard peckers to glance over from their screens in one synchronized motion, as if choreographed. "Love is the excuse these people use! Love is what they *use*!"

I marveled at how different Jessica suddenly seemed. She grimaced and rolled her eyes in an almost teenage way, raking her fingers through her hair and causing her normally impeccable strands to stand up at cockeyed angles. It threw me to see Jessica Hendy so abruptly mussed and upset. In that moment, I only wanted to calm her, drain the tension from the conversation so we could get back to the business of being friends.

"It doesn't matter," I told her, "because he's never coming back."

Jessica glanced around the room, taking a break from the conversation, trying to decide whether to keep haranguing me or let it go. It would cost her something to keep it up, I could see. It had already cost her poise, her equilibrium, in some fundamental way. We both took a quiet sip of coffee. By the time she turned back to me, she had arranged her features and was back to her ladylike self.

"Listen," she said. "I have some good news."

It turned out that silver-haired Nate had called her just that morning, sounding sheepish. He said that if she felt at all strange about it, he would understand. But the fact was, he and Jason could not dislodge the thought of Irene Petrie's house from their minds. If she, Jessica, was still even doing business with the monstrous homeowner who had assaulted her in the driveway, they would like to make an offer.

30

discovered my sister at one of the long communal tables where I'd left her, only now she was contentedly rolling colored clay beneath her palm. She'd roll it and roll it until it started to resemble a worm, and when she felt she was finished she'd hand the worm off to a fellow crafter, who would shape it into hearts and rainbows and the like. There was a candy-colored array of Kelli and her partner's creations spread out on the table in front of them. The most elaborate one was a face—one big long worm to form the circle of the head, two little circles for the eyes (with two tiny clay balls that had been squashed flat for the irises), a couple of worms curved into C's for the ears, and plenty of long, skinny ones for hair.

"Who is that?" I asked, pointing to the face. I was so delighted by Kelli's output, I wanted to engage with it somehow, ask questions, and this was the only question I could think of.

Kelli's partner, a woman in her forties in a yellow velour tracksuit of the kind I remembered J.Lo and Britney Spears wearing in the early aughts, turned and beamed up at me. "Iss you!" she declared. We had not been introduced at that point, but I went along with it.

"It *does* look like me," I said, smiling down at the circular face and Medusa hair.

"Karie dat," Kelli confirmed with an air of satisfaction.

Around us, balls and drums and beanbags were being gathered up and put away and chairs were being pushed into the tables, their feet scraping musically against the floor, as everyone prepared to go home for the day. Marlene was no longer around, but Lina reported to me that Kelli had been so taken by the craft portion of the day—the Play-Doh shapes—they had allowed her to just sit and roll out worms alongside her tracksuited collaborator for the entire afternoon. They had offered her a drum when it came to drum circle time, but she'd turned up her nose and, as I'd predicted, showed no interest whatsoever in the exercise portion of the day. The modeling clay, however, had been a hit, and Lina explained to me that when something went over as big with one of their participants—especially a newbie—as the clay did with Kelli, their motto tended to be "If it ain't broke, don't fix it."

I couldn't stop looking at the figures Kelli and her partner had produced, the multicolored assemblage of clay snakes and rainbows, hearts, flowers, and trees. *Kelli made these,* I had to keep repeating to myself. Maybe not the shapes themselves, but the raw material for the shapes. She had rolled out the worms of various thicknesses and lengths like a champ. She had collaborated with a peer on an artistic endeavor. My sister had created something. And it was only her first day.

What's more, Kelli liked it here. She didn't want to leave. Prying her away from the table, where she was wedged beside her new tracksuit-wearing bestie, would have been impossible if it weren't for the fact that dinnertime was looming. Lina and I had to explain, over Kelli's objections, that it was time to go home. Even as I argued with Kelli and bribed her with promises of spaghetti, I couldn't stop smiling. My sister loved the day program. It was an overwhelming success. The people were great. The program was great. This was working, and it was going to work.

If Kelli would have permitted it, I'd have taken her in my arms and waltzed her across the parking lot to the car in all my euphoria. This on top of the news about the house. When Jessica told me about Nate's call, it was as if the ceiling of the coffeeshop had cracked open, spilling forth a profusion of balloons. The thing I had wanted so badly for so long was finally happening. It wasn't a dream—or a fantasy, as I had so often feared. And somehow I hadn't managed to sabotage it, even with my behavior in the driveway. The house would go. It was going, and soon it would be gone. Gorsebrook would work. Kelli and I would live nearby, somewhere nice. Somewhere just for us. And Jessica Hendy would be our friend. Yes, things had ended a little awkwardly with Jessica after our coffee, but that was to be expected. I had been so thrilled about the house, so grateful to her for being willing to give our friendship another chance post-slap, that I had maybe overstepped when we'd said good-bye. I'd ambushed her with a hug, which I could tell, as I held her, she wasn't quite up for. So I held her a bit too long to compensate for her lack of enthusiasm, squished her against me to let her know how appreciative I was, but this was the wrong instinct. Jessica went from stiff to limp in my arms, and finally she gave my back a little pat, after which I let her go, feeling like I had physically coerced the gesture.

I'd shaken off the feeling as I'd walked back to Gorsebrook. Jessica would come around. The point was, things were finally getting back on track. Life would go on. It wasn't even that life would go on. It would start up again. At last.

Just as I got Kelli belted in, my phone rang.

"Karen," said Eleanor Mallon, turning businesslike once we'd gone back and forth about the weather a couple of times (noticeably chillier!), "I wanted to let you know I followed up on some of what we talked about the other day. I made inquiries about Bestlife and Gorsebrook Residential, as we discussed."

"Actually," I told her, "we're just leaving Gorsebrook. Kelli spent the afternoon here."

"Oh! And how did she like it?"

"She loved it," I told Eleanor, girding myself to have my good mood quashed. *Please,* I begged silently, *let there be no lawsuits, disapproving health inspectors, media exposés on ponytailed Ian's secret, pervy history of interfering with—*

"I'm so glad!" said Eleanor. "I wanted to assure you I've heard nothing but good things. I really think the incident with Jeremy was a blip."

"I heard he was actually fine the entire time," I said, fizzing with relief. "He was with a family member, it just wasn't logged."

"Yes," said Eleanor. "That's what I heard too."

"But thanks so much for looking into it."

"About Bestlife," she said, and paused. "I think you could do better."

Given Eleanor Mallon's consistently upbeat demeanor since I'd known her, these six words struck me as positively damning.

"Many people I spoke to in the home care industry," she continued, "didn't approve of the practice of pairing male workers with female clients. It's funny, considering the opposite situation is so commonplace . . ."

"Women taking care of men?"

"Yes. Just goes to show . . ." Eleanor trailed off. What did it go to show? That women taking care of men was the natural order of things. Whereas the opposite bordered on perversion.

"However, Bestlife has a lot of staff turnover," continued Eleanor. "Which is a bad sign in itself, I think."

"So you're saying Trevor ended up being assigned to Kelli because they didn't have enough female workers?"

"That's right," said Eleanor. "And that's not normally done. Even your mother had some concerns on that front."

I had placed Eleanor on speakerphone and put the key in the ignition, figuring we could talk as I drove home, but now I stopped, took her off speakerphone, and held the phone up to my ear. It wasn't so much that it mattered if Kelli heard any of the conversation. It was just that I did not want to be distracted; I did not want to miss one word of what Eleanor Mallon said next.

"My mother had concerns? About Trevor? Where did you hear this from?"

"I know a couple of—"

"Did you talk to Margot?" I asked. I scoured my memory for Margot's last name. "Margot in admin? Because she told me—"

"I didn't speak to Margot, no, but I do know some people who've worked there, and they were nice enough to speak candidly with me."

Oh, Miz Petrie. Your mother never gave us any trouble at all. I was going to kill Margot, I decided.

"What were my mother's concerns? Did they tell you?"

"Well, at first she was wary of having a man assigned to your sister, of course."

"But she was fine with Trevor after that, wasn't she?"

"Oh—I think she was," said Eleanor. "She definitely grew fond of him, and everyone said he had a great rapport with Kelli. But your mother did call the office at one point early on to ask if they'd . . ." Eleanor paused. "Not reprimand him, exactly."

The phone was becoming hot against my cheek.

"She didn't want him taken out of rotation," continued Eleanor. "And she was very clear that she didn't want them to mention she'd even called. But she asked that they switch him out with another worker maybe once a week. Just so he wasn't coming over quite so often."

It was at this point that Kelli, who'd been huffing and puffing with impatience in the seat beside me, reached a breaking point and started demanding to know why exactly the car was not moving forward, toward the spaghetti I had promised her for dinner.

"Just a second, Kell," I snapped. "I'm on the phone." After which I took a deep breath, kicking myself for snapping at Kelli within earshot of Eleanor Mallon.

"And did they?" I asked Eleanor. "Did they switch Trevor out with someone else?"

"They didn't," tutted Eleanor. "They told her they didn't have another worker available at the time."

I tried to imagine Margot's face, even though we'd never met. Pasty and soft, like bread dough. Tart, slappable mouth calling you "dear."

"And what," I pressed Eleanor, "did my mother say? When they told her they couldn't switch him out?"

"I believe she told them that she'd manage."

"So that was it? Nothing was done?"

"She didn't call again," said Eleanor. "She assured them she'd be fine."

———

Kelli and I drove home. I ignored her as she complained at all the stoplights—she always did this, taking umbrage at the idea that something as arbitrary as a glowing red circle could arrest her forward motion. "Geen," she would command, every time we hit a red light. "Light geen now, Karie." Normally I would engage, explain that the light was not yet green but red. And Kelli, even though I was pretty sure she knew the difference, would argue about it until the light finally did switch over. Then she'd settle back in her seat with an air of smugness as if she'd been right all along—at least until we hit the next red. But now I had no patience for our usual routines.

We drove across the Angus L. Macdonald Bridge, where there were no lights to antagonize her, and Kelli lost herself for a time, gazing at the downtown cranes and cruise ships in the harbor.

"Do you think she even liked Trevor?" I said.

Kelli glanced at me. "Trebie gone."

"I know," I said. "But I don't know what makes me feel worse. That he looked after her when I didn't. Or that he didn't. Or maybe he did—but she didn't want him to."

"Comin' back," said Kelli.

"Karie," he said. That was it. No deep cuts from the Karie catalog this time, no Karie-me-home or Karie-that-weight. Maybe he'd run out. He answered the phone with a solemn, formal air, like a funeral director.

"Hey, Trevor," I said. "Can we talk?"

"You're goddamn right we can talk," he rejoined, warming up a bit. "You get my note?"

"I did," I said.

"You want me to come by? I can come by tonight. I'll pick up a —"

"Tomorrow," I told him. "How about the Tim Hortons at the bottom of the hill from us? The one I take Kelli to all the time."

"Well, well, well, an afternoon out, eh?" He was thrown by this but tried to sound jovial, as if my insistence on neutral territory in a public setting meant nothing, was simply a novel treat, like when we all decided to go for fish and chips.

"One-thirty or so?"

"Sounds good," said Trevor. "Bringin' ol' Beaner along?"

"No," I said. Kelli would be at Gorsebrook. I experienced a brief compulsion to explain this to Trevor, which I stifled. I could feel his confusion practically humming through the ether, and it gave me satisfaction.

"Okay then," he said. "Good, good."

"I'll see you then," I said. And hung up first.

What was I planning on doing, exactly? People always stop me, when I get to this part of the story, to ask that question, because I can never quite articulate what it is I had in mind. *I was just mad* is what I usually tell them. I remember feeling deceived. Wanting to know the truth. But I know I also wanted to tell Trevor a thing or two. Maybe I wanted to tell him how great things were going with Gorsebrook. How much Kelli loved it. Oh, and that the house had sold. That we'd be moving. That everything was going to change. Then maybe innocently mention how my good friend Jessica Hendy and I—we were friends again, by the way—had discovered the identity of the man who'd shouted abuse at Kelli in the parking lot, and we'd be passing that information on to the cops. Oh, and by the way, Irene never wanted you.

And if Trevor got angry at any of that, if he started looking around the Tim Hortons for a water jug to brandish at me, that's when I would ask: Is that what you did to my mother? Did you fling dishes onto the floor, weigh the jug in your hands at a sick old lady who just wanted you out of her house? Did you berate her for letting other people clear her driveway? Did you say you were her son to make those people go away?

I couldn't have articulated those thoughts at the time. My pulse was going too fast, pounding in my temples, as I waited for him to pick up. All my thoughts and impulses just sloshed around in a kind of undifferentiated stew. If you'd asked me back then what I planned to do when I saw Trevor the next day, I wouldn't have been able to tell you. Just like I can't tell you now what I did end up doing. Because the meeting never took place.

31

B ad guys," exclaimed Kelli, wide awake and smiling to herself as she hovered at my bedside.

I wasn't surprised to see her, exactly—I'd suspected that Kelli might have trouble sleeping after all the excitement of her day at Gorsebrook. But Gorsebrook wasn't what was on my sister's mind this night. Kelli, it seemed, wanted to talk about Arun Gill. She was practically bouncing from foot to foot. It felt almost as if she'd been lying awake obsessing over the man.

"Bad guys Misser Gill's garage," she said.

Kelli brought up Mr. Gill a lot these days. She'd been excited by all the neighborhood action the night the Gill garage was vandalized, and lately she often asked me about "bad guys"—specifically "bad guys in Misser Gill's garage"—because that was how I'd explained the incident to her. It wasn't so much that Kelli was afraid of these bad guys as that every time she thought she heard a noise now, she believed she knew the cause and, furthermore, she hoped that she was right because it had been so much fun seeing all the cop cars on the street, not to mention the neighbors in their bathrobes out in the middle of the night. In short, Kelli was hoping for a replay of poor Arun Gill's misfortune.

"Mr. Gill's probably asleep now, Kell," I said. "He got rid of all the bad guys. Did you hear a noise?"

"Noise," agreed Kelli.

Maybe the ghost is back, I thought, still half-asleep. Which was a funny thing to be thinking, because I hadn't thought about the ghost for weeks. Yes, Kelli still got up from time to time, but she always woke me when she did—just as she was doing now. But there'd been no nocturnally rearranged furniture or messed-up closets since I'd joked about it on the phone to Jessica. I had put the ghost out of my mind—at least, I thought I had.

"Bad guys Misser *Gill*," insisted Kelli, becoming impatient with me because I had closed my eyes again.

"I don't think so," I told her, sitting up. "But go take a look if you want."

Kelli darted back to her room to peer out the window. I could hear her murmuring to herself as she surveyed the street.

"See anything, Kell?"

Kelli lumbered out of her room, whispering. She stood in the hall for a moment or two, rocking slightly, meditative.

"Where those bad guys, Karie?" she asked at last.

"I don't think the bad guys are out tonight."

"No bad guys, no," Kelli allowed, disgruntled.

"Which means maybe it's time to head back to bed, what do you say? Wanna be rested to see your friends at Gorsebrook tomorrow, right?"

I thought the mention of Gorsebrook would light up her eyes, but Kelli just paced and rocked some more, preoccupied. I pulled my covers up to my chin. My goal—as it always was during these episodes of wakefulness on Kelli's part—was to get through this bout without having to get out of bed myself.

"Baffroom," Kelli announced, as I'd known she eventually would.

"Fill your boots," I told her.

But Kelli didn't budge. She just kept weaving and glancing at me, and I got a sinking feeling.

"Baffroom, Karie?"

Which meant she wanted company.

In these instances, Kelli basically just wanted someone to stand in the doorway and banter with her while she did her business. But tonight she was particularly talkative, like she'd just awoken from a thrilling dream. She kept pelting me with bad-guy-related questions, and even though I made my answers as soothing and soporific as I could, nothing seemed to slow her chatter. I was starting to despair of getting her settled down again. As I leaned against the doorframe, rubbing my eyes, it occurred to me to try to troubleshoot. Ever since Kelli had started getting up at night, I realized, I'd been shrugging it off as just another Kelli thing—something she did without rhyme or reason, like rocking and whispering. But everything had a reason, no matter how invisible it might be to me. If something was keeping her up, why shouldn't I be able to discern that something? Why hadn't I even bothered to try before now?

"Why're you so awake, Kelli?" I murmured.

"Bad guys," said Kelli.

Perhaps, I thought, it was something in her diet. She'd been eating a lot of beef lately, due to all the barbecues with Trevor—maybe it was messing with her digestion.

"Your tummy okay?"

"Tummy," said Kelli noncommittally, and yanked a too-large wad of toilet paper off the roll.

But then, thinking of the meals with Trevor, I remembered something else: the pop. Trevor had introduced No Name cola to the household the same time he'd introduced rum, and he'd been handing over tumblerfuls of it to Kelli whenever she so much as inclined her head at the bottle. Now that Kelli had a taste for it, I'd started doing the same. Of course! The caffeine and sugar had to be what was keeping her up. And drinking all that pop was probably making her have to pee. Eureka.

That was when I heard it. *Tink*. Very faint, almost whispery, but entirely recognizable as the noise of an ice cube nudging the side of a glass. Specifically, it was the sound that occurs after the glass is raised and is tipped toward a mouth for a sip to be taken. For a moment I thought perhaps my mind had done something nifty: instead of conjuring up a mental picture of a tumblerful of No Name cola, it had offered up an aural one. I felt, as you do at these times—these times when something completely out of the ordinary is happening and your brain is struggling to provide an unalarming explanation— that maybe I had experienced some kind of psychological anomaly.

Because, of course, I knew the brain didn't normally do that—conjure aural as opposed to mental pictures. But the other thing I knew was that you didn't just hear the sound of an ice cube tinking against the side of a glass when there was not someone nearby tipping a glass with an ice cube in it.

These thoughts went through my head in a microsecond, and I was peering into the darkened living room before I had even finished thinking them—knowing what I was looking for, and seeing it. I didn't feel dread, just comprehension, an almost satisfying feeling like when you're trying to figure out how to assemble something, a confounding piece of IKEA furniture, say, and in a moment of inspiration you maneuver Incomprehensible Fragment A into Mystifying Chamber B and everything snaps into place. That sense of: *I get it.* The mellow streetlights glowed beyond the windows and Mr. Gill's new LED spotlight glared from his garage across the street, and together they cast a somehow stark yet buttery glow around the room, so that the furniture was slightly haloed, outlined as shadowy but recognizable lumps. Along with the shadowy, recognizable lump slouched in the center of the couch. Just as I made him out, he took another sip.

I turned and cajoled Kelli into bed, whispering reassurances about bad guys—because she wasn't finished talking about them, not by a long shot. I assured my sister that the bad guys were in bed, so she should be too, but added that maybe they'd be out in the morning and she could watch them from her perch by the window before heading out to see her friends. After a few further, whispered inquiries, Kelli finally said good night, slumped back into bed, and allowed me to pull her bedroom door almost completely shut. I knew she wouldn't go to sleep, not right away. But she would lie there, whispering excitedly to herself for a while, and those whispers would fill her ears, I hoped, drowning out whatever might be going on down the hall from her room.

I went to my bedroom, pulled on a robe, and grabbed a box of Kleenex.

I didn't turn on any lights. I took a seat in the cushioned armchair—its old springs whimpering as I settled my weight into it—and placed the Kleenex on the coffee table without speaking. I flashed on a memory of a therapist I used to see when I was going through my divorce. She'd had this way of wordlessly placing a box of tissues in front of me every time I started to snivel that I'd found, for no good reason, infuriating. She never rolled her eyes, exactly, but I somehow read contempt in the way she thumped the Kleenex down.

But Trevor didn't seem to read anything into it. He was beyond that, maybe. He just jerked forward and yanked a fistful of tissue from the box, which he jammed against his running eyes and nose.

"Ah, fuck," he gasped. He leaned into the wad of tissues a long moment. His shoulders bounced and he made labored heaving noises. He couldn't even talk.

We sat in the dark as Trevor sobbed noiselessly. Eventually I told him, "It's okay." It was not an appropriate thing to say, but I was letting instinct guide me. The priority was, of course, to get him out. That was my instinct above all else—I had to get him out. But my instinct also told me to go slow. To act like this was nothing out of the ordinary. To be kind, solicitous even. To this day I shake my head at those instincts. I shake it right along with all the people I tell this story to—the people who demand to know why on earth I didn't grab my phone the moment I spotted Trevor's silhouette—or a heavy object, suitable for bludgeoning—as opposed to a bathrobe and a box of Kleenex. But then I feel guilty, as if I have betrayed someone. What right do I have, after all—a comfortable person seated at a desk in the secure present, spine lovingly supported by my ergonomic chair—what right have I to look askance at this other person, shifting squeakily around in her mother's ancient rocker, flailing in the moment? I am at a distance now—she wasn't. I am operating on pliable memory and cool reflection—she was operating on adrenaline in the dark.

Trevor lifted his face from the wad of Kleenex and blinked at the ceiling. He took a breath.

"Sorry," he whispered. "Didn't wanna wake up Beaner."

"It's fine," I told him.

"It's not fine," he said. Then he struggled a while before he could say the next thing. "I'm fucking this up and I know it. You think I don't know it?" His face disappeared into the clot of tissue again.

"You're not fucking anything up," I whispered.

"I was a prick."

"It's okay."

"It's not okay."

How long could we go back and forth like this?

"You got angry," I told him. "And I got angry. It's okay. People get angry."

"I just care about you guys so much," said Trevor.

"I know."

"I don't got anything," he said, his face contorting. The extremity of his expression was amplified by the shadows cast by the streetlights and the LED outside, and he looked abruptly like a gargoyle. "I don't got anything," he said again, and shuddered.

The strange, keening rhythms of this conversation, its singsong, whispered repetition, gave me a feeling like Trevor and I were performing some kind of spontaneous poetry together, here in my mother's darkened living room, or improvising a ritual, a magic incantation. It reminded me of the feeling I'd had the first time Trevor got angry at me, when we sat eating cookies and drinking tea and I felt as if, in my effort to win back his approval, I was following a script that he'd already memorized and I could only intuit.

I knew how he wanted me to reply, but I wasn't going to follow that particular script this time. "You have Mike," I told him. "You have your brother—your family."

"I push everyone away," he told me. "I don't wanna push you guys away too."

"You haven't pushed us away," I assured him. "We're right here." I figured this statement was factual yet noncommittal enough that Trevor could take what he needed from it and I could still feel that I was keeping him at arm's length. The conversation required every ounce of my concentration; it felt almost like a physical ordeal, like rock climbing, hoisting yourself inexorably upward, every thought devoted to where you'll next place your hands and feet.

"Promise me," said Trevor.

"I promise," I said. "But you need to go home now, Trevor."

"I know," he said. "I just need to know that I'm forgiven."

"You're forgiven," I told him.

"I'm so sorry." He mopped his face again with Kleenex and sat with his elbows on his knees, drawing cleansing and, I hoped, sobering gulps of air.

Then Trevor asked, "Can I just get a hug?"

"Yes," I said. "But then you have to go."

Trevor stood up and I stood up. He came at me before I was ready and took me in his arms.

It was as if he had been stuffed into an oven and basted in Captain Morgan; the liquor fumed from his pores. He held me tight, squashing my chest against his, heedless of my boobs—most men, when I was hugged in polite circumstances, discreetly rounded their backs to avoid that kind of squashing contact, as I discreetly rounded mine for the same reason. But I was incapable of rounding, or any other kind of movement, for that matter, as Trevor leaned into me. I stood there, half holding him up, breathing his alcoholic perspiration and his inadequately applied deodorant—some corporate chemist's idea of what the ocean should smell like. All I could do was swallow my claustrophobia and wait to be released.

"You are so dear to me," he breathed into my neck. "You and the Bean. So, so dear. Do you know that?"

I thought it was a rhetorical question, so I didn't answer. But then his arms tightened and he dug his chin a little into the crook between my neck and shoulder.

"Yes," I said. "I know that. We both do."

His arms loosened. He took a step away at last and immediately lost his balance and fell over onto the floor, knocking against an end table as he did and causing the framed photograph of my father riding a horse in Bermuda to forward-roll onto the carpet.

"Whoops!" said Trevor, and then he put his finger to his lips, admonishing, "Shhh!" at the surrounding furniture. It struck me then that Trevor was a mess. A drunken mess. He would not remember any of this tomorrow. The realization hollowed out a pit in my stomach—a visceral memory of how my ex used to blindside me with the degree of his drunkenness in exactly this same way. He'd appear in the bedroom doorway sometime after midnight, call my name until I woke up, pontificate for a few lively minutes on something called "schizoanalysis," and, when I finally gathered the wherewithal to yell at him for waking me, would become incensed and tell me this was my problem exactly, I simply did not *care,* I was indifferent to the things that truly mattered—no, not indifferent, in *terror.* I was a coward and all I wanted was to bury my head in the sand and avoid avoid. To wake up in the morning, every morning, and simply be permitted to *fake it.* Fake peace. Fake quiet. Fake well-being. Fake compassion. Fake devotion. Fake emotion. Fake humanity. And once I was good and awake, roiling with adrenaline, because that's what happens when you are under attack in the middle of the night, when your fight-or-flight reaction is initiated—that's when, reliably, he would sink to his knees at the foot of the bed, slouch against it with his upper body, and fall asleep.

I dropped to my knees on the floor beside Trevor then. He gazed at me, surprised and with an air of expectation, as if we were about to sit cross-legged across from each other and play some kind of children's game.

"Trevor," I said. "Did you send Finny?"

Trevor stopped smiling and let his head loll back against the carpet. He looked up at the ceiling awhile.

A kind of fog descended in my brain. *Just get him up,* the fog dictated, *get him out of here and go to bed.* The fog didn't want me to dwell on it. The fog was eager for me to get some sleep. The only other thing I was sure of, inside that fog, was that Trevor would never hurt Kelli. He loved my sister, after all. Just as he had loved, however pushily, my mother. His love was what had made it all negotiable, forgivable, for so long. And that was why going to sleep would be okay.

This was a dumb, drunken stunt he had pulled, but a minor irritation in the grand scheme of things. Right now I just had to get him out.

Only Trevor wasn't going anywhere. I stood up first, still holding his hand but pulling on it now, saying I would call him a cab. Trevor allowed himself to be yanked to his feet, but as soon as he was up he fell against me, reeling and chortling and forgetting that he needed to be quiet. I tried to heave him upright but instead ended up just shifting his weight enough that the momentum carried him back to the couch, onto which he unresistingly flopped.

"Ohh," said Trevor then, pulling his legs up onto the couch along with the rest of his torso. It was an *Ohh* of pleasure—drunken Trevor liked the couch, the couch was good, it welcomed him. He would be passed out in moments.

"Trevor," I whispered helplessly, "don't you dare throw up on my mother's carpet."

"Wouldn' dream of it," he slurred. In the dark, I could tell his eyes were closed. They no longer glittered at me.

He snored as I unfolded a tartan throw that Irene had always kept on display over the back of the cushioned armchair and spread it over him. There was nothing to be done about him now. But tomorrow, I resolved, we would have the serious talk I'd intended us to have at Tim Hortons. Trevor would be ashamed of himself, horrified by his behavior, and I would finally ask him, with total justification, to return the key. Strictly speaking this was breaking and entering—I would tell him that. I still fully intended to get the locks changed, even though I now knew we'd be out of here in a matter of months—maybe even weeks, depending on the keenness of Nate and Jason to move in. Still, demanding the key would be a symbolic gesture, a long-overdue one, to let Trevor know that he had stepped irrevocably over the line this time.

In the meantime, I just had to get through the night. And since it was three in the morning, the night would be short—it was practically over already. I rooted around beneath the kitchen sink and pulled out a bucket, the same orange bucket Jessica had grabbed too late the night Kelli got sick. I went back into the living room and placed it on the floor near Trevor's purring head. Finally, I picked up his glass—which was empty—and brought it to the kitchen. The boozy fumes wafting up from the glass made me scowl—reminding me of performing this exact chore for my passed-out husband.

I enacted these rituals in the dark, as if they were shameful instead of merely practical, domestic. Typical, even—the same rites that sober people had performed in service of the drunk since time immemorial, that parents performed for children, women for men and vice versa, everywhere on the planet, throughout all of human history, I suppose. Inevitable and eternal. *World without end,* as my mother and I once droned in unison at Mass. These were the routines that made life orderly and coherent from moment to moment—the covert connective tissue of our days. Sometimes they made you feel weary or taken for granted, but dirty glasses had to be rinsed out, pristine carpets needed defending from bilious onslaughts, and the inescapable fact was that someone had to do it. You didn't have to like it, but you had to do it. That was the lesson at the end of the day. For morning to come, for the future to take place, there always had to be someone scuttling around in the background with a broom and dustpan. Someone had to suck it up. It was very early but not yet dawn, maybe five-thirty or six in the morning. I hadn't heard him come in, hadn't felt the give of the bedsprings as he lowered himself down or felt the breeze created by the bedclothes being shifted. My back was to him and, as I came awake, my body seemed to solidify into the fetal position I'd been sleeping in—I didn't shift or budge, because it felt like I was made of rock. My muscles locked up and I thought, weirdly, about the ancient people of Pompeii, caught unaware by exploding Mount Vesuvius, which killed them instantly in an ungodly blast of heat from the center of the earth. How they all curled up, the way I was curled up—providing perfect stone casts of themselves, for posterity, after the lava had hardened all around them.

Sunbeam

32

And then I was standing. I didn't remember moving, or thinking, but now I was standing by the bed and looking down at him.

"Get out," I said. Looking back, I think these words were the first I'd ever spoken to Trevor in the whole time we were acquainted that I had not weighed in advance before opening my mouth. They just came out. "Get out of there. Get out. Now."

Trevor rolled onto his back and looked at me. "That couch," he said, "is too friggin' hard, you ask me."

It couldn't have been more than three hours since he'd passed out, but Trevor was sober now. Completely sober, it seemed. His eyes were bright, unclouded. He sat up and rubbed them.

"Ah, well. Guess we might as well get up, if we're up."

"Get out," I said again. I'd slept barely a handful of hours, but it felt like I'd had twenty cups of coffee.

Unhurriedly, Trevor flung his legs over the side of the bed. "You having a shower?" he asked.

"No, I'm not having a fucking shower!"

"Go on if you want to," said Trevor. "I'll get some breakfast going." He stood up, stretched again, and lumbered out of the room.

"No," I said, but he was off down the hall.

I threw on some clothes and went into the living room to look around. Normally, I kept my phone on the bedside table, but it wasn't there this morning. It wasn't on the coffee table either. I went down into the foyer and dug into my purse. It wasn't there. I was going to have to check the kitchen next.

I went back upstairs and stood in the entryway as if I wanted to talk to him.

"I want you to go now," I said, scanning the countertops.

"All right," said Trevor, scooping coffee grounds into the filter. "Let's just have a cup of joe and then I'll haul my hungover arse on outta here, okay?"

"No!"

Trevor yawned and grimaced simultaneously. "Don't get all shrieky, you're gonna wake up Beaner."

"I'm gonna call the cops if you're not out of here in the next five seconds, Trevor," I said.

"You're not gonna call the cops on that phone with the broken screen," said Trevor, flicking on the coffee machine. I knew from the previous morning he'd spent with us that Trevor's coffee was going to be terrible. I always made it in single servings with a pour-over filter I'd brought from home, but Trevor's way was to dump an obscene amount of grounds into my mother's rickety Canadian Tire coffee-maker and balance that off with an even more obscene amount of water. The resulting gallons of muddy liquid were like nothing I'd ever tasted.

I was thinking about this, I guess, to delay thinking about the fact that Trevor knew about my broken screen. Which meant, perhaps, that he'd seen my phone—and maybe even knew where it was.

"The phone works fine," I said.

"Pfft," said Trevor. "I'd love to see you make a call with that cracked-up piece of shit." Turning away from the coffeemaker, which creaked and hissed as it expanded with heat, he leaned against the counter to face me.

"Where is it?" I said.

Trevor shrugged. "How would I know where your phone is?"

I turned away from him, went down into the foyer, and pulled on a pair of sneakers. This was dumb, amygdala-driven instinct. I didn't know exactly what I was doing—it was feeling like I needed armor. Trevor came to the top of the stairs and watched me.

"Goin' somewhere?"

"No," I said, standing there with my shoes untied.

"Good," said Trevor, "'cause I think I hear Beaner gettin' up to see what all the excitement is out here." He turned away and went back to the kitchen.

Since Kelli was up, Kelli had to be fed. I sat sipping the nightmare coffee as Trevor placed sizzling slices of bacon to blot on a doubled-up piece of paper towel. Kelli and I almost never had bacon, because of the nitrates, so this—on top of the surprise of Trevor greeting her when she woke up—made for a thrilling morning for my sister.

"Trebie bacon," she murmured when he put the plate down in front of her.

"Now, you take it easy with that," said Trevor. "Don't inhale it all at once."

"Cut it up into pieces, Kelli," I advised.

"Cut it up small," Kelli murmured. She whispered this a few more times to herself, hacking away at her plate until the egg and bacon and toast Trevor had served up was a pulverized, slimy yellow hash.

"I love a woman of appetites!" Trevor declared. He put the next plate in front of me and then sat down with one himself and began to eat.

"Surprised you have much appetite after last night," I said after a moment.

"You kidding?" said Trevor around a mouthful of egg. "This stuff is the ultimate hangover cure right here."

I watched him chew. He glanced at me.

"You gonna eat?" said Trevor.

"No, I'm not gonna eat," I said.

"Look," said Trevor. "Let's just get through breakfast, okay? Then we'll get Beaner all settled in her chair and we can have a good talk."

He picked up his toast and mopped at the swirl of yolk and ketchup on his plate.

As Trevor cleaned up, I decided to eat everything on my plate after all. There was nothing I wanted to do less, but the bad coffee was sizzling away my stomach lining, so I gulped the greasy food like medicine. It was the same impulse as the one that had driven me to the foyer to pull on my sneakers. A feeling like I needed to be fortified. I sat with my eyes closed, willing myself to keep it down, as Trevor teased Kelli. She had gotten stuck on her way to the living room, the way she sometimes did as she moved throughout the house. "Putting herself on pause," my mother used to call it. Kelli just sometimes stopped on her way to wherever she was going and decided to linger for a while, wherever she happened to be. Now she leaned against the doorframe, running her hand along it almost thoughtfully and whispering to herself. She looked interested, engaged. You could imagine that she was having a conversation with some entity residing in the walls.

"Whup!" said Trevor. "She got stalled, Mother! I had an old jalopy used to do that."

Kelli ignored him. She was intent on whatever it was she was doing there against the doorframe, whatever prayers or benedictions she was whispering. Perhaps she simply didn't want to leave the room. To leave me alone with Trevor. I let myself imagine, for just a moment, that Kelli was feeling protective. That she was looking after me, for a change. That she had paused, in the doorway, in a show of solidarity.

We faced off over the kitchen table. "Are you going to leave?" I said.

"Not until we work this out," said Trevor.

"We can't work this out," I said, "until you leave."

"Now, Karie, you and I both know that doesn't make one goddamn iota of sense."

"You can't just show up in the middle of the night. You can't just climb into bed with—"

"I am a member of this family," said Trevor, speaking loudly to drown out whatever I was going to say next. "That's what your mom wanted. And that's what you wanted, until you got all these ideas in your head."

"That's not what I wanted," I said.

"Oh, so you just wanted a manservant, then, is that it? It's fine having me around as long as I'm bowin' and scrapin'."

"I never wanted that either!"

"What did you want then, Karie? You tell me, because I'll be fucked if I can figure it out. You want a shoulder to cry on and you want someone to save your ass from Adult Protection and you want someone to look after your dying mother because you're too much of a big shot to come home and do it yourself—"

"She never wanted you," I blurted. *My god,* my rational mind said then, *don't argue with him. Don't actually rise to his arguments—this isn't about justifying yourself, this is about getting him out.* I bit down on what I wanted to say next, but Trevor's eyebrows descended and he glowered at me.

"You don't know what the fuck she wanted. How could you? You weren't here."

"You bullied her," I said. "Just like you're bullying me."

Trevor reared back in disbelief. He touched his chest as if to say, *Moi?* Then he shoved his face at me.

"You listen here. I woulda cut my heart out for your mom, and that's the truth."

"You don't know how to do it right," I said.

"What the fuck is that supposed to mean?"

"Nobody wants you to cut your heart out. Nobody's asking for that. That's not how you help people. You don't know how to help people. All you know how to do is crush them."

Trevor stood up so suddenly it made me flinch. He was like an animal under attack trying to make itself seem bigger.

Why didn't you shut up, asked my rational mind, *when I told you to shut up?*

"All I fucking do for you Petrie women," he said, "is give. I give and give and give. And I keep thinking, *Maybe now? No. Okay, how about now? No, eh?* Okay, so what exactly do I have to do? Tell me what I have to do, Karie. What is it you people actually want from me?"

"I want you to *leave*," I said.

Trevor turned and went into the living room, where Kelli was.

When I got there, he had yanked Kelli around in her stool, away from the window, and was kneeling on the floor in front of her, his hands gripping the sides of her seat.

"That what you want, K-bean? You want me to leave? You want Trebie to go and never come back?"

Kelli's reaction to the surprise of this was to stare hard into her lap, frowning and muttering.

"What's that? Speak up so your sister can hear you, Bean-o."

"Leave her alone," I said.

"No," said Kelli loud and clear.

"What's that? You don't want Trebie to go away?"

"No Trebie," said Kelli, scowling at his proximity.

"She wants you to get away from her," I said.

Trevor ignored me. "Whaddya say, Beaner? Want me out of here?"

"No," said Kelli again, placing her hands over her ears.

Trevor straightened, triumphant. "Two against one!" he declared.

"Come back into the kitchen, Trevor," I said. "Let's talk, okay?"

"No," said Trevor primly. "This is a family discussion, and I think Kelli should be a part of it. Right, Bean?"

But Kelli was full-on rocking and whispering now. She had removed herself.

Every now and then, I'd glance out onto the street. The sun had risen and the streetlights had faded out. The LED at Mr. Gill's clicked off, and moments later a woman emerged from the house, Mrs. Gill, presumably, to water her flower pots, overflowing with spindly pansies, blown out from summer. Then she went back inside, and the street was quiet again. Soon there'd be dog walkers. One or both of the Gills climbing into their cars to head to work. Marilyn too. Maybe not Noel, since he was retired. The point was, there'd be people on the sidewalks within the hour, going about their morning only a few feet away from us.

"We need to make a plan," Trevor was saying. "Just one example: We wanna keep this house or not?"

"The house is sold," I said mildly. I was trying to keep everything I said mild.

"You sign the papers? 'Cause nothing's a done deal if you haven't signed the papers. You can still back out."

"True," I said after a moment.

"I mean, this is a great fuckin' house," said Trevor. "Let's face it. Lots of room. Pretty good neighborhood. Beaner likes it, eh, Bean?"

Kelli hummed, gazing out the window.

"We could give it a nice makeover if you don't like the looks of it anymore. Get rid of that fluorescent in the kitchen—I know you don't like that. Strip the wallpaper. Maybe pull up the carpet out here, put down some nice hardwood. Modernize the place a bit."

My heart began to gallop.

"Yes," I said as if thinking about it.

"Might be a fun little project for us both," said Trevor.

For us both. "You want—to move in?"

Trevor shrugged, not as if to say, *I don't know* but as if the question itself were a no-brainer. "No sense paying rent on a place when I'm here half the time anyway."

"Did you move in with Mom?" I asked, to stall.

"Rini wanted me to," said Trevor, "but we ended up having a tiff about that. I wanted to pay rent, and she wasn't having it. So I told her until she came to her senses, I'd be holding on to my place." Trevor leaned forward and clasped his hands. "That's what I want you to understand, Karie. I pull my own weight. We're partners in this. I do for you, and you do for me."

I took a breath, as deeply as I could without opening my mouth or letting my shoulders rise too explicitly. I needed to seem calm. I needed to keep him calm. I needed to change the subject, but I also needed to assert some kind of authority in this situation. I kept my face neutral, but my hands in my lap felt like frozen, knuckly chunks of meat.

"We need to talk about," I said, "what happened this morning."

Trevor leaned back. "That was not my finest hour."

"I don't know what that was," I said. "But it can't happen again."

"I guess I was just trying to move things forward," Trevor explained. "I was a dummy. I'm a man, I had to make a move. You can't blame a guy for trying."

He didn't put it down to being drunk. He wasn't even bothering to pretend that he'd been drunk anymore. He was pretending something else now. *Trevor,* I wanted to say, *you are not attracted to me, and you know it.* I understood this with more clarity than I understood anything else about the situation.

"Won't happen again," promised Trevor. Then he amended the promise: "We'll take things slow."

And everything did become slow, from that moment forward—unbearably slow, the way people describe experiencing car crashes and other inexorable disasters. The three of us sat together in the living room as the morning ticked away while Trevor elaborated on what our futures together held. Sometimes I felt like my mind was racing, whereas other times it felt as if it had completely shut down. In the racing moments I mostly wondered why it wasn't *giving* me anything—some kind of strategy. I'd always thought that in a crisis, a person's mind was supposed to sharpen, become focused. But then I realized what the problem was. I *was* focused—entirely focused on Trevor. His sunburned forearms and his gingery five o'clock shadow. His lordly, spread-legged couch sprawl and bloodshot eyes. I'd become hypervigilant, and that was taking up the entirety of my mental bandwidth—helplessly fixated on Trevor's every flinch and utterance.

The sticking point was Kelli. I could bolt, maybe, when his back was turned, when he stepped into the hallway bathroom to "drain the dragon" (as he liked to announce), but Kelli could not. Kelli required work to dislodge—which Trevor knew. If I took off on my own, if I defied or angered him, he'd go for her. He had already showed me that. I didn't know what he'd do, exactly, but I knew that much. He'd turn to Kelli. That was the threat.

Eventually, it was almost lunchtime. I'd watched the neighbors come and go throughout the morning—cars being ejected from garages, cats being let out and then let in. Noel emerged from his own garage on a ride-on mower and sat like a general on horseback as he putt-putted in circles across his lawn. It turned out that Marilyn stayed home on weekdays; she emerged to do some gardening and banter with Noel for a few minutes before both went back to their yard work.

Maybe, I thought, if I pretended along with Trevor that all this was normal and fine, he'd start to actually believe it, as opposed to trying to force it into being, and therefore relax his grip on us a little. So I tried suggesting that we go for a walk—all three of us—thinking I could wave to someone if we did, maybe stop and say hi to good-neighbor Marilyn, for example, who, I recalled, had been so alert to danger the night Mr. Gill's garage was broken into. And Trevor wouldn't be able to do anything about it, or do anything to Kelli, because we'd be in public.

This was my lone gambit, after hours of mostly nodding and blank-minded panic. I asked, the inside of my mouth feeling gluey, if Trevor wasn't getting restless from all the sitting? Kelli, I said, would probably love a walk before lunch—her bad knee could use a bit of exercise and I could too, come to think of it, and look what a lovely, long-shadowed end-of-summer day it was.

"Ah, now, Karie," said Trevor. "We haven't even got started on this whole thing."

Since breakfast had been heavy, I opened a couple cans of soup. Normally I'd throw together a salad, but I didn't want to antagonize Trevor with rabbit food. I buttered some buns and Trevor set the table, but when we called Kelli to come and get it, she didn't budge. Trevor went to the doorway to check on her.

"Coming, Beaner?"

"No," said Kelli, staring at her lap again.

"Let's go," he said, clapping his hands. "Gonna be hungry later."

"No Trebie no," said Kelli. She bent forward and started to hum.

"She's just being stubborn," I said. "She'll ask for a snack in an hour or so."

Trevor frowned but eventually returned to the table. "Don't like seeing our girl go hungry."

Afterward, tucking the leftovers away in the fridge, I pretended that something had just occurred to me. "We're low on a few things," I said. "Should maybe grab some groceries today."

"I can pick 'em up tomorrow," said Trevor. "We got enough to get us through till then."

Not knowing what else to do, I filled the kettle. Now that we were in the kitchen, I felt a little more secure—I felt like I wanted to keep him here, away from Kelli, even though I knew he could bolt into the living room at any time and be at her chair again in a few quick strides.

"I'm making tea," I said. So Trevor, in that Pavlovian, Maritime way, got comfortable.

"You know that thing you said about me bullying your mom," said Trevor, as I placed a steaming mug in front of him. "That hurt my feelings."

I sat down across from him, filling my own mug from the teapot. "I apologize for that."

"Someone tell you that?"

"No," I said.

"That Paki across the street?"

"I was just being a bitch," I told him. "Trying to upset you. I'm really sorry."

"You were talking to Bestlife," Trevor decided, nodding. "You wanna talk bitches. That bitch in the front office had it in for me from day one."

"I don't like them either," I said. "We're not using them anymore."

The moment after I said this, blood rushed into my face. At first I didn't even know why. *Wait,* I thought, as my brain caught up to what my nervous system had already realized. It wasn't actually true that we weren't using Bestlife anymore. Because I hadn't canceled them yet. I'd been intending to, after Eleanor Mallon's call, but I hadn't had the chance. Kelli was still booked for baths, two afternoons a week. Meaning someone from Bestlife should be arriving—when? What day was today?

"You all right?" said Trevor. "Tea go down the wrong chute?"

I put my cup down and started nodding, coughing. I waved a hand in front of my face.

Trevor got up and poured me a glass of water from the tap. I took several long, uninterrupted gulps so I could think. Kelli started Gorsebrook yesterday. Was it yesterday? Yesterday seemed like months away. But it was yesterday. And yesterday was . . . a Tuesday. Therefore today was Wednesday. Meaning today was not bathing day. Mondays and Thursdays. Those were Kelli's Bestlife afternoons. Which meant no one was coming until tomorrow. There'd be no one till tomorrow afternoon.

33

The silent hours dragged. We could have been on the moon, it felt like, or in an underground bunker with all of civilization nuked to smithereens above our heads. No one came to the door all day. My phone, wherever it was stashed, didn't ring once, and neither did Trevor's. Sometimes a car would honk in the distance. Sometimes we'd hear a muffled neighbor calling to another down the street. Once, a couple of dogs on leashes got into it briefly, and we were all startled by the sound of their frantic, feral yelps and snarls tearing up the afternoon silence. Trevor and I went to the window and stood beside Kelli to look. Eventually the dogs got yanked apart, tense human apologies were exchanged, and things became quiet again.

With Trevor in control of the house, he could now do and say what he liked, and what he mostly wanted to do was rhapsodize about Irene. There was an element of compulsion to this process—of self-soothing. If he could convince me of their happiness together, of their mutual devotion, he could believe in it fully himself. He wouldn't have to yell and bluster anymore. He would banish all doubt from both of our minds. My job—or should I say my function, since *job* makes it sound as if I had a choice—was to sit absorbing this onslaught of bullshit until, essentially, it wore me down enough to where I would at least pretend that I agreed with it.

Up until now my desperation had made me cautious beyond anything else. But caution didn't seem to be getting me anywhere. The afternoon felt like a spider's web—fleeing was impossible; staying still was doom. But you had to do *something*. Something that wasn't quite either of those options.

Around three-thirty I suggested we have a drink. Trevor grinned and rubbed his forehead.

"Little early," he said.

"Just one before dinner," I said. "We'll be civilized about it."

Trevor winked and stood up, rubbing his hands together. "Good thing Rini's not around to see this." This was a continuation of the one-sided conversation he'd been having with me for the last hour or so. His days of splendor with Irene—barbecues, weekly doctors' appointments and trips to the mall, drives out to Peggy's Cove or Lawrencetown Beach on weekends, to give Irene and Kelli a nice oceanside walk and hit of salt air. At one point he came over and knelt beside my chair, pulling his phone out of his back pocket to show me some photos he'd taken over the past year. I stiffened as he approached. The photos were all selfies, the perspective always from the end of Trevor's extended arm. No one else had ever been asked to take these pictures. His other arm was usually around my mother, if not Kelli too—and Kelli, of course, was always reluctant, always cutting her eyes away from the camera.

My mother looked shrunken beneath his arm. In a photo taken in front of the Peggy's Cove lighthouse, she was wearing the oversized Jackie O sunglasses she favored and her white hair streamed across her face in the wind. Her mouth was the only thing remotely expressive, remotely readable, in that photo. Somewhat puckered, as if she had been in the middle of remarking *Oh!* Or *No.*

"Did she use to get at you for your drinking?" I asked.

Trevor paused on his way to the kitchen. "Oh, you know your mum. She might not say anything, but you knew when she disapproved."

Bullshit, I thought as he went into the kitchen. When Irene disapproved, you heard about it. She knew how to make herself heard. She may have made passive-aggression a high art when dealing with me, but she'd always been an enthusiastic lodger of complaints—she wrote letters to MPs, MLAs, various newspapers back when people did that sort of thing. Her letters were always direct, grammatical, and well reasoned to a fault. She began by listing her credentials—a widow, a former nurse, a lifelong Nova Scotian (such bona fides were important to Nova Scotians), a full-time caregiver and single mother of two splendid girls. *I have earned,* her written preambles always seemed to declare, *this small, particular instance of complaint. Hear me and I will trouble you no more.*

Of course, no one did that these days. All the rules of engagement as Irene had once understood them, of carefully staking out one's status and accompanying worthiness to speak, were out the window; I couldn't even think when, exactly, this had happened, it had been so quick and so complete. Letters to the editor got replaced by barbarous Comments sections, furious tweets. My mother was a fighter, but these days she'd be like a Marquess of Queensberry boxer tossed into an Ultimate cage-fighting match. She'd been taught to fight a certain way. She hadn't been told there were other options. And she certainly had never been told how to fight against someone who threw the rule book out, who cheated, who was no gentleman and could not be trusted to fight clean. Thinking about it made me furious on her behalf.

In spite of everything that was happening, there was something about this day that was drawing my mother and me closer together. I felt like I was starting to see her in a way I hadn't before—in a way that felt clear, sharp-edged, for once.

I heard ice cubes tinkling into glasses. Soon Trevor came out of the kitchen with a drink in either hand and bowed at the waist to hand me mine. We clinked.

"To starting over," he said.

The doorbell rang midway through our first drink, the sound, for me, like a jolt from a cattle prod. Trevor swung his head around. "You stay put," he murmured, getting to his feet. "Keep Beaner entertained."

He went down the stairs, disappearing step by step into the foyer. I heard the screen door wheeze open, a gruff accent, a hearty "How's she goin'?," to which Trevor gave a fulsome fellow workingman's response. The word *buddy* was exchanged a couple times, and the weather was acknowledged to have been beautiful these last few days. Eventually it dawned on me that it was my mother's fish guy. He brought haddock and Atlantic shrimp up from the docks every couple of months, and his stuff was ten times fresher than anything you could get at Superstore. The first time he showed up, I bought a bag of boiled shrimp from him on a lark, having no idea what to do with it in terms of putting together a meal. But then I sampled a couple from the bag—they were sweet as berries—and ended up devouring half of them just sitting and surfing the Internet.

"Fish for dinner!" Trevor called up to me. I used this as an excuse to move to the top of the stairs. The fish guy, whose name I had never caught (Jimmy? Hughie?) grinned up at me through his salt-and-pepper stubble. "Fresh in today," he said. As if he would be here selling it if it weren't. I looked him in the eye—his eyes were very blue, offset by a squinty, sunburned face, and I willed them to catch mine and linger. But men like this weren't the kind to seek out eye contact with a person like me, and Trevor hadn't stopped bantering with him this entire time, keeping Jimmy or Hughie distracted. Something about the weather out there on the water, Trevor heard it had been rough this past week, and Jimmy or Hughie said yes, but he didn't get out onto the water no more himself, hurt his back a few years ago, slipped on the goddamn deck, and that's why he was "workin' the front end" these days, hawking fish door-to-door. Worked out just dandy as he was a more social type anyway, loved having a yak with people, and now he didn't have to be away overnight—so the wife was happy anyhow. For once! Jimmy or Hughie winked.

"Ah, it's all about keepin' them happy," said Trevor.

"If we know what's good for us," agreed Jimmy or Hughie, digging around in his cooler and withdrawing what looked to be a couple of choice fillets. "Now, sir, you wanna talk happy? Wait'll she tries these."

He was, I guess, talking about me. My happiness. I came down the stairs with my hand extended. "I'll put those in the fridge." But Trevor had already handed the guy a twenty and taken them from him. Instead of achieving significant eye contact with the fish guy, I got it from Trevor as he handed me the bag. "Good, good," he said, unsmiling. Which meant I was to turn around now and go upstairs. But I stayed, instead, to see Jimmy or Hughie out the door. I needed to look past the open door and view what was beyond—the oblivious cars, the placid houses across the street—to see if there was anyone I could raise a hand to. Someone who would see me.

Kelli was peevish at dinner, even though Trevor had made a great ceremony about the beautiful haddock he'd pan-fried especially for her. Just before he'd called her to the table, he had made the mistake of remarking that fresh haddock was "better than fish and chips" when cooked right, and all Kelli had heard in that sentence was "fish and chips." When a monochrome plate of haddock and mashed potatoes was placed in front of her, she started hollering. Where were the fish and chips? It made me feel gleeful. It was such a rookie mistake—how stupid did you have to be to mention fish and chips to Kelli moments before suppertime if it wasn't on the menu? You were just asking for trouble.

Trevor busied himself buttering Kelli's roll and pretending not to be taken aback. "Well, well," he said. "Someone's got an attitude on her tonight."

"It's because she skipped lunch," I ventured.

"Keep it up and no dessert," said Trevor, placing the roll at the side of Kelli's plate. His mouth was a prim, hurt line. I was the one who gave him trouble; he expected it from me. But he and Kelli were supposed to be a team.

Even with half her roll in her mouth, Kelli managed to snarl, "Want dessert!"

Trevor shot me an exasperated look. "We gotta do something about the table manners around here!"

"It's been a weird day for her," I said. "The early start. Missed lunch. Hasn't moved all day."

"No excuse," grumbled Trevor. "If I ever caught Mike throwing a snit like that at the table, dinner'd be in the garbage before he could blink."

Kelli brought her face closer to her plate, the faster to shovel food in.

"Slow down, Kelli," I said quietly.

"No," said Kelli around the fork in her mouth.

"Listen to your sister," said Trevor, "and slow the fuck down."

Kelli started griping loudly again, spewing potato particles from her mouth. "No Trebie no she don't want to slow—"

Trevor reached over and, with just two fingers, flipped her plate over and onto the floor.

"How about that?" said Trevor.

Did he think this would quiet Kelli down? At the sight of her supper flung across the linoleum, my sister started hollering again, outraged in earnest. Trevor watched her rail for a blank-faced moment. He'd never encountered this level of defiance before.

"Leave the table," he roared, slamming his palm down, sending the dishes and cutlery jumping.

But Kelli just roared back at him. A rapid-fire stream of *no*s and *Trebie*s and *Kelli's supper*s. She was not remotely intimidated by the red-faced, table-slamming man beside her. When Trevor realized this, he turned to me.

"Get her the fuck out of here."

"Kelli," I said. "Let's go sit."

"No Karie no Karie no K—"

"I'll bring you a nice snack in your chair," I promised.

Grumbling, she shoved back her chair and lumbered to her feet. She kept saying Trevor's name—*Trebie*—over and over again, drained of all affection, spitting out the two syllables with the same coldness Jessica had that time we fought in the driveway. Trevor watched as Kelli blundered out of the kitchen. His red face faded to pink, and his fury began fading into something I had to look away from—the last thing I wanted to feel toward Trevor was pity.

"She never acted this way when your mother was around," he told me.

"Fair enough," I said after a moment.

"'Fair enough'? That's all you gotta say?"

"Things have been a lot different since then," I said. "It's going to affect her."

"It was up to you to keep things on an even keel," said Trevor. He got up and went to the counter to top up his rum. "Sure as fuck screwed the pooch on that one, though, eh?"

The smart thing to do, and I knew how to do it now, was soothe and appease. All I had to say was that Trevor was right. That I had gone about things all wrong. I had gone about things all wrong because I had not had Trevor to tell me what was right—or I had, but I had not appreciated him, had not listened to him. But now, thank goodness, he was here, and everything would be okay. But something about Kelli's outburst—how it had wounded him—made me want to rebel. Of course, it was dangerous to wound him like that. Kelli could get away with what I couldn't. But it had been so invigorating to witness! In a long, endless afternoon dominated by a terror so low-key it was downright monotonous, Kelli's dinner table fuck-you to Trevor had given me a thrill of goose bumps.

So I talked back.

"Hard to keep things on an even keel," I said. "With you constantly trying to scare the shit out of us."

"Don't start in about that bullshit with the water jug again," said Trevor. "I apologized for that. I gave you a goddamn written apology."

"I'm not just talking about the water jug," I said. "I'm talking about Finny."

Trevor cocked his head in a faux-quizzical way that was so actorly—*Whatever do you mean?*—it almost made me laugh.

"We talked about Finny last night," I said. "Do you remember?"

"I don't remember a whole hell of a lot from last night," said Trevor, sitting back down at the table as if ready to resume eating.

"Bullshit," I said.

Trevor put his fork down and spread his arms in exasperation. "Why is everyone ganging up on me today? I thought we were all gonna have a nice dinner!"

"You're trying to change the subject," I said.

"Actually, you're the one who's trying to change the subject," said Trevor. "The subject is how badly you been fucking things up ever since you got here. Your mum had this place running like a well-oiled machine—meanwhile, you can barely keep it together."

"How have I not kept it together?"

Trevor snorted. "Oh sure, you did a great job. So good, Adult Protection has to come busting in."

He picked up his fork and started eating again, calmly, as if confident that his final point had ended the conversation once and for all.

"*You* called Adult Protection," I said. I hadn't even known I was going to say it. Or that I did, in fact, believe it to be true. Not until that moment.

Trevor looked up from his plate. "If I did," he said, "you can't very well blame me, can you? Beaner gettin' sick every other day. You selling off the goddamn place, your sister's home, piece by piece, in front of her eyes? No wonder she got sick! Did you even think for five minutes how that would affect her? No, you didn't. Because you don't think of anyone except yourself. If you needed a good swift kick in the arse to come to your senses, maybe that's what had to happen."

I was onto my feet before I could think about it. Anger had shot me out of my chair like a boulder from the guts of a volcano. It would have flung me across the table at him—to slap, or throttle, or god knows what disastrous idiocy I would have performed, and how he might have felt justified in retaliating—if fear hadn't caught up and kept me rigid.

"Sit down," said Trevor, "and eat your supper. It's in the past now."

"And Finny had to happen?" I said. "Terrorizing Kelli in the parking lot?"

"Enough with this Finny bullshit," said Trevor, waving a hand.

"And you got him to cook the books with Gorsebrook too, so we'd think they lost Jeremy. So I'd be too spooked to send Kelli there."

"Enough," said Trevor, his temples flexing. He was clenching his jaw again. But I couldn't shut myself up.

"What else did you do? Because this is insane. Do you even know how fucking psycho this whole thing—"

In one motion, Trevor stood, placed both hands against the table, and shoved it away from him. A couple of plates jerked forward and landed on the floor. A glass toppled over and rolled, almost lazily, over the edge. It was one of my mother's shatter-proof glasses from the seventies. True to the brand, it didn't shatter when it landed. But it did when Trevor kicked it across the room and into the wall. It shattered utterly, disintegrating like a windshield—too many pieces to count. I would be sweeping them up for the rest of my life.

"I just want to have my supper," said Trevor, and sat back down.

As I was cleaning up, he poured us both a conciliatory rum. This was Trevor's pattern, I was starting to understand. First, he tensed, and the tension would build—and it was up to you to intuit that tension early, to defuse it by any means possible, with some kind of appeasement or distraction. If you didn't succeed, what came next was always your fault: Trevor would explode, shutting down all possible dissent or insubordination with acts of noisiness and violence—violence that always implied there could be more and greater violence to come. And finally, once you, his tormentor, were completely cowed, the way he liked you, he made nice. He forgave and forgot, expecting you to do the same. The roller coaster ride was over for now, but soon it would begin again.

He didn't want me to be mad at him, he said. He understood that I'd been upset about my mom. That I was still upset. He let me clear away the dishes on my own as he spoke. The rum was making him loquacious, philosophical. Guilt, Trevor told me, was a hell of a thing. Literally, it could be hell. "When you feel like you haven't done your job by someone? That you've let them down? Fuck me if that isn't the worst feeling in the world. I've been there, Karie, Christ knows. I'm not one to judge."

I swept up the shattered glass and emptied it, tinkling, into the garbage.

"Leanne. My brother. I know I made my brother out to be an asshole—oh, and he is, by the way, a gaping asshole—but, you know . . .

he's younger than me, and I should be looking out for him. I know I need to be the bigger man. I need to reach out, apologize for poppin' him that time. But I just don't have it in me yet—I can't put aside my anger. I'm not there. And that was your problem too, Karie. You waited too long with your mum. And now you're beatin' yourself up for it. But there's no point to that anymore. It doesn't get you any-where—it just has you going around in circles, making dumb deci-sions that end up hurting everybody."

I began rinsing the excess grease off the dishes and loading them into the dishwasher.

"I used to say the same thing to your mother. You can't just sit around moaning about the past. You got a life to live, you got a girl to take care of, and you got someone here who's ready and willing to help you. So quit yer bellyaching, Mother, I used to say to her. Quit beating yourself up and get on with it."

I closed the dishwasher door, flicked it on, and leaned against the counter, thinking about this. It seemed as if he was getting me and Irene mixed up.

"Wait," I said. "Why was she beating herself up?"

Trevor shrugged and slurped his rum noisily, as if trying to cool it, like he'd forgotten he wasn't drinking tea.

"Oh, you know—we all feel bad sometimes. You felt bad about her, she felt bad about you."

"But what did she feel bad about? Our fights?"

"Sure," said Trevor. "Your fights. She was sorry as all shit you two fought so much back in the day."

"But you said she was beating herself up. Did she blame herself?"

"Oh, there was plenty of blame to go around," said Trevor. "You know that as well as I do. But here's my point—"

"But I'm asking," I said. "Did my mother feel guilty?"

Trevor became still and put his glass down. "Okay, look," he said. "We all feel guilty. But I told her, like I'm telling you, that's no way to be. Know how you stop feeling guilty? You do your job. You do what's right. Cryin's not gonna help. Makin' calls in the middle of the night isn't gonna help—"

"What calls?" I said. "Calls to who?"

"Calls to whoever!" said Trevor, getting to his feet. The tension was back in his jaw, which was my warning to back off—but I couldn't, because a certainty was boiling up in me now. Trevor started clearing the table; there were still a few items left: the butter dish, the salt and pepper grinders, the bread basket, cradling a single, deflated-looking roll. His face was sullen, and he wouldn't meet my eye.

"Wait," I said. "When was she crying?"

"For fuck's sake!" Trevor slammed the salt and pepper caddy onto its spot above the stove. "Your mother had a hard time of it, okay? When *wasn't* she crying, that's the better question. You really wanna hear about it? Everything she went through? You weren't there, that's all you need to know."

"She felt guilty," I said. "And she wanted to call." All I could see in that moment, against a background of red, was the photo Trevor had shown me on his phone. One ruddy arm around Irene, the other extended, snapping the picture. Irene's massive sunglasses, her small, hidden face. The pursed *no* of her mouth. "She wanted to call me," I said. "And you wouldn't let her, you fucking bully. You wouldn't let her do anything, would you? You kept her fucking prisoner, like you're doing to us right now."

A look came over Trevor that indicated the roller coaster was starting up again—the pre-flipping-over-of-the-dinner-plate look. Next, I knew—from the water jug, from the moment before he knocked the dishpan into the sink—his eyes would bulge and a stillness would overtake the room. At that point all you could do was brace yourself for what would come next. But this time felt different, bigger. This time Trevor's nostrils actually flared, and the stillness felt unending, like a time warp. It was like when you feel a sneeze coming on, how the *ah* gets drawn out before the eruption of the *choo*. The longer the *ah,* the bigger the *choo*. It felt as if a very big *choo* was on its way.

But I didn't even register this, not consciously, anyway. My heart was pounding so hard I could feel its throbbing pressure behind my eyes. I was so furious—dangerously furious, I thought later. Because whatever came next, it wasn't just that I was convinced I was ready for it—it was that I *wanted* it. I wanted the big *choo,* the explosion, the irrevocable thing I'd been so frightened of and desperate to avoid these past twelve hours. Now—fuck it. Bring it. Let it all rain down.

Shreeeeeeee—ehhhhhhhhhhhhrrrrrrrkkkk!

The noise was something between a shriek and a death rattle— high-pitched and grinding. It wasn't coming from Trevor. I leapt away from the counter in alarm, because the counter was trembling. The noise was coming from the dishwasher.

Trevor's eyebrows plunged. "Jesus, what's—"

The moment he spoke, the death shriek of the churning Sunbeam dropped to an almost reassuring whirr, then became a less reassuring gurgle, then, just when it sounded like it was about to give up the ghost, it soared back into an eardrum-piercing yowl. I backed away from it, plugging my ears. At the same time, Trevor lurched forward, reaching for the dishwasher's off button. But before he got there, his face contorted.

"Agh!" he said, and spasmodically lifted one leg. He grabbed himself by the ankle and peered at the bottom of his white-socked foot.

"Fucking piece of glass!" said Trevor, and he collapsed, writhing, into a chair.

I moved without thinking. I went into the living room and almost bashed into Kelli, who had risen from her perch and was lurching toward the kitchen with an affronted look to complain about the noise.

"Let's go, Kell," I said, and took her hand.

34

Things happened very fast after that. Not the things I wanted to happen. In my mind, from the moment I took Kelli by the hand, events would unfold something like this: Trevor had not heard my words to Kelli over the last gasps of the dishwasher. As I pulled her down the stairs into the foyer, I'd explain to her that the dishwasher was broken and therefore we were going out to dinner—at Swiss Chalet! Considering that Kelli had to be starving by that point, I figured that this would light a fire under her. Trevor would have his sock off, examining his foot. Maybe he'd still be distracted enough by the noise and the pain not to notice what was going on. Descending the stairs—me in my sneakers and Kelli in her slipper-shoes—I'd try to remember if my car keys had been in my purse when I'd gone rifling through it for my phone this morning. I couldn't remember if I'd heard the usual jangling sound they made in the always-open zippered pocket where I kept them. But I wouldn't stop to check. I'd just grab the purse, stick my hand in to root around as Kelli and I kept moving, through the front door, and if, by the time we got to the car, I had not found my keys, we would simply keep going across the street—*Change of plans, Kell!*—and start pounding on Mr. Gill's or Marilyn's front door.

But Trevor had come out of the kitchen before we even made it to the top of the stairs, and he grabbed Kelli around the waist in a bear hug and lifted her briefly off the ground. Like he was being playful.

"Where ya goin', darlin'?"

Predictably, Kelli started hollering, and by the time Trevor had frog-marched her back to her perch by the window, she was more than ready to take it up again.

"Put her down," I said.

"That's what I'm doin'," said Trevor. "Calm down. You're the one who's getting her all worked up."

Kelli glared at the window, whispering in outrage as she methodically, rapidly rocked herself back into a feeling of security. Trevor reached past her to pull the curtains closed. It was starting to get dark now.

In the kitchen, the Sunbeam gave a final, groaning shudder and at last stopped dead. The house was silent again, and I knew I couldn't stand it. I couldn't stand another minute of it. I went back to the kitchen and yanked the dishwasher open to survey the carnage within. Gray water sloshed out, sudsy and festooned with food particles, and got all over the floor.

Behind me, Trevor was in the process of saying, "Jesus, don't open it! It's gonna—ah, fuck, now see what you did?"

I took out a plate and flung it away from me. Not at Trevor, just away from me, without much interest in where it would end up. It ended up in the dining room and smashed impressively through the window of my mother's china cabinet. A twofer, I thought.

"Jesus Christ!" yelled Trevor.

"Leave," I said.

"Or you'll break all the dishes?" said Trevor. "Why should I give a shit if you break all the dishes? Fuckin' all we do is break dishes around here."

So I kept breaking dishes. I smashed them into the sink. I smashed them against the table, the walls. I flung a few more into the dining room—some of them smashed, some didn't. I avoided the foyer because I wanted to leave it clear, I wanted there to be no impediments to departure when the time came. With every fling, I told Trevor to leave. "Leave," I said. *SMASH.* "Leave. Leave. Leave." *SMASH. SMASH. SMASH.* Trevor crossed his arms and stood there, off-balance because he was trying not to stand on the ball of his right foot where it had been gouged. The bottom tip of his sports sock, I saw, was bloody. He didn't flinch at the shattering plates, even as Kelli railed at the noise from the living room, no doubt rocking even faster than before and covering her ears. He just watched me, shaking his head. *What a pitiful display,* he seemed to be saying. What a sad shambles this house has become.

"Who's gonna clean this—" he tried to interject at one point.

"Leave!" I screamed, and hurled a plate against the big kitchen window, which overlooked the backyard and the houses beyond. The plate smashed, the window didn't, but this seemed to shake Trevor out of his bemusement, and he yanked the next plate out of my hand. I went to open the cupboard for more ammunition, but he got there just in time and slammed it shut. We stood there together, me furiously yanking at the cupboard handle, Trevor with his hand flat against the cupboard door, nostrils flaring. And that's when the doorbell rang for the second time that day.

Trevor wanted me to answer it this time. At first I didn't understand why. I thought it might be because he didn't want to hobble down the stairs on his cut foot. Or maybe he was trying to keep up appearances, intuiting that if a strange man was the only one ever seen coming to the door at Irene Petrie's house, well-meaning neighbors might ask questions. At any rate, I was to go down and answer the door, and Trevor would, he said, "be right here," leaning against the kitchen doorway, where he could "keep an eye on Beaner." This position had the added benefit of blocking the view of the kitchen from down there, the broken glass and jagged white plate fragments covering the floor like a layer of splintered bones. I swept my eyes across this glinting carpet before heading down the stairs, kind of amazed. Who had done that? Me? I had a feeling like I'd just been shaken awake. That's when I understood why Trevor had sent me to answer the door. Because he knew if he hadn't, I would've kept going—would've yanked open the cupboard door the moment he stepped away and kept right on smashing dishes.

I went down the stairs, wondering how I looked. Trevor hadn't told me to straighten myself up, so maybe I wasn't as mad-eyed and disheveled as I felt. Then again, the doorbell kept ringing, and perhaps Trevor was unnerved. Maybe he just wanted me to get down there and make it stop.

Noel was carrying a clipboard. "Oh—how ya doing," he said when I pulled open the door, looking up from it, at me, over his bifocals.

"Good, Noel. Hi," I said, thinking, *See me.*

"Didn't catch you folks in the middle of your supper, I hope?"

"No, no," I said. "We just finished."

"I try to time it that way." Noel waved the clipboard at me apologetically. "Hate this door-to-door BS, but folks along the street here are usually nice enough to put up with it once a year anyhow."

I stared at him, trying to understand why Noel would be selling something door-to-door.

"Raffle season!" he said.

"Raffle season?"

"For the hospital. Lions Club holds it every year. Your mom always liked to put in."

It took me what felt like a very long time to decipher these words. "Are you," I said slowly, "a Lion?"

Noel closed his eyes and nodded. "I am a Lion." He said this in a serene way that struck me as out of character. I was used to seeing Noel fired up, his face in a pissed-off knot, ready to fight. "Going on about thirty years, it pains me to say." He glanced up at Trevor. A neutral glance of casual dislike, obligatory acknowledgment. "How's it going?"

"Good-good," said Trevor.

Noel turned back to me. He was a big man—I'd noticed it before, had assumed his size was what made him so pugnacious. I'd figured Noel was a man who had gotten used, during his young manhood, to being intimidating. He'd never had to develop debating skills or learn to negotiate assholes, like the rest of us. He plowed through the bullshit of life, as was the prerogative of the large and muscular. But he was old now, living the soft, lawn-mower-riding life of a retiree. Putting on weight, going outside only to putter in his yard. He wore bifocals and had a bad hip. Or knee. Whatever it was that gave him that limp.

Noel coughed.

"Um," I said. "What did my mother usually give?"

"It's a raffle," repeated Noel patiently. "You could win a house! Tickets are fifty dollars."

I grabbed my purse off the coatrack, just as I had fantasized about doing moments before. *But I don't want another house,* I thought distantly. *The house I have is killing me.*

Above us, Trevor couldn't help himself. "Fifty dollars," he said wonderingly. "Jesus Murphy."

Noel flicked his eyes up to Trevor, his features flattening into hostile neutrality again. "For a *house*," he repeated. "To help the *hospital*."

I had my wallet in my hand and stood there staring into it. "I don't have fifty dollars," I said in what I could hear was a fretful, almost panicked voice. Because I didn't know how to do this. I didn't know what I was supposed to do. This was an opportunity, but I had no idea how to take advantage of it.

Noel turned back to me, his face kind and, for the first time since I'd known him, fatherly. "I can just take your credit card number, dear."

"Oh boy!" yelped Trevor from above us. "Someone's on his way to Fiji!" Noel's face contracted into the pissed-off knot I was familiar with, and he jerked it up at Trevor to retort something sharp. But then he noticed something.

"Foot's bleeding there, buddy."

I glanced up at Trevor. He'd been leaning against the doorframe, balancing all his weight on his left foot in order to avoid putting any on his right. But now the bottom of his right sock was soaked through with blood—I wondered if he'd got any on Irene's carpet when he'd been frog-marching Kelli back to her stool. He had to have, I realized. A single bloody footprint stamped haphazardly across the pristine off-white like a boneheaded clue in a cheesy murder mystery.

"Arse," remarked Trevor, glancing down at his foot.

"We broke a glass," I explained to Noel.

"Okay," said Noel, watching with something like contentment as

Trevor, wincing, leaned against the fridge and pulled off his sock. "Should get some Polysporin or something on that."

Trevor was already reaching above the fridge, where, he apparently knew, Irene had kept the first aid kit since Kelli and I were kids. His face was twisted in irritation at Noel's advice—it was clear that Noel rubbed Trevor the wrong way every bit as much as Trevor did Noel. They were two snarling alphas, like the dogs who'd had to be scolded and pulled apart on the sidewalk earlier that afternoon.

But before Trevor could snarl a remark at Noel, a pot fell out of the cupboard and hit him in the face—this happened with a combination of speed and surprise that felt surreal to me in the moment. It was only later that I registered that this surreal quality was *comedy*—that is, the pot had comic timing. It even made a sound like *bonk!* as it bounced off the bridge of Trevor's nose.

He shouted in pain, doubled over—and just as he was about to straighten up again, another pot and a lid fell out, as if they'd somehow been teetering there, biding their time. It was the same thing that had happened to me when I was cleaning the kitchen, and I couldn't quite comprehend how it could be happening a second time. The pots bounced off the back of his head and upper shoulders and Trevor howled again and I knew I had been given another chance.

I turned to Noel. "Can you go get your shotgun?"

35

Life isn't like the movies. You want the big *choo,* in a story, but in life it never quite arrives. Or if it does, it's terrible. It's not cleansing or cathartic. It doesn't bring you that nebulous, perhaps imaginary thing they talk about in self-help circles: closure. Or else it brings you a hideous kind of closure—the kind you'd be perfectly happy to forgo and live the rest of your life without. In stories—successful stories, anyway—endings always feel right, satisfying, even when they're sad. But in life, endings—the big-*choo* kind of endings—uniformly feel awful. They're the incidents from which we must recover, the cascade of events that feel unexpected even when they're not and divide our lives into the innocent, oblivious before and the annihilated after.

Trevor's departure wasn't really like that, though. It wasn't nearly as annihilating as, say, the departure of my mother—which was so quiet and unobtrusive in contrast.

What I should've said to Noel, instead of *Can you go get your shotgun?* was *Would you please go to your house and call the police?* Whenever I tell this story, I try to make this point before the person I am telling it to can. The person's eyes always get big, just as Noel's did after I said those words to him, but then my listener will stop me there, because he or she has objections to raise. A gun changes everything, in a story, even a gun as silly as Noel's Remington 870—if you can call a shotgun silly. I read up on it online sometime afterward and discovered that hunters mostly like the 870 for shooting ducks and geese. Which somehow seems ridiculous to me. Once, when I told this story to a man, he burst out laughing at the evocation of the shotgun. He'd been riveted up until that moment, holding either side of his face during the whole dish-throwing episode, as if to calm himself. But when I told him what I said to Noel in the foyer, he reacted as if the entire story had been the setup and *Can you go get your shotgun?* was the punch line. "All of a sudden it's *Pulp Fiction*!" he exclaimed, meaning the movie or, maybe, just the genre itself. Either way, he somehow couldn't take me seriously after that.

"I'm just telling you what happened," I say to people like that man, people who argue with me at this point in this story, as if I've been doing okay up until then, but suddenly I've started telling it wrong and they need to nudge me back on track.

I know that it's perverse, the pleasure I get from this whole process. That's why I've told this story as many times as I have, to so many different people. It's one of those pleasurable if not quite healthy compulsions, like picking obsessively at your cuticles. Once, riding the bus, I watched a young woman across the aisle frown at her bare forearms until at last she could no longer stand what she saw. She pulled out a set of tweezers and started plucking at the invisible hairs of her arm. It went on for a full ten minutes—just plucking and plucking at herself without once looking up. My compulsion to tell this story has always felt a little like that. Although I've never told it this thoroughly or ruthlessly before, which I think means I'll be done with it for good once you and I are finished here.

When there's a gun in a story, the wisdom goes, it has to go off. That's another thing this story does wrong, because Noel's gun never even made an appearance. For the second time since it was evoked, the Remington remained locked away in its cabinet—it turned out that Noel had never managed to unearth the key. He'd taken a good look around for it after Arun Gill's garage was broken into, become frustrated when it didn't turn up, and then forgotten all about it, as busy and distractible people will.

That said, the gun still *worked*. It still managed to work its annihilating magic—the magic guns bequeath to every story, true or fake. The ability to bring things to an end.

It wasn't so much my informing Trevor that Noel had gone to get his shotgun that ended our standoff—it was simply that now somebody knew. Thanks to the moment of Trevor being distracted by fall-ing pots. I was able to say to Noel: *Can you go get your shotgun?* And, in the next moment: *I can't leave Kelli here alone.* Twelve words that punctured the bubble of unreality my sister and I had been trapped inside for the past eighteen hours. Noel's eyes flared in that moment of comprehension, and he fast-limped across the street, carrying the truth of our situation with him. As he went rummaging through his house, Noel babbled what was happening to his wife—a level-headed woman (in contrast to her excitable husband) whose name, I would later learn, was Phyllis. And it was good old cool-as-a-cucumber Phyllis who called the police.

Trevor left, and that was the end of our time in the bubble, yes. But it wasn't the end. The ending just went on and on—in fact, for a while there it didn't feel like much of an ending at all. There would be police reports. Court appearances. Brief jail time. Then the reappear-ances, followed by restraining orders. There would be long, plead-ing e-mails and Facebook messages, notes in all caps slipped beneath my windshield wipers, all in violation of the restraining orders, even three years later. Over those years, information would come tumbling out of places like Bestlife, the police department, and Eleanor Mallon like so many pots from a high cupboard. News that Trevor had done this sort of thing, to a lesser degree, with home care clients before us ("got a little clingy," in the enraging words of Margot) and Bestlife had looked the other way. That his ex-wife, Leanne, had taken out a restraining order on him too—more than one, in fact—well before I did. That Trevor had a habit of picking Mike up from school on days that did not accord with his custody agreement—one of those being the day he first brought Mike over to meet Kelli and me.

There were appearances in the Gorsebrook parking lot and out-side our condo—I'd made a point of getting a place with a twenty-four-hour security guard who had to buzz people up. And broken windows at Gorsebrook sometimes—he hated Gorsebrook because it soon became our second home, the residents and workers like family, and he only ever wanted us to have one family. He accused Gorse-brook of all sorts of things, referred to Marlene as "the brainwasher in chief." Spray paint appeared across the door one morning—SEX ABUSERS WORK HERE. A happy face in the o. He showed up at Jessica Hendy's house too. And once at Martin Hendy's school. Jessica also endured her share of pleading Facebook messages. She also took out more than one restraining order. There were more court appearances. Fines. Brief jail time. Honestly? It went on and on—world without end. When it finally stopped, I knew it was because he'd found another. Someone who needed what he had to give. So, really, it didn't stop at all.

The screen door wheezed shut, and I watched Noel hotfoot it across the street as fast as his bad hip or knee would allow. Once he reached his front door, I called up to Trevor to tell him what I'd said—what Noel now understood about our situation. And so the bubble was punctured, and Trevor knew it. He looked down at me from the kitchen doorway, one hand clapped over his nose, blinking away tears of pain, his bare foot bleeding.

After a moment he said from beneath his hand, "Fine. If you're gonna be like that."

"So you should get out of here now," I said loudly, thinking he didn't understand.

"Fuck, *okay,*" said Trevor. He hobbled into the living room, favoring his bad foot. I bolted up the stairs. He was going for Kelli.

When I got there, he was kneeling in front of her for the second time that day. Kelli looked alert and troubled.

"Trevor," I said, "you're bleeding all over the fucking carpet." I glanced at the window, and through the crack between the curtains I could see that the main floor of Noel's house was blazing with light—as if in a single gesture he'd turned on every lamp he owned the moment he'd crossed the threshold.

Trevor was whispering to Kelli now, in the same prayerlike way she often whispered to herself. I made out "Beaner" a couple of times.

He was looking not at her but at his own hands, which were clasped in her lap. I had a feeling that he would have liked to have been holding her hands but had stopped himself from taking them in his. Trevor, it struck me, was showing Kelli a little respect for a change. That is to say, he was respecting her aversion to eye contact, to physical manhandling. Yes, he had clasped his hands against her knees, but he hadn't grabbed her, he wasn't plowing through her boundaries the way he usually did—I thought about the first day I'd ever laid eyes on Trevor, being amazed and discomfited when he'd demonstrated how he'd trained my eternally hug-avoidant sister to embrace him. But now he was getting as close to Kelli as he could, communing with her, without violating any of her personal taboos.

As I stood there not knowing what to do, Kelli bent toward Trevor as if curious to hear what he was whispering. She cocked her head to the side. After a moment, she started whispering along with him.

I glanced through the curtains again, to Noel's house. Now the entire place was lit up, from the basement to the second floor. I saw him rush past a window. Then a woman followed, gesturing in a patient, unruffled sort of way. What was happening over there? I realized I didn't even know what I wanted—for Noel to hurry or for Noel to take his time.

As Kelli got caught up in the rhythms of whatever she was whispering, she began to rock. To my surprise, she was growing comfortable there with Trevor in her lap. Something about his reverent whispering had put her at ease. I wasn't sure how long I should let this ceremony—if that's what it was—between Trevor and my sister continue. Then again, I wasn't even sure it was a question of *let*. Trevor still hadn't left, though he had said he would, but he had said that many times before. Noel still wasn't here. There was still no shotgun. There was only the threat of those things. I didn't know if I had the upper hand or not. If there was even such a thing with Trevor.

"Trevor," I said.

Distantly, I heard a siren. But we often heard sirens in the distance. He started whispering more loudly, as if to drown me out. *I believe in you,* I heard him say. He was now rocking in synchrony with Kelli. *I believe in you. I do. I do.*

"Trevor, you have to leave now." There was panic in my voice, because I think on some level I understood what Trevor was doing with this repetition, these avowals. He was attempting to eradicate the immediate future—the consequences of everything he'd done up to this point. Or maybe that doesn't make sense—to say that Trevor was trying to eradicate something that hadn't happened yet. Maybe it makes more sense to say that he was fortifying himself against those consequences. He was seeking, and drawing, strength. So that he could stand against them when the time came. So all his love and delusion could remain intact.

"I believe in you—"

The siren hadn't died away. It was louder now, and I took a gamble on it. "Do you hear that?" I said. "They're coming."

"You can't make me not believe in you."

"Leave," said Kelli, quite clearly.

I was amazed. I'd never heard Kelli issue an order like this before. Trevor raised his head, mouth open, and in the same moment my sister raised her hand and placed the back of it lightly against his forehead. As if checking for a fever. Trevor closed his eyes. He leaned into her hand and grimaced—but it was, I saw, a joyful grimace. He was overwhelmed. And at first I didn't understand.

"Trebie leave," said Kelli again. I felt a cautious thrill. I wanted to pump my fist—*Way to go, Kelli! Tell him!* But Trevor's expression didn't change. If anything, it became more beatific.

"I do," Trevor avowed. And then I knew—I knew before he even said it. My sense of panic thickened into something more dismal: a certainty.

He broke Kelli's rules then, clasping both her hands in his. "I *do* believe," he said.

Kelli reared away from his grip, but Trevor didn't notice. He'd already turned, beaming, to extend a hand toward me.

Author's Note

I don't usually play favorites when it comes to my characters, but Kelli is my favorite character in this book, in the same way that my uncle—who inspired many of Kelli's mannerisms and speech patterns—is one of my favorite people in real life. I haven't seen many full-blooded depictions of people like my uncle in books very often, perhaps because we're used to recognizable types when it comes to fictional characters. And someone like Kelli wouldn't be all that recognizable to your average reader. She, like my uncle, is an original. That kind of originality can sometimes be tricky to get down on the page.

This is all to say that I worked hard to do Kelli justice as a character, to never reduce her to a type. Karen's frustrations and impatience with her are, I feel, a pretty honest depiction of the kind of thing a family member and caregiver of someone like Kelli would struggle with. I wanted to be straight with readers about that. But I knew it wouldn't work if I couldn't show Kelli to be as complicated, multifaceted, and lovable a person as my uncle is. I hope I succeeded.

Acknowledgments

In November 2016 I did a residency at Artscape Gibraltar Point on Toronto Island. It was a hell of a November in a lot of ways, but the weather that month was stunning, and I spent a lot of time just gaping stupefied at the clear, vivid sky. I came back from that residency feeling wrecked and depressed and like I had accomplished precisely nothing, but it was probably some of the most important writing I did for this book, so thank you to Artscape.

Thank you also to the people who spoke with me about caregiving and social services of various stripes, including Mark MacLean and Christy Ann Conlin.

Thanks to Christy Fletcher and Sarah Fuentes for their encouragement and essential early feedback. Anita Badami was an invaluable first reader. My editor, Melanie Little, is made of solid gold, as far as I'm concerned. I'm forever grateful to Sarah McLachlan for her steadfast enthusiasm and support of the things I write.

Love and thanks to Rob Appleford for being there throughout.

The caregivers in my life who I'd specifically like to single out for thanks: Phyllis, James, and Clint Coady.

Lynn Coady is the critically acclaimed and award-winning author of six books, including *Hellgoing,* which won the Scotiabank Giller Prize, was a finalist for the Rogers Writers' Trust Fiction Prize, and was an Amazon.ca and a *Globe and Mail* Best Book. She is also the author of *The Antagonist,* winner of the Georges Bugnet Award for Fiction and a finalist for the Scotiabank Giller Prize. Her first novel, *Strange Heaven,* published when she was just twenty-eight, was a finalist for the Governor General's Literary Award. Her books have been published in the United Kingdom, United States, Holland, France, and Germany. Coady lives in Toronto and writes for television.

A NOTE ON THE TYPE

This book was set in Granjon, a type named in compliment to Robert Granjon, a type cutter and printer active in Antwerp, Lyons, Rome, and Paris from 1523 to 1590. Granjon, the boldest and most original designer of his time, was one of the first to practice the trade of typefounder apart from that of printer.

Linotype Granjon was designed by George W. Jones, who based his drawings on a face used by Claude Garamond (ca. 1480–1561) in his beautiful French books. Granjon more closely resembles Garamond's own type than do any of the various modern faces that bear his name.

Composed by North Market Street Graphics,
Lancaster, Pennsylvania

Printed and bound by Berryville Graphics,
Berryville, Virginia

Designed by Cassandra J. Pappas